A Questing Stranger

by Marshall Thompson

www.trafford.com

North America & international
toll-free: 1 888 232 4444 (USA & Canada)
phone: 250 383 6864 ♦ fax: 812 355 4082

Hunnish Expansion from the 5th to the 7th Centuries.

The Left-hand army remained over China while the Right-hand extended further West in conquests.

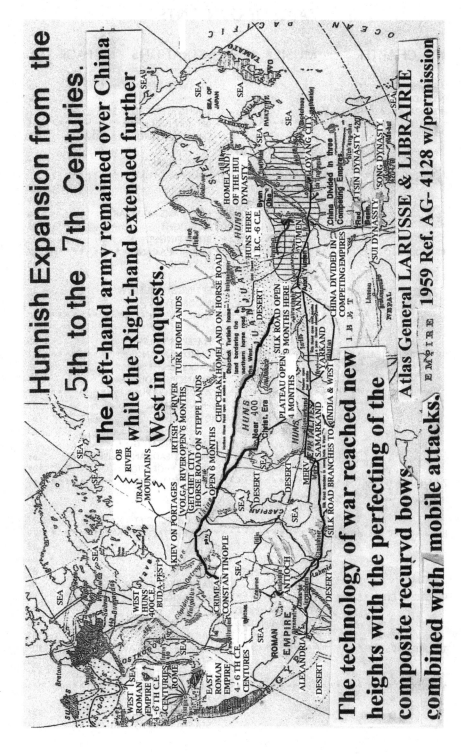

The technology of war reached new heights with the perfecting of the composite recurvd bows combined with mobile attacks.

Atlas General LARUSSE & LIBRAIRIE 1959 Ref. AG- 4128 w/permission

TABLE OF CONTENTS

* CHAPTER * MUSIC * ILLUSTRATIONS * PAGE *

INTRODUCTORY REMARKS

Adventuring with Kaya is fun. When the book became a series of three parts, I was tempted to fill a few lapses of time in his travels, from east to west. The historical significance of Eastern Europe, especially the Ukraine, sailing the Black Sea, Rumania and Hungary made the additions necessary. All these areas were conquered by the Huns.

This fill-in became a block of brand-new, beloved characters each different and interesting. First comes feisty, but polite little Olga the Goth. Second. Merien Papasian is the governor's daughter, with her 'yes' and 'no' added to her conversations. Saraijik, is the smart, haughty, daughter of "Munzur Khan, the Terrible", and scornful wife of her guardian Evran. These took on a reality I couldn't ignore. Each had a quest and a manner of proceeding on it. These flights into culture and character development added pages to the book, but, I hope interest to the reader; whose comfort and enjoyment is of prime importance. It required new songs and pictures to illustrate the times.

I thank my wife for her endurance and help. As well, many friends: Margaret Ryan, Joy Martel, Suzanne McGillivary, Lois Campbell, Barbara Maseberg who proof read and remarked on the novel's music and illustrations as the book progressed. Trafford Publisher's advice, contacts and services are of great importance. My thanks to each and all.

So, here we have the completed product: <u>A Questing Stranger.</u> One of my proof readers read it through for work and after, again, for pleasure. I hope you enjoy it, too.

Sincerely,
Marshall B. Thompson Jr.

PS: The foreign words are printed in italics in the glossary and text. Accents shown at the beginning of each chapter will not always appear in the text. They are spelled in English phonetics for your convenience. They will not be so spelled in their own dictionaries. MT

HISTORICAL CATCH-UP

In the 5th Century of the present era the Huns were wide spread conquerors of many areas of the world. Their technology and tactics had placed them high on the list of cultures able to impose their will and way upon much of the civilized world. Material riches fell under their control, and their command of herds and slaves equipped them to rule subdued peoples in China, India and Middle Asia, as well as Europe. This trend of Central Asian dominance started in the 4th century and continued through the 14th century until the changes in technology, tactics and moral attitudes caused the crown of conquest to pass to other hands in other lands.

Today, we live with the obvious influence of these later conquerors, but beneath and permeating the present situations are ancient concepts, and practices still alive and enduring, under many guises, in the populations once ruled by those Central Asian powers.

This book concerns the earlier epic of recorded domination, although earlier occasions surely existed, un-recorded and registered only in folk legends of its perpetrators. It is my pleasure to present those days in story form for your reading enjoyment.

Christianity was one of the competing forces present in the thousand years, the time that Central Asian people repeatedly conquered and ruled the great lands of the east, south and west of the Eurasian Continent. It is recorded sketchily in most history books. Its early growth we can only surmise, but its presence is well attested to. This, perhaps, links A Questing Stranger to western accounts of similar quests in the early history of those days. The warrior profession was almost universal at that time. Protection of the people of each culture was a major concern by all leaders in government, whatever their social structure.

This credible story takes the seeker from the borders of China with the capital In Loyang of the Northern Kingdom to the plains of Hungary. The cultural details have been kept as accurate as the author could make them.

This book is historical fiction written for your pleasure. Enjoy it and share it around with others. The saddest fate of any book is to sit on a shelf in some house unattended and unshared.

SPRING STEPPE FLOWERS

PEOPLE, PLACES & PLOTS IN CHAPTER 1

Al'tom: means 'My Gold', the name of Kaya's mare.
Bol'dar: commander of the East Huns (Left Hand Horde).
Few soon: loses her knife to an enemy's need.
Jo'mer: the merchant loses horses and goods.
Ka'ya: leaves his herd to solve a dilemma and find a friend.
Koke Ju: commander of a Chinese fort hit by a Hun attack.
Koosta: bandit leader, a rival of Kaya from school days.
Ma Chan' Zi: agent for Jomer's trade on the Yellow River.
Oz'kurt: Kaya's friend expects trouble and finds lots of it.
Ters'in: is appointed by Koos'ta to destroy Kaya's trackers.
Yown'ja: 'Clover Blossom,' the baby name of Kaya's love.

GLOSSARY:

bash'ooze-two-nay: I'll do as you say; I obey, immediately; yes, sir; literally: it's on my head.
gok'te-key: heavenly made; sky manufactured; an ancient metal-smith style.
hoe'sh gel'den-iz: you came happily; welcome; glad you're here.
hoe'sh boll'duke: I arrived safely; I got here fine; glad to be here.
kangal: a large dog were used for herding by many tribes.
Ye'su gel: God help me; protect me, Jesus.
Yea'shu: Jesus name in the local Chinese dialect.

BROKEN TRUCE

Kaya awoke to the call of the gray wolf, the wail of salute to the setting of the moon and the momentary dark before the pale of morning and the rising of the sun. He had dreamed of his life as a cub among his brothers. He had spent two years with the bears and it had changed his manner of living. Then, his place in his tribe as the child of promise and later as heir to the commerce of Jomer the merchant prince of Epec Kent, Silk City, had brought new opportunities into his life. But it was the two years spent at the Hermitage, where the hermit taught useful arts that gave moral shape to his young life. Now he was taking a herd of golden horses down the chain of Altai Mountains, crossing the Gobi to the north loop of the Yellow River in frontier China. The Kingdom of the Hui needed horses. At the same time his intended bride was accompanying Jomer in his caravan. They would meet soon near the northern city of Jining. He sighed; his foster sister was a joy not only to behold, but to work around. She was as bright as her flame-red hair.

Again the wolf howl echoed from the desert. He roused himself more as he heard the restless snort of the horses and the nervous growl of his faithful, great herd-dog, a *kangal*, part wolf, but mostly dog. He quickly unsheathed his knife and reached up for his bow and quiver placed just above his head. Suddenly, from across the valley below their table mountain, there came an answering call of a wolf, which tightened his stomach and brought him to his feet. In one smooth motion he moved into the darkness near the brush, and had strung his bow and notched arrow into it. A soft chuckle sounded beside him from the depth of a scrub willow.

"That man's call might have fooled a frontier guard, but not a hill man," whispered Ozkurt, his companion. Ozkurt, a skinny-hard mountaineer with a five-year lead on the youthful Kaya, was already overshadowed by the great bulk and overwhelming height of the tribe leader's son.

"Was there nothing earlier," he asked, "sound or sign?"

The hill man grunted assent, "Too quiet, but only you slept, everything else was awake and waiting. Were you dreaming about a tiger?"

Kaya only smiled, it was an old joke referring to a time when he had faced off the predator and been knocked unconscious for it. He returned no comment. It was part of his name for confidence, that he could sleep before battle, or while men fumed or fretted over the slowness of time. The words of his teacher came to mind, 'Never hurry, never worry. Trust God, wait, then, act in His will and time.'

"Did you make the circuit before the moon was down?" he asked, more in the way of continuation than curiosity. He knew that Ozkurt would have poked his scrawny head, with four weeks growth of hair on his scalp and face with a walrus moustache, into every clump of trees and stream bed around the herd of golden horses. The herd stallion snorted again and the mares circled nervously in the center with their foals, while the fillies and bucks paced the outer edge of the herd testing the air. The light started to grow steadily. Kaya's mare, Altom, meaning 'My Gold,' came over to nuzzle a greeting.

"Everything has been the same as now, it ...," he said, suddenly breaking as the squeal of goose-quilled whistling arrows sounded in the distance, and the high call of a brass Hunnish war horn sounded in the valley about two miles distant. The roar of war dogs followed with the scream of wounded men. Shouts and the rallying cry of a Chinese war trumpet and clashing cymbals rose as the frontier guards sought to rally the contingent against the sudden attack. Just as suddenly, the noise stopped, only to start again after a few minutes of calm. Then the quiet of death, followed by the crackling of fire on wood, told the end of the military border post.

Kaya and his men were riding in wide, quiet circles about the horses, crooning soothing sounds and calming their animals' strenuous efforts to depart the plateau. They had allowed them to rush toward the upwind of the valley so the smell of smoke and blood would not further excite them. They were restless and calling, after their stampede and moved along the stubble grass crest of the mountain edge. Some men sat on their horses, pointing to where the smoke of the buildings could be seen. Kaya motioned to Ozkurt, "Leave Tezlee in charge with orders to shoot anything that moves," he said. "We are going down to see what's left. Bring five men."

The roofs of the stone, brick and clay buildings were still burning and bits of bamboo and thatch smoldered on the clay floors. The fire had been brief, violent, until the combustibles were devoured. Guards' bodies were scattered randomly through the buildings and grounds behind the walls and the arrows still adorned the bodies in ones and twos in throat or chest. The shooting had been accurate and economical.

"Huns for sure," Ozkurt remarked, "see the arrows." Kaya grunted, looking at the corkscrew pattern of feathering. Then, suddenly straightened up and moved deliberately toward the large pagoda building towering three stories above the open drill ground and the barracks. The invaders had left almost without looting or even recovering the spent arrows.

"There may be survivors in the tower area." Here too, however, all had suffered the flames. Outside the main building, they came upon a man dressed in the silks and wools of a person of high rank, stretched with several retainers upon the ground, whose shields were filled with arrows. A simple animal-headed knife rested above the heart of the noble, through the armored leather breast piece.

Kaya drew a breath of surprise. "Old *gok'tekey* manufacture," he said, "the leader of the tower sortie was killed with one of our knives." He reached down and pulled the long necked animal head easily from the seam between metal plates, wiped it on the material and brought it up for examination. At that moment the fallen warrior groaned. Ozkurt pulled his knife.

"Shall I end his pain?" he asked. Kaya motioned 'no' with an upward jerk of his head. He knelt beside the fallen warrior.

"Let's see if the armor didn't deflect the knife." Kaya started to un-strap the buckler from the side. Ozkurt frowned, suddenly impatient. "Besides, this is my sister's knife. I need the face of the man who used it on him." How well Kaya remembered the discovery of the knife. He let his mind linger a moment fondly. Yownja had loved it and used it constantly; the antique, wolf-headed knife from the ancestors.

> - - - - - - - >

The officer groaned again and licked his lips. Kaya motioned to Ozkurt and they carried the man inside the building to a wall bench of brick where they deposited him. Kaya brought up his ayran bag and gave the man a sip. The man stirred and tried to take more. Consciousness and awareness appeared on his face.

He was dressed in Chinese military fashion, but his features were Northern, for these barbarians differed as much from the Han Chinese as the western Barbarian from the Roman. The Northern Dynasty, nobles and army were still largely Tungus and Hunnish. They fought political, not ethnic, battles with the northern and eastern Huns.

As the man had his wound treated by Kaya, who had lived in a medicine woman's yurt, he began to carefully answer the questions. Would these be his captors or saviors? He was respectful, but guarded and, occasionally, evasive and vague.

"Yes, I am commander of the frontier guard." "No, I did not see the size of the total force. Only about 40 men appeared in sight, but outer buildings were being set on fire while I parleyed with the raider's leader." "Yes, they were Ordos Huns." "No, there was no great treasure in the fort, only normal tax and customs receipts from merchants entering and leaving our jurisdiction." "Yes, I think the inspectors and treasurer are dead, and I'm sure the money was robbed."

"But what did they want? What did they take?" Ozkurt interrupted the interrogation.

The commander looked carefully at him and then answered slowly. "He wanted a merchant and his daughter."

Ozkurt's jaw dropped and he stood, speechless while Kaya filled in with an observation. "You were not making a sortie; you were talking, making terms with the raider's leader when stabbed."

Uneasily, the Commander nodded slowly. "After I was stabbed, they broke the truce and fired volleys at my men. I watched the attack overcome my men and after that, I remembered no more until you woke me." He closed his eyes, as if faint.

"Attack a fort and kill a hundred men for a couple of travelers, who could be picked off on the road?" Ozkurt broke in again. "I can't believe that."

"The merchant and his goods were being held by the fort. The horses were commandeered for the army at Baotou. The army is preparing to drive north for the Hun's military base at Bayan Oba if the peace effort fails. This attack may be the first of the war." The man watched the faces of his questioners carefully. He noticed the incised ivory swan badge of office that hung from Kaya's neck. The officer pointed to it and asked. "You are allies of the Huns?" As both men jerked their heads up in negative unison, the commander seemed to relax a bit and asked for more ayran to drink. "My name is Koke Ju, herbalist," he laughed, "named for my grandfather who was an herbalist." After drinking more, he looked at the wound and at Kaya, "Was it poisoned, do you think?" He looked at the short copper knife which Ozkurt now held.

"It's old, but clean," stated Ozkurt, "a few inches lower, and it would have done the job. You have good armor."

"My mother will burn a whole basket of incense at the temple." The man smiled.

"What of the man and girl?" Kaya interrupted.

"The terms were the surrender of the man, girl and goods. They didn't realize that the horses had been sent on the day before and only the garrison horses remained. They attacked the center and killed the soldiers in the last redoubt." He motioned at the pagoda round him.

"You are lying," Kaya stated, staring hard at the man, "There was treasure here." He pointed to an open door into an inner room, some Chinese script paper money and a thin silver bar lay where it had fallen in haste. "You tried to palm off the man and girl and keep the treasure, but they must have known your trick."

The commander's face changed color, he turned his head away and murmured, "It was a bribe to bring the Mongols of the east to attack the restless Huns on their flank and cause a diversion. They were to come to Jining to collect. Now the money is lost, and I will be in disgrace. It would have been better to die." His face reflected his despair.

"Not if you make contact with the Mongols in time to tell them what has happened to their money and put them on a hot trail," Kaya retorted. "True, they might be angry enough to kill you, but they would have a reason to fight the Huns." Kaya tested the bandage and replaced the armor.

"It's worth trying. Even if it fails, I am credited with merit for attempting to retrieve our loss of face. Will you provide me with horses and men?" The commander stood up and braced himself. Kaya nodded and motioned to Ozkurt. "Dispatch four men with provisions to escort the officer to within sight of the river and Jining, but they are not to enter. They must return immediately to the herd." Kaya turned to Koke Ju. "Before you leave, tell me of their leader and how the blow was struck."

"I signaled a truce after the initial surprise and defeat. It was accepted. I took the prisoners with me. The woman still had her personal knife. As a responsible officer, I could not leave her defenseless. The Hunnish leader was tall and tough, but very young for such a responsible position, even as you are. We talked and I tried to persuade him to take the prisoners for ransom and their goods, pretending we had no other treasure. However, they had information of our project and the man reached over and drew the woman's knife and struck me while ordering his men to attack mine."

"But," Kaya insisted, "the look of the man. How was he? Describe him."

"The Hun was arrogant, angry and confident; he had a short thumb on one hand, they called him Koosta" reported the commander.

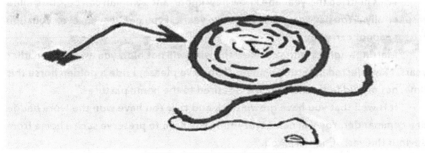

SHIELD AND BROKEN ARROW

The trail led them east, parallel to the river. This wild country around the north loop of the Yellow River was for centuries the wild west of the Han dynasty, and all other dynasties of ancient China. A special, hearty type of people lived there, squeezed between the mountains of Tibet and the deserts of Mongolia, living in caves and houses of yellow-mud-brick and stone. They cultivated the yellow terraces of fertile but dry, semi-arid soils. The Great Wall cut through the bottom half of the great river's loop. It was excluded militarily and culturally from the real China, the eastern wet lands. Yet it contained the oldest evidences of what was to be characteristic of Chinese culture. It was an uncharacteristic heartland of drought and ethnic conflict; persistent farmers against insistent herders and nomads. Stubborn merchants kept a channel of communication open to the west in spite of rapacious plunderers and warring tribes. The open, north-west frontier was the source of continual conflict, and devious strategies were developed to defend an ancient civilization from crudeness, strength and greed of conquest. Only from this north corridor could foreignness threaten the ancient culture. The Great Wall was more than a physical barrier. It marked the limit of Chinese rule, but not the extent of their influence.

Kaya pulled up his horse, Altom, to await the party of Chinese herders. They were coming from the northern bank of the river. The Ma family, who were followers of Yesu the Redeemer, provided the factor, the agent, for the sale of the horses and would help the Chipchaks get the animals to the government posts. Handsome, young Ma Chan Zi rode ahead of his men to meet his friend. He bowed low in the saddle and gave greetings in Hunnish.

"*Hoe'sh gel'diniz*, Where is the herd?" He inquired curiously.

"*Hoe'sh boll'duke*, Two hours behind us and shorthanded. We were forced to rescue a fort Commandant and send him with escort to the nearest post. We pursue the abductors of my patron and fiancée," Kaya replied.

"I will join the pursuit and my brother will lead our men to move the herd." He turned to face his disappointed younger brother who, protesting, led the men on Kaya's back trail. Chan Zi and another man joined Kaya, now making a party of ten men.

"I was married this year and know how important a woman can be," he smiled respectfully. "You have grown taller in two years. If you get heavier, even your lion horses cannot carry you."

"Marriage agrees with you. Now the wind will not blow you away as in earlier years," Kaya jested in return, smiling. "Observe please, I ride a golden horse this time, not my old faithful black. She is retired to the home pastures."

"It is well that you have grown thick and tall. You have won the ivory badge of a commander. You will need everything you have to preserve such a horse from envious thieves," Chan Zi joked.

"She is named Altom, My Gold. My fiancée and I trained her. She is the envy of everyone in our camp."

"If she were my gold to ride now, I would run away and you would have lost all your treasures in one day."

> - - - - - - - >

The Huns" trail was easy to read. North and east it cut over dry mountains and desert hills toward the sands. Kaya had left the majority of the men with the horses to continue toward the purchasing agent of the Tungus Chinese government. Although they ran the risk of being commandeered, the presence of Chinese herders might shift the suspicion. After a day's riding north, the night came as they reached a small seepage spring in the desert. The small party shared the water with their mounts and ate their travel rations. Chan Zi caught Kaya up on their lives and family news. "At this time the people suffer with the wars of the three kingdoms and general disorder. God has prepared many hearts to find refuge in *Yea Shu*, the Anointed one, He has healed many and comforted more, but there is sporadic persecution by the state and much jealousy by the favored religions. Even our hospitals and charities are disrupted."

Kaya observed sympathetically, "It's strange how people will cling to old habits and indulge their lusts rather than seek those things which benefit their spirits and minds. They are afraid of a way of salvation that demands commitment, discipline and obedience. Our faith seems foolish to the unthinking, self-sufficient traditionalists." Kaya lay watching the stars, his head on his saddle. "A shaman in a frenzied trance impresses them more than a praying, saintly a*postolos*. Evil is a short cut to the wealth and indulgence they crave. They know but dimly how it will fasten on them and enslave their will and reduce their freedom to choose." He sighed. "Gold weighs down, but prayers lift up."

"I wish our faith were more militant, and we could fight against those who oppress and plant evil habits among the people. Put the fear of God in their hearts! We wouldn't have to put up with this persecution and discrimination." Chan Zi's voice was angry and resentful. "Why be finicky about shedding the blood of unbelievers? They go to hell anyway. What matters a few years?" he snorted.

"Try to control the work of God? Decide who should die and who live? Kill those who might with time repent? Take life from the potential believer... helpful genius... generous patron... serving sage... godly preacher and healers of the ill? These you might destroy in your anger and self-righteous fury. 'Judge not', the Scriptures say." Chan Zi sat up and faced Kaya.

"But it says we will judge angels. If we can tell good from bad in these higher beings, then we know enough. I can tell good people from bad easily."

"We are commanded to turn the other cheek, to flee to the next city and to pray for those who despitefully use us. Yesu doesn't promise an easy road, but he calls it the road to God. 'If we don't obey, we'll miss the way,' the song says, remember?" Kaya sat and sang the hymn softly:

> 1. Yesu, Lord and Savior come and help us.
> Grant us safety, guidance and protection.
> We acknowledge all our sin and weakness.
> Grant us now both victory and completeness.

> Chorus: Heed our prayer. There is none to help beside You.
> Hear our call. Come and save us by Your grace.
> You alone can guide, protect our footsteps.
> We will thank You for Your grace and glory.

COME AND HELP US

Ye - su, Lord and Sav - ior come and help us,

Grant us saf - ty, gui - dance and pro - tec - tion.

We ac - know - ledge all our sin and weak - ness.

Grant us now both vic - t'ry and com - plete - ness.

Chorus: Heed our prayer. There is none to help be - side You.

Hear our call. Come and save us by Your grace.

You a - lone can guide, pro - tect our foot - steps.

We will thank You for Your grace and glo - ry.

2. Save us, Lord, from hatred, lust, and envy,
Keep our minds and hearts upon Your treasures.
With Your blessing we will find true pleasures.
Joy in loving, trust beyond all measure.
Chorus:
3. Master send, we pray, Your Holy Spirit.
Teach us all the love of truth and goodness.
Heaven is for those who work for Your day.
If we don't obey, we'll miss the sure way.
Chorus:

Chan Zi's face softened and both lay back on their pallets. "We have to endure to prove ourselves, but I still say there are limits to what kind of provocations we have to endure. You can't wait until a man kills you if you're to protect those you love," he spoke quietly.

"That's why we pray daily, before the moment of crisis arrives that we might be saved from wrong actions."

"Yes, I don't know what I wouldn't do to any who touched my beloved." He sighed and then chuckled, "She was so frightened the first time our families brought us together at the wedding feast. I had seen her before, but thought her plain and mousy. She thought me rough and loud. We soon found how much each pleased the other. Love is a garden of discoveries."

"And I fight for the recovery of my promised one. I wonder how long it will take." Kaya sighed.

"When you find the ones who hold her, remember your good words about loving your enemies," Chan Zi chuckled.

Ten men for the pursuit were too many to feed easily, yet not enough to effect much in a fight, but Kaya and Chan Zi continued next morning on the track north. As Kaya expected, after four hours the trail divided. Two parties of four went left and right from the main group of about sixty going northwest into the Gobi Desert. At least one group could circle around and trail them. Another four hours the same pattern was repeated. Now, between eight and twelve men would be trailing or flanking them. One group may have been the prisoners and guards, but some would be planning an attack. The prisoners would be hustled off to a main camp near water. The main body might turn back to attack or simply dissolve into a hundred small trails. To wait for the Mongols to arrive was to lose all hope of rescue.

After twelve hours on the trail, Kaya suddenly veered north and left off trailing the attackers. Within an hour they crossed the trail of four going north and in another half hour saw riders before them.

Dismounting to remain hidden, they walked their horses, following in the low spots between the dunes and hills. The small party ahead seemed unaware of their presence. As darkness and shadows spread, they grew gradually nearer.

At this point Kaya split his forces. Taking Ozkurt and his two best archers, he explained his plan to them, and they took horses and circled ahead toward the northwest. Kaya and his remaining seven men started to creep closer. Suddenly in the last light before dark, Kaya rode up on the top of a hill in plain sight of the travelers. Chan Zi crouched behind, his bow drawn.

"You are surrounded, and we wish to parley with you. Lay down your weapons, and we promise no damage to yourselves or your goods."

A clear commanding voice replied, "You have our compliance, but whose promise do we have?"

"Kaya the Bear, of the Chipchaks gives his word," the confident reply came.

"I have heard of this bear who sells the golden lion horses to the Emperor of the north, our sometimes enemy. We have much to talk about," the voice replied as a small, old man moved his horse to a hill top and dropped his bow case to the ground. He motioned for his men to do likewise.

At that moment a goose-quilled whistling arrow shrieked overhead. A third voice joined the conversation from behind.

"Now you will surrender to us. We have trailed you for hours, and you will not escape," it snarled.

"Do you offer us the same guarantee of life and goods as we have given our prisoners?" Kaya asked.

"We offer nothing to prisoners, but what it pleases us to give," the voice snarled again.

"The kind of mercy given the frontier garrison you slaughtered?" Kaya said sarcastically. "Then everyone dies, for you are not so many that we might not take you too, here in the dark." There was an uncomfortable pause.

Then the commanding voice rang out again. "A parley has been called for. I, Boldar of the East Huns, call a truce. There will be no fighting on pain of exile; hear and obey." There was a long pause, and the sound of argument.

"'Bash-ooze-two-nay,' as you command," came with slow reluctance from the leader of the raiders.

As he spoke fire arrows with goose-quill whistles came from the east beyond Kaya's advanced scouts and made an arc above the three parties. An answering volley of fire arrows streaked from the opposite west side of the crowd and fell beyond them. All knew they had been encircled by a larger force. The weak had become the strong and held their lives in their hands. Escape would be difficult even in this moment of increasing dark. The blackness returned. Tanra or fate had dealt a new hand which they must now play. Life or death lay before them! Would they see the light of morning? What would it reveal?

FLAMING ARROWS

PEOPLE, PLACES & PLOTS IN CHAPTER 2

Ahjit': the leader finds difficulties in organizing the caravan.
Al'tom: the mare arouses others to envy and jealousy.
Blind singer: provides inspiring songs of bravery.
Bol'dar: denounces raiders at court before the high lord.
Kaya: seeks Koosta, who has taken treasure and his bride.
Ma Chan'Zi: friend, agent and buyer for Jomer's trade.
O'nat bey: commander of the Royal Guard of the Huns.
On'basha: a corporal in charge of the guests or prisoners.
Op'tal and Pesh: entertainers in China at the Yellow River.
Ordos: the arid land enclosed by the north loop of the river.
Oz'kurt: expects more trouble and finds it.
Soldier/priest: begs that others may gain merit.
Ters'in: explains the actions of the young warrior society.
Wei: a kingdom in northeast China, ruled by the Tungus
Hui dynasty from the capital, Loyang.
You-chel': High Lord of the East Huns in the Gobi Desert.

GLOSSARY:

hey' be: a woven, wool saddle-bag. It hangs across the horses' back with room for useful packets.
kar'ma: fate; a portion by lot; one's part by others' decision.
kar' num-match: My stomach's empty; I'm hungry; Feed me.
onbasha: a military title for a corporal; leader of ten men.
ye' tish-tear benny: reach out to me; Help me; be generous; give me something.

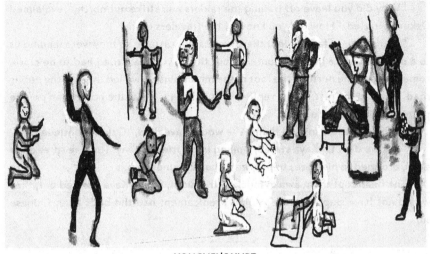

YOUCHEL'S YURT

Onat, chief of the royal guards, had come to meet his lord and escort him to camp. He had lightly netted his lord's preoccupied opposition and had a circlet of archers about all the bands. They were first disarmed, then, allowed to make their way to the Hun base camp and town.

Like giant beads on a string, they rode following each other, but did not mix. First came Boldar's party of authorities and reinforced guards. Kaya's party of herdsmen-warriors came second with Onat's guards accompanying them. Half the body of raiders, minus the leader and booty came after, a poor third, following with their guards. Each group was distrustful of the others and self-contained; nevertheless, they were compelled to keep to the same trail and destination. The first group was talkative and animated, the second, attentive and watchful, and the last, reluctant and disgruntled, murmuring their discontent and curses quietly, lest the rear guard hear and censure.

In three hours they arrived at the main camp, an extensive city of yurts and tents. Orders were given for the accommodation of the travelers, names were taken and billets assigned. At midnight the city seemed deserted and empty, only the well-armed patrols of the overlord moved in the streets.

Ozkurt rode beside Kaya and shared some bits of dry food from the saddlebag and the last of the ayran from the leather carrying bag. Chan Zi ate his dry, boiled millet as escorts took them to their tent. The accommodations were Spartan simple, but not particularly clean. Dust covered the fabrics, floor and rugs. Ozkurt requested sheep skins for sleeping and the leader of the patrol, an *Onbasha*, directed his attention to a pile of dirty skins under a rug in one corner and left them.

"Why did you leave off trailing the raiders and strike out north?" exclaimed Ozkurt, puzzled. "How did you know of the travelers there?"

"In the hour of fading light they would surely attack, so they were leading us to a deserted place in the mountains, but the west to east road had to be close, somewhere to the north at the foot of the mountains, so we led them to the public road. God did the rest," Kaya replied with a shrug. "It was the hour when people press to arrive at a safe camp."

"What if we had missed them? We would have died," Ozkurt continued.

"But we didn't," Kaya stated, smiling in his friendly way. Then he spread the skins, dropped to his knees to pray and Chan Zi joined him.

The fleas kept them awake much of the night, but as Kaya pointed out, they would not have slept soundly in their predicament had the beds been Chinese silk.

> - - - - - - - >

The next morning before dawn, Onbasha took the herders to the military cantonment for a breakfast of soup and tea.

"My Lord will see you at the hour of the hare. A morning meeting has been called of the heads of families and generals. You will be available for questions. Ready yourselves." Onbasha who followed the Chinese courtesies and etiquette bowed deeply and left them as they bowed in return.

The Onbasha returned at the appointed hour, and escorted them to the presence of the lord in a great tent full of guards and seated dignitaries. They were allowed to sit on the rug before the dais. There they waited and conversed in hushed tones as the leaders of the Hun raiders were conducted into the tent. Angry glances were exchanged and the wait continued.

There was a sudden stir of company as orders were harshly called. Everyone rose to their feet and bowed from the waist as the honor guard entered the tent and then all went down on their knees, bowing as the princes entered. Finally they were down flat on their faces, when Bol'dar appeared with the tribal lord. Guard and audience bowed in submission as the high lord, family and counselors entered in a body. Their faces were northern and pale with mustaches and beards, but the court administration and etiquette were as Chinese and as demanding as the courts of the Tungus Wei or as any other assimilating border people.

The high lord, You'chel, took his seat on a satin covered divan on the raised dais and the counselors sat lower beside him on cushions on the floor in a semicircle. Below the dais the witnesses sat and guards stood on the intricately designed floral-patterned silk and wool rug that covered the floor of the tent. Behind the dais stood servants and attendants, ready for any service at a motion or call.

As the audience resumed its sitting, the Lord Bol'dar stood, bowed and began an address to the high lord. His words contained few honorifics and evasions. His speech was direct and dynamic. Chinese and Hunnish scribes waited to write any commands of the high lord and to keep minutes.

"My Lord You'chel knows of the treachery of the three kingdoms. To this is added treachery within the membership of the Warrior Society, some of whose members, without permission, have raided a fort near Jining on the Yellow River. Money intended for ourselves, to finance war against the intruding Mongols of the northeast, has been stolen from the fort and in this way from our coffers. These witnesses to the outrage were being hunted by the robber band, when we intervened to save them and bring their pursuers to justice." The Lord Bol'dar concluded his presentation, glaring at the culprits and bowing to the high lord.

The accused was permitted to speak for his band. A young warrior, Tersin by name, angry and sullen, stood, bowed and began to speak.

"My Lord You'chel knows that rumors have flown like birds through the camp as to the coming military action of the three kingdoms. The Tangut Sui, from the Tibetan mountains, continue to expand in our area. The Wei, Tungus rulers of the east, have paid us as allies to resist. Our leader had news through spies of a shipment destined for the Mongol enemies and intercepted it. We captured foreign persons who were to convey the treasure to our enemies under the pretext of taking horses to the Wei rulers of the East. We know this to be a lie, so we hold both treasure and prisoners. We were in the process of eliminating the last of those who pursued us and win the golden horse, when Lord Bol'dar interfered. Our intentions were to protect the tribe and enrich it."

The Lord You'chel looked carefully at young Kaya and his ivory swan that signified high office, before saying, "You are permitted to speak now. Tell where you are from, your purpose in traveling. Tell your reason for being in our territory and all you have seen at the fort."

"I am Kaya, the bear, of the camp of Erkan of the Chipchak brotherhood, south of the Altai Mountains," he stated, bowing his powerful young body deeply. He was happy that all the preliminaries were over and talk could begin. "I am but a traveler with horses to deliver to the King of the East. Half of the herd was ahead with my master, the merchant Jomer and my foster sister Fewsoon."

The picture of their last parting came to his mind, her great eagerness to be with the first contingent when the treasure of gold and jewels would be received from the Prince of Wei. Her delight in commerce and travel seemed most unusual in the daughter of a Chipchak warrior. But there was no doubt of her love for all this.

"The first herd was confiscated on the pretext that they were destined for the Prince of Wu in the far southeast. This calumny is demonstrably false, as shown by the choice of roads. We would have taken the route over the mountains to arrive in the Red Basin if we were to trade in the south. Instead, we came to the Ordos and the north bank of the Yellow River. We found the frontier fort destroyed and our party, prisoner of the raiders. The commander of the fort was wounded, but lived to tell us of the leader of the raid, Koosta Short-thumb. The commander spoke of funds for the Mongols, stolen in the raid. We trailed the raiders to recover our people, and here we are," Kaya, after bowing, continued standing to await questions.

"You came for the treasure and for vengeance," accused Tersin, the raider lieutenant, "we should have finished you off earlier. You were in our trap."

"Stolen goods are returned to the owner," Kaya stated calmly, "Vengeance belongs to God, who can deliver men out of traps."

"The question at this point is: to whom does the treasure belong?" interrupted Bol'dar, "I say it is for us, and the fort commander said it was for Mongols. Do the Chipchaks claim it too?"

"No," You'chel boomed out in a powerful voice, "The question is: where is the treasure now? The possessor owns the wealth now. Later, in consultation with our Tungus ally, the Wei, the treasure will be disposed of. The Tibet Tanguts continue to advance and we are pressed eastward. The treasure is required now for defense."

"Lord You'chel," Kaya's voice cut in, "You know that the treasure is with Koosta and that raiding party entered the Gobi a few hours before my trackers. The men in your possession were to ambush my party and to rejoin their leader west of here. They are holding my kinswoman, Fewsoon, and the merchant Jomer for ransom."

"Searchers were dispatched last night, young warrior," You'chel cautioned, "guard your manners and your tongue."

All bowed and a brief silence ensued to restore harmony. Lord Bol'dar bowed again and with the assent of the high lord commenced on a new point. The assembly hung on his words.

"Our guests are anxious for friends, but we assure them that our young warriors are within our grasp. They are dutiful slaves of their master, Lord You'chel. No harm will befall any but the guilty. Let us use the time to talk of the need of horses by the high lord." He bowed, yet again, to the autocrat. "Old friends may grow forgetful, and new enemies rise like thunder clouds in summer, but the feel of trained horseflesh under a warrior's thighs is as joyful as a return to the yurt after a long journey."

"Arrange the details with our Chipchak friends," commanded You'chel. "We will return the captives and punish the guilty and send the necessary apologies... that is, explanations to the Wei."

> - - - - - - >

The enforced stay with the Huns produced a trade treaty negotiated reluctantly by Chan Zi and Kaya. A modest banquet of roasted game and blood sausage was enjoyed. A blind musician with a long-necked lute played an old song in the manner of the Wei people, extolling the heroes and ancestors.

1. Hear this story of the brave days
    When our fathers faced the foe.
    They were mighty men of valor;
    We their children know.
    Brave to face the awesome beasts,
    Courage rise with danger.
    Riding always in the hunt,
    They faced hunger, too.

Refrain:
1. We will remember and tell others too,
    Of the brave deeds people do,
    Of their faithful lives and true.

WE WILL REMEMBER

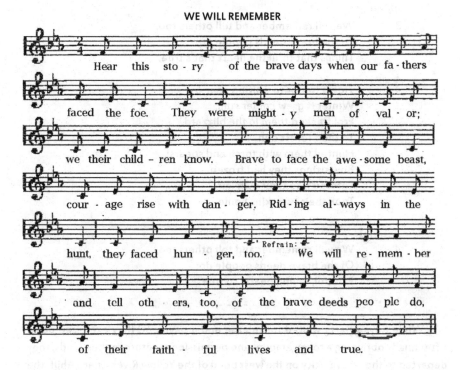

Hear this sto - ry of the brave days when our fa - thers faced the foe. They were might - y men of val - or; we their child - ren know. Brave to face the awe - some beast, cour - age rise with dan - ger. Rid - ing al - ways in the hunt, they faced hun - ger, too. Refrain: We will re - mem - ber and tell oth - ers, too, of the brave deeds peo - ple do, of their faith - ful lives and true.

2. Weather wild and large beasts too,
    Filled their days with fright and dread.
    Sickness frequent, danger constant,
    Filled their lives with pain.
    They were forced to fight the foe
    With the odds uneven.
    Men were brave and women bold
    All their whole life through.

Refrain:

2.   We will remember and tell others too,
        Of the brave things people do,
        Things unusual, but true.

3.   Erol was an orphan boy who
        herded with his brother old.
        Tigers spooked the stallion herd and
        Others bears had killed.
        In the snow and blowing wind,
        Off he went to save them.
        Fought the bear with knife in hand,
        Brought the horse herd home.

Refrain:

3.   We will remember and tell others too,
        Of the brave deeds people do;
        Things that thrill the heart that's true.

4.   Tigers too were waiting near-by,
        Winter it grew colder still.
        Erol tracked them in the blizzard
        To their forest den.
        Hunted them with torch and spears;
        Bow strings they had frozen.
        Entered into their own lair,
        Took their two skins home.

Refrain:

4.   We will remember and tell others too,
        Of the brave deeds people do;
        Faithful, loving hearts so true.

> - - - - - - - >

While Kaya's party waited for release and a payment, they exercised daily. After finally obtaining a token amount and permission to return to their lands, they departed to the caravan city on the west bend of the Yellow River. There Ahjit, the caravan master, was living with the Christian Ma clan. He waited with the purchases made from the compensation he received in exchange for the confiscation of the first horse herd. The glad encounter was marred only by the news that Koosta's band of Hunnish raiders had crossed the Gobi Desert to the Silk Road and was fleeing west. They made ready to follow.

Kaya's stay with Chan Zi and his shy wife was short, but pleasant. The caravan, formed for pursuit, carried the lightest and most valuable goods only.

As the travelers neared the city gate, the assembly point of departure for the pursuit, at an adobe and stone inn, they heard the sound of music. A pipe and drum beat out a southern tune from India. There, gathered before the gate near a fountain, was a crowd of travelers, local men, women drawing water, and children. They were watching the antics of a small brown bear as the two musicians sang.

COME TO HINDUSTAN

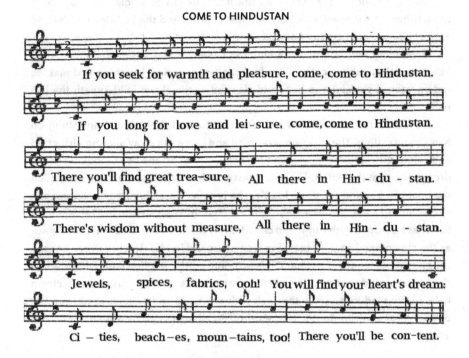

If you seek for warmth and pleasure, come, come to Hindustan.
If you long for love and lei-sure, come, come to Hindustan.
There you'll find great trea-sure, All there in Hin - du - stan.
There's wisdom without measure, All there in Hin - du - stan.
Jewels, spices, fabrics, ooh! You will find your heart's dream:
Ci - ties, beach-es, moun-tains, too! There you'll be con-tent.

If you seek for warmth and pleasure,
Come, come to Hindustan.
If you long for love and leisure,
Come, come to Hindustan.

There you'll find great treasure,
All there in Hindustan.
There's wisdom without measure,
All there in Hindustan.

Jewels, spices, fabrics, ooh!
You will find your heart's dream:
Cities, beaches, mountains, too!
There you'll be content.

They sang it repeatedly, for no one seemed to tire of it. All knew the whole of it by heart within a few trials. More people pressed in to gawk and listen to the strange music of the foreign men. They laughed heartily at their antics, but kept their distance from the bear.

The children - Chinese, Hun, Tungus, and Tibetan - danced and played as they imitated the dancing bear and then the flutist began to juggle four cloth balls before them. He started well, but soon lost control, and the balls fell on his head as the children laughed and pointed.

Screaming and taunting the children called: "Long nose, catch the balls." "Black monkey can't juggle." "Big fool can't play good." Laughing and making rude gestures, the children bent and clapped as the clown fell beneath the last ball.

Suddenly the bear roared and charged toward the prone man falling on him and wrestling. The children screamed and some ran away and the girls cried and called out, "Help him," "Don't hurt him," "Call off the bear," looking at the drummer and at the victim. The bear-master suddenly pulled the chain and called the bear off, beating the drum loudly. The juggler-victim jumped up. Running in circles hiding a bladder of water under his coat, he let it stream out between his hands as he yipped with fright and called shrilly for help. The children leaped back as the clown peed at their feet, Everyone laughed loudly. The bear then chased the man to the length of its chain. The boys and adults laughed and pointed while the girls giggled with heads together, ashamed and embarrassed. The clown held up the bladder to show the trick with one hand and held his miter-like cap out open for contributions with the other. Small copper coins were given by the adults.

MUSICIANS AND BEAR

As the crowd began to move, Kaya found himself again staring at the bear. It had grown but little in five years.

"What happened to the old bear?" asked Kaya, concern in his voice.

"By the Buddha, look who has come our way. Aren't you the bear boy, heir of the merchant, Jomer?" Optal, the bear-master exclaimed, with delight.

"Look how big and strong you have become," chortled Pesh, the comical friend, "and you're dressed like a Chipchak warrior. How fierce you look. You'll frighten all enemies away."

"The old bear," Kaya asked again mildly, "Did he die?" He looked from one man to the other.

Sadly, the old man nodded his head. The clown too, nodding, pulled out a large cloth and dabbed his eyes exaggeratedly.

"He got too old and irritable to work well," the bear-master said quietly, "so, we let him sleep that winter, but he never woke." The drummer moved toward the inn, "Come, I'll tell you about it." The clown moved rapidly before them to open the door and indicate the near corner table, summoning the inn keeper with another flourish and bow. Ahjit Bey followed Kaya and Ozkurt into the inn cautiously. Then, after looking inside, he returned to speak to his men who settled down to eat and make final preparations for the trip. Then, as he returned, he saw a hard-ridden Hun pony, head drooping, muzzle frothing, reins dangling, too exhausted to move, heaving at the rear of the inn. At that moment a small boy came out of the compound to lead the horse to the stable.

Inside the inn Ahjit saw no new arrivals. His hand on his waist- band dagger, he walked to where the juggler was quaffing a drink greedily. The drummer was already well launched into the story of the bear's demise, his hands shaking as he justified each decision and medicine used up to the end. The juggler watched Ahjit bey through narrowed eyes. Suddenly he leaned forward deliberately and spoke. "You are the leader of the merchant's caravans. I have seen you many times in E'peck Kent. But you are Chipchak too. Are you related by blood?" He motioned toward Kaya.

"We are from the same camp, but I left when he was but a child," Ahjit replied.

"Tenacious warriors, the Chipchaks. We were in their camp once, years ago, after a great battle involving thousands." The juggler shook his head marveling, "They won great riches and did great damage to the Persians."

Ahjit's laughter filled the inn. Then he sucked his breath in and bowed slightly, "Sorry, I forgot myself. It was only a modest skirmish with both sides retiring. The merchants and marauders kept most of the goods. But I do recall your presence in the camp."

"Yes, by Tanra, now I remember you," exclaimed the juggler, his face showing shock. "You were with the two pretty girls; the blond sang and danced for us."

"Yes, I remember. It has been a long time." Ahjit's face showed sadness with his smile.

"You were the lieutenant, Yuzbasha of the camp, so you must have led the attack against the marauders." The man's eyes showed bright excitement and interest. "You are a great warrior, Yuzbasha. I have heard stories of the attack, how quick and decisive your actions were." The man continued respectfully, "You won great honor against the raiders."

"Those events belong to a past life, not to my present one." Yuzbasha shifted uncomfortably. "God has made me a master of caravans now, although I still fight bandits sometimes."

"*Karma*, Yuzbasha, our fate is written before the gods." The man stated automatically, suppressing his excitement and taking another long drink from his cup.

Beside them, Kaya was feeding the bear and listening to the bear-master.

"You have survived many dangers, young master," the old man was saying. You say you arrived home after the Tartar attack on the Chipchak camp and your friends, the Prince Kutch and his father, were in the north Sayan mountains. How miraculous was the survival of those people. Everyone trembles at the power of the Tartars." The man placed his palsied hand on his face and added thoughtfully. "I hear they have moved west again and will move beyond the Ural mountains. Their Khan Bata is old and the young Prince lacks experience to resist others." He shook his head.

"Yes, honored sir, that is correct, by all accounts," Kaya stated, "so danger lies east for us rather than west at this moment. The Tanguts continue to descend from the mountains of Tibet pressing against Kansu province and the oases cities, the Tungus from the east plains are pressing west and all press on the Huns in the north and the Nan dynasties, the Wu, of the Chinese people in the Yangsi."

The drummer shook his head sadly, "When the elephants fight, where do the ants go?"

"Deep underground, hidden for a better day," answered Kaya with a smile. "But tell me of yourselves. Do you venture farther east?"

The drummer moved his head up sharply in a negative nod, "The competition gets greater eastward, the language changes and the differences of face make us less popular, so we never go beyond the Ordos Desert, and the loop of the Yellow River where Hunnish is still understood."

"I understand that things are tense inside the Great Walls, the rule of the Northern Tungus grows weak and the invasions of the mountain Tanguts is feared," Kaya confided to the bear-master.

"Where life and wealth are at risk because power lives with uncertainty, the people are irritable and angry. The Wei dynasty will end." The bear-master was whispering now, and abruptly he stopped as a manservant passed near to serve them. Kaya held a morsel up for the bear to beg for and attention shifted. When the servant passed, the drummer continued, "Take the north route through the desert for your return. Tangut troops of the Sui kingdom are gathering in the south, near the garrison towns. They could strike east or west."

"We must leave now," Kaya said, "We have a long journey until we make camp." They thanked the innkeeper with bows and silver. The musicians, with more bows and full stomachs, said, in bad Chipchak, "*Goo lay, go lay*, go happily."

As Ahjit and Kaya readied the caravan and moved out on their horses, a servant came from the inn with a package. He bowed deeply and extended the gift to Kaya.

"My master sends provisions for the road and thanks you again for your generosity," he stated. Inside the wrapped cloth were dried fruit and small, flat, cooked wheat cakes. The fruits Kaya placed in a bag at hand, near the ayran. Then, with thanks, rewrapped the cakes and stored them in a *heybe*, a woven wool saddle bag, on the back of his spare horse to eat later. He mounted Altom for the long ride.

Every man had two or three spare horses and changed mounts every two hours. Normally they would rest and eat with the changes, but today, after a huge, early breakfast, they were full and hurried, so they ate only some dried fruit for its sweetness and drank ayran.

Travelers on this part of the Silk Road attracted little notice and the travel papers written up by the Lord Boldar's scribes, passed them along swiftly from post to post.

DOG FIGHT

They arrived at sunset to a caravanserai on the edge of the desert. The bearded innkeeper received them at the door with an invitation to supper and promised an abundance of fresh provisions for the road. As they wearily unpacked for the night, a skinny, crippled old soldier in a tattered orange robe came near holding out his hands with a small bowl. He said "*Kar num match. Yetish tear benny*, I'm hungry. Help me."

Kaya, remembering his spare supplies, gave the man, a begging Buddhist monk, some of the wheat cakes and some fruit. The old soldier-monk thanked him and while walking away, stumbled and dropped the cakes. As soon as they touched the ground two scavenger dogs were eating them and their fighting with other hungry dogs sent the old one sprawling. Kaya helped him to his feet and gave him the entire package of remaining food.

Entering the inn they were served an acceptable meal: meat and bulgur, boiled wheat, which formed the core of many meals there on the desert's edge. In the morning, as Ahjit went out to prepare the caravan's departure, he found the bodies of two of the dogs near the front of the inn. From the smell and strained look of their bodies, poison seemed indicated as the cause of their deaths. Immediately, search was made for the beggar.

They found the old monk where the innkeeper had suggested: inside his lean-to of brush, lying on his back, beside a smoldering hearth fire, dead, staring at the sky. A bit of unfinished wheat cake lay in its cloth wrapping. Kaya rekindled the hearth and placed the remaining cakes on the fire to be destroyed. They burned slowly.

"Someone seeks our lives," Kaya said gravely, "They have missed the mark, but another has taken our place and warned us. We must pray for the repose of his soul."

"It must be Koosta's people," interjected Ozkurt angrily. "They fret for the safety of their treasure." Kaya shrugged, knelt and making the sign of the cross, started to pray. As he finished Ozkurt asked, "Why do you pray for one who is not of our faith and is barred from the Yesu's Garden?"

"God used this man to save us. We should be thankful. I wish him repose, knowing his life has saved others, even though he did not know of salvation in Yesu."

They paid an extra fee to the innkeeper to have the body buried and left immediately, following the trail west.

BLIND SINGER

PEOPLE, PLACES & PLOTS IN CHAPTER 3

Ajit: the caravan master hurries his men for a return home.
Emperor of the Hui: a young man of great talents, but easily bored with court procedures.
Lord Secretary of External Affairs: is an old experienced hand at foreigners' threats.
Kai Ya: Chinese way of dealing with the name of Kaya.
Koo Sta: Chinese name of Koosta.
Mai Ling: the Emperor's new favorite in the Royal Harem, a Tungus princess.
Wei: a kingdom in northeast China controlled by the Hui dynasty and supported by Tungus warriors.

GLOSSARY:

Ak'koon: the White Huns, an elite army of the West Huns expanding into India.
chay: tea, a popular drink.
Ye-shu kel: Jesus come; (Eastern Turkic dialects exchange K for G and broaden the S to Sh.)

EMPEROR'S CAGE

A tense, vigilant caravan traveled at top speed along the Kansu corridor toward the west, Ahjit and Kaya at the head, Ozkurt and the best archers at the tail. This living body of men bonded to the same purpose and mutually dependent for survival, moved through societies that were dependent on supplying other's needs in transit. It was a mutually helpful dependence as long as greed did not overcome good sense and help turn to harm.

The thin, tenuous, hilly road trailed from city to city. Each center was almost but not quite independent of the others, however proud and separate each might feel. They all existed for the reason of trade, the link that depended on the sensibility and goodwill of the larger part of their inhabitants. This was only one of many requirements for survival. Soil was needed that would yield sustenance for the grower and a surplus of food that could be sold to transients. Water and supplies were the body of their life, but commerce was the blood.

Squeezed between the pastoral societies of the deserts to the north and the herders of the high mountain pastures to the south, this narrow road of cities prospered. Each was highly individual by reason of topography: water supply, protecting mountains, quality of soil, local climate, ethnic composition, linguistic affiliations, customs and gods. Each city was part of the channel by which art, knowledge and faith could stimulate men's minds by their transmission with the goods of high intrinsic value.

The value of interdependence was evident with the rapidity of the spread of ideas. There was the stimulation of competing thoughts: Greek, Hindu and Chinese art forms were evident, as were temples of Buddhists, Taoists, Christians,

Manicheans, and local deities. Men and women in different regional dress with varied racial and cultural characteristics walked the streets and rode every kind of imaginable contrivance and animal.

The cities were rich, some more than others, and the rich set the standards. Ostentation was everywhere evident: pride set few limits to the heights of extravagance. Ambition and common interest tried to link the cities politically, but the only civilization capable of linking them was China, at this time hopelessly divided.

The Sui dynasty ruled in the Red Basin and southwest. Control over some of the corridor cities was in their hands, patrolled by the army of Tangut mountain men and imposed authorities. These authorities lacked the power to enforce obedience outside their cities and agricultural districts.

As Kaya traveled, the evidence of fighting in west Kansu province produced beggars and bandits in large numbers. The first lined the roads and city gates, whining piteously. The later appeared suddenly, armed to demand tolls arrogantly. Loyang, the northern capital of Wei, was losing control.

Kaya knew that local information was provided by the inns; each knew their section intimately, together with the latest travel news. Two weeks had passed since they left the Yellow River's northern loop at Laoling. The route was no longer under control of the Huns. The authorized passes of Boldar were no longer accepted and were retained only as proof of their successful arrival at the Hun camp. Other documents from E'peck Kent took their place. As much time was spent in passing garrisons as was passed traveling on the road. However, to return to the desert north to avoid passing garrisons meant suspicion and rough treatment farther along the line, and winter on the desert without sufficient provisions meant death. Even the fleeing Hun raiders would have to make contact with the towns and repeat their story and answer the inevitable questions.

> - - - - - - - >

The clatter of a horse's hooves in the courtyard advised the Emperor of Wei of the arrival of urgent post. The hum of voices carried a sound of urgency. The news would have to pass the secretary and ministers and be copied down for filing before arriving to his ears and his decision recorded.

He rolled his shoulders round and suppressed a yawn and thought, 'Buddha, how boring it was with all the traditions and protocol.' He thought of the beautiful Mai Ling, his newest favorite. How she could play and sing like a nightingale; thoughts of her wit and charm caused him to sigh. At once, an attendant bent over to inquire of his comfort. He shrugged and was suddenly annoyed. He longed for the private quarters of the women's court.

The commotion of the secretary's entrance to the Hall of Ceremonies brought him out of his reveries. The grossly fat, bowing figure desired to speak, and he nodded his acquiescence.

"Oh Most Serene and High Emperor of the Wei People and rightful heir of all the Han Empire and tribes of the northeast, I beg your indulgence for the news of the barbarians of the north and west," began the old minister's preamble.

The Emperor's nod was just perceptible as he waited. He wondered if one of his younger companions could be posted in the old minister's place. He sighed. The bureaucracy had itself hedged about and was protected from disruption by capricious whims. He had started his favorites as high up the ladder and as fast as the unyielding structure of rules would permit him. 'I am a prisoner in the city of Loyang, in a cage constructed of ministers and protocol,' he thought.

"Speak, oh worthy one," commanded the Emperor as he motioned an aid for a bowl of deep red tea known as *chay*.

"The agent of the people of the lion horses has received full compensation for the animals confiscated and delivered at Baotou. Both herds are composed of superior beasts, and we have compensated at full value, surrendering our advantage." The old man's manner was intimate and smooth, only a trace of smugness showed... just enough to annoy the enthroned youth.

"My ancestors of the glorious Mu Rong grew to greatness by the generous use of northern tribes. Set aside some breeding stock from the herds and speed the herders back, away from the Huns." The Emperor was cool and assertive as he claimed the advice of his counselors.

"There are no golden stallions among the herds and the mares were isolated before travel. None are with foal except a few used in breeding the meat ponies; those set aside only for consumption." There was a slight hint of triumphant, 'I told you so,' in the manner of the minister.

"Send the best mares to our herds and make sure the Huns do not get any of them. These allies need not have the best, though they bargain for it."

"The commander of the destroyed garrison, Koke Ju, has been demoted and assigned to work with those tracing the raiders. In spite of wounds he rides with the advanced party." Here the voice and manner of the minister was flawless and impassive; the Commander was a nephew.

"Yes, Koke Ju has a burr under his tail. He will ride far and fast," the Emperor's face wore a sneer as he prodded the proud, tender spot in his minister.

"Poison was used in an attempt against the Turk leaders. We lack knowledge of the planners. It may have been the revenge of the relatives of the renegade, Koo Sta, who is now under ban by the tribe," the minister bowed again knowing that the gruesome details would be expected in full. "The raiders cut across the desert to tribal and Sui towns in the west. We are alerting agents on the Silk Road."

"I want Koo Sta in our special torture chamber. I had tribal friends in the school near the wall who remember his tricks and bullying. It is a bad example to let him take the Emperor's wealth."

"My Lord knows that the notorious rebel and leader of the dissatisfied young men, Koo Sta, is outside our reach. He is into the west of Kansu among the barbarian cities fleeing farther west. We may try to strike him down, but to force a return is impossible. We are now just able to delay him in the alien towns. He uses his new wealth generously."

"We have agents outside our borders. What are they doing? Our wealth is stolen and our diplomacy in tatters. Both friends and enemies may discover our plans for the disruption of the northern tribes. The tribe defrauded will talk and denounce. The tribe betrayed will know us for enemy. Someone must pay." The Emperor's voice rose in indignation and rage. "We cannot be sure that the wealth was not overlooked by the raiders and taken by the herders who would be doubly enriched at our expense."

"New wealth burns men's purses to be spent. The hunted ones are leaving their trail in greased palms. We are now sure they are running for the land of the *Ak' Koon*, White Huns, who live in the deserts north of the Hindu Kush mountains, near where the Gupta Empire has expanded. The White Huns are aggressive and need mercenary warriors for strikes along the borders. My Lord will remember from his history tutor that they are part of the old, right hand Hun army by their own peculiar designation, and like all Huns for the last 400 years, they are a menace to civilized peoples."

"This Kai Ya of the Turks, who wears the ivory badge, can we speed him to revenge us?" inquired the Emperor eagerly.

"The band is capable of a strike, but there are a few complications. They seek two held for ransom. If they are returned, they might be content. The man is a Christian and does not seek revenge. My Lord must remember the last conversation about this subversive faith spreading among the caravan cities." The counselor eyed the indolent young lord carefully. It was such a struggle to train up a good Emperor, but his own future depended on it. He sighed, and prompted: "The dying god who carries the sins of his people; the one who will come to set up a righteous kingdom."

"Oh, yes. A god tortured to death by his enslaved, but expectant people, killed for sedition against the Romans. He's a crucified god, eaten repeatedly in ceremony, and a goddess of mercy, beautifully tender, praying for repentant sinners." It was the Emperor's turn to sigh. The counselor's face puckered with worry.

"Yes, High One, it travels far and sets kingdoms on fire. It is accompanied by riot and uncontrollable changes. Its faithful show a contrary disposition. They do not always act as one would expect."

"But so far away is its source. The goddess is so sweet and appealing, so feminine in concerns." He remembered at this moment the graceful statue that Mai Ling kept in her quarters. "The man is heroic and good. How could such a charming story of domestic and national tragedy be dangerous?"

"Sire, this god is appealing, but inflexible. He demands all, and his standards are absolute. He will accept anyone, regardless of past life, but makes the same demands on all. He offers to all the same fantastic rewards. He condemns totally what he calls sin, and is offensively impartial to rank and condition. This is why our laws are so stringent against this foreign innovation. Let not the matter of distance fool My Lord. Buddhism comes from far Hindustan, and it is powerful in our land, but has the advantage of being pliant, man-centered, ignoring the gods."

"Yes, my dynasty, the Hui, has grown great by promoting the great teachings of the Buddha, and the self-disciplines are better for a properly obedient population. They have our support and no new beliefs must be allowed to confuse the mind of our people." There was a pause while the Emperor considered the full implication of his statement in relation to Mai Ling, but decided a few exceptions would not bend the rule. "If the band of Kai Ya will not revenge us, we may as well consider the value of the money they carry. In that case, the messenger's news of the poison's failure would be bad news."

"Unless, Lord, the value of the promised horses is greater for our future needs. If we promote the Tungus and Mongolian tribes against our late allies, the Huns, we will need the best possible advantage in trained mounts. The miserable, grubby merchants and middlemen cannot supply the quantity obtained directly from the source tribe."

"All the barbarian tribes raise horses, Counselor, but few have ready cash on hand. We need cash, and also Kai Ya is reported to have visited the Hun headquarters riding a golden horse fit for an Emperor. What agreements would he have made there? We await our agents' reports. We must think more on this. It must be highly secret, however. It would not be propitious for Heaven or the Hui dynasty if it were known that I, the 'Son of Heaven,' was less than completely honorable in negotiating government treaties."

"We have carrier pigeons for your agents in the west at any time," agreed the old counselor, reluctantly. "We must not act hastily for it involves dangers to the throne itself. If Koo Sta is going to the White Huns, north of the Hindu Kush Mountains, he follows but one known way. Kai Ya must follow. We have agents in two places, ample time and thus a double chance with each party." An avid eagerness crept over the Emperor's face; the intoxication of the hunt. The old one sighed at this sign of barbarian Hui weakness. Should he resign? The ruler was corrupt; he had just confessed it. Confucius teachings were clear. The dynasty will fall.

"We will lay plans tonight after moon-rise." Mai Ling had been kept waiting long enough, and the business of court was tedious, except for moments of intrigue, when it came to planning men's deaths. Then, power over other's lives became exciting and pleasant. He could gain a golden horse and the price of two herds.

> - - - - - - - >

Mai Ling's division of the Women's palace was sumptuous, as befits the status of a favorite. There were servants, especially chosen and trained from childhood for particular jobs, a few mutilated for greater security, who were permitted liberty of movement in the apartments. A few spied for a price, but most were loyal and their own future rose and fell with their mistress. They had groomed her assiduously every fold and hair was in place. She was beautifully proportioned and strong; a confident young woman of limited social experience from a northern tribe, but indulged by a doting family, trained by experts in all the arts.

She sat before the dais bed where the Emperor lay replete with the banquet meal, served by a host of anxious servants, his every whim indulged. She wondered that he was so quiet and thoughtful. He stared through the open door at the moon gate of the garden. Soon the moon would rise, the gate framing its summer rising. She was not the center of his attention, but she had a special treat to wrest it to herself again.

At her sign an instrument was brought to her. She pretended to fuss over its tuning, sweeping several chords in succession, but it was all readied before hand. She struck a sweeping cord and bowed for permission to start. The Emperor smiled his assent. Her high, child-like voice was warm and whimsical as she sang:

1.   Little frog sits on a lily pad all alone.
   She'll watch the world hop by, with a sigh.
   One's passing by. She tries to catch his eye.
   Come to me.
   Would you love me ever; share life's endeavor?
   Tell me true.

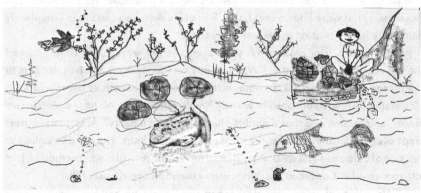

SHY SEEKERS

The music cast a spell over the room and the new favorite had the eye and ear of everyone in the quarter. Some who had heard her practice, smiled with pleasure at her accomplishment, poise and performance; others hid disappointment from envy and rivalry secretly felt. The harem is a narrow world of intense intrigue and competition. The moment belonged to Mai Ling and she filled it beautifully as she continued her appealing song.

2.   Little bird sits on a nesting site, all alone.
        She'll watch the world fly by, whistling high.
        One's flying near, she tries to catch his ear.
        Find me here.
        Would you love me really, and share life's feelings?
        Tell me, do.

3.   Little fish swims near the ocean floor, one alone.
        She'll watch the world swim by, bubbles high.
        One's darting by, she shows her brightest light.
        See the sight?
        Would you love me truly, and share life's duty?
        Love me, true.

4.   Little heart waits doing daily chores, cries alone.
        She'll watch the world pass by, smiling dry.
        One's going by, she shows her talents bright.
        See me right?
        Would you love me truly, and share life's beauty?
        Love me, do.

WOULD YOU LOVE ME

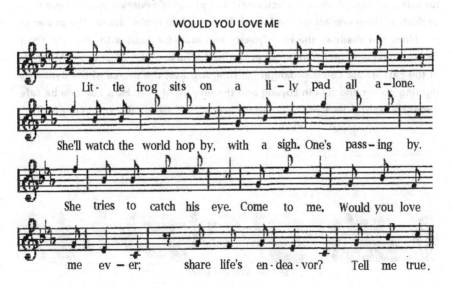

Lit - tle frog sits on a li - ly pad all a —lone.

She'll watch the world hop by, with a sigh. One's pass - ing by.

She tries to catch his eye. Come to me. Would you love

me ev — er, share life's en - dea - vor? Tell me true.

The first glow of moon-rise touched the Emperor's face and the room simmered in the growing light. The man sighed deeply, and turned his gaze to the face of the slim beauty.

"This sign must not be on display anywhere. It is forbidden." He reached out and touched the Tau cross that graced her neck. "I must go now," he said softly, "there is interesting work awaiting me. I will be very late. Do not wait up for me." She bit her lip and bowed her head in assent. She knew her defeat, and the answer to her song; there would be other favorites. She would dream of a youth she might have had, had she known, but ambition spurns the obvious.

Mai Ling alone held the key to a small room near the garden. Flowers decked a small shrine where the statue of the Goddess of Mercy presided beneath a cross. She made the sign and knelt before the statue. She removed her necklace and placed the cross at the feet of the image. "Lady," she prayed, "I should have listened to you, and to my heart. I have sinned and now repent. This is a matter to place before your son, Ye shu, only He can save me." A blush crept up her neck into her face.

"He knows, but I shall have to tell Him anyway." She crossed her hands over her breasts, bowed deeply and murmured, "*Ye-shu kel.*"

> - - - - - - - >

The Emperor sat in the private chamber with his counselor, but his mind wandered to the moon gate and the song. He could feel her hurt now. He cringed at his callous behavior. His mother would scold him for such discourtesy.

"Perhaps, at another time, in another life," the ruler thought, and sighed again. "Buddha, life is too complicated and binds a man to murder and extortion for safety's sake." A thrill of excitement swept him. Power was his to move men or destroy them and affect the future. The kingdom is not secure. The power of the Huns still shadows the Hui dynasty and must be dealt with strongly. Their destruction might give dangerous power to the Turks of the West or the Mongols of the East. These could endanger his Tungus tribes; the source of the dynasty's fighting power and rule in Loyang and the empire of Wei. How can one be safe under Heaven? Where lies the road to salvation? How could I cripple them all?

SPRING STEPPE FLOWERS

MOON GATE

PEOPLE, PLACES & PLOTS IN CHAPTER 4

Ah'jit: the caravan master handles his men skillfully.
Emperor of the Hui: is perplexed as plans go wrong.
Fang' Nu: an agent of the Hui government in the city is a local enforcer and executioner.
Ka'ya: tries to raise morale and keep clear of trouble.
Mai' Ling: risks by trying to help, and finds more freedom.
Oz'kurt: is resentful over delays passing cities in their pursuit.
Soy' Lee: a special performer at the city's farewell banquet.
Tash: a desperate farmer for sale, with special talents needed by secret agents.

GLOSSARY:

bonze: a spiritual head of Buddhist monasteries.
choke al'tun var: They have lots of gold; They are rich.
tash: a stone; pebble; a small particle.

FANG NU'S AGREEMENT

Kaya yawned, stretched and looked across the room at his companion. Ozkurt looked back and shrugged. Neither felt like talking; the waits to fulfill all legal requirements between journeys seemed longer the farther west in Kansu one went. Non-agricultural areas were of slight interest to troops. The Tangut warlords, who ruled in the name of the southwestern Sui dynasty, controlled the fertile frontiers areas with great vigilance. Each Lord tried to balance free commerce and control of the local population. One town would obey the Sui, the next, with strong walls, the Wei, or some local oligarchy. Loyalty was tenuous, conflicting, changeable and frequently for sale.

"They travel as slowly as we," Kaya said suddenly, "With even more delays and perhaps bigger bribes."

"Like us, once out of the corridor, they'll avoid towns for desert travel," returned Ozkurt sourly, "*Choke al' tun var,* they have lots of gold. They have millions to make heads bow and open the road."

"The scent of gold brings a thirst not easily quenched," stated Kaya smiling, "'My gold' is surer and faster," he quipped. "Koosta has more armed people, but Yownja will be creating distractions, and their lies will not be believed without price. Commanders will dally over the price of passage, versus the price of reward from bilked relatives and rulers back east. The troop is too large to go long without re-supplying. Even the weak towns will exact delays, while we draw nearer."

"Herd owners have gold from sales too," objected Ozkurt, "We'll pay, too, and have nothing when we arrive home, worn and poor."

"'God, family and friends first.' my teacher would say. 'Then land and goods.' We exercise legitimate commerce. They will want us to come again. More than that, they see us as the arm of authority to recover the loss of the defrauded." Then he grinned mischievously, "I intend to keep 'My Gold' regardless of our remaining coins."

"It is taking too long. They will disappear into the desert," Ozkurt complained despondently.

Kaya shook his head slowly, but persisted with a sad smile.

"Even with that, they must find tribal friends and allies. Believe me, we will run them to earth," Kaya affirmed positively. "Ahjit is with the commander now. He is well known, being a caravan master. We'll go to the next garrison."

"Why does Ahjit live in the midst of the men while we live apart?" Ozkurt continued.

"A good commander knows his troops and keeps an eye on the morale and condition of his men. In this we differ from others. Our men get only the best equipment and care. In those things we are all equals," Kaya smiled wryly, "But as the elder son, I, the Heir of Promise must have special treatment."

"I am only an ignorant man from the hills beyond the Chipchak steppes. I do not know protocol," Ozkurt commented frowning.

"You are my chosen friend and companion," Kaya laughed, "but you would have our caravan shrouded in gloom if you were billeted with them."

>- - - - - - - >

The city elders nodded and conversed behind their fans. The excitement was evident and even Ozkurt looked animated and alert. Kaya sat patiently at the center of a circle, of largely town's people, but with his key men seated behind him.

The wealth of Yumen city was shown in the dress of the councilors and the large room's furnishings. It was superficially Han, but the features, language and dress of the people showed important differences. Most spoke Hunnish, Tibetan and Northern Han Chinese, but other languages were evident. The divisions thus demonstrated made it possible for local political maneuvering to take place within the oligarchy by both the Hun and Tungus dynasties. It had also provided the diversity where Christianity entered and was slowly growing in the mix of tribes and religions.

The arrival of a worn, hungry pigeon meant communication from the Emperor of Wei, ten days flight east. Relays were set up so each bird was to do one day's flight, but occasionally one was delayed overnight. It was rumored that the message would enrich the Town Council. Secretaries of both Han pictographs and Sogdian script were seated behind their low tables, ready for official decrees and actions.

The Spokesman/Ruler entered in a sea of bows and salutations. His rich silk robes reflected the light of the summer day and the wealth of the oligarchy.

Everyone remained bowing until he was seated on the dais, and the interview began. The Spokesman called the names of the Chipchak and caravan leader.

Ahjit protested the delays imposed by the city leaders and the inflated passage tax. Most of the caravan goods were not of a perishable nature, but supplies were being used up and needless cost and delay involved. The caravan leader Ahjit was well known and merited considerate treatment. The Chipchak herdsmen were acting as guards on the return journey. When questioned about the price of the purchased horse herds, Ahjit claimed that the money had remained with the agents, who purchased for the merchant Lord Jomer. The bankers and buyers had retained the money for debts and new purchases.

Had Kaya's party been smaller or less well known, a forced search would have been in order. However, the town of Yumen had imperial connections and a message was awaited. All the town cried out in admiration as an Imperial carrier pigeon fluttered down at the cote. The town buzzed with excitement. A messenger ran into the gathering and thrust the message into the magistrate's hands. Heads together the elders consulted the new orders.

"The Son of Heaven declares your freedom to proceed and prays your prompt return in peace to trade with our kingdom." Everyone bowed and smiled and a farewell feast was announced to celebrate the righteous decision. In the preparations for the feast, no one noticed that another imperial pigeon arrived hours later at dusk with new, secret, contrary messages for special agents.

Kaya had the caravan in a flurry of preparation. The men worked with a will for they had been bored, but they nevertheless complained bitterly about being sent ahead. They would miss some tidbits from the banquet. Only the chief men were invited, but prized bits were passed round and the regular ration was larger. Ahjit would not listen or relent. He jollied the men with jokes as they packed.

"You complained about staying, now you complain about going. What will please you? When we arrive in E'peck Kent the banquet will be for you, my word on it! Then, you can eat it all. These people don't eat the good dark red horse meat that satisfies. They will eat dog meat or rat, my word.... Have you forgotten that nice wife of yours? She must be longing for you now... Home cooking in another month, and presents to surprise them... Why delay?"

Only Ozkurt would not be jollied and Kaya had to relent lest he carry the whole camp into rebellion. It was decided that Ahjit would beg off and start the caravan while Ozkurt was toasted as lieutenant. He and Kaya would leave Yumen late and join the caravan that night along the main route.

The caravan departed and the town turned out to watch and cheer them on their way. They got some farewell gifts as town folk pressed small presents of food on them and wished a safe return. Caravans and trade were, after all, their lifeblood. The herders were friendly, simple tribesmen, but their loyalty was outside the town, and they could become feared enemies by a command. Their continued goodwill was important to the town.

> - - - - - - - >

In the same town of Yumen, another agreement was being made. The large, powerfully built man, who sat on a dais, stared at the small wiry man sullenly sitting on his haunches below. The big man, wearing an ivory badge of office, was the local enforcer of imperial edicts and was known as a 'hatchet man.' He was not above personally executing imperial justice on chosen targets. Fang Nu was not liked, but was certainly feared. He was a man who enjoyed his work, and no man felt safe from his envious eyes. The little man well knew his reputation. The big man worked in secret and met his new tool in a small room above the banquet room. There below, he too, would enjoy a meal honoring his newest victim.

"You have been selected because of your special qualities. The plan is understood? The timing must be perfect." The cruel-faced man watched the small man carefully. He could see resignation in his whole manner and face.

The man, *Tash*, nodded wordlessly. He understood. He would not fail. He made a sign with his head. He had the patient look of the farmer, the stubborn quality of men who planted where crops could fail, except for the cleverness and ability of those who cared for the plants. He had the look of men living on the margins, making the desert bloom. His name, little rock, *Tash,* spoke his hardness.

Tash knew the quality of the prey. His father's fields had been burned by herdsmen riding horses that gave them speed and distance to hit those who encroached on their grazing rights. They were cruel to farmers whose future could be ruined in one night of burning and plundering.

There developed over the centuries a flexing line of cropland, with sufficient rain for harvest yields three out of four years. This line set margins, which marked the end of normally productive farmlands. The farmers kept a few small herds of animals on the arid, less productive meadows on the desert side, which served them in good, rainy years. In bad, dry years they quickly slaughtered their surplus animals.

Farmers dealt with the bearded nomads obtaining salt, hides, dried meat and young animals in exchange for wheat, barley, fruits and vegetables. Barter existed and coin facilitated business, but it was an easy step to robbery in hard times.

In bad years the nomads entered the farmer's fields to save their stock; the drier the year, the deeper the penetration and the harder the fighting. It was a question of who had the right and power to live. From this uncertainty and occasional conflict arose the need for strong Emperors and great walls.

There was the question of shortages as well; the need for women and children when death struck hard at a tribe. Violence was a substitute for bargaining and loss of valued goods by trade. It avoided the risk of rejection and loss of face.

Tash had lost two sisters in this way. As they had grown to maturity they were snatched away and taken to an alien life far from their home. He bore the scar of an arrow on his shoulder from one such conflict. It was then that the fires of revenge had burned unquenched in his heart. Peace had left him, and he practiced with the knife and cleaver until he could split a bean inserted in the bark of a tree at ten paces using either hand.

His father's death during a raid in his boyhood had left the farm without enough hands. The loss of the sisters had compounded the damage. The authorities were hesitant to possess the land for unpaid taxes, but knowing the man's good qualities offered him to the enforcer. That great man, Fang Nu, now offered the chance to eliminate his debts and revenge himself at the same moment. It was a unique opportunity, even though his old mother pleaded for reason and integrity.

He knew the money lenders to be lazy leaches, fattening on the labor of others, but he could escape them. Kill a tribal leader and get money for it. Here, truly, one got two birds with one stone. He made sure of the enforcer's money, canceling all the debts. He was paid and the fact recorded in his favor. He had gold enough to pay the cost of a strong wife to help his old mother. Whatever the outcome, he was content.

The giant enforcer, Fang Nu, relaxed, well pleased. The plan of assassination was perfect. No others knew of the plot. Theft and murder were common in the city. The local citizens would be shocked for a moment, but so many nomads came and went, the death of a few would only cause the people to appreciate the protection of the government more. Moreover, he would be close behind to make sure the man died. There would be a bonus and a golden horse for his reward. His smile almost made him look happy.

The banquet was attended by some of the prominent business men and landowners as well as government. The horse trade was aristocratic, and the breeding of mules was a lucrative pastime. Altom attracted their attention and admiration. However, the cold deserts did not produce good horses. For that, one needed grasslands.

Women were afraid of the barbarian tribesmen and were not normally present at civic functions anyway; just men came.

Peace and prosperity were spoken of and wished to all, with long life and many descendants. Those present were richly dressed. They sat on cushions on the floor and ate off low tables. It was a business dinner, friendly and jovial, but that did not mean it was without its attractions. There was a very pretty youth there who would provide the entertainment, since women were not present.

Soy Lee sat cross-legged with a zither like instrument on his lap. He was dressed as a woman, with kohl eye-shadow, in beautiful silks and without a beard looked very feminine and appealing. Several men seemed fascinated by him. His high falsetto was clear and sweet. He announced his song as: a riddle for the children and for the wise.

1.　　　　She kissed me 'neath the willow tree.
　　　　　She kissed me twice and fled.
　　　　　She kissed me and I wanted more,
　　　　　And so I seek her always.
　　　　　Beside the flowing waters there,
　　　　　We met and fell in love.
　　　　　I didn't even learn her name,
　　　　　And yet I seek her always.

THE RIDDLE

2.   Sometimes in dreams I see her there,
            Beneath the willow tree.
            I talk she answers not a word,
            Although, I seek her always.
            I live beneath the willow tree.
            A home I built in vain.
            She never has come back again,
            But still I seek her always.

The singer stopped expectantly, looked round the room and asked in a shy voice if someone had learned the name of the woman and where she lived.

One of the younger boys at his father's urging spoke up. "Is it the willow woman?" he asked blushing. The father threw his head back to laugh and hugged the boy happily. The men exchanged smiles and Soy Lee nodded and continued to sing.

3.   The willow woman is her name.
            She lives inside a tree.
            I carve my name into its bark.
            Now she is mine forever.
            I know my friends believe me not,
            That such a thing should be.
            I smile and show our children then,
            My sprouting little willows.

A shower of silver and bronze coins followed the performance. Laughter was hearty and general. Several sent script or paper money with their personal seal stamped on it. Perhaps they offered an invitation for another performance.

Servants entered and departed with the numerous trays of food and drink. Among the servants was the small wiry farmer who was awkward with his work. He passed the broad back of Kaya and the slender form of Ozkurt, and he studied their faces from the side. The ivory swan identified the tribal commander. Tash was not required to continue to serve. It was enough that he knew his target. He withdrew to wait at the caravanserai building where the men would leave to join the departed caravan westward. The stable master was well-paid to call.

The small Tash sat in a corner of the room, waiting the call of the stable master. When the call came: that the horses were prepared, the men would move down the long corridor where the rooms branched off. They would come toward the stairs down to the main floor. The target was the broad-chested young man who was a tribal leader and man of influence among the peoples beyond the northern desert; the essence of the mobile enemy whom all northern Han people feared. Men moved in the corridor, but no call came. There were the sounds of horses in the courtyard, but no call. There was the sound of shouting outside. Finally, the call came. "Sir, your horse awaits, come." There was the sound of haste in the corridor. The time had come.

Cleaver upraised, Tash leaped into the corridor to see the giant form of a man wrapped in a riding cloak, wearing an ivory badge, hurrying past the stairs toward his room. The throw caught the silhouetted man in the head, although his hands were up before him in protest and protection. The enforcer, Fang Nu, toppled back and down the stairs with a crash. The startled Tash turned back into his room and crawled through a small hole to the roof. A nearby tree offered shelter in the increasing dark. Before dawn he was able to descend and pass the city gates at first light, like any farmer returning from a day in the city. By dark he had walked the distance to his farm on the desert's edge where he waited to spend his reward.

Kaya and Ozkurt followed the river northwest from Yumen between the wall and the river. They had hurried to get away as early as possible after the dinner, gotten their own horses and had ridden at top speed. There had been an uproar at the inn after they left it, but they did not turn back. Their horses were exhausted when they joined the caravan near midnight. They got little sleep the camp was up and moving by dawn.

> - - - - - - - >

Mai Ling and her women were waiting, food warmed and instruments tuned and ready. The Emperor sat long faced and meditative, ignoring the tantalizing odors from the kitchen. When he heaved a sigh, May Ling dared to speak,

"Two can bear a burden with greater ease than one."

He raised his head, "Even the world cannot bear an Emperor's failures."

She ventured sweetly, "The God who rules over all can turn ill to good for those who humble themselves to accept His decrees."

He stared at her, "Heaven does not approve of what I attempted. So, it has ceased to smile on my efforts."

She nodded sympathetically. "Confession is Heaven's road to salvation and new blessings."

He laughed and kissed her hand. "It is ironic that the religion I have favored has repaid me with treason. Yet yours is full of forgiveness. Three Buddhist monasteries are found hoarding arms and the *Bonze*, directors, are implicated in plotting to rise and remove the dynasty because of our foreign origin. For this reason, I'll rescind the harsh decrees against your people. Some of the more traditional governors have been over-zealous; fines will be rescinded and prisoners freed.

"Besides all this, there is the unexplained loss of an agent, Fang Nu, in the west and the failure to eliminate a rich enemy, who has made some kind of agreement with the Gobi Huns. They are now lost in an area where the Tanguts press from the southern mountains on the west trade route. Instability there means loss of revenue. The men I wanted are almost beyond my reach now. There is but one more agent at the end of the corridor." He shook his head, "The old one has promised success on our last try or he will resign his position." He smiled, "It might be worth a failure." And then, he covered a yawn and stretched. "Come, pillow my head and let me nap. I need your comfort." As she placed his head on her lap, he looked up, touched the bare neck and asked, "Where is your talisman? Do you not wear it? Wear it now. I like it! Why should we favor one way of the gods over others?"

EMPEROR'S REST

PEOPLE, PLACES & PLOTS IN CHAPTER 5

Da vut': is an honest youth, son of Neshe bey and guide across the Pamir Plateau.

Jomer: suffers loss of strength, as do his enterprises.

Ka chak': is a boy you have to watch as a known guide and smuggler.

Ka'ya: meets some good news, and at the end more bad news.

Mert'ler: is organizer of the hunt, a friend of the royal family.

Neshe bey: is a happy old merchant, able to redeem an old friend for health and freedom.

Oz'kurt: tires of cold and dust and longs for excitement.

Ser'dar: the twelve-year old son of a Khan loves to hunt with his grandfather.

Tek'han: is the wise old grandfather of Ser'dar, his only weakness.

GLOSSARY:

dee-cot': careful; attention; be cautious; be alert; look out.

em'dot: help; emergency; give me aid.

gel' ya: come now; come here; come on.

hanjers: daggers used in fighting, or for utility, the fine point opens seams.

kim'sin: who are you? who's there?

seer'seery: vagabond; tramp; vagrant; bum.

AMBUSH AT AN XI

At the west end of the corridor, beyond Kansu Province, was the ancient city of An Xi, beyond the last section of the great wall. Here the mountains of the south squeezed the alluvial trench of a river between the Gobi rocks and sandstone, forming fault lines, rugged country. To the west the high, mountain-surrounded basin of the Tarim River system opened. It is an area never Chinese in blood or culture, but always deeply influenced by them. The river runs west into the lower basin, desert country.

The time had come to decide on the parting of three ways. Northwest lay the road to the Dzungarian basin and the homeland, below the Altai Mountains. Due west, lay the road to E'peck Kent and the north side of the Tarim Basin. Southwest of An Xi lay the drier southern route to Yarkand and the Pamir Mountains. Here the caravan shifted to the north side of the river preparing to bypass the road to the city and continue west. The decision, however, was taken from them and given to others. Those men were hidden in the rocky bottoms of the north cliff of sandstone and boulders on the Gobi's edge.

The first warning was the unnerving scream of Tibetan whistling arrows, followed by the savage roar of huge, mastiff war dogs armed with collars of sharpened spikes, and impelled by three days hunger. The arrows were aimed for the men of the caravan, but the dogs following the sound of the arrows were interested in the animals burdened with baggage. Dust, blood, screams and kicks were only a small part of the chaos that occurred simultaneously near the river.

The first two volleys arrived before the dogs and tore into the ordered ranks of men and animals. Screams of terror and pain followed with the wave of dust from running feet. Some of the column ran back toward the river. Others ran forward to some boulders for shelter. Ahjit called encouragement from the edge of the line of rocks rallying the men and readying his bow against the dogs. All efforts were spent in gaining the shelter of the rocks and defending the burdened animals against the attack of the giant dogs. The arrows' whistle advised the dogs of the trajectory, and they always avoided the line of fire. The better trained animals attacked those with weapons first, decimating the defense. Dogs less disciplined went hungrily for the bloodied animals.

Those who foolishly attempted to retreat over the river were dropped in the shallow water, and only about half reached the far bank. Kaya and Ozkurt had just formed their small body of horse after the crossing, so endured the rain of arrows behind their small round shields. The whistling arrows now warned their targets of their danger and took less blood. Kaya set their mounted troop in action against the body of Tangut men who, after the fourth volley, had followed the dogs on foot in a charge against the main body of the caravan.

The defense was disorganized and individual, each using his weapon against the dog or man who was attacking him. They would have been overcome immediately except for the charge of Kaya and his mounted archers. The charge caused the first ripple of dismay among the foot troops, many of whom had discarded their bows for hand weapons of close combat. Part of the Tanguts completed their attack afoot and engaged in hand-to-hand combat with the caravan defenders, but the other part stopped. They again drew bow or retreated to the shelter of the rocky cliffs as the squad of mounted bowmen ran the length of the battlefield and returned.

The force of the attack was broken, and the indecisive enemies were picked off by Kaya's troop who charged the area between the cliff and the river, clearing it of men. The caravan defenders gave a better account of themselves among the rocks by the river, and any enemy who ran was killed by the archers. Several of the dogs sated their hunger on the bodies of animals killed in the first attack and were easily destroyed after the worst fighting was over. Kaya refused to allow his men to pursue the fleeing Tanguts among the cliffs.

Retreat was organized: part of the mounted bowmen guarded against a renewed attack by the Tanguts. The wounded were treated, goods gathered, the dead comrades hurriedly buried in a mass grave in a crevice. They recrossed the river before night to an inn nearby, outside the walls of An Xi.

They had lost half their men. Everyone had wounds. Ahjit hobbled around on a wooden crutch, while the long slash on his thigh wept bloody water. It was sewn shut with washed hairs from the horses' tails. Ozkurt, too, had taken an arrow in his upper arm.

> - - - - - - - >

The fine days of summer passed as health returned, and new men and animals were sought. Harnesses of the dead animals were secretly opened to extract silver coins hidden there for payment of the new purchases. Word went round that the caravan was paying in Chinese silver. Local prices increased and wandering men soon outnumbered local citizenry. Thievery increased in the market and once, a riot broke out over the sale of cattle. A number of animals were lost to the owners and driven off. The local judges and police were unable to maintain justice for those who came to market.

It was in the dark just before dawn that the first hint of trouble came. The sentries posted by Ozkurt were waiting, impatiently or sleepily, the change of guards. One heard the faintest sound of movement near the inn gate. He called a challenge in a normal voice.

"Kim'sin orda? Who's out there?" His answer was a bronze blade in his throat and as his body was laid quietly down; the shuffle of many feet moving rapidly was heard by the guard inside the gate.

He had time to cry: "*Dee cot, em dot*, attention, help," The crash of the gates announced the entrance of enemy into the caravanserai's courtyard. The invaders knew the interior plan of the area. One group ran toward the stables to get animals and harness, another attacked the inn door with the battering ram used on the main gate.

The garrison was now awake and busy dressing and arming. Lights flared up here and there as men searched for equipment and enemies in the dark. The chief groom and his apprenticed helpers grabbed some two-pronged hay forks and attacked the first men that burst into the stables. Several died on the hardened wooden prongs, but the assassins' dread hanjers, long knives, soon sent the survivors scurrying to hide with the weakest boys under the hay.

BACKS TO THE WALL

The door of the inn was sturdy and resisted several charges by the attackers' battering ram. Defenders filled the hall entrance, fumbling in the torch light.

Kaya's voice filled the room with calm authority. "Everyone back and touch the wall with your shoulder. Make a big circle with every one at the wall and find your neighbor and friend. When the door opens kill everyone before you who is not at the wall. Don't leave your place. Understand?"

"Now take the torches to the other room," Kaya ordered. He didn't wait for complete dark, but pulled up the cross bar on the door. He dropped it at his feet to stop the doors sudden swing open as the ram hit the freed door and swung open hitting the wooden bar with a loud bang. This propelled the charging men into the blackened room unexpectedly and slammed the rebounding door into part of the attackers. The ram fell from their hands, throwing them off balance. As they tottered to get their balance, some fell against the men at the walls and were stabbed. The smell of blood and sound of shrieks filled the room.

Kaya pushed the door closed again from his place at the wall behind the door. Those still outside had paused an instant in the sudden turn of events. A rough voice in Tibetan Tangut commanded a charge, and the door again banged open. A body of men pushed into the dark entrance. Those behind shoved those before them causing them to stumble over the bodies of the dead and the wooden ram. The room again filled with the sounds and smells of dying. Kaya was unable to close the door again for soon the press of those going out was as great as the press of those going in. The threshold became a point of congestion and was filled with the points of blades and the bruising of bodies seeking passage in the dark.

Suddenly, the entrance was empty and no others blocked the door, but there were bodies and blood everywhere underfoot. Some were still groaning curses and faint supplications.

Kaya shouted for light and cautioned the men to stay in their places. The light flared in the hands of those men who were in the room behind and were unable to get into the main room. Anxious for their share of glory and action, these men waded out through the carnage to empty into the courtyard.

"Seize the main gate where they will have to exit," shouted Kaya as they rushed out with torches. Only a few heard and fewer obeyed. The others wandered around in the dark, a danger to themselves and others, seeking prey and being sought.

The clatter of horses' hooves warned the men that goods were being stolen. A few had the light sound of mounted troops, but more had the burdened sound of heavily laden caravan mules being led away. Kaya took a torch from the hand of a sarai servant and lifting it high as he ran, shouted her name.

"Altom, *gel ya*!" First light revealed a horse bucking its rider free and kicking him, as she turned to run toward her master.

Kaya and other men were running toward the gate where a single torch flared, but the action preceded them. Shouts and the clang of metal announced the fight. The neighing of horses and shouts of victory encouraged the runners, but the sound of animals passing outside the gate confirmed that a handful had succeeded in the effort to breakout. Kaya swung on to Altom's back and raced out the gate. The loaded animals were moving away in different directions. Kaya met a rear-guard who hacked at him as he drove his horse into the path of Altom. The animal and rider went down, but Altom stumbled and stopped as Kaya fell also. Pursuit proved vain. The successful raiders had divided the animals and vanished. Ringleaders would never be discovered. The dead remained unidentified. The day was spent counting losses and tending new wounds.

The town mayor visited Ahjit and Kaya for an evening meal and lingered to talk. "We can no longer guarantee safety to our known citizens. Countless new `seer seery,' vagabonds are entering the area. The council and I agree: the prolonged drought is the reason failing farms are losing their workers. We conclude that you are, in part, the reason; rich merchants make tempting targets. Somehow, your presence here has been advertised. For our safety and your own, you must leave. Secretly make your escape; otherwise, there will be more attacks as autumn advances. I will undertake to protect those wounded who can't yet travel. We will send them on to you in E'peck Kent, later. The Huns you seek are a month's travel ahead of you on the southwest road." The mayor was right.

Ahjit agreed to leave immediately and Kaya ordered a dawn departure westward. They left money for the care of the many wounded and a promise of more money as needed through the primitive banking system.

> - - - - - - - >

The stretch of low hills to the north wore a desert aspect the roads of the silk corridor had lacked. They were completely barren. No struggling streamlet braved its way to the edge of the sands nor any rough shrub offer leaf or branch for grazing or fire. Here the trail led.

They turned further south as they entered the Tarim Basin. Scant information and a few witnesses provided evidence that the south road was being followed by the escaping Huns. That route would take them through the Pamir Mountains into far Khoristan or following passes south into the Lands of the Gupta Empire to Kashmir.

It was October when they passed the drying Lop Nor Lake. Ahjit, still pale from his wounds, took the road north by the scant Tarim River to home with the caravan and herders as guards while Kaya, and Ozkurt alone took the road west to Yarkand city and the Pamirs.

The trick was to pass the mountains before the eternal cold of high country turned stormy. Summer monsoons stopped in the Hindu Kush Mountains. Depressions from the far Mediterranean brought storms and winter moisture to the Pamir region. Late spring to early autumn was the open season for caravans to make the safe passages, but dangers were present all year.

In the city of Yarkand they were told October was too late for a crossing. Koosta and the Hun mercenaries had passed leaving one man ill in Yarkand. Kaya sought an old caravan friend of Jomer, a veteran of many passages. The tall, blue-eyed, old one, Neshe bey laughed when he heard the request.

"Yes, it is late for the merchants, for with loaded animals it is a difficult passage now. For a handful of young adventurers, it is possible, but take lots of warm clothes. I will send my grandson with you. He knows the way and a friend of his is to marry in Perikanda. He has been anxious to celebrate with them. Offer to pay him and he will bring a companion and leave tomorrow." And so they agreed, but the old man continued with a chuckle.

"I have a surprise for you. Have you heard that the Huns left a sick man here? Yes? He is a Christian friend, so I paid a ransom and took him in, lest he die or become blind. He has the Han plague that passed first in the time of my grandfather. The old ones had stories of the thousands that died in a week in his time. It touched me too, as a child, so I can visit him and cheer his isolation and darkness. You cannot enter his room lest you too get his pox. Have you guessed his name? Jomer your protector! He is here, but you cannot visit him; this disease is a dragon that eats all who have not braved its fire of fever before. It will cheer him to know you have come. He reports that the girl, your promised one, has come to no harm. She now bosses the troop as if she were a clan mother. They walk in fear of her." He laughed again, called for tea, and for his grandson, Davut, a strapping youth, to meet his new travel companions.

> - - - - - - - >

The wind was always blowing, the mountains were bare of cover and the stream beds were often dry. The heights were clear, cold and devoid of vegetation. Ice fields were crossed and the needle-sharp ice and sand fragments were a torment to the eyes and feet. All water and food were carried. Even the hay and straw for the animals were loaded on their backs. At the last inn under the rim of the plateau, they were warned.

"It is better to start whenever the wind calms and travel day and night without stopping to the nearest inn. If you stop more than an hour on the open plateau, you can freeze. The crossing holds the danger of getting lost in the dark, but there is the fording of the Murgab River, which flows north across the road. You must follow the river west to safety at the next inn, after the river turns. The river road is served by inns with food and fodder for a price. It's the two days and the nights where the great fatigue and danger occurs."

They got lost twice in the night, but the two guides soon brought them back into the road and once crossing the river the second day were able to trudge to the next inn. There one of the horses that had fallen on the ice at the river had to be left. They borrowed one with the payment of rent and a promise to return it by the guides. Some inns were closed for the lateness of the season. All were surprised at the arrival of travelers from the East.

> - - - - - - - >

The Kash'ka Dar'ia Valley is a rich land of orchards, fields and fine horses. In November, however, the cold blankets everything. The smoke of the winter fires hugs the valley floor and produces fog. On the mountain slopes the grass is brown and the view of snow-capped mountain is spectacular. A rich party of White Huns were there hunting the musk deer that follow the descending band of dry grass below the frost and snow. The deer pass the winter eating the stem-dried hay. In the spring they will follow the return of the new grass to the high mountains.

A boy of twelve and a white-haired, scarred grandfather stood together overlooking the valley as their huntsmen organized. Combining profit and pleasure, they hunt the shy deer with the valued musk sack located on its abdomen. Used in the fixing of scents, it was in constant demand.

The boy laughed and rubbed his hands together. "We will be richer than my father if we get the deer today, Grandfather."

"That is a dangerous policy; never exceed the wealth of the ruler lest he envy your prosperity." The gray mustache quivered upward in a chuckle of delight.

"But I will be ruler someday. Must I fear my father and ultimately myself?" The boy grinned at the ruggedly built man who stood unseeing, a fond expression on his face.

"A wise man fears all powers above him, and to fear one's self is to guard from arrogance and folly." The old one turned back toward the sound of horses behind them.

"I wish Father would come hunting with us sometime. He only has time for the treasury and the harem," the boy complained, looking at the valley still.

"I will make the request of him on my death-bed," the old man grunted. "He won't be able to refuse it. Let it be a last gift to you." He coughed spasmodically.

"I don't want you to ever die, Grandfather." The boy spoke sincerely, still looking over the valley.

"It's the way of all flesh," the old one shrugged. "Come, the party is returning. They must have placed the flags and perhaps have news for us. Be my eyes, Serdar." The man stretched out his hand nearest the boy and took several careful steps until Serdar had scrambled forward to take the hand. He looked at the lord shrewdly.

"You never wait for help," he accused.

"Khans are leaders. If one delays, another will take his command. I hear the voice of Mertler. All will be in readiness." Together they hurried down the trail from the hill to a party of horsemen, who saluted them respectfully.

"Tekhan bay, we have seen the deer tracks, and we have placed the flags. If you bring the hawks, we are ready to flush one." The man's voice held excitement. "I chose a good place in arrow range to wait."

"Lead; we follow." Serdar placed the old one's hand on the horses back and he mounted unaided. Serdar handed up the hawks from a limb of a small scrubby tree where they had been left. The birds screeched hungrily. Serdar mounted and took his own bird, following Tekhan bey who rode beside Mertler.

> - - - - - - - >

The cold wind blew dust in their faces as Kaya, Ozkurt, Davut and Kachak moved up the valley northward. The guides were in consultation as Ozkurt complained,

"We suffer unbearable cold for six days, and now we eat gravel four days. When will this suffering be over?"

"When we enter paradise," Kaya responded with a pounding on Ozkurt's shoulders that almost spilled him from his horse. Straightening, he raised a fist in mock defiance. "You lead to Perikanda or to hell, I'll follow, but I like better food than dry earth," Ozkurt roared, spurring toward Kaya, who also started his Altom ahead.

"This way, an old trail over the mountains," shouted Kachak who, starting from before them, left Davut, and galloped toward the hills to the north. They followed in a rush, while Davut reluctantly brought up the rear with the pack horses. They climbed into the mountains and the dust disappeared, but the wind was still cold and fresh. Brush and small trees and grass on the south facing slopes caused them to regroup and assume a more relaxed mood.

"This is an old smuggler's trail," complained Davut. "In the caravan season it is frequented by government people and bandits." He shook his head in disapproval.

"We are out of season, and I have only a few personal items for friends and presents for the wedding," Kachak shouted resentfully. "There is no profit for such as travel with you, Davut, so full of prayers and goodness." He dismissed him with an angry gesture and rode ahead again, leading the way in the wild, uninhabited country.

CHANCE ENCOUNTER

PEOPLE, PLACES & PLOTS IN CHAPTER 6

Da vut': being a true friend and guide is never easy when temptation calls.
Ka chak': 'runaway' proves well named, a boy you have to watch.
Ka'ya: finds new friends, but not old ones.
Mert'ler: the organizer of the hunt is a busy courtier.
Oz'kurt: finds life can get tedious anywhere.
Ser'dar: the twelve-year old son of the Khan learns new things.
Tek'han: the wise old grandfather of Ser'dar is blind, but brave.

GLOSSARY:

barish: peace; welcome friend; greetings.
dee' kot ed' en: be careful; take precautions; watch out.
Hephtalite: The Latin name for the White Huns.
nay o' lure?: Please; why not?; What's the harm?; Let me (pleading).
Nay var?: What's this? What's happening? What up?
ta-mom': okay; enough; that's fine; good job.
ya-bon'jee: foreigner; stranger; derived from the word for wild or savage.

A SMUGGLER RUNS

The hunting party was spread over the mountain side. Serdar sat with Tekhan in sight of the waving flag on a pole, just in arrow flight, but behind some small trees and brush to be hidden. They faced into the west wind watching the north and south flanks of the hills. Behind them on the south slope an old trail passed. Mertler quietly rode up from behind them. He spoke in a quiet voice.

"All is in readiness, and the animals are in the brush behind the flag." He looked round cautiously, "*Nay var?* What's this? Strangers approach from the southeast."

"Downwind? The *yabonjees* surprise us. The keen stalkers are stalked." The old man chuckled at the awkward interval. "Are they close? Are they armed?"

"Sire, they are travelers with pack animals. They have just seen us and are equally surprised. One rides a golden horse. They are not preparing for action, but one man is taking his pack horse and departing down the slope. Stay and I will intercept them." Mertler whirled his horse in pursuit. Serdar feathered an arrow in readiness, turning to face the advancing party of three.

"One man must be smuggling illicit goods, but it sounds like the others are continuing to advance; perhaps there are still honest merchants," Tekhan mused.

"Mertler talks with the men. They seem friendly. They ignore the fleeing man. They come laughing," the boy reports. "They say, 'Kachak has lived up to his name'."

"I know that name, an impudent, reckless youth of many scrapes and adventures on the borders of our land. I'm pleased that Mertler didn't leave all to pursue him." The old man shook his head thoughtfully, "They are brave men to pass the mountains at so late a season. Few can survive the trip even with the help of a smuggler." He listened to the approaching horses and shouted, "*Barish*, peace," as they drew up to stop before them. Serdar sheathed his arrow.

"*Barish*, you are hunting musk deer. I smell them upwind. You will have success," Kaya began. The old one burst into laughter, which the boy quickly joined.

"You must be a gray wolf to know it from here," Tekhan said wryly. Serdar studied the burley Kaya and his mount with interest. The ivory swan hung around his neck indicated a military award. Davut stayed carefully behind tending the pack animals and spare horses.

"The gray wolf is the Chipchak ancestor, but I learned from the bears," Kaya laughed easily.

"Tell us of your travels and adventures," suggested Tekhan as he motioned to Mertler, "Bring a skin of wine and some cakes. We must wait for the deer's curiosity to overcome their shyness of the flags."

> - - - - - - - >

It was an hour later when the party of travelers took their leave. They departed up the north trail, giving the flag and brush a wide circuit. Mertler rushed off to check the waiting drivers and gather news of sightings. The old man turned to his grandson.

"They are Christians, a strange, divided people. Do you know anything about them?" he inquired gruffly.

"Father taxes them heavily for they are mostly merchants. They are Suriani, Armeni, and others of Mesopotamia that live among us. They are a sect persecuted first by Constantine and his successors for differences with the Orthodox. The Sanassids give them refuge as do we. They are generally despised by the priests and devout of local religions for their differences with customs and traditions. I hear they are intolerant and believe that all but themselves are doomed to a place of fire. Their leader was killed by the people of Rome, but they claim he still lives. They all seem honest, quiet and peace-loving like these men." He shrugged and looked at Tekhan closely to see if the recitation was acceptable.

"They need watching. They have a different nature from the others. Don't be fooled by their meekness. They can be persistently stubborn and tenacious against anything that goes against the obedience to their God. The new converts, and they seek them from any part of our society, are fanatical and faithful. Though often very humble and poor, they make surprising changes in their condition. They speak much of sin and ask their God for daily needs. They pray often, but can move from quietness to surprising action. They make much of the sick and unfortunate and are well received by widows and orphans," Tekhan paused.

"I have seen the hospital they maintain near the church building. How do poor people build such lovely buildings and maintain their charities?" Serdar interjected, curiously watching the backs of the departing strangers.

"The first generation is spirit-minded and direct in speech and life. They believe Yesu the Christ has forgiven their sins. They establish churches and institutions and contact new people boldly. The second generation is different. Better educated and trained, they are thinkers and prosperous benefactors; they supply intellectual leadership, apologetics and money. The third generation is different yet again, and are artistic and discriminating in temperament. They refine and beautify their homes and churches, services and vestments. Very compassionate, they find the actual work with poverty and illness depressing and choose to support others to do these things. They are socially-minded and associate with the highest classes where possible. The fourth generation becomes casual in faith. Gradually they grow indistinguishable from the others who prosper in the city."

"So they cancel themselves out in four generations? If that be true, why worry that they differ from the general society?" Serdar smiled proudly at his quick deduction.

"Because new converts continue to augment the first generation so all four types coexist at the same time in the churches. Types skip a generation in some families and others revert to the world sooner than the fourth generation. According to their zeal and faith, some families will be faithful for hundreds of years. They propagate the stories of Yesu and his righteous kingdom." Tekhan shook his head in utter bewilderment, "They are intolerant of any god but their own and any other customs. Even persecution does not bring them under control. It simply thins and scatters them. It clears them of dead wood and revitalizes them." The old one snorted his distrust. "I'll wager there is a dispatch from the East about this young warrior. If he has been off seeking his kinswoman, he will have made a wide trail. All for just one woman, but he thinks he has God's help, brash fool."

HUNT'S END

- 59 -

"Perhaps he has, Grandfather. Let's ask about it."

Tekhan grimaced in anger. "You heard him suggest it was necessary for me to seek God's will at my advanced age and condition: to lay my own plans aside?"

The boy suppressed a laugh to reply meekly, "Yes Sir, I thought you took it with your usual kindness when your will is crossed."

"Leave the jokes to the court fool, Young Sir. Such matters do not concern him."

The sound of a running horse interrupted the thought. The hunt master came swiftly up. "*Dee-cot ed-en*, careful Sire," Mertler shrilled from behind them. "The deer break cover behind the flag, out of arrow range," he panted as he passed them on the run. "Launch the hawks, or we lose them." In one motion the deed was done, and the two hawks battled for height. The horses eagerly leapt forward, and the two riders followed the sound of the echoing hooves.

In the first confused rush, Serdar looked up to see the buck poised at the edge of rocks and brush while the females and young lost themselves in the maze. The hawks swooped at the face of the deer to blind it. Serdar loosed an arrow to bring down the buck. It was at that instant his grandfather's horse ran under a short, stubby tree. The impact of the man and the arrow were almost simultaneous; both man and deer fell without a sound. The hunt had ended in death for two creatures.

> - - - - - - - >

The city guards admitted Kaya's party, but once inside disarmed them. They were also refused permission to leave without the authorization of the Khan. However, they released them into the city.

Amazingly, Kachak turned up at the friend's wedding celebration. He evidently had means of access unknown to any outside his trade. He avoided Kaya and Ozkurt at the party. He made plain his deep difference with Davut in another argument they overheard between them. They were out in the garden area of the great house in the evening.

"Davut, if you despise the gold they pay, you could have, at least, thought of the loyalty you owe. The Khan offers refuge for those of your church. Those who are imprisoned as heretics in other lands can enter. They admit them here to be free. They want the commerce. You owe something to the Royal House for that alone. It'll be an adventure to carry dispatches; you don't have to do the spying. It's not like smuggling or dealing in contraband. The government helps you."

Davut shook his head, annoyed at the pressure. "My father says that we should not mix into the political ambitions of the men of this world. The attitude towards my church could change again with another Khan."

"Davut, they aren't asking your father to go. You know the trails, and they trust you. I'd take it in a minute if I got the offer. Don't be a fool."

Davut shook his head, "I'll have to keep it a secret from the family. I don't think I can live that way."

"You have never tried, and you are too big a coward to try now." Shoves were exchanged here, and Kachak left.

Kaya was disappointed to learn that Koosta's band of mercenaries had been turned away from all the cities because of illness among his men. The pox-ridden men were kept outside the cities of the Khanate and eventually had gone on west to winter, but permission to follow was withheld by the authorities. Davut, however, was able to leave and disappeared for weeks. At the same time the old hunter's grandson called on them regularly and took them on tours of the city. He showed them where they could exercise their horses, and he took a particular liking to Altom. He never mentioned his family directly except to say the grandfather was away hunting in a wide land.

Christmas was not celebrated generally in the Amu Daria or the Syr River basins, areas already filled with Zoroastrian and Buddhist temples, but a large church was found in Perikanda (later named Samarkand) largely composed of the Syriac commercial community. There, January sixth, Epiphany, was observed as the day of giving gifts. Davut was living with friends. Kaya had not seen him since the wedding feast where they had enjoyed the status of guests. He returned to fill their hours now, and he offered no explanation of his weeks of neglect. He wore a new Kashmir suit and spent freely. Davut was impatient for the arrival of the feast day. Special music had been prepared, and the Episcopes had a children's choir trained to participate. They would sing an antiphonal part with the older choir, and he assured them it would be wonderful.

Epiphany dawned cold and clear with sun, after a light scattering of snow to settle the dust. The church was unheated except for some lamps and candles lit before the icon paintings of Saints and Virgin. There were no seats except at the front of the church for visiting clergy. The congregation stood in a semicircle around the church and the Episcopes sat awaiting the special music. Kaya's party, including Serdar, had arrived late and stood near the door with the cold at their backs, but the deep voices of the men boomed out the special Christmas song.

1.   Stars and angels sent to serve Him;
        All announced Messiah's birth.
        Mary, virgin pure, obedient;
        Heard and rejoiced, the King is come.
        Guards the temple flocks are watching:
        The perfect lamb is born today.

2.   Distant scholar's gifts are bringing;
        Offerings of purse and soul.
        Judah's King and great men puzzle;

A gracious king is born to save.
Come, you weary, heavy laden;
God's perfect lamb will die for you.

3.   Shepherds, wise men hear the message;
     God will take the form of man.
     Joseph, trusting, cares for Mary;
     Finds for their bed a cattle stall.
     Angel chorus tells the story;
     The Christ is born in Bethlehem.

4.   Trembling, Herod seeks to kill Him;
     Many more will have to die.
     Come forgive your sinful people;
     We will rejoice and bless Your name.
     Peace to all who seek God's purpose;
     God's Living Word is born to stay.

CHRISTMAS PROCLAMATION

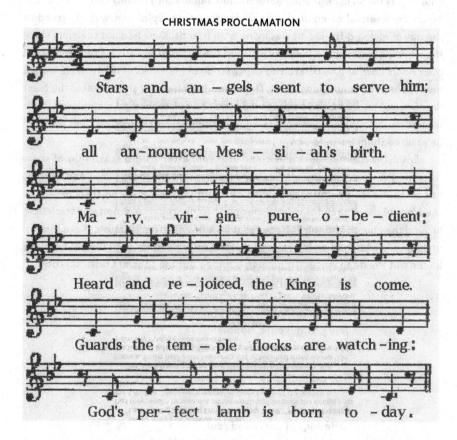

Stars and an – gels sent to serve him;

all an – nounced Mes – si – ah's birth.

Ma – ry, vir – gin pure, o – be – dient;

Heard and re – joiced, the King is come.

Guards the tem – ple flocks are watch – ing;

God's per – fect lamb is born to – day.

The four verses finished the anthem and its story, but the celebration had only begun. The high excited voices of the children answered. The adult voices entered softly, but gradually took up the anthem and filled the church with their rich warm depth:

> Let's adore and glorify Him.
> Let's all praise His heav'nly love.
> Kings and servants bow before Him.
> They obey His gracious will.
> Christ the lamb will never change.
> Halleluya, Halleluya,
> Halleluya, Christ is born.
> We will rejoice, His kingdom comes.
> Halleluya, Halleluya,
> Christ is born in Bethlehem.
> God's perfect gift is meant for you.
> Halleluya, Halleluya.
> Jesus Christ is born today.
> God sent His Son to die for you.
> Halleluya, He loves you.

GOD'S PERFECT GIFT

Let's a-dore and glo-ri-fy Him. Let's all praise His Heav'n-ly love.

Kings and servants bow be-fore Him. They o-bey His gracious will.

Christ the lamb will never change; Ha-le-lu-ya, Ha-le-lu-ya,

Ha-le-lu-ya, Christ is born. We will re-joice, His king-dom comes.

Ha-le-lu-ya, Ha-le-lu-ya, Christ is born in Beth-le-hem.

God's per-fect gift is meant for you. Ha-le-lu-ya, Ha-le-

lu-va. Je-sus Christ is born to day. God sent His Son

to die for you. Ha-le-lu-ya, He loves you.

No one seemed to stir as the music and incense filled the air. The cold dark building with its candles lighting the icons picturing the life of Yesu, now seemed to swell with light.

Many in the congregation began to move forward and leave gifts before the railing, which the attendants received and carried forward to place on the altar. They brought dried fruit and flour in bags, food of many kinds, artists' work from men's shops, precious metals of many kinds. Fabrics and cloth, both precious and common, draped the rails. It was a day to give: the priests and hospital would be provided for all winter with the gifts coming now. Everyone shared from their wealth or poverty; all gave.

The singing started again in joyful cadence. The children's answer and the choir's final statements brought the singing to an end. The joy of the people and the friendship the visitors met there was warm and real. Most spoke Hunnish, so they got many invitations that winter. Several merchants hired them for guard duty at their stores.

> - - - - - - >

"*Tamom*, alright Serdar, you've had three circuits of the park, time to rest." The boy passed at a lope and continued around.

"*Nay o-lure*, please, what's the harm in another turn. She isn't even sweating yet," Serdar pleaded.

"I don't want her to sweat in this chill wind. Come now." Kaya's voice was calm and pleasant and the young noble circled back reluctantly.

Ozkurt patted the horse. "She, at least, never gets out of condition. She flourishes under the attention of two young men. I never thought she would let another ride her."

Kaya laughed softly. "She is a princess who knows the heart of those who love her. Only true devotion is acceptable." Kaya moved forward to share a treat with Altom. "My sweetheart, Fewsoon, also has red-gold hair, a bright fire that she is forced to braid and hide away or it stands out like a sun's rays around her face."

Serdar looked at Kaya seriously but hesitantly. "There are so many women you could have. Why pursue just this one?"

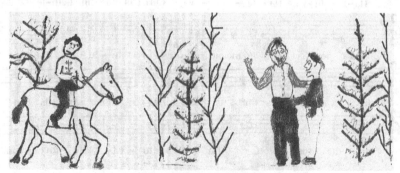

EXERCISING MY GOLD

"Why love one horse above all others? Performance, style, and looks, all are personal qualities that can be known only in intimacy and trust. Love is a magnet that pulls only sensitive souls, like the love of God; it is selective. Tanra binds such a discovery with a special warmth and attraction that is hard to explain or deny. It is always felt and becomes one wonder-filled and binding attraction, in a world of distraction and loneliness. Love is the discovery of God, or some of His qualities in a person whom you feel to be necessary for your life to exist. You will recognize love when it comes."

Serdar brushed Altom vigorously. "How I wish I had another like Altom," he said reverently.

"When Yesu completes his purposes and allows me to return to our yurt home with bride and horse, I will send you a yearling to love and train." Kaya responded.

Serdar's face glowed, "Would you really do that? I would have my own gold to ride in Hindustan."

"You're sure of your destiny then?" Ozkurt queried.

The boy nodded. "Father says the Guptas grow weak and corrupt; they will crumble before us. There, in battle, I will win my ivory badge and command."

"I too, enjoy the tests of skill and bravery that combat offers one," volunteered Ozkurt. "That's why I get so restless cooped up in the city where opportunity is lacking."

"But such a desire leads one to a constant seeking of conflict and opposition," protested Kaya. "Is there no place to say hold, enough, I'm satisfied?"

"It isn't the fighting I enjoy, but the flow of heroic deeds well done. Good administration and right decisions make a nation happy and civilization prosper," Serdar offered.

"My teacher, the hermit, said that we should love and follow only one good desire that Tanra plants in our heart. That all else is distraction and vanity." Kaya paused then stated, "We live like plants in a dry land. We can fulfill our destiny only as the rain of God's presence revives us to grow and bloom. We wait on Him."

Ozkurt sighed, "I hope He'll move us before I die of boredom."

PRAYER BEADS AND GOSPEL

> - - - - - - - >

Perikanda had grown large and prosperous on the booty captured in the growth of empire as the *Hephtalite* Hun capital city. War, as a struggle for fortresses and harvests, was waged in a yearly fashion with the Sanassids and Gupta Empires in the area located southwest and southeast of the irrigated valleys of the two rivers. In the heights of the Hindu Kush Mountains, around the oasis of Merv and the Iranian Plateau, war was a permanent condition.

The cycle of droughts pushed the nomads toward southern lands as it damaged all the empires dependent on the year's rainfall.

The cultivation based on irrigation and canals was less affected by the sparse years. There was always more water than needed to irrigate the flat flood plains. The surplus water ran to the shrinking lakes to evaporate. However, damage to the canals and loss of lives by war did permanent damage to some of the villages. Manpower for the armies was assured from the young and displaced herders or farmers.

Agah Khan of the *Hephtalite* or White Huns was aware of every wind of policy that blew upon his exposed desert land of rivers and oases. Although he was a bit indulgent and spent much time in the harem with his women, his administrators were zealously active. His spies were everywhere. Accurate information was rewarded. Davut lived well. Agah's ministers were careful to strip Koosta by heavy passage duties and to send him out of harm's way through to the Sanassid border. The Sanassids would repeat the process and exactions to send them to Dagistan around the southern end of the Caspian Sea. Agents were sent to misrepresent the situation to Kaya. They were also sent to make offers of service under the Khan's system of recruitment. The rewards for service were extravagant, and high positions were offered if they would comply. They were badly wanted, but could not get permission to leave the city. Serdar showed them anything they were willing to see. They even got a tour of the Royal Court in audience, being led and directed by a page of the court. In late winter everything flagged except Kaya's humor.

Finally, Kaya concluded that Koosta and his men had departed with Fewsoon for the camp of the West Huns, who were now conquering beyond the Ukraine and beyond the Carpathian Mountains of Europe. They needed recruits and horses. The pay was good. Opportunities opened for warriors needed in the west. Fewsoon, too, would be there with her captors. They needed to pursue and find their enemy. Yet Kaya's problem remained the same. How could he escape the city?

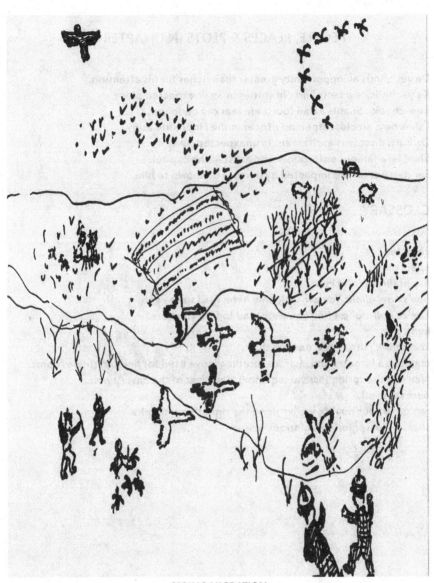

SPRING MIGRATION

PEOPLE, PLACES & PLOTS IN CHAPTER 7

Da vut': finds an opportunity greater than riches for his attention.
Ka'ya: finds new facts and old stories in an unexpected place.
Koo-chook': Shanla's frail fourteen-year old daughter.
I'shak bey: an old, respected officer in the Hephalite army.
Oz'kurt: discovers excitement in unexpected places.
Shan'la: a famous entertainer and artist in the capital.
Ser'dar: has his life impacted by persons unknown to him.

GLOSSARY:

chay: tea
epec: silk
hephtalite: White Huns
hoe'sh gel-diniz: You are welcome here; glad to see you.
hoe'sh boll-duke: I find you well; glad to find you here.
kent: city
koo chook'; little; wee one; small.
man'gel: a large, round charcoal burning stove used for heating single rooms.
Nev'ruz: the spring festival (equinox) New Year of the East Aryans.
peri: fairy; elf.
sah'ol: to your health; you've done the right thing; thanks.
shanla: glory; glorious; glorious one.

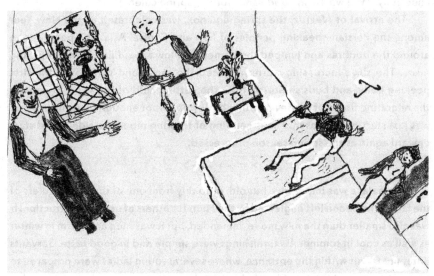

VISITORS' WELCOME

Davut came running to the inn where Kaya and Ozkurt were staying. He was out of breath and excited as he bowed and stuttered out the words. "Shanla wants to see you. Imagine the honor; she invites you to her winter home." His face was flushed and he panted as he babbled.

"Who is Shanla, and why are we honored?" Kaya inquired with a smile. "Get your breath before answering."

"Shanla is queen of the entertainers. All seek to hear her. She performs in the old theater. It is said to have been first built by the Greeks under Alexander who conquered this region over 700 years ago. The Greeks and Persians who live here are crazed with love for her. She speaks their languages as well as Hunnish. The city lies at her feet; she commands all. Even the Khan is said to offer her half his kingdom to marry him, but she stays true to her public who love her. She performs in the summer season, but is busy rehearsing and training new girls now during the winter. She has heard of Chipchaks in Perikanda and requests your attendance on her for *Nevruz*." Davut's eyes bugged with excitement.

"Why should she wish to see Chipchaks? Are we some curiosity to be wondered at?" complained Ozkurt.

"She didn't say, but any man would be considered crazy if he didn't accept. You would offend the townsfolk."

"We accept with joy and pleasure that we should satisfy so great a lady's curiosity," laughed Kaya. "When will we come bearing appropriate gifts?"

"Tomorrow noon I myself will guide you," Davut exulted proudly.

"The thing I have seen you do repeatedly without errors," confided Kaya cheerfully. "We will be in good hands for this spring celebration."

The arrival of *Nevruz*, the spring equinox, was celebrated as the New Year among the Persian-speaking peoples of Iran and Central Asia. The people sang around the bonfires and jumped the flames. The low areas filled with smoke and mists. The sun's increasing warmth heated the sands and stimulated the first peeking bulbs and buds sheltered from the cutting cold of the wind. Overhead the migrating flocks of geese and other birds were proof enough that winter's grip was just starting to loosen. The green ring of thawing mountain side would start upward again as the spring season progressed.

> - - - - - - - >

The palace was impressive but old, probably from one of the earlier rulers of the land. It had been left neglected by the Huns for others of newer construction. It was also smaller than the new mode demanded, but it was snug and warm in winter as well as cool in summer. Its furnishings were simple and in good taste. Servants detained Davut within the entrance, where several young ladies were prepared to entertain him, and the two Chipchaks were shown to a warm room over a garden with a balcony whose door had panes made of bladder, admitting light.

A mature woman of great beauty, wearing a fine wool dress with trousers, looked up expectantly from before a large charcoal burning *mangal*. Her fine blond hair and light eyes shone in the contrasting glow of charcoal and the darkness of the winter room. Her voice was melodious and controlled. However, she was thin and coughed occasionally.

"*Hoesh geldiniz*, come welcomed," she said in Chipchak, standing and smiling into their shocked faces.

"You know our dialect!" exclaimed Ozkurt forgetting to bow or reply.

"*Hoesh boll duke*, we find you well?" inquired Kaya with a low bow which Ozkurt hastened to imitate.

"*Sah'ol*, to health," she smiled her greetings, motioning towards a divan covered with a fluffy warm material near the mangal. At her call a young girl came with *chay*, tea to warm their bodies and hands. With the hot tea bowls in their hands, they sat entranced by the beauty and art of their hostess. Her knowledge left them open-mouthed.

"So, you are both from the Chipchaks, one from the upland hills and the other from Erkan's band on the north horse road. Little Kaya grown large and pursuing the Huns, who hold his beloved sister. As I remember, Koosta was always a rival. He nearly won in the spring race by whipping off my son, Kutch, so you were able to pass them both. I remember it well. Where is Kutch now?"

"You are the wife of Erkan, my father?" gasped Kaya breathlessly, leaning forward to peer intently in the face of the handsome woman and taking inquisitive sniffs.

"Once a bear, always a bear," she laughed holding out a daintily perfumed hand toward his face. "The perfume is new, but the flesh is familiar."

"Forgive my doubt," he took the hand and kissed it, pressing it to his forehead. Ozkurt followed suit.

"Your beauty is legend among the tribes," Ozkurt stated shyly, blushing, "but I had not imagined you thus."

"Imagination always fails reality. God is greater than the mind, but come give me the home news first."

> - - - - - - - >

The banquet-like meal finished and the hostess again directed the conversation.

"My son, the hermit's assistant, would no doubt condemn my greed and excesses, as well as my profession."

"His joys are of the mind and spirit, Lady, feel no sorrow for his choices. He is content." Kaya was solicitous of the ease of the lady. "My father too, complains much of his past losses, but prospers, as does the tribe."

"I found no contentment or rest there with the tribe, but have found great joy in fame and fortune here. When sold by the Tartars to the old prince, Ishak Bay, I became his entertainer and gradually his administrator. With his help I was able to finance my start in the theater. From there I have had all my youthful dreams realized."

"It must have been difficult to rise from slave to the most famous woman of the Hephtalite Empire," murmured Ozkurt, admiringly.

"My greatest crisis was when I saw myself, very young, betrayed into the power of the Khan, your father. I knifed my master for that offence, but I did not kill him, another did that, not I. Onder didn't love me. He started a child with Vashti and would have traded me for the horse. How I hated them." Her voice was petulant and resentful.

"Lady," Kaya started up, "I understood that East Huns killed the merchant and that Lady Vashti bore the child of Yuzbasha, the Khan's man." His face reflected concern.

"The only East Hun was one come to take the horse back to Onder's master as the price of forgiveness. He chased me into the woods after I knifed Onder. It was Yuzbasha's knife, so I left it that it might seem his act. I know it was wrong of me; I was terrified. After that the East Hun died and the knife vanished."

"Here it is with me," stated Kaya producing the knife from his belt. She took the knife gingerly from his hand and shuddered, holding it at arm's length.

"Yes," she agreed, "The wolf head is the same, but see how the blade flexes. It turned in my hand and stuck in the chest bone. The East Hun laid hand on me, and I bit his hand and ran. When I came again, all had changed."

"But the girl Fewsoon is the Lieutenant's daughter," Kaya insisted, "She is my milk sister and promised bride."

"Yownja, the flame-haired one is Chipchak in spirit and training. We will say no more about it," Shanla the actress laughed and gestured to the cups. "Let us enjoy another for old time's sake." She herself served them. Kaya spoke slowly.

"The Yuzbasha disappeared after his yoking and was never heard from again. He took your penalty, Lady; he saved you." Kaya pressed the point very seriously.

"He quarreled with Onder first and shot the wounding arrow. Then I compounded it, but I think another finished it. God will be the judge. Besides, I know that Yuzbasha obtained work and still lives, though he changed his name. He is prosperous." She looked at Kaya's troubled face and continued. "Packets and news were brought to me by the traveling musicians twice. Inside the sealed cloth, he had placed a gift piece of silk material: e'peck, A bit of dried brick used in city constructions means kent: city. A strap of harness used in a caravan indicates work. There was a coin of gold meaning prosperity. A bit of broom straw suggested a kitchen and family life. A summer packet held the little blue flowers of remembrance: forget-me-nots. It was clearly an invitation to come to E'peck Kent and set up house, with him doing caravan work and providing support. She, however, stayed with you two children and soon after was taken prisoner by the Tartars." Her eyes snapped with excitement as she remembered the story. "I do owe him my thanks and prayers, whatever they are worth."

"After that I almost became content with the life of a Khan's wife. But the boy I bore the Khan was small and bookish and the little girl sickly. Ah, little Kaya, you will never know the despair you produced in me when you returned to become the heir. All the fantastic stories they told about you as the child of promise. It took away all my joy in high position. Truly I was ready to go when the raid took me." She laughed at his doleful expression.

"No, don't look so sad; it was not your fault. We must try to fulfill our dreams. My place is here where God has brought me. Come, I have some one who is frantic to meet you. You will never guess who it is. She was not healthy enough to run around after you, but Kutch told her so many stories about you that she has never forgotten. Yes, I mean Koo'chook, do you remember her name? She knows yours. She was of little value to the Tartars; they expected her to die. I think that is when I learned about prayer. She still lives, but not vigorously. It is a day-to-day gift. Here in this room."

Two sides of the room held large windows and a door that opened to the south garden. It would be light and bright in summer and was even now. A child of perhaps fourteen years lay propped by pillows. Her pallid face was somewhat flushed. Her hand held a needle with which she worked on a flower design. It seemed finished to Kaya.

"Oh, Kaya?" She said and seemed incapable of saying more. He became aware again of how much he had grown since the capture of the family. He took her hand, kissed and pressed it to his forehead, and she blushed.

"Yes, Koo'chook, I am a big, bumbling Kaya now. The bear has grown up to full size." Her little laugh was like the tinkle of bells. She smiled sweetly and sought her voice. "Such stories as Kutch used to tell me, were they true?" She whispered.

"Very likely, little one, he was never a good liar, but he could always make the fun stand out."

She held out the embroidered flowers done on white silk.

"I knew Fewsoon and loved her. She would visit me and make me laugh. I want her to have this for her wedding. You will take it to her and tell her it's from me?"

He gently took the offered piece and looked closely at the work. Then he smelled it. "With all my heart little lady, it bears your work and your scent." She sighed in her contentment and seemed to be thinking of other things.

"She caught me a wild bird once, and it sang sweetly, but its songs were sad, so I set it free. I never told her. Would she be sad?" A single tear marked the edge of Kaya's eye.

"No Princess," he said, "she would be glad."

Shanla was moving toward the door. "Koo'chook dear. We are going to sing like the birds tonight. You can listen or sing from here. We will sing you to sleep." They moved back to the large room again.

"The raid of the Tartars had a very strange air to it. They knew my name and told me to come and bring my child. They knew where our wealth was stored. They killed only those who resisted. Anyone could run away and they let them, unless it was a young woman. There was no rape and plunder such as usually occurs in raids of revenge. Yurts were burned, but nothing wasted. They even seemed to know that the Khan and chief warriors would be gone."

Kaya felt the hair on his neck rise and he seemed to smell skunk for an instant. He found he was breathing loudly. He demanded, "The leader of the raid, what manner of man was he?"

She noted his agitation with concern. "Tall, blond and very confident in his control of the action. He was — efficient and effective - they took everything they wanted and burned the rest."

Kaya nodded, "I know the smell of him, and I sometimes dream of his hunting me."

"Slave raiders usually kill the sick and all small children to make their escape faster and easier, but this man did nothing like that. They let Koo'chook live and we traveled on a camel to market. He even made sure we were sold together to someone who could afford to keep us. It is strange how I can owe so much to a Chipchak and a Tartar, enemies who did me good."

Kaya sighed and seemed to search for something to say. "Do you permit visitors? I mean is Koo'chook able to visit with younger friends?"

"The girls are in and out all day, when they have time. They love her and have such fun. They call her a *Peri*, fairy, little elf."

Kaya nodded and proceeded with more confidence. "I have a young friend who needs to know one such as she. He's a younger, lonesome boy from a rich military family. I would bring him so you may approve his character and his acceptability as a playmate for her."

She stopped and studied him carefully. "You're not match-making are you Kaya? She will not have the strength ..."

"Not at all, it is for both. He knows weapons and their uses, horses and their care, but the harem is the only feminine side he has seen, and it shows no affection..."

"Only collection," she finished for him. "Perhaps it would suit both. Of the men she has known only her brother was a friend. Bring him. How will he take it?"

Kaya stood thinking, "He has never mentioned a woman, only his grandfather and his father who enjoys the harem life too much to attend to his training."

Shanla sniffed disdain, "Very rich military indeed. They are finishing a period of mourning the death of the Khan's father. They will be plunged back into blood sports again, after it ends. Better he come now, before that. Bored minds are more easily captured and refined." Shanla laughed and then reiterated, "Bring him." Kaya nodded his gratitude and yawned.

"Now, Kaya, enough of history, escapes and obligations. You will seek a dark corner and sleep if we continue in this way. We promised Koo'chook music, and she'll be waiting. Come, I will sing for you. Get Ozkurt and your guide Davut. Call them in. It's an old favorite from the camp, `Crazy Love'. It will bring back memories of the fire-side and the yurts." They awaited Davut's arrival.

"I have heard that the Khan offers you a commission with high pay and honors. There are Chipchak mercenaries to command and chances of spoil against the Gupta and Sanassid. You will not stay near by? There are many enticements and advantages." She smiled beguilingly.

"I have rejected the offers. My quest must proceed. I will not be distracted from my promise." He eyed her shrewdly. "You hear much for a woman convalescing in winter quarters." Davut, laughing, entered the room with a girl on each arm, apologizing for delays.

"My house is always honored by your presence." She spoke, looking at Kaya. "I will be sad if you don't come often. I need your happy presence." She smiled for all. "First I have a new song that everyone loves here. It makes them cry, and I love it most. It is named, 'Regrets.'" Her attendant friend picked out the melody on a harp while she sang. Her voice held a vigor and brightness that seemed a contradiction to her size and age. It was a vigorous contralto yet conveyed the tragedy felt by the singer lost in her role. They joined her on the ending refrain which varied slightly each time. It started with an introduction, sung only once, followed by three verses and the endings.

Introduction:
       I remember old times and old faces;
       And they know me.
       They must remember how I loved them.

1st verse: I think of old friends where we used to live then.
       We had old dreams of what we'd be;
       And new loves we hoped to see.
       We knew how great our lives and plans would make us.
       We thought no God would interfere,
       We would make it all appear.

1st ending: Old days and old ways with old dreams
       And old loves to guide us. And they know me.
       They can remember how I loved them.

2nd verse: I dream of old joys, zest and human folly;
       So full of jealousy and hate,
       Love and vice we blame on fate.
       We chose to live deceit and confrontation.
       It didn't matter that all knew;
       It was just something to do.

2nd ending: With hearts ablaze, loving our ways,
       Anger and hate, regret came late: heartbreak!
       So we parted. They don't remember I still love them.

3rd verse: New lives, new faces came to fill their places.
       It didn't matter what we'd do
       We would just try something new.
       It got so boring with the same old story.
       I couldn't find the reason why
       Life had now become so dry.

3rd ending: How my heart cry's out for them;
       God remembers. And I pray for them.
       How my heart aches.

I re-mem-ber old times. and old fa-ces.

And they know me. They must re-mem-ber

1st verse I think of old friends
how I loved them. I dream of old joys,
New lives, new fa-ces

where we used to live then. We had old dreams of
zest and hum-an fol-ly; So full of jeal-ou
came to fill their pla-ces. It did-n't mat-ter

what we'd be; and new loves we'd hoped to see-
sy and hate, love and vice we blame on fate.
what we'd do we would just try some-thing new

We knew how great our lives and plans would make us
We chose to live de-ceit and con-fron-ta-tion.
It got so bor-ing with the same old sto-ry.

We thought no God would int-er-fere, We would make
It did-n't mat-ter that all knew; It was just
I could-n't find the rea-son why life had

it all ap-pear.
something to do. Old days and old ways with old
be come so dry.

dreams and old loves to guide us., And they know me.

They can re-mem-ber how I loved them.

SECOND & THIRD ENDINGS

With hearts a - blaze,   lov - ing our ways, , anger and hate,

re - gret came late: heart break.   So   we   part - ed.

They don't re - mem - ber   I   still love them.

How my heart cries out for them.   God re - mem - bers

and I   pray for them   How my heart aches.

So they celebrated *Nevruz*. They sang old songs, laughed and cried as they told stories through the night; a night to remember.

KOOCHUK'S GIFT

PEOPLE, PLACES & PLOTS IN CHAPTER 8

Agah bey: Khan of the White Hun Armies, a wise father takes his responsibility.
Da-vut': makes some important decisions about his future.
Ka'ya: keeps to his quest in spite of the distress of many.
Koo chook': finds two birds in her bush, to her delight.
Jan'o-var: monster, a merciless raider of flocks.
Mert'ler: organizes the hunt and encourages the hunters.
Oz'kurt: finds more than he intended when he prayed for excitement.
Shan'la: gets as much as she can handle with her guests.
Ser'dar: is charmed and frustrated by the events of his life.
Village head man: complains of the dangers found in staying home.

GLOSSARY:

han'um: lady; misses; madam; a term of honor.
jan'o-var: a monster; horrible creature; hideous thing.
Sultan va'li-de: Sultan's mother; wives' mother-in-law. Often the ruler of the harem.
Tanra: an ancient word for the Creator, personified in the everlasting blue sky.
yeet: brave young man; bold hero; he-man.

HAWK ATTACKS SWANS

"I have my young friend Serdar here, and we thought we would make a short visit on your kind invitation, Shanla *hanum*," Kaya's voice boomed cheerfully.

"Welcome honored guests," the doorman and presumably household guard said. He was tall and gaunt, a tower that might sway in the wind, but never fall. Beyond him the mistress of the house moved solicitously forward.

"Happily you have come, Kaya: this is your friend?" She paused and a look of uncertainty passed her face. "I have seen you before. Where have we met?"

The boy was examining the entry hall and view of rooms critically. He shrugged indifferently. "You are the *Sultan-valide* of the harem?

"he queried. He knew that the mother of the Sultan, as the ruler of the harem, always took charge. After all, a man might have many wives and concubines, but only one mother. What man would offend his mother for a mere wife, "Your establishment is very nice," he said.

"There is a garden here on the south side," Kaya proclaimed. "There are early bulbs and tulips beginning to show; come and see." They moved through the dining room to the door of the garden. It was still cool outside and had the winter look.

"It's all small, but very nice." He commented generously.

"I know you are the entertainer, but where is your lord?" He asked.

"She was the wife of my father, the Khan, robbed in a raid. She became the trusted administrator of Ishak bey, and he financed her theatrical presentations," Kaya hastily explained.

"I manage my own house," Shanla added, "we are not a harem, nor a house of pleasure. We are more like a school."

"You said Ishak bey, what of him?" A puzzled look dominated the face of the boy.

"He died many years ago," Shanla explained, "His sons were killed in battle and I manage the estate, which I bought from the nephew. I train young ladies for the stage and as artists. In the summer we perform for the entertainment of the public."

The boy stood thinking, "I have known nothing like this before." He looked at Kaya, "How do we proceed?"

Kaya chuckled again and patted the boy on the back familiarly. "We proceed to see the works of art, listen to the music and meet the artists. Then, we could offer to finance one of them in her career. You can enjoy a meal with us now, and visit again when you need someone to talk to or share confidences." Kaya paused, "They are good at keeping secrets, and have lots of good advice for the young."

"I should like that," Serdar exclaimed.

Shanla smiled broadly, "I have just the person, only a little older than you, to share confidences with." Kaya and Serdar followed Shanla expectantly. Kaya brought something out of his pouch.

"Look Koo'chook," he blurted out, "I brought you a bird that will never fly away and leave you." He waved a small wood-carved bird the size of the girl's fist. It was painted blue and yellow and had a straw or pipe stem entering through the back.

"Oh Kaya," she laughed, and the bells seemed to tinkle again, "What is it? Let me see." He smiled shyly and put the stem to his lips and blew. A bubbly, warbling whistle came from the open beak of the bird.

Koo'chook clapped her hands and whispered, "Let me, oh, let me do it, please." Kaya laughed and passed her the bird.

"Careful, don't spill the water on you. The breath passes through water to sound from the beak. It is a plaything of the Dolgan people." She produced a series of long peeps and warbles, and her face was flushed with excitement. She stopped, out of breath.

"Koo'chook, this is my best friend in Perikanda. Serdar, we wanted you to meet. She knows many stories about me when I was only a cub just learning about yurt life," Kaya explained.

Serdar had stood open-mouthed taking in everything. He blurted out, "You knew her in the tribe?"

Kaya stopped to think about this first. "No, I knew of her, but not to talk to or visit. Her brother came to the mare's pasture to talk and play. I was not allowed..." He stopped abruptly and looked anxiously at Shanla.

"Come Kaya, you'll be embarrassed if she tells one of the stories now," she ordered. "We'll be back shortly, dear. Don't bore Serdar with too many wild accounts." They sat in silence for a moment. Then, she piped the bird again and laughed. She offered it to him. Without a word he took it and blew a long, loud blast. Water sprayed the room and both children started to laugh uncontrollably. Those outside listened with satisfaction.

"Oh Kaya, you continue to perplex and amaze me. You have no idea who your little friend is, but I know. One of my girls, the daughter of the palace cook, has recognized him. You have a prince as sponsor."

Kaya nodded and smiled. "I wondered about that, but I too, am a child of promise, and it doesn't affect who I choose for friends. He must learn to rise above rank and prejudice."

"Yes, we all learn. I don't compel my girls down the path that I was forced to go. They make their choices: marriage, career or lovers with advice about each road. I don't know if you understand what I'm saying, but *Tanra* has been generous in spite of pain and sorrow."

He stood nodding his head, smiling. Then he looked around sniffing. "Yes, I have food being prepared, you wonderful bear-man. I shall take the children their share first, before I let you at it." She laughed and left him.

> - - - - - - - >

The children's voices shrilled again in loud laughter and more bird songs warbled loudly. "My brother swore that every word I told you is true, Serdar. Now you must tell me a story about yourself."

Serdar passed her the wooden bird and sat thinking. "Have you ever seen a swan? Kaya Bey has one cut in ivory on his talisman. It says: 'A leader decides when and where to descend for the good of all; in order to feed his flock.' I like that! Real swans are giant birds too big and wild to hold in both arms." He illustrated the holding. "They are the most beautiful birds in the sky, except, of course, my hawk. They weave patterns in the sky and fly as a flock together. They're always perfectly aligned and never crowd each other in flight. Would you like a swan feather? We go hawking in three day's time."

Her smile was broad, and she let the toy bird pipe her approval.

Then the smile faded, and she asked somewhat timidly, "You won't have to kill the bird to get the feather, will you?"

He stiffened. "Part of the beauty is the swoop of the hawk and his attack on the flock as he gets through the formation to pick out one single bird. They fall in an arc of flowing plumes to splash down. It's so exciting."

She now looked sadder and objected, "The feathers would be wet and stained. I shouldn't want one."

He protested, "I don't hunt for blood, but for beauty. Don't worry; your feather will be shed." She tweeted her bird again as lunch was brought to them.

> - - - - - - - >

The Khan and his son, Serdar, were armed with hawks and shivering attendants as they rode by the marshy lake where the sound of feeding geese and ducks proclaimed the migration and courtship activities in progress. Out before first light, they had an ample load of bird carcasses, which would suffice the palace occupants and staff for several days. When Agah Khan called a halt and ordered a fire started, the attendants gutted the prey, and the lord permitted the hawks to feed on the heads of the catch. Serdar, however, held his hawk apart wanting one more go at the flocks, but uncertain which way to launch his bird.

"Look south, Sir, here they come." Mertler pointed to a formation of wild swans that were bearing in over the lake. The boy stared long, in wonder at the magnificent sight, then quickly he launched, and his bird fought for height as the great white swans swept over the marsh. At the same moment the hawk dived to intercept, a trifle low and slow. The great birds rose from their glide and without breaking formation began evasive flight. Serdar jumped up and down in excited anticipation.

The hawk tried for the nearest bird now over the center of the lake. Lacking great height or surprise, the hawk made a side rush at the head of the bird, but it retracted its head, rolled away from the dive and brought its great wing down on the head of the plunging raptor. They seemed to fall together for a moment. Then the swan resumed its great wing beat, and the hawk spread her wings in a braking action just before she hit the water.

The Agah Khan chuckled as he looked on and shouted, "You hesitated, and you lost. You must give your bird time to get in position. Time must be used to your advantage." The prince, up to his knees in the lake, seemed to be about to plunge into the icy water to save his floundering bird, but the hawk was flapping vigorously and had pulled herself clear of the surface. Exhausted, she arrived at the bank. Serdar gathered his hawk to him and took off his turban to dry his friend: stroking, patting the wet feathers dry. A broken white feather clung to its coat.

"Feed her now," said his father, "she performed well; the fault was not hers."

The pouting boy reluctantly surrendered the bird to an attendant and carelessly rewound his turban, replying, "We got half a hundred. Why magnify only one failure? The bird was tired." He tucked the white feather away; the owner lived. There was no blood. It would be a fitting gift.

"Right, yet it becomes a lesson from Tanra if we listen and learn." The Khan walked over and embraced the lad, facing them toward the lake where the swans had settled on the farther side. "They are beautiful birds, and it was an exciting lesson."

"I've been told you are going to let the man who wears the swan talisman escape you, Agah bay."

The man dropped his arms at the use of his name. He turned to face the boy. "The Chipchak? Does that Turk mean so much to you? An unwilling mercenary is

- 82 -

worth no more than a war prisoner. You will get no service from him that will equal the damage he can do."

"But you, too, have lost your swan, father."

"On the contrary, I give him freedom and the chance to become *Yeet*, a hero; to make his name live. Dead or alive, that is no small favor." He glanced to see the attention on the boy's anxious face. "Suppose you kept your hawk always in the mews and never on the wing, how would you know its merits?" He smiled at the boy's reluctant nod. "It's not weakness for a questing stranger to pass up easy promotion and riches."

"When will he be allowed to leave?"

"Late Spring, after the Christian's Holy Week." He did not mention that they would be sent out to the north through the desert near the Aral Sea. There were monsters there to tempt the foolish or heroes.

> - - - - - - - >

The church was packed on Palm Sunday with believers and their friends. Some held palm branches and others had them woven into the form of a donkey. Others held miniature pictures of a man riding a donkey through cheering crowds.

RUN AND SEE

1,   Run, we'll run and see on the city streets,
      Something is happening there right now.
      Hear the crowd's loud echoes sweet.
      Join them to praise the king who comes.
      Palms and robes are laid for him
      At the donkey's feet.
      See Him ride on so joyfully, to the temple hill.
      God protects our people here.
      We stay in His care.
      In Jerusalem there is peace.

Male voices took up the second part. It formed a refrain after each verse and presented a kind of complaint in a chant.

Refrain: Please come away, work and don't play.
          It's not important, so don't go and stay.
          We're busy living now, we can't delay.
          Let angels think of it, not our affair.
          We'll leave it all to God: don't go out there.

DON'T GO

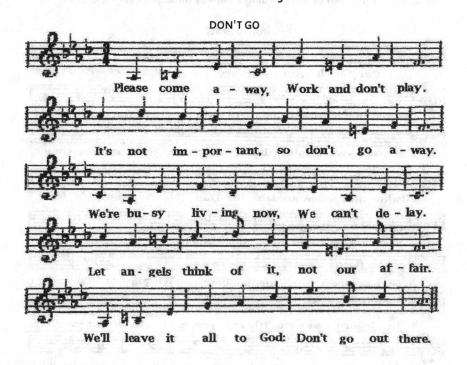

Please come a - way, Work and don't play.

It's not im - por - tant, so don't go a - way.

We're bu - sy liv - ing now, We can't de - lay.

Let an - gels think of it, not our af - fair.

We'll leave it all to God: Don't go out there.

The children's choir sang the antiphony in crisp, clear voices stating heaven's viewpoint.

SING LOUD PRAISES

Hal - le - lu - jah, Hal- le - lu - jah. Sing loud praises
to the lamb. Hal - le - lu - jah, Hal - le - lu - jah.
Sing, Oh sing Je - ru -sa - lem. For the blood of the Mes- si-
ah, shed to set God's peo-ple free; For the Love of
the Al - migh - ty, Lasts for all e - ter - ni - ty.

Affirmation:　　Hallelujah, Hallelujah,
　　　　　　　　Sing loud praises to the lamb.
　　　　　　　　Hallelujah, Hallelujah,
　　　　　　　　Sing, oh sing, Jerusalem.
　　　　　　　　For the blood of the Messiah,
　　　　　　　　Shed to set God's people free;
　　　　　　　　For the love of the Almighty,
　　　　　　　　Lasts for all Eternity.

The end brought a new beginning and the total choir started again with soft anticipation building the suspense.

2.　　　　　Watch, we watch at night from the city wall.
　　　　　　Something is happening now out there.
　　　　　　See the burning torches move,
　　　　　　Out to the olive garden, where
　　　　　　His disciples fight and flee.
　　　　　　Leaving one alone.
　　　　　　See how he stands with head held high.
　　　　　　Will they try him now?
　　　　　　God protects the innocent
　　　　　　With His watchful eye.
　　　　　　In Jerusalem there is peace.

Again the male voices followed by the children sang their parts in the complaint and hallelujah. Then a new verse follows.

3.   Hear, we hear at dawn from the courtyard square.
     Something is happening now in there.
     Hear the sound of whip and thong,
     Count the lash that cuts to bone.
     Council meets, they him condemn,
     Standing there alone.
     Pilate wash, you will not free,
     All shout crucify.
     God protects our righteous men
     With his truth and grace.
     In Jerusalem was there peace?

After each verse, chant and chorus the voices filled the church with the echoes of contrast in the refrain.

4.   Look, we look to see in the city street.
     Something is happening there right now.
     Guards are marching to a beat,
     Felons are marching with their cross.
     Mobs are screaming their contempt,
     To the place of death.
     Guards nail Him up above the crowd,
     See Him thirst and die.
     God looks down with tender eye,
     While the guards stand by.
     In Jerusalem there's no peace.

Some of the women were crying now and the congregation was in the grip of the story.

5.   Hush, we hush to hear, whisperings come clear.
     People are moving to the tomb.
     They are whispering everywhere.
     Jesus appears, they've seen him there.
     Touch and feel that He is real.
     Death has lost its power.
     He sends them out with truth and light
     To the harvest fields.
     Now he calls us every one
     To salvation free;
     To Jerusalem He sends peace.

The conclusion sent thrills of anticipation through the audience of worshipers. On Sunday, the cries of 'Christ is risen,' answered by, 'He is risen indeed,' filled the small cathedral.

The group of Kaya's friends came to be with him on his last day in the city. Kaya and Ozkurt had been given permission to leave Samarkand by the northwest road. They would have to pass the Kyzel Kum Desert of red sand.

"Go happily on your journey, Kaya bey, I too will travel back to my home beyond the Pamir Plateau. It has been my pleasure to guide and work with you," Davut said.

"Will you leave your present employment and go back home?"

"I'm not easy in this work. It was a mistake to accept it. I'm sorry now and need to go home and be with my parents. Tanra has helped me understand the shame of it. You have given me one glory to boast about: I have met Shanla and been received and entertained in her palace. I will never forget it. Go with God and my prayers for your success."

It was near summer when they arrived at the mouth of the Amu River where it entered the brackish waters of Lake Aral. The deserts hemmed them in on every side. Only the water from the mountains sustained life by irrigation.

At the last village the people complained. "Why all this rush to go west? We are in need of the presence of warriors here. Now at the time of the orchards blooming, the *Janovar*, sand monsters, will appear. Thin and greedy from the winter's sleep, they will eat our flocks and even our shepherds, but our warriors go west or south for glory and gold. Who will help us for a farmer's thanks? We have only our food and animals."

Making close inquiry, Kaya and Ozkurt found the facts about the *samovar* shocking. The young were as large as the greatest kangal herd dogs and adults, from nose to tail, measured over six feet. When rearing on two feet propped by the long snake-like tail, they were as tall as the tallest men. Their teeth were retracted and curved toward the inside of the mouth, and they seemed to have several rows of teeth. He was shown shed teeth and claws of the feared monsters.

"They can be killed with spears and arrows when trapped or found in their caves, but on the sands they are fast and fierce. They attack, scatter a herd and kill greedily. The uneaten prey they hide under the sand after they decimate a flock. We will provide food or whatever you need for travel if you will help us now." The elders of the village proposed a plan to send out one large flock. The village men, Kaya and Ozkurt would guard it. The other animals would stay near the village. They agreed to scout on the Kyzel Kum Desert to the east and then on the Ust'Yurt Plateau on the west.

While they laid a trap in the east, the village was hit from the west. Reports of three dogs and ten sheep missing reached the men. Trackers were put to the trail and several burials were found close to the kill. An excavation was made near the first spot and all the buried carcasses brought there. Sticks driven close together were made to ring the top of the hole. Two entrances were left open and sharpened stakes were weighted with a filled oil pot to fall down and close the entrance gaps. A couple of torches were prepared for burning, and a pot with burning coals was kept at hand with those set to await the return of the large lizards. Kaya searched for their den, but the dogs showed anxiety and failed to keep the trail.

Two days later movement was reported near a different flock to the west. Both men went together to verify the report. As they reached the horizon, a shout behind them caused them to turn. The monsters had returned at the warmest hour of the day. One was eating in the pit and another entering from one side when the stakes fell. Oil spilt and coals scattered. The frightened creatures thrashed around inside the pen. The lighted torches came arching in as thrown by the village men. The oil caught fire and the thrashing increased in the pen. The animal caught under the stakes began to back out, spilling more oil.

As they watched the one escaped running with head and shoulders ablaze toward the area where they had not searched the previous days. Ozkurt whooped and put his horse in full gallop toward some hills at the edge of the plateau. The village men with spears were finishing the one in the pit.

Kaya followed his friend, arming his bow and notched an arrow at ready. Ozkurt and the wounded animal were set on a collision course, when, as Ozkurt loosed his first arrow, another monster reared up out of the sand at his horse's feet. Hissing in rage, it struck Ozkurt's chest and sent him flying out of the saddle. His horse ran on and then quickly dodged out of the way of the blazing creature ahead, writhing with Ozkurt's arrow in its side.

Kaya bent, urging Altom on. Ozkurt lay stunned and breathless trying to pull his long knife. The Janovar paused hissing, her mouth now open and tongue flicking out. She seemed reluctant to attack. Coiling defensively around her nest of large white eggs, she sent forth a low, loud hissing sound; both defiant yet urgent, appealing.

On the crest of a bluff above Ozkurt's head a tall figure of the male drew into a crouch and leaped with a grunt toward the downed man. Kaya rode between and released his arrow at the eye. He heard the thud of the arrow and the neigh of terror of Altom, who skidded to a halt trembling, trapped by the three monsters.

As Kaya turned to look back, he released his second arrow at the female. It took her in the open mouth. She was now moving forward, toward the fallen man. Then he felt, rather than saw, the rise of the burning figure near him. Altom reared as a huge mouth grabbed Kaya's cloak just behind his neck and shook him savagely, plucking him up off the horse's back. Altom kept running, kicking up sand and dust as she escaped. Ozkurt was rolling away from the female's nest and had his knife drawn. There were his spilled arrows scattered everywhere, so he grabbed one and tried to move toward the bluff's base, away from the thrashing form of the male.

Kaya grabbed his long knife and struck back, over his shoulder, under the jaw of the animal that held him. His cape was choking him, and he fought to catch his breath. The shaking continued. Ozkurt shouted defiance, but he was distracted with the female and the agonizing male. Kaya seemed to lose track of what was happening. The smell of burning flesh and blood filled the air. A short hissing exhalation of breath sounded in his ear. He caught the sight of a mounted village man rushing in before him. Dangling, he saw the headman thrusting a spear at his heart. Kaya tried to twist out of the way. Then, darkness.

JANAVARS' ATTACK

PEOPLE, PLACES & PLOTS IN CHAPTER 9

Ben Isha'ak: a rich Jewish merchant and custodian of Judith at Gechit City.
Il'kin: a militant prince of the ruling Khazar family, guarding territories on the Don River.
Judith: a young Jewish heiress, deeply in love.
Kal'mash: an owner of the Golden Pond Inn in Gech'it City's Jewish district.
Ka'ya: seeks friends to explain the city's composition.
Khan Kinner: a strict ruler of the Khazar Empire.
Oz'kurt: weary of traveling, seeks a moment of diversion.
Op'tal and Pesh: appear with a gift from Jomer bey.

GLOSSARY:

Adoni: Lord; a Hebrew substitute for the name of God.
dee'cot: caution; attention; warning; be careful.
gehenaya goyim: hell-bound gentiles; go to hell you aliens.
Hav'rah-dar: It's a Synagogue; a Jewish building for worship and education.
janum: my soul; dearest; beloved; for family affection.
Kah ra man': an acclaimed hero.
of-fad-dair' sin-is: pardon me; forgive me; "excuse the question, but..."
Rume: the name used for the East Roman Empire and its citizens.
Shabat: the Sabbath day; Jewish Sabbath from Friday sundown to Saturday dark.
Shabat goyim: gentile servants who do work prohibited to practicing Jews.
soos: hush; quiet; shut up; calm down.
yeet: brave youth; hero; known and admired he-man.
you-rue: walk; keep moving; go on; keep going; move.

A FAIR RIOT

Kaya awoke to the sounds of celebration, drums beat and the sound of pipes and strings filled the air. His head and neck hurt, and he felt queasy; his stomach hurt. He touched his ribs and groaned. He lay still and listened to the singing:

1.   We sing of heroes, we sing of love.
      We sing of pale hands as soft as a dove.
      We hail the brave ones who risk and who try.
      Stars rule the heavens, but you rule my eyes.

2.   Men love their beauties; soft, loving, sweet.
      Women love heroes who fall at their feet.
      There are deceivers and people who cry;
      All seek a hero to measure their lives.

3.   Good men love daylight to work aright.
      Dark deeds require the cover of night.
      Heroes find victory through tests and by trials.
      Women fall victim to flattery's wiles.

4.   We hail the bold ones, knowing and bright.
      The sun rules by day, the moon lightens night.
      Evil confronts you, truth brings you to fight.
      God in His Glory tests men in the light.

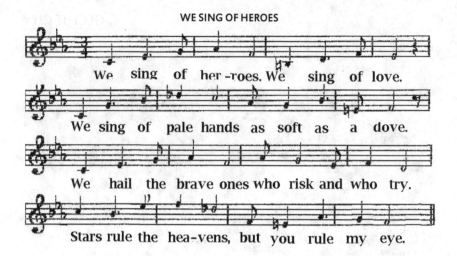

WE SING OF HEROES

We sing of her-roes. We sing of love.

We sing of pale hands as soft as a dove.

We hail the brave ones who risk and who try.

Stars rule the hea-vens, but you rule my eye.

Ozkurt came into the hut laughing boisterously with a girl on his arm. "Awake finally? *Yeet*, my hero and brother, you've missed most of the party. We must leave tomorrow for the river town, Gechit, the crossing. It's on the Volga, the mother of rivers. Do you know that there, the Khan has a palace of wood that is higher than five yurts? The Jewish merchants have gold rings on every finger? They call it the new... no, the second Jerusalem!" He shook his head in disbelief as he illustrated each statement clumsily. "I have drunk lots in advance of the desert journey. I'll never be thirsty again. Let me tell you how I finished off that giant female defending her eggs." He staggered and turned to the girl. "I'm thirsty again, Can you get me something?" He collapsed next to Kaya and slept.

Departure took longer than Ozkurt thought. The local people would not let them go. They got two perfect skins and a skeleton of the Janovar to keep as trophies. They were sent on their way with all the travel supplies their horses could carry. They would cut across the Caspian depression where formerly water had flowed during the last Ice Age when all the seas and lakes of Middle Asia overflowed to enrich the grasslands around them. The trail now led over desert and short grass steppe where sheep and goats got scanty fare. Summer passed, leaving them brown and tough with constant travel.

They viewed the Volga, the Mother of Rivers, from the high eastern terraces. Awed by the endless, moving water they sat waiting, but the waters never varied as they flowed lazily to the Caspian Sea. Reluctantly, they left their view and rode down to the city, a strange mixture of expensive wooden or stone buildings surrounded by the omnipresent familiar yurts of felt or hides. Animals and people thronged the streets. They moved toward the central core where more than one building was three times any yurt in height. They vainly sought news of Koostah's band or of hostages seen or sold.

Approaching a large building of stone, they found a prosperous young man walking slowly, thoughtfully, toward an inn facing an imposing building. Ozkurt spoke first.

"*Of fad dair sinis,* your pardon, Sir. What is this large building? What part of the city is this?"

"*Havrah dar,* it's the Synagogue, Beth Shalom. You're new in town. If you seek a Caravanserai, the Golden Pond is the best here on the edge of the Jewish section. It's kosher and well located for business." The youth's speech was cultivated, indicating an upper class Khazar.

Ozkurt objected. "We are poor travelers, with only a few silver coins for our stay. We are rich in adventures, but poor in wealth." He looked at Kaya keenly, "I have a lovesick companion who scarcely endures the days," he laughed.

"Then the Golden Pond is the very place where all these needs are met. And if misery loves company, your friend will find such a one with me. I, too, have suffered the loss of a dear one." His smile belied his suffering. "I have a plan laid to change all that." He motioned toward the inn.

"The sector we have passed seems to hold some Christians. We have seen different churches." Ozkurt ventured, as they rode to the inn and dismounted.

"Our town has grown by reason of the persecutions among the Byzantines. All *Rume* is ablaze with the expulsions and riots. Jews and heretics are escaping wherever freedom lies. We have three types of Christians. Each refuses to associate with the other kinds. They have only insults to offer those who hold a different opinion. Gechit is a bucket of oil and water; none of these people will mix with the others." As they entered the inn, the youth was greeted with great deference by a portly man, obviously the owner or manager. He came forward solicitously.

"Ilkin bey, welcome again, we are honored." He bowed deeply and then looked behind the guest, "Ah, this is an unofficial visit, no guards," he inclined again.

"If you continue to bow and scrape, everyone will know I am here privately," His voice seemed to puncture the man's suaveness. "I bring two friends who require a room and will eat with me on the upper terrace tonight."

"Sir, will there be a lady visitor this time? Should I make preparations as before?" The noble shook him.

"*Soos,* Kalmash! Hush, will you tell everything you know? My father will hang you by your toes, and the master of the Synagogue will burn your inn." His eyes held fury.

"Yes, my Lord, forgive me." Kalmash was reduced to a mass of quivering servility. "Come gentlemen, you'll wish to wash the stains of journey from you. The baths adjoin the inn, and we have a private entrance." He led the men away.

"So I have made preparations to rescue my dearest *Yahudit*, Judith, from the control of her guardian. He is a man of great wealth and power in the city, concerned with all the affairs of his community. That provides the key to his weakness and loss. Once our marriage is consummated, I think we can come to an arrangement satisfactory to my father and to the Guardian," Ilkin smiled confidently.

"I see little we can do to forward your plans, or repay our debt to your hospitality." Ozkurt replied.

"Your stories and the persistence of your pursuit speak wonders to my heart. I know you will maintain your faith and succeed in your purpose. My beloved is willing, but the fine line is that the guardian, Ben Ishaak, the master of the Synagogue, remain away sufficient time for our planned elopement. With your experience you can lengthen the time of discussion and keep control of the situation, so it does not get out of hand. Ben Ishaak will be there first and foremost to the end; he loves an argument."

"We will help any way we can," concluded Kaya. "Tomorrow at dawn we will be at the fair site." They sat, and from their terrace, continued to look at the great stone building, the city streets, the gardens, and over the river,

> - - - - - - >

"My booth goes here. I have the authorized papers from the supervisor of the fair," affirmed a tall husky man to the elderly Jew. The Jew was richly dressed. He wore a turban with curls showing about the temples and full beard, also carefully curled. He wore gold rings, but the objector pushed him aside. "This is my spot."

"You are mistaken sir. I have the papers and the bill of receipt," replied Ben Ishaak. "My men have already started their work and all is arranged with the authorities. Call a security guard if you like. Let him see your papers, but you are wrong, and I will allow no delay in our work."

"You arrogant old fool, you are wrong, but you refuse to look at my papers. You people fill our land without invitation and take our places assigned by our Khan. You will finish nothing until you see these papers."

As the volume rose, the security people started to move in that direction, as did Ozkurt and Kaya. A crowd of the idle, the curious, and workers formed about the two men and some cat-calls and mocking voices joined the tumult.

"Damned foreigners."

"Refugees and refuse from the south."

"Go home, take the Christians with you."

"This is Khazar land."

"Go home," became the chant. The crowd began to jostle and push. The security guards had raised loud voices trying to quiet the crowd. "*Soos, deecot,* order."

"Disperse, go about your business."

"*You rue*, move on," but the noise increased. Now other voices were heard as Jewish workmen and owners added their words to the tumult. "Leave him be," they protested.

"Don't listen to the pagans."

"*Gehenaya goyim*."

"Uncircumcised scum."

"Philistines."

Monophysites, Arians and Nestorians in the crowd now seized the opportunity to gain favor with the Khazar whom they too, privately, called pagans.

"The Jew's papers are forgeries."

"They buy favors with bribes."

"Christ killers."

Blows were exchanged indiscriminately. The violence started.

Kaya and Ozkurt, who would never walk a mile without their horses, mounted and moved toward the center of the melee. The animals became skittish, and those who were jostled pulled back. Each man took out his quirt. Gripping the flexible tip, they used them like clubs swinging them back and forth above the horse's mane in a figure eight, to force the people to dodge and scatter. In this way they vigorously pushed forward to the two men who had been the reason for the confrontation. Each horseman seized one of the protagonists and left with his startled prey mounted before him, retreating to the Golden Pond. Behind them the fighting ceased. Mounted Khazar guards moved in tardily to restore order and to aid the security guards with their arrests.

The subdued men agreed to go together to the fair master and lay the matter before him. It was late evening before Ben Ishaak got home to discover his loss. He went directly to the Khan Kinner with the complaint.

Outside the inn a crowd had gathered. The sound of music brought still more people. A small brown bear was dancing to the pipe and drum. The music spoke of a far, almost mystical country where riches and pleasure was the portion of all: Hindustan, land of legend.

> If you seek for warmth and pleasure,
> Come, come to Hindustan.
> If you long for love and leisure.
> Come, come to Hindustan.
>
> There you'll find great treasure:
> All there in Hindustan.

There's wisdom without measure:
All there in Hindustan.

Jewels, spices, fabrics ooh,
You will find your hearts dream;
Cities, beaches, mountains too,
There you'll be content.

COME TO HINDUSTAN

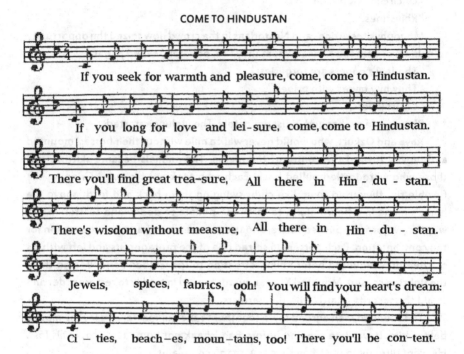

If you seek for warmth and pleasure, come, come to Hindustan.

If you long for love and lei-sure, come, come to Hindustan.

There you'll find great trea-sure, All there in Hin - du - stan.

There's wisdom without measure, All there in Hin - du - stan.

Jewels, spices, fabrics, ooh! You will find your heart's dream:

Ci - ties, beach-es, moun-tains, too! There you'll be con-tent.

In a moment a thin emaciated man began to juggle three large knives while balancing an apple on his head. Children gathered: Jewish, Christian, Manichean and Pagan Khazar. Each wore their local dress: curls and skullcaps; ear-flap hats; wearing Cross, fish, amulet, blue bead or Star of David for protection. They laughed and played at imitating the bear's dance. Pesh and the bear wrestled. Optal stormed. The music wailed. Everyone enjoyed the presentation.

Kaya rode up when the performance was at its height and sat watching the antics of children and entertainers. When the fortunes were told, the people resumed their movements. Kaya leaned over to speak to the watching Kalmash, owner of the inn. He nodded hesitantly and entered the inn. Kaya dismounted and went to the bear master, took his hands and pressed them, kissed his hands and touched them with his forehead. Optal's smile was broad.

"Kaya, my friend, God has smiled on us today. We have found you," he embraced him and kissed his cheek.

"Yes, we looked for you here, and now we have found you. We recognized your golden horse." Pesh nodded vigorously. "We always meet and eat, while you feed the bear." He giggled and looked about expectantly looking around for a food stand.

"Were you seeking me? Why? What would you have?" Kaya looked at them in a puzzled way, but made a motion toward the inn with his hand.

"We have important tidings from your city and a present from your patron. He is home and healed. We will carry back any messages."

"Come, we will eat on the terrace. I have a Janovar skin to send to Jomer bey. My companion, Ozkurt, is doing a favor for a friend. He will not be here till evening. Of course, you will stay for supper." Kaya gave his horse, Altom, to the inn's groom.

"They call you *Yeet, Kahraman*, now," Pesh reported, "young hero." It was a great, long, story-filled meal which Ozkurt joined with news of success. Music continued late that night.

> - - - - - - >

"You were present at the quarrel. You were prepared to rescue the two protagonists from the riot. You subdued the fighting by your prompt action. You both were seen later in the morning at the house of Ben Ishaak when the girl, his ward, was abducted. One of you remained there and led the men who pursued in the wrong direction. You were recognized easily by your lion-colored horse. I want to know where the girl was taken. Her guardian wants her back. I will have the man who did this and you in dungeon. If you would spare yourselves pain, explain the gold we have found in your room. If innocent, you have nothing to fear." Khan Kinner, grim-faced and angry, looked down at the two prisoners kneeling, in chains, on the ground before him. "You will stay here until I am convinced you have given me all the information I demand. Then, and only then, will I give you a proper trial."

> - - - - - - >

The prince stretched lazily on the bed when the dark-eyed, long-haired Judith came to the door of the room.

"Where have you been, *Janum*, my soul. I have been here pining away for your love," Ilkin stretched his arm toward her appealingly. She uttered a little laugh.

"You have been asleep, you callous monster," she teased. "And since you love me so little, I have sent for my family's *Shabat Goyim* to give me the news. But they, less one, have departed long since. She must work here tonight. The food is prepared, and we will enjoy our first Sabbath together." He sat up slowly and cocked his head to one side.

"I don't think I've ever observed Saturday. I see others doing it, but it will be a new experience."

"I have no doubt *Adoni*, the Lord, will have to exercise much grace for your many violations of His Day. It starts Friday night with the candle lighting."

"Why do we have to keep *Shabat*? You're married now to a Prince of the land. You can do anything you please." She laughed again and went to his side, brushed his hair back out of his face and kissed him tenderly, sighing.

"I was a Jewish girl keeping *Shabat* seventeen years before I met my beautiful prince. One year of devotion and love for a prince does not cancel the earlier years. It pleases me to keep *Shabat* and the ways of my fathers even though I married a man who has other traditions." She smiled her prettiest.

"We don't really have to do any inconvenient things, do we? We could let it go till next week. It's only three days since our elopement. We are just getting to know each other intimately. We have lots of time to learn." He held out his hands appealingly.

He pulled her down for another kiss. She yielded graciously, but then, when he sought to hold her even closer, rolled over and evaded him neatly. Laughing, she sat up and dodged his grab for her. Shaking her head she said softly, "It's time to light the candles and too late to delay. We will abstain from the flesh for the moment. Get up and put on a clean outfit, then join me in the dining room. Your lessons are about to begin." She swept out the door before he could prevent her. He was left alone and thoughtful as he dressed.

> - - - - - - >

Ozkurt sat looking through the barred door that held them, waiting for the sound of people or of food. Kaya sat facing the high window where the sound of birds and movement penetrated. They had been three days in confinement. Ozkurt groused; "We don't know the place where they can find the Prince Ilkin. How can we give information we don't have? We told everything we know. They don't believe us. We were duped. We didn't know it was the Khan's son who carried off the girl. She seemed eager enough." Ozkurt's anger seethed as he rattled the bars.

"Take any man's treasure, and you run risk and pay the full consequences. We were bored with travel and eager for adventure. Now, we pay. I shall occupy myself with prayer and meditation. I recommend them to you." Kaya was calm and tranquil. He whistled a bird call, and one came to the window and cocked its head. It found a crumb tossed there.

"They took the gold Jomer sent us. Optal and Pesh have disappeared. No one can confirm the source of the gold. They'll keep it." Ozkurt's hand gestured angrily. The bird flew.

> - - - - - - >

"Tell me more of the two easterners who helped you. They sound like unusual men. They were not paid agents like the others. Why did they help?" Judith sat on a divan. *Shabat* was over so she did handwork.

"As I said, they are on a quest. One pursues his kidnapped bride, the other comes for adventure and friendship. They sought to help from sympathy and perhaps boredom of travel. They are from a land where there are few Christians or Jews, and they asked questions about our situation here. Christianity is not politicized there and they could scarcely grasp the idea of Christian groups seeking to replace each other for power and favor. The strangers did not see how doctrine could define the groupings. They asked if there were differences in worship or practice and since there are no large differences, they were more puzzled." Ilkin smiled as Judith went into hearty laughter.

"As a curious, disobedient little girl, I went with some of my *Shabat goy* friends to the churches secretly, and there is no real difference in teaching or ritual between them. I heard the same teachings of Yesu in all of them."

"Who are these friends who helped you defy your father's wishes?" Ilkin asked, and she looked at him closely.

"You become concerned, now that you hold the father's position?" She queried laughingly. Then she smiled, "The gentiles, those of other nations, are hired to do the tasks the law has barred us from performing on *Shabat*. Many become close friends and confidents. We learn from each other."

"So you were not against such tasks being done. You were against doing them yourselves. Why so?"

"As people of a special purpose and standing before our Maker, we Jews were barred by our law from doing them. Others suffer no such prohibitions and incur no penalty. They earn, and we are more comfortable. *Adonai* is glorified."

"What of Yesu and his teachings? There you disobeyed your father. Was that against the law and custom of your people?" Ilkin pursued the subject further.

"Yesu, I love, he is a wonderful Jew, and his teachings are a summation of the best of our laws and prophets. His claims are fantastic and, if true, fulfill the hopes of my people. However, I consider the churches jealous nit-pickers." She stopped and laughed. "That sounds arrogant and judgmental; forgive me. Who is more divided and nit-picking than our self-righteous little cliques and sects in Judaism? I have only our heritage as a child of Abraham. I would be shamed and perhaps, shunned by some people for my girlish escapades and present opinions, but I have risked more in our marriage: you are esteemed a heathen by all. You're feared and obeyed as a superb warrior and ruler, but still scorned for your ignorance in things spiritual, plus your superstitious customs."

"My father follows the Ways of the Ancestors, and I have no desire to promote any religion. In Byzantium, I have seen the shifts between the striving powers; first Arius and his party were in ascendancy, then Cyrus and the Orthodox. Preference brings problems, strife and refugees."

"I hope you will never be forced to prefer one over the others, but life is full of compelled choices. Had I chosen a church, I would be considered dead by my people. Like the believing thief on the cross, I am not baptized. An anchorite might do it secretly, but I would still fall between the stools. Instead, I married you, so I'm dead." Judith paused, sighed and added, "We have strayed from our subject: the Turks from the East. They are not barbarians then, these distant relatives of your people? They are compassionate and sensible?"

Ilkin smiled broadly and chuckled. "They are refreshingly open and honest. The one, wearing an ivory swan insignia, claims to have been raised by bears. He feels like a bear living in a man's body, so he says. Yet he seeks his promised one for two years now. He rides a magnificent golden horse. He was full of the sayings of the leader of a hermitage school for children. He is a delightful man and his companion is an eager adventurer whom I would have in my army, if my father would allow me such command."

"Your father has kept you in a golden cage. There are other sons whom you cannot trust. Such circumstances come from those leaders who favor harems of women. You have promised to forego such accumulations." She leaned over to kiss him. "We are family enough until God provides more through me. The brothers will grow together--one family."

"May it be so, we must face my father's fury." He frowned and sighed. "They'll find us soon enough and we'll have to suffer humiliation. We were married by the itinerant Rabbi, who your people will esteem as mad. I bribed the Shaman for a ceremony. And the priests will not recognize the blessing of the Anchorite at the Don River woods. My men were witnesses of all three; at least it will impress my people."

"How long do we have?" She looked longingly at him.

"Two more days, I ordered my men to return to my father, after the week and report our location. I wrote a message requesting him to free the two Turks and send them to me here. They'll winter with us. If father sends a troop to take us, I have my guard division whom I have fed with all our estate's money. It might come to a stand off. I'm sure father's spies have reported our position as well as the enlarged forces. My message includes a pledge of personal loyalty and submission. I hope it's enough to stay his hand. I stand on the frontier of his hopes; if I can make the Huns withdraw beyond the Dnieper River. We will make a forced march there to claim it this winter. Our two easterners will lead a hundred."

> - - - - - - - >

"You boys would have gotten better treatment if you had told all you knew immediately," the jailor remarked as he opened the door to their cell.

Ozkurt looked up angrily, "The inn keeper gave you everything you needed. We told you everything we did, except the name of the place. We didn't know that! You were just having your fun. You wanted an excuse to keep our money. So you said the man lied about the gypsies coming, even though there were crowds watching."

"We don't doubt they came. We doubt that beggars carry gold to give to other people. It isn't reasonable. It's usual for collaborators to cook up stories about how they get gold. But we won't get it - Khan Kinner will; he can squeeze blood from a turnip." It had been a long week and they were bruised, dirty and hungry.

"Are you giving us the chains?" Ozkurt held up his wrists.

"Last thing on the list." The jailor smirked, "We'll take the leg irons now. I'd keep the horses and ivory too if it wasn't for our law and traditions. Our Khan would be richer for seating you on stakes."

> - - - - - - - >

"I am suspending your trial and sentence until the day I see you again." Kinner bey's face reflected cold control of his anger. "Go, then, west to the River Don, where my son, who has shamed me, is staying. He will attend your needs as he pleases. Your gold goes to Ben Ishaak bey for the daughter you helped steal. I should yoke and sit you on sharp stakes as meddlers deserving painful death. Get out of my sight, now and forever. To see my face again is to die." The hard old man turned his back and left.

The two stood and hurried to recover their goods and horses. Two men waited at the stable to guide them out of the city, to cross the great waters of the Volga and ride to the Don River. Across that water lay an army of Huns protecting the Dnieper River crossings from more pressure, invasion from the East. Heroes who kill monsters are only a bit of foam on that tide of people moving west.

JAIL BIRDS

PEOPLE, PLACES & PLOTS IN CHAPTER 10

At-illa: a scout with a common name, combining the words of horse, father/ancestor, and God.

Go'chen: a giant of a man, cynical, crude and ambitious.

Han Lee: an East Hun warrior, serving as a mercenary.

Ilkin: a prince of the Khazar people, pushing west.

Judith: a Jewish ward of Ben Ishaak, who eloped with Ilkin.

Kaya: continues his quest to find and rescue his intended bride.

Ozkurt: a weary adventurer accompanying Kaya to the Ukraine.

Sherbet: a slave and kitchen girl for the Huns.

GLOSSARY:

Adoni: the Lord, Hebrew, used in place of the name of God.

aya; pronounced i-ya: a bear; also forms part of Kaya's name.

baba: father or dad, used with an suffixed -m in direct address.

bayan: formal address, used before a woman's name; lady; madam.

chabuk ol: quickly, be quick.

dough rue: correct, right, of course, sure.

do'er: stop; hold still.

ha-mom: a Turkish bath with steam, hot and cold water.

havra: a synagogue; place of Jewish worship.

koo-mool-da-ma: don't move; stay where you are.

sherbet: a sweet frozen or liquid drink.

soos: hush; quiet; shush; silence.

tom-mom: okay; I agree; that's fine.

ya-bon'jee: foreigners; outsiders; strangers.

HAMAM DOORWAY

"You must be the prisoners our Prince has freed, ignorant scum from the east to dirty our *hamom*. Stand aside, I never give way to fools." The large man filled the door to the clothes lockers of the public baths. Kaya, stepping back, watched the advancing Ozkurt receive a bump as the man passed.

Kaya turned to his friend, who was angered by the bump and about to push the matter farther, and said, "I always give way to fools. It's prudent. We can't repay our host by quarreling with a rude guard."

The ride to the Don River estates had been a pleasant week's outing after confinement in the Gechit City dungeon. However, both Kaya and Ozkurt were on their best behavior when they met their royal sponsor, who had saved them from the wrath of Khan Kinner. Arriving just before dark, they enjoyed the *hamom* steam baths used for the troops and they were provided temporary uniforms by the resident tailor until their own could be made. It was evident that the estate was really a military garrison defending the east side of the Don River, now claimed by the Khazars.

The cultivated land lay on the north-east side of the river around a large wood-framed building facing the southern, lowering winter sun. The barracks for the troops lay slightly above on the rise to the higher ground that lines the eastern side of the Don, the Volga and all the Ukraine river systems. Across the river lay the flatter west side, where the brown grasslands invited viewers to come and see what the plains were hiding. That landscape was empty of human life both farming and herding. The Huns had come, devastated, occupied and gradually abandoned it as the lure of more productive lands moved them inevitably westward. The Khazars were giving land to cultivate or graze in an effort to reclaim the deserted fields.

"My offer of land for military personnel is real and the acreage is considerable. You are welcome to sign on as supporters and land owners, but you must populate the estate and provide military help on a permanent basis. This is a great opportunity for young men like you. Both of you can become rich and famous working with me." Seated on the floor, around the dinner dish, Prince Ilkin was launched on his favorite subject: the repopulating and incorporation of the land in the Khazar Empire.

Ozkurt responded with enthusiasm as they finished the meal.

"We have heard of the repopulating of the Chopper valley, and now of your hope for the Don valley. But where do you find surplus people?"

Ilkin laughed loudly and rose to gesture broadly. "The poor live crowded into forest lands to the north and mountains to the south. The promise of food and protection brings them in. Often poor in quality but abundant in numbers they will fill your halls and try your patience, yet they will build your prosperity as you nurture them."

"My dear, let the guests enjoy their food and talk of their travels. You have spoken amply and covered the subject several times." The lady Judith was forthright, but smiling fondly.

"Oh, my dear, can one ever hear enough of the marvelous opportunities we face?"

"You can see why I love him so," she addressed the guests, "he has style, words and brave actions to define and conquer his dreams -- aside from being a handsome prince."

"His father would not deem him so, Bayan," quipped Kaya "the words I heard from that source would not bear repeating before a lady." All laughed appreciatively at the reminder.

"Father will not continue to think that way if we continue to gain land west along the Don River. He will come and dance at the birth of an heir, if we make him the present of the steppes all the way to the Dnieper or Bug Rivers." The guests leaned forward excitedly.

"You are confident in your pursuit of the Huns then?" queried Kaya, curiously.

"When they have finished with a land, it is always sterile, depopulated and impoverished. Greener pastures, cattle and people are further west. That which will not profit them they abandon."

"All their troops are withdrawn?" questioned Ozkurt.

Ilkin laughed again, "New recruits are trained, where the seasoned veterans disdain to serve. There are no riches or glory here, but hard service in a picked over land. A new band has just arrived from the capital. But I don't know if some veterans have been withdrawn. War in the west presses hard, so they take the best. A new yuzbasha is in charge. He will be zealous, but a novice, susceptible to mistakes."

"How can we best use this intelligence when we make a new incursion?" Kaya smiled nodding,

"By enticement and ambush, we gather direct intelligence and capture a few prisoners first to know the real strength of the enemy."

Judith rose from her divan with a sad shake of her head. "You boys will have your fun and make your plans. I'll get my beauty rest. But I will have one question answered before I leave. Are there any of my people, the Jews, living in your eastern provinces? What do you know of us?"

Ozkurt and Kaya exchanged glances and Kaya nodded, electing to answer her. "We know of you through the gospels. You are a moral and religious people, waiting for a God appointed leader, but you didn't recognize your Messiah. Jealousy and envy, pride and prejudice exist in every community, religious or not, and there, the failure lay among those who should have known," Kaya concluded.

"Ask a direct question, wham, a direct answer, slightly softened by way of courtesy," Judith smiled,

"Lady, there was sufficient reason for the difficulties. There was the presence of a foreign army, betrayal by the local rulers and religious leaders who prospered by collaborating with an empire that forced ruinous taxation. They wanted a war leader."

She smiled again, "You are really a lovely young man trying to relieve my distress. Be assured, I am not distressed. I know the weakness of my people. But I assume that you know no Jews personally."

"There are a few along the Silk Road, but they don't have a *havra*, a worship place."

"It requires ten men and considerable wealth to formalize our worship in a proper building. When scattered we have our sanctuary in our homes."

"We get a day of rest that I have learned to enjoy, especially when she lets me sleep." Prince Ilkin smiled at his wife.

"The Lord requires it. Besides that, every ambitious man ought to get one night's sleep a week without distractions and late planning sessions till all hours. Go ahead, but don't let the fire go out. I'm off to bed," she replied. They rose and said their thanks and bid her rest easy. She took a lamp to light her way, leaving the room darker. The men brought their heads together and the prince used the table settings to illustrate his plan.

"I don't think there are any troops left. We have ridden for an hour, no one is around," Ozkurt protested to his companions. Gochen, the rude giant rode with the troop and answered him with contempt. "There are eyes everywhere. If we're not seen we soon will be, riding and raising dust."

"Then it's a good time to stop and have a good look around ourselves. The tallest hill is to our right. We could climb it and have a look." Kaya indicated a curiously rounded hill near by.

"It's thought to be haunted and bad luck to go to the top without an offering. It is called the Breasts. There is another like it behind to the west. A war camp is sometimes set up behind this hill. It hides them from the river's view and there is water." Gochen laughed, "A place to rest between the breasts," he quipped crudely.

Kaya made a motion meaning up and away to an outrider on the flank, "We can go up," Kaya offered "and have a look for you." He rode ahead on Altom to accompany the scout.

"Your friend's a fool, if a patrol comes around the base they'll be cut off from retreat. They'll take his gold," Gochen sneered.

"He may surprise you. He fools me constantly." Ozkurt drew up to stop and then spurred ahead. "I think I'll join them and enjoy the view," he shouted. "No one will be there. You wait a while."

The climb was steep and they led the horses when scrub and rocks forced them to dismount. The steep riverside slope blocked them out and they decided to move around to the side.

"We can see the camp area soon," the scout promised, "It's a good place to camp: water and wood as well as grazing. I'll bet a copper coin they have moved in, but they won't see us."

"Save your money, Ozkurt," Kaya replied, "he's right, I can smell the fires."

"Is that the trail to the top?" Ozkurt asked. A trail of dark earth showed between the scrubby trees.

"*Soos*, hush, no more talk," whispered the guide. They started to follow the path up the hill. From above a voice sounded and a stout figure was seen before a stone out-cropping. There a warrior stood bared to the waist in the chill air.

"Hear me, oh, Tanra, accept my offering and give me my petition. Here is drink," the man held a small bowl of kumis that he lifted above his head. "It is good," he stated, demonstrating his words by taking a sip from the bowl. Then he poured the liquid over the rock he faced. There on a rounded surface just over his head was the shape of a giant face. The growth of lichen and moss had delineated the shape of eyes, nose and a wide sneering mouth.

STONE FACE

- 106 -

The scent of alcohol touched the air as it dribbled down the rock chin and fell on the scree below. He smashed the bowl on the rock and the shards fell into the pile below the boulder. The image was not carved, but natural, the eroded remains of the hill's core. "I give my blood and that of my sacrifice," he proclaimed. Unsheathing his dagger, he placed the point over one breast and tapped the handle. A tiny dribble of blood rose and trickled down the breast. He repeated the process on the other breast. Then, again on the dimple at the base of the throat between the chest bones, pressing downward ever so slightly. He now was marked by three tiny trails of red on his exposed chest. "Here, oh Tanra, is your meat and drink." The powerful warrior extracted from his medicine bag a tiny, squalling, striped kitten, which he held by the nape of the neck before the image. The kitten hissed and struck out as the man raised the dagger point to its neck.

At that moment Kaya moved behind him. "*Do'er, koo-mool-da'ma*, stop, don't move. Drop the knife. Now, put the cat in the bag." Ozkurt moved behind the man to remove his sword and search for other weapons. At that moment a Hunnish war horn blared its alarm from the taller hill beyond the camp below.

Kaya nodded, understanding the new development. "Gochen hasn't waited, but has moved and been seen. Now he'll have to run for it."

"Shouldn't we get out and join them?" inquired Ozkurt.

Kaya laughed and the warrior said, "They will expect me to join the pursuit. You would do well to surrender to me now."

"You'll remain silent. Your troop will be in a hurry and not wait for laggards. Does your lookout on the other hill join the pursuit?" The warrior grunted by way of answer and they listened as the troop formed below. Horns sounded again and voices called orders. The whoop of excited men filled the air. Someone called up the hill in an urgent command. It was the man's name. "Han' Lee, the troop is ready. Come!" The shout faded unanswered and the sound of running horses drowned any further communication. The troop had gone.

Kaya walked up to the man and put a hand on his broad shoulder, then he touched his neck hair and pulled a few hairs out to sniff them. The man stiffened surprised.

"You smell of millet and rice. You're an East Hun. Do you know Koosta, short thumb?"

"He's our commander. How could you know? We've only just arrived."

Kaya's look grew intense, "You had a girl captured on the Silk Road. What of her? Is she with you here?"

The man looked suspicious, "How could you know a thing like that unless..." He grew pale and looked Kaya up and down carefully. "You're her foster brother, the bear, Kaya *Aya*. She would threaten us with what you would do when you found us."

"I'll do worse, if you don't tell me where she is."

"We left her in the capital with Munzur Khan, when he accepted us as mercenaries and dispatched us here to hold the borders."

Kaya made a deep growling sound. "You came to replace others sent to the capital. You're to attack the Khazars and keep them off the Ukraine steppes. Is Koosta with the troop that just left?"

"No, he follows with reinforcements."

"More recruits like you, boys needing training."

"I'm a warrior. I've come all the way from the Gobi and the great wall to help conquer the world. Our people's greatness will live forever. Everyone fears and serves us," he proclaimed proudly.

"Now Han Lee, tell me how you treated the woman Fewsoon. What were her duties? How did she act?"

"She was kept well guarded and respected by Koosta. He knew that she was necessary to guarantee that you would follow us. He hopes to revenge himself on you. Only the girl would assure your coming after us. I would have left her with the sick old man near the Pamirs, but he would keep her. She was sure you would catch us any day and he hoped you would. She acted like a shrew and commanded us with harsh words and constant criticisms. 'Clean up!' 'Keep guard!' 'Groom the horses.' 'Clean the plates.' 'Bury the garbage.' 'Gather fire wood.' 'Shake out your blankets.' All the time she was at it. Even after a long day's travel. Yakaty yak, all talk and complaints against us! I was glad she stayed behind."

Kaya's face wore a strange smile as he listened to Han Lee complain. "I have a message for Koosta which you will give him when he arrives. All you have to do is obey us now, and you'll be here to see him when he arrives. I leave vengeance to my God. He's the Tanra you mistakenly tried to invoke before the idol. The stone did not hear you, nor will it answer you. The true Tanra, whose symbol is the everlasting blue sky is a living spirit that gives us better than we deserve. A perfect sacrifice has been made once and need never be offered again: the blood of one perfect man for the ones needing healing and restoration. Have faith in Yesu. He will supply your needs. He forgives your sin. Yesu waits for spiritual, living sacrifices by his followers. Remember these words. They will save you from futility. What favors were you seeking from the image and the spirit world?"

"I love a girl who was sold to the cook by her parents. I need money to redeem her from her slavery."

"Will a stone pay a dowry? I will get you the money and land to graze as well. The Khazars are paying big for warriors to settle the land and use it for stock and crops: someone to defend the settlements in war. You could have a new start here, any warrior is welcome."

"Even a Hun? Wouldn't they kill me at the river?"

"Come with a woman, a white flag and my name. They'll welcome you to freedom. It's better than the Gobi or Munzur's capital city."

The man looked thoughtful. "I'd have to talk it over with her first."

"Tanra invites you through me, it's better than a stone idol. You won't find any other riches here."

"*Soos*, hush, someone's coming," whispered the scout. They could all hear the footsteps of someone out of breath, panting as they ran up the hill. A girl dressed in shalvar pants and bright embroidered blouse burst into the clearing before the rock. She stood staring at them. "The troopers have left and you stand here talking? You'll never catch up if you delay anymore."

"Sherbet hanum, you must go back quickly to the kitchen. Your master will punish you," the warrior called.

"Your onbasha will fine you for missing the attack, they are going to pursue them across the Don." She caught her breath as she took in the difference of face and dress. "You are not men of our troop. You are *ya-bon'jee*, outsiders." The girl whirled around and sped down the path shouting: "Intruders, aliens have come. They're on the hill top."

Kaya grabbed Han Lee. "Quick, tell me who is left in camp." He pushed him on toward the path. Ozkurt notched an arrow.

"Cook and kitchen help, cart and supply workers and a few women," he shouted. Already you could hear the women and men screaming and running away to hide. Only a few clumps of people were prepared to defend themselves with the warriors gone. Kaya grabbed the medicine bundle and descended to the flats between the hills. There they mounted their horses and Kaya rode Altom to the kitchen, dismounted, and taking a flaming wood brand had flung it on the supply tent. The scout took a torch and carried it to the armament tent and fired it. Ozkurt raided the command tent for letters and on foot, pressed some of his arrow heads into burning wood fragments and shot them onto some of the tents. The cook came charging out of the tent with a cleaver raised, but Kaya picked up a flaming branch and held it before the man's face. Ozkurt aimed an arrow, but Kaya shouted a 'no' and the cook broke and ran behind the tent. Kaya threw the branch onto the tent and mounted again. Then they left at a gallop going north rather than east.

On the western hill of the breasts a horn sounded. "That will divide the attacking party if they notice it." Ozkurt shouted.

The scout raced ahead, he knew the country and would take them to a ford across the river, but the river was deep even there and they would surely have to swim. Behind them a plume of smoke and the braying of a horn marked their departure. Kaya wondered how close Koosta and his reinforcements would be. Behind he saw a small dust cloud forming: pursuit for sure.

> - - - - - - - >

"Ride for your lives," Gochen shouted, "the Huns are here at the camp." He had been careless of Ozkurt's advice to rest, and had advanced almost around the hill. The war horn echoed its warning. "We can't stand against a war host. Run for the river," Gochen ordered. The Khazar patrol ran their horses at full gallop while the emerging Huns, in a column of four abreast, trotted their horses. Each troop of fifty horses maintained a disciplined block that rode forward patiently waiting for the pursued foe to weaken and tire before their relentless pressure. Their horses were fresh and the river far away still. They had five such troops: two hundred and fifty men. They heard the renewed braying of the lookout's horn, and the last troop was ordered back to investigate where the first traces of smoke smudged the morning sky. Unlike the pursuers, those who returned to camp rode at top speed.

> - - - - - - >

"They may catch the fool, they have far to go." Ozkurt said.

Kaya made a negative head jerk, "We came walking, paused to investigate. If they have the sense to go easily they'll make it to the river. We've split up the opposition which is good for the plan. Some will chase us and others stay to help guard the camp."

The scout looked back as they rode and gestured, "By the dust cloud I'd say they have put about ten men on our tail. The fires have been put out. We can slow and trot now. We have a good lead on them. There's a thicket ahead that has some hidden trails. We might lose them there, if they're new recruits." Later, they stopped and dismounted to enter the dense underbrush and the three were soon hidden from view.

> - - - - - - >

"Here they come, scattered and demoralized, just as we planned. The big man's driven his horse to the limit. I don't know if he'll make the river," Prince Ilkin reported.

"It's easy to see he's no leader. What of the two Chipchaks?" Judith requested from her seat near by.

"Don't see them. That golden would be easy to spot. They're elsewhere or downed. The first rider has reached the river. The last few are getting shot at now."

"Should you signal the boats now?" she asked.

"Too soon, we want them fully committed before we act. We have our full force here. We should be able to handle them, unless they have been reinforced. We've allowed no one to cross the river for a week. We hope it's a surprise." The prince struck his palm with a fist, "Look, the big man's horse is down. He's running now. The last few men are passing, one has caught an arrow in the shoulder, the horse has slowed and the running man has caught the reins. He's pushing the rider off! He's dumped him and is mounting and running it to the river."

The Huns first line launched their arrows at the swimming men and horses and then plunged into the river to continue the pursuit. The farther bank was empty except for a few of the emerging men and exhausted horses. In a minute the entire first Hun troop was in the water.

The second paused but an instant and they too were ordered by their yuzbasha to continue. The pursuit would become a raid on the enemy. As the last of the Khazar squad emerged from the water and slogged away toward the higher ground, the first wave of the first troop of Huns emerged. Just at that moment a flag was run up behind the highest hill of the eastern ridges. A shout arose from the ground and slopes along the river which was heartily answered from the river above the struggling swimmers.

Three long boats appeared with warriors paddling down on the swimming Huns of the second troop. Close by and in easy arrow range they dropped anchors and the rowers took up bows to pick out the swimming enemy. The third troop was in the act of plunging into the river as the arrows dug into their ordered ranks. The fourth troop broke formation and moved up river to attack the nearest boat. The first fifty had now emerged from the river and were trying to remount and arm their drenched weapons. However, a bee swarm of arrows buzzed in on them from every side from men almost invisible, hidden in trenches. Only their heads could occasionally be seen as they took aim and loosed the deadly shafts at their struggling foes.

The first troop spread out in a general attack on all fronts, but seemed to go down like standing grain before the reapers' scythe. Only a few even shot a return arrow. The second troop was already aware of the waiting barrage and maintained their formation on emerging and they charged straight up the ridge following the road. However, the arrows from the boats cut into their backs while the side ranks were penetrated by the entrenched bowmen.

The lead managed to charge several trenches, but the bowmen seized spear and crescent pike to skewer the riders.

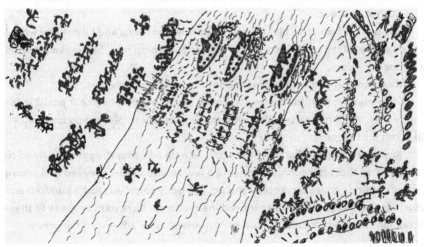

DON RIVER DEFENCE

The beach and slope were littered with dead and wounded. The third troop dissolved like salt in the river. Half the troop had not fully entered and those entering tried to return. The boats made short work of such. The combat between the boats and shore was more equal and those boats nearest the bank, where the fourth troop spread, were showered with arrows. But this encounter, too, was of short duration. The Huns used troops of all peoples under their power. Mercenaries are willing to train, do guard duty, and risk for money, but very few are willing to die for cash. Their commander ordered a quick retreat. The wounded were expected to fall on their knives rather than suffer torture by the enemy. Many of them did.

> - - - - - - >

"I'd say the Prince has had a great victory, Kaya. Look at the bodies spread around the riverside," Ozkurt remarked with pride. Kaya seemed quiet and distant as he looked with distaste at the corpses stripped of clothing and valuables by the victorious Khazar troops. They rode up in time to hear the heated argument between their hosts. The prince was proudly examining a jewel studded sword from the Hun commander.

"You can enjoy the gains of victory, but you can't leave those bodies out on the beach and in the river to rot. Adoni is not pleased with filth left on the ground. You must bury them," Judith insisted.

Ilkin shrugged, "Scavengers will finish the remains. There will be a few days of bad smells and after that nothing."

"The river water will make people sick. The earth is corrupted, contaminated. Adoni will not bless your efforts. Bury them, now, today," she demanded.

Ilkin was annoyed and showed it. "The warriors have fought their battles and are celebrating. No one will be willing to bury defeated enemies. My father once said that the stench of the enemy is the perfume of the victorious. It holds the scent of wealth and power."

She put her face up to his and said, "Adoni will not bless and I'll not stay where the dead are left to rot. I'll leave here if no one will help me." She looked around and saw the riders.

Kaya rode up and held out his hands in supplication for quiet.

"We made it possible for you to come, bayan, we must make it possible for you to stay. We'll fill the trenches with the bodies and so please you and Tanra." Ilkin left for the party.

Kaya persuaded Ozkurt and the scout to help and they dragged the dead to the trenches that afternoon. There were a few wounded that they fed and whose wounds Judith's house servants bound up. The body count was just a hundred and fourteen dead and twelve who survived their wounds. Kaya went to speak to them at twilight. The lady Judith listened with approval as he addressed the group.

"For some unknown reason Tanra has spared your lives today. Now you must find some reason to justify his mercy to you. Many of your friends are dead. You too, could have been with them underground tonight. The fact that you are here demands some debt of thankful gratitude on your part. Tanra has spared your life, how will you repay Him? Yesu calls for his believers to make spiritual sacrifices: to use their bodies for God's good purposes. I leave you free to make such choices and to decide how you will live. I think you have suffered enough and I will not keep you as war prisoners. You will be helped across the river and be free to return to your camp as you can. The Khazars are offering land to those who will do military service and populate the estates. If you are tired of war and would change sides, the Khazars are prepared to give you jobs on estates. Return when you are healed and have thought through this offer. I am Kaya Aya, the bear. Say that I have called you forth when you return. Prince Ilkin guarantees you a place."

> - - - - - - - >

They arrived at the house worn and tired, ready to tell their story. The prince was occupied at a victory banquet. The Lady Judith brought them into the kitchen for food and talk. Ozkurt soon left.

"Lady, I have a special request for a little friend." Kaya brought the medicine bundle from Altom's back and opened it before her on the kitchen table. "Here I have rescued a near victim of sacrifice at a stone idol. It is both hungry and wild and cannot be trusted yet, but it has the potential of friendship and usefulness." He held the mewing kitten by the scruff of its neck, carefully.

"How cute, yet, as you say wild and frightened. A bowl of milk and bread might be a wise start to the long process of domestication," she said, smiling.

"I gave it some dried jerky this afternoon, if you have bread and a bowl we can quiet the pangs of hunger and thirst," Kaya stated. Judith suited actions to his words and the kitten was too hungry to run and hide.

"I have a basket in my room that will do for a den, It will learn the attractions of the kitchen soon enough. Wait and see." Bringing the basket from the master bedroom the lady uncovered the top to place the kitten inside, topped it and left it by the fire.

She sat and indicated a stool. "Now you won't be planning war, they are celebrating the victory, but I still want to hear about your quest and the one you pursue." Kaya was glad enough to tell it all.

> - - - - - - - >

"It's a glorious victory, the first of many to come," the voice was slurred and the steps that approached the door were erratic and faltering.

The lady smiled and arose, "The celebrant arrives and needs our attention." The prince fumbled and almost fell as Judith opened the door. "Here Kaya bring him in and help me remove the coat." she ordered. They undressed the protesting Ilkin and had tucked him away still raving and celebrating. Then Kaya went looking for Ozkurt to repeat the same process in their quarters. Few were up at a decent hour in the morning and a counter attack would have carried the estate and all troops with them. All victories reveal weaknesses.

> - - - - - - >

"I'll not share my gains with anyone who was not present at the retreat and the fight." Gochen proclaimed in a loud course voice. "The men that claim to have climbed the breast and fired the camp can get their loot from those places. They'll get none of ours." The custom of shared pillage is an old one. All nations that permitted looting came to a sharing arrangement between officers and men. Usually the soldiers robbed the bodies. Then they displayed their gains to the corporals and sergeants who chose their share, a portion of which they passed on up to their officers. Sometimes the superior ranks extorted a fixed sum per battle from those gaining. There was opportunity for fraud, theft and extortion under these rough conditions. But the opportunity to become rich existed and many took advantage of it, one way or another. The Khazars permitted sharing of loot and about one fifth of the treasures had to be passed on up the chain of command. Each man selecting a portion to buy promotions, favors, or repay debts and obligations to those who were in positions of authority-- who can grant the giver a favor: his personal wish. Every man kept a mental list of loans, favors owed and promises made. Men killed each other while fighting for the same cause or master, because of these gains and losses. Men might give lip service to honesty, but where riches were concerned, every sly practice was exercised. Gambling was an entertainment common in every army. A winter on the Don River would be passed in this way. Boring duties and food; dull companionship; competitive, money-centered games; occasional fighting the enemy abroad and personal quarrels and fights in quarters were always as perennial as the penetrating winter chill.

"It's not right," proclaimed Ozkurt, "We were in as great a danger as the rest of the squad. More danger really, three men in the midst of the enemy camp. We split the attacking force by burning the camp. They've no right to keep our part of the gains." Ozkurt insisted, "We forwarded the plan at danger to ourselves."

Kaya sat smiling at his rage. "But did you notice Gochen's concession to us?" Kaya interjected. "He states that the hill and camp hold our part of the compensation. All we have to do is collect it. If he recognizes that our loot is there, let's go and get it. We can promise a part to those who help." Their defrauded scout, Atilla, was able to get a number of his impoverished and bored friends to go with them. And the squad left the squalor of winter camp behind for the icy sunshine of a December day. The river was low and they rode easily through the forming ice. They met no troops guarding the road. They climbed the hill and surveyed the camp. The grounds lay empty and the ruins of the burned tents were clearly unoccupied. The clutter that lay between the ruins showed a rapid abandonment by the Hun's troops.

"They must have left right after the battle, sir," reported the scout. Kaya nodded and ordered, "Take five men and ride straight across the camp without stopping. Go to the other hill where the lookout was stationed and check out the post and the area behind the hill for any concealed troops. It could be a trap. Use your horn to signal an all clear. Ozkurt will help me with the work here."

Kaya moved to a rise before the stone face and started digging a hole with his sword, Then he ordered, "Bring a trenching tool and make this hole knee deep. One of you men cut a tree trunk the thickness of a thigh for a pole twice my height, and let another of the same thickness be cut for the cross bar. About my height will do and we will put it opposite the shrine so people will have to face one way or the other. They must turn their back on one of them." The men moved to obey, but Ozkurt objected.

"Why don't we tear down the idol and deface it? Leave the cross to dominate the hill." Kaya cocked his head and then threw it up negatively, saying,

"God requires us to choose what is best. Some will not believe and we have no right to impose our choice. When all believe the face will be only a curious rock again." The listening men exchanged glances. Consideration and personal choice was not usual. The blast of a horn announced the absence of danger on the other hill and the men moved restlessly toward the path.

"Now men, you will clean out the camp. Pile the refuse together for a great burning and all you salvage lay in a circle with each man standing before his pile. We'll come and make sure of a fair sharing before we return to quarters. Ozkurt and I will finish here and be down after you. Don't quarrel. Be alert for the enemies return and save your strength for them. Go ahead, dismissed." The men whooped like small boys on the descent to the camp.

Ozkurt grumbled a bit as they lifted the butt for the drop into the hole. They packed the earth to make it stand up. They finished by putting the bar across the top of the pole. "Now, let's get down before everything's gone," Ozkurt shouted with joyful excitement.

Kaya nodded his consent with thanks. "You go and have fun, I'll pray you find something good. I'll be down in a little while." He moved several small trunks and branches of wood to form a line before the cross and knelt there before the new symbol of faith. Finished, he too ran down the trail to the camp.

> - - - - - - - >

"*Tom-mom*, okay men, lets see what you found." The scout, Atilla, displayed his finds first. Arrowheads, a wrist guard, bow strings and a shield were from the burned armament tent. Kaya noted that everything was in good condition and valuable. "You've done well. What do you wish to give to your officers?" The young man smiled brightly and held out his hand with several gold coins for inspection.

"I found these near where the official tents must have been. They were buried so someone's got to be planning to return and claim them later. They departed in a hurry and left a lot around for us," he reported gleefully.

"Keep some for yourself." Kaya advised cheerfully.

"Oh I did, don't worry the bag was full." He then displayed the total extent of his riches. "I want my fifth to go to you sir. Only you would have the confidence to return here so soon. I'll share drinks for all with the troop who came back with us today." There was a ragged cheer and looks of envy around the circle. Most of them had found food, some military gear and weapons lost or abandoned during the hasty retreat. Ozkurt had found some personal items, letters at the foot of the path up the hill. Some, who won much, shared with those finding little. All were excited by the excursion. Kaya assigned Atilla to take the troop back, but asked for volunteers to go an hour further to check the roads for Huns. He got four who wanted to venture further. The rest wanted to start the bonfire and get home quickly with their gains. As Kaya and Ozkurt rode farther into the steppes, a black column of smoke rose behind them.

> - - - - - - - >

"*Chabuk ol*, quickly, take cover, someone's coming," Ozkurt called. The men scattered about and armed their bows. Kaya crept forward for another look over the rise. Then he stood and waved, an answering shout echoed in their ears. Three horses and two riders gradually appeared riding at a trot leading a pack horse.

"Han Lee, you have decided to become a Khazar supporter and have brought a bride." The man laughed heartily as he rode up into the small company.

"Aya, I got the money for the legal purchase of Sherbet, and I even hid money for a return to camp."

"Your hide-away gold has been found and divided, but, no matter, you are here safe. Will you be followed?" Kaya asked.

The Hun jerked his head up sharply, "I'm accounted a rescuer because I was there to put out the fire. I saved the cook's personal stores and part of the kitchen goods. We lost the supply, command and the armory tents. Koosta came with new, green troops and not in numbers large enough to hold the camp, so we retreated. The cook sold Sherbet to me for my help and we married two days ago. We were sent away for a few days of joy, so we have come back. This winter will be a hungry one. There is talk of retreat west. Munzur keeps on withdrawing his veterans. Newcomers are left to gather as they can for themselves."

"Prince Ilkin provides warm housing and land. You'll see." Kaya assured him. "Besides the breast, is there another camp abandoned or goods still about? My squad here got little loot at the old camp."

Han Lee thought briefly. "There's a camp an hour north of here. They were called back two days ago. You can see what was left there."

Ozkurt was immediately interested and rode ahead with Han Lee and their troop. Kaya rode after them with the girl and pack horse. He hummed a tune, then, said quietly, "Have you heard anything about Yesu in your camp or family?"

The girl shrugged, "A Hungarian cook used his name to swear at any mistake I made, but you easterners know only Tanra."

"You mean the Creator or the rock face?"

Again she shrugged, "There are different ways of getting what you really want in life. Sacrifice seems to get more answers."

"But one must consider what is important to sacrifice and to whom it should properly be made, *bayan*."

"I know little about such matters," she said sadly.

"But you would be willing to learn, wouldn't you?"

"Naturally, we all have dreams and needs to gain."

"I'll give you these prayer beads and the most important prayer to start it. We call Tanra, the creator, our father; because he wants us to. Was your *baba* a good one, bayan?"

Her nose pointed up in a negative gesture. They rode a moment in silence. Then Kaya continued. "The father of creation is Tanra --God and He's good. You can tell by what He made. He does not fail us or hold grudges in anger. He forgives us in Yesu whom He sent to be our sacrifice. He asks for obedience because He knows what's best for each part of His creation. The prayer ends by asking Tanra to deliver us from the evil one."

"I would like that," she murmured. "Are the others as good?"

"My teacher, the hermit, taught me many other prayers for the beads. I'll teach you those when you have the first one down by memory."

> - - - - - - - >

"What's in your pack, *Bayan*?" Kaya asked as they came in sight of the deserted army camp. Ozkurt held up a bag of coins for them to see. Han Lee flourished a jeweled sword he had found.

She laughed, waved encouragingly and listed, "Clothes, food for a week, his war gear, and a few other personal things."

He nodded easily, and went on, "I thought I heard movement, sounds." He paused.

She laughed and covered her mouth, modestly, "My man breeds racing pigeons, He won bets on them when we were celebrating our wedding day: a gold coin."

"It was a day of many victories indeed. Koosta bey was present for the occasion, no doubt?"

She nodded enthusiastically, "He's now Yuzbasha in charge of the Donetz and Don districts."

PEOPLE, PLACES & PLOTS IN CHAPTER 11

Atilla: a scout, newly rich, with Kaya's troop.
Gochen: a giant warrior whose ambition knows no restraints.
Han Lee: a Gobi Hun changes sides for the Khazars.
Judith: a Jewess married and pregnant at Don River estate.
Kaya: finds himself at war in a winter world.
Koosta: finds new problems in his planned victories.
Ozkurt: finds more action and weather than he likes.
Prince Ilkin: overreaches and learns the consequences.
Sherbet: a girl sold by parents, freed and married by Han Lee.

GLOSSARY:

Adoni: the Lord; in Hebrew, used in place of God's name.
barak: leave; stand aside; leave alone; stand off.
bayan: lady, a title of respect; Miss or Mrs. used <u>before</u> a name.
bekley'en: wait; just a minute; hold on; wait up.
bir dakika: one moment; wait a minute.
bow'za defa: a hot winter drink of slightly fermented millet.
dough roo: correct; you're right; of course; sure; oh yes.
ha-mom': a Turkish bath with steam, hot and cold water.
han'um: the equivalent of Mrs. used <u>after</u> a given name.
hoe'sh-gel-den-is: welcome; happily you've come.
ked'y: kitten; small cat.
loot'fin: please; if you please; by your permission.
man'ta: a boiled wheat wrap with a tiny meat center.
Rume: Rome; East Roman Empire; Constantinople.
status quo anti bellum: Latin, a return to pre-war status.
vah'she: a wild beast; savage animal; abandoned child,

DEADLY DEFEAT

"*Barak*, leave off, stand aside, I have to pass. You easterners are smarter than I thought," Gochen exclaimed. "I'll go with you next time you venture out. I should've known you'd hide some booty when you disrupted that camp, after we lured them away, like we did. Cunning, I call it, hiding on the Breast and then swooping down when the troops were away in pursuit of us." He shook his head as if to dispel a bad dream. Gochen passed through, pausing to make the comment, before exiting the *hamom*.

"We step aside, but he'll step with us in the future," Kaya quipped. "We got his attention and he doesn't want to miss out on anything."

Ozkurt laughed, but showed his perennial resentment against the rude giant that had first greeted them some weeks before. He had never forgotten that experience. "As long as he's running from the enemy, I like it. But I get tired of that sneering look and curt talk," he mumbled.

"Why let a fool get your goat? He presumes on his size to get him what he wants. He's grown up a big bull in a small herd. He'll learn in time that it doesn't count as much as he thought."

Ozkurt, however, didn't listen.

> - - - - - - - >

"Well Kaya, we have two camps we can post advanced guards to hold. You have done well by us."

"*Dough rue*, right, Sire, You are on the other, western, side of the Don River now. ''m sure Han Lee's information is correct, a definite pull out is indicated."

"Yes, and we'll help them hurry it a bit. Harry their supply lines and disrupt their raids." Prince Ilkin was happy and stood preparing to run to the door. "Gochen is about to leave with a troop. I must speak with him."

Kaya nodded, "I didn't think Gochen could hold followers."

Lady Judith observed, "He's rough and coarse, but he went back to help the man whose horse he took and gave him part of his loot. So, he really tries to make up for wrongs and quarrels. His men are awed by him. I think success and gain may help him."

Ozkurt stood and followed the prince to the door to exit.

"Tanra gives men insight into truth, if they are willing to accept it," Kaya quoted. "The hard part is accepting the evidence of what our spirits see."

"I always thought that the search for truth was a Jewish trait, but I see it exists in you as well," Lady Judith offered.

"It may have to do with the promise of a thousand years for my tribe and family," Kaya said modestly.

"I remember, now, your story about the boat people rescuing your band and the blessings they left behind. We Jews know a lot about unmerited favor, we've had our share during our long history. Though we like to think we earned it by our merit. Which of the favors impressed your people most?"

"My father mentioned three; the golden horse, the golden-haired wife and the golden child, which is to say a child of promise. But the gifts came at the price of loss and suffering. Actually, my half-brother Kutch, will make a better Khan than I. The golden wife produced a boy of golden mind and spirit. He knows how to administer and direct."

"Nevertheless, you seem to have your portion of good and brightness. Your quest will succeed; you will find your love." She patted his hand affectionately.

"What is this love you speak of, wife?" Ilkin's voice cut into the room with cold fury. He stood at the door with anger in his face. He walked toward Kaya.

Judith rose haughtily and turned coldly to face his approach. "Had you entered, instead of hovering around the door to eavesdrop, you would understand that I refer to his lost, foster-sister and bride."

Ilkin gestured brusquely, "And, were you not pregnant with our child, I would call this boy out and finish him."

Kaya rose slowly, "No offence intended, my Prince, I miss our clan mother for counsel and comfort."

Judith's face was cold. "If I am the mother of a dynasty and a nation, I deserve more trust and support from my ruler and mate. I have your confidence or I have nothing."

Ilkin paused, realized he had offended, and made excuses. "Your beauty and talents rule my heart. I was jealous. You do seem to be together a lot and I envy his time with you."

Lady Judith relaxed somewhat, "His interest in *Adoni*, the Lord, is our basic link, I belong to an eternal people and he has the promise of a thousand years for his; this creates a bond of interests between us. It helps pass my winter and my condition. I'll not have it taken away from me. We have Hanukah and Christmas to plan, as different expressions of our one faith in Messiah. Your jealousy is foolish and unworthy of a prince."

He winced, and appealed. "Judith, my love, -- my love is overpowering and I know that I am not worthy of your love. To lose you would mean my death. I want to be first in your regard, so I am jealous even of that kitten you have adopted. When you pet it my heart rages. I'm consumed by this passion."

"The child I bear you will divide your passion; age will bring tolerance and sweeter expressions. Endure it for now. I will not part with kitten or Kaya as companions, and I'm adding that sweet new bride of Han Lee. She is as tasty as her name and, though ignorant of many things, is teachable and adept. Otherwise, I will die of boredom and then where will you be?"

The prince's face worked and he sighed and then laughed as his mood changed. "I must say welcome to a kitten, a bear and a sherbet as part of my wife's cravings: *kedy, aya ve sherbet, hoe'sh geldinez.*" The others laughed with him.

> - - - - - - - >

"Han Lee says that our troops are going seven days ride past the camp now. Abandoned camps are emptied of people and animals, but there are always valuables to gather. Atilla bey, the scout, has found gold three times now." Sherbet hanum gossiped as she set the table for the officers as Bayan Judith came in for an inspection of her work. She smiled her approval of the job. The two women were suited in taste.

"Ilkin is delirious with joy and mercenaries are flocking in to volunteer their service," Judith replied. "Our numbers have grown to five hundred, but we lack space for them."

"How I thank Tanra for the opportunities here. Retreat is a hard road to travel." Judith acknowledged her reply and sighed. It was dark and the men would be late.

"Training new men is always hard business, even if they are veterans of other battles. Ilkin seems determined to make one more push before spring."

The sound of men on the back entrance silenced them. Four tired hungry men entered the room and took seats on the floor around the table that stood in the center of the room with only space enough for legs under its slightly raised surface. Sherbet hanum brought the large pan of *manta*, boiled dumplings. It was placed in the center and the plates of bread and sauces were placed around the sides within reach of all. The flat bread was used as a scoop for the meat and sauces. Only Kaya paused to make the sign and pray silently before joining them. The women did not join them, but continued to serve and replace emptied side plates.

"Our scout will soon be richer than a prince," Ilkin joked. "I may have to borrow money from him." All laughed.

"I find this strange," Kaya objected. "The Ak-Hun never kept large amounts of money in their camps; it invites theft and attacks. They pay when the troops come home to the capital. Why should these Huns act differently? It smells like a baited trap. Gold in three camps?"

Ozkurt paused to correct him. "Four camps, Gochen got the gold in the last one. He's bragging that all the new finds will be by him. He's got more men under his command. He's liberal with his goods." All nodded agreement; their mouths were full.

"Atilla is staying with your command isn't he, Kaya?" asked Ilkin, "I haven't heard of him hiring troops."

"He sent much of it home to his family farm, here in the Don valley and he has been generous to all in our troop."

"So you too are enriched. Perhaps you will consider loans now? The fifth I collect won't service half the new recruits. I'll have to go to my father or Judith's guardian for more."

Judith laughed as she came with new bread. "Ben Ishaak would be happy to put the squeeze on you. He likes to venture cash on new enterprises, but you will pay high interest and be obliged for years to come."

"Father will be no less strict and will interfere with my war plans as well. He'll put his men over the new territory to develop it."

Judith stood behind him as he ate. "Why go into debt at all?" she asked, "Why not develop what you have without more troops and war?"

"Han Lee thinks another push will break Koosta." His nod indicated the quiet Gobi warrior. "Too many green troops are left without veterans to steady them."

"Too much land brings complex problems that are not necessary if we would let expansion alone and develop what we have without new expenses," she insisted.

"Staying home, farming and grazing is a dull way to gain fame and fortune," stated the prince.

"Men need to meet the challenge of danger and strife to prove their abilities," Ozkurt agreed. "Superiority is demonstrated in conflict: the winners show the indisputable proof of victory."

"Superiority speaks of pride and contempt, the two poisons of human relationships," sniffed Bayan Judith.

"Love is proved in small considerations and helps," ventured Sherbet hanum timidly, "it doesn't need great displays as proofs."

The men rose to sit on the trunks and boxes around the walls of the room. Hot *bowza defa* was served. Talk had slowed when the prince roused to say: "You are right about having more than we can handle. So, just one more push, it will be our last, I promise. I can't let these men go without one final proof of our training and their valor." Han Lee and the others nodded in smiling agreement.

"Just one more big push and we'll settle down to work what we've gained. It will mean more for everybody."

> - - - - - - - >

"This is where we started, this is the base camp. Here Koosta took up his command and the veterans departed to the West," Han Lee reported, as they rode to the top of a valley. They had stopped the five hundred on a knoll that overlooked the camp. A stream ran down from below this high point forming a small ravine just beside and below the hill. It broadened into an abundant water supply as it passed the camp to flow into the Donetz River. To the east the hills rose above them. The valley lay somnolent or dead before them. Kaya felt the hair on his neck and arms rise, he sniffed the air suspiciously. Nothing moved in the camp. No sound that they had not brought with them greeted their arrival. A village of tents, yurts and soddy huts rose before their eyes, invitingly undefended.

Han Lee smiled triumphantly, "See, it's all waiting for us," pointing broadly. "Let's go take it." He suited his action to his words and rode around the hill and down the valley at a gallop. Gochen and the troop he led, sixty men, followed him from the right wing.

"*Bekleyen*, wait," shouted Kaya, "reconnoiter first. We saw enemy scouts yesterday. They know we're here. It must be a trap." He rode to the top of the knoll to see the race for the camp. Han Lee had crossed the stream above the camp and moved toward the hills. Gochen's men lost formation.

"Sound the 'rally to me,' on the horn," commanded Ilkin. "Kaya's right, this is too artificial, something's wrong. We must investigate." The horn sounded a return and one group led by a veteran onbasha turned back, he too, suspected something.

A low rumbling sound commenced near by. Mounted riders moved to the tops of the eastern hills. A line, a thousand strong, appeared ready to close the trap. The Khazar army took a shocked breath of surprise. Ilkin took it all in at a glance.

"Form up around the knoll, behind the ravine at hill base. Lay down all the horses, backs out, behind your packs. Cover the heads. Make room for some movement. The Huns will be densely packed. Shoot for bodies and horse's heads. Keep it low on the first ranks. Don't draw until I give the order. They'll have to charge packed. Rapid fire, don't aim, shoot straight ahead unless danger threatens. Stay cool and we'll get through it. Tanra, Tanra, Tanra ..."

> - - - - - - - >

"Well done, Han Lee," Koosta shouted. "I knew it would work, even when all your pigeons came in on the same day without news. We fooled them. They're trapped! Why didn't they move on down?"

Han Lee looked back on the Khazar troops as they drew up in defense lines around the knoll. He pointed, "There stands Kaya on the hill downing the horses.

He suspected something. They're going to defend. He left the yellow mare to foal a colt. He's as wary as the girl, Fewsoon, said. He's caught up with us. He says he leaves vengeance to Tanra, but he came to see it."

"He'll never see anything again, nor any on that hill." Koosta snarled. Below them the ranks moved forward. "I'll take care of my own vengeance and not leave it for others," Koosta bragged. "Let's move in closer to be in on the final kill. You got to see the `vah-she' close up. Now, come see him die."

Han Lee nodded, he almost regretted this closing moment. The bear man had been generous.

They heard Ilkin shout. "Here they come. Hold, hold, now, pull; let fly all." A solid wall of charging men on horses collapsed in a welter of tumbling legs and arrow-filled bodies fifty yards from the defense line behind the ravine. The succeeding wave jumped them and fell before the rain of arrows. The third rank was disrupted by the vast quantity of bodies and melted away as the charging line moved right up the slope toward the top to surround them.

A small counter current of wounded men and horses moved down to the stream which was now starting to change color as the ravine filled with bodies. A few of the unhorsed men tried to move forward to find the enemy, but the newer, green troops sought to escape. The returning onbasha had arrived just in time to fill the gap left by the Gochen's right wing desertion. The thinning ranks of Khazars were able to keep up the fire, but fresh, angry Huns continued to fill the ranks of the fallen. They rode around the blood drenched knoll. The wounded Khazars started gathering spent arrows for their comrades that could still use the bow. The Huns were still packed too tightly to maneuver and suffered the consequences. The crescent shaped Khazar pole knives cut off heads.

About two hundred Hunnish troops had turned down into the valley to ride on the village. Fifty men of Gochen's troop arrived before they realized their situation. In the middle of the village, from a large command tent, a group of fifty Huns emerged with pikes and bows at ready. Each pike man had a bowman beside him, each protecting the other. They blocked the street with a double line of defense.

Most of Gochen's Khazar men, hurrying for spoils in an abandoned village, were held by this sight of a guard troop awaiting them. The riders pulled back while others caught up. They formed a mob of men frustrated in their hopes. The last riders had seen the Huns sweep in from the hills and were shouting warnings. The comrades were drawn up uncertain about what to do. Gochen now recognized the trap and was searching for a place of safety. His closest place of cover lay away from the camp and attackers in a section of scrubby brush used by the Huns for calls of nature. The latrine smelled of urine. They plunged behind the first line of bushes. They were hidden, even being mounted. In frustrated anger they met the onslaught of the two hundred Huns. They, through necessity, had to split into single lines to enter between the trees. The maze was well covered by Gochen's troop and the Huns started taking heavy losses even as they rooted out the Khazars. The Hunnish Yuzbasha thought of a solution and commanded the pike men to come with torches and fire the brush while they awaited with pikes at the trails' exits. There was only a little breeze so the fire advanced slowly.

The riders did not appear as expected, but a sudden volley of fire arrows were launched from the scrub into the tents and yurts of the winter quarters. The Huns, now with casualties, were spreading thin. They were surrounding the area of brush and fighting fire in the village. The heat forced the pike men back. More flaming arrows were shot at huts.

Koosta refused to send men from the battle of the knoll to help the village, so it burned down. Gochen made a break out with about half his men. They were pursued by over half the encircling Huns. The running fight continued up to the knoll where over half the original Khazar force had died. Gochen was met by a portion of the right wing troop who cut their way with hand weapons through the faltering Huns to bring in ten of Gochen's starting force. At this point Koosta called off the attacks to reform his morale-shattered battalions of green troops.

The Khazars started cooking horse meat from the slaughter to get strength before night fell. Already the air above the knoll was filled with predator birds and the meadows with varmints that would feast by night. The heavy frost assured a short time of pain for the seriously wounded: the anesthesia of numbness.

Under the cover of night the Khazars crept away. In the morning the pursuit would begin, so the main body kept together. Messages were sent ahead to warn the home folks. The wounded lagged behind. Many were forced to walk or lead exhausted and wounded horses with what they considered priceless from their personal packs. Food was better than gold, weapons no better than clothing, for the cold kills as well as the enemy. A track, as visible as signposts, pointed the army's route home. The commanders were tossed on the horns of the dilemma: to wait or not wait for the weak and wounded. Compassion called for delays. Survival called for speed. The victorious enemy will pursue and harass all who retreat. With hundreds of eyes seeking those who hide, only one in ten would be able to fool the enemy as to where they were hidden. Death awaited every discovery with torture or humiliation as by-products of pain and hate. Death, easy or hard, awaited them all.

Questions stated in various ways filled every mind: 'Why me?' 'Why not me?' 'Why him?' 'How did it happen?' 'I saw it coming.' 'I didn't see it.' 'It was so sudden!'

The unexpected moment that changes everything in one's life: present and future arose. New, un-weighed decisions, made on the basis of happenings that never crossed one's mind, before the fateful moment, were required. A god or fate, seldom considered, loomed large in the crisis of the event. Confused minds filled with pain sought reasons and justification for the happenings; failures and successes.

Kaya, a son of the medicine woman's yurt, found himself with the traveling wounded. He had a bloodied bandage around his head. Those who could walk did. Those who couldn't rode or were left behind to crawl away to hide, or to fall on their knives. There remained a choice between suffering a quick or slow death. Hope was often the deciding factor.

Those who pursued would by-pass the easy prey and spend their strength on the main body of the enemy. Recognition and rewards were not gained from the destruction of the weak and wounded. Even here, however, choice remained a factor. Those impatient for revenge had their opportunity. Small pickings and pay-back always attract those who have little desire for any recognition or hope of collecting a big reward. It's the coward's opportunity to prove he can kill.

Koosta, too, found himself on the horns of a dilemma, and it carried possible rewards or blame. The winter camp was totally destroyed. He had failed to take this possibility into consideration. Where would they winter? A new location was urgent. The old site was devastated and the nearest safe haven was a three day ride west beyond the Donetz River, guarding the fords of the Dneiper River. Perhaps he could move to the Breasts, which lay a perilous hour from enemy lines. Could he be sure that the enemy was destroyed and could be defeated on their home ground? Should he send troops to build a camp for winter safety or continue to utterly crush the opposition? Which would gain the better reward?

Politics now entered the decision making process. Munzur Khan was intent on western expansion. The problem lay in keeping the reputation of being all-conquering warriors and holding ground against eastern pressure. It was important not to lose face, nor to experience defeat on the battlefield. The defeat at the Don River crossing had been erased by a victory through ambush. Was it enough to satisfy pride of place and royal expectations? Would `status quo ante-bellum,' lead to promotion? Or would pride demand a greater punishment of the transgressing Khazars? One man's choice: his, would lead to good or bad for thousands. The future lay in Koosta's hands and the Khan's reply. Dare he delay for a reply?

> - - - - - - - >

"Continue on the trail Onbasha, I'll stop and catch up in a moment." Han Lee commanded his aide. The hundreds of trotting Hun troopers looked with disdain at the broken, slow moving crowd of wounded. Such trash as they saw would not bring serious concern to warriors out to catch and finish off the strong, but retreating, core of the Khazars. Trash such as these, would be disposed of on their victorious return. They snarled their contempt as the onbasha kept up the pace and they soon outdistanced the unfortunates. Han Lee found Kaya leading several horses with mounted wounded behind his horse. He was not riding Altom, but another borrowed gray pony.

"What a pity, you didn't bring your gold. I could have had her." Kaya plodded on as Han Lee rode up.

"She's due to foal, and has never been trained as a war horse. She wouldn't know how to kill. She's safe at home."

"I can bring her when I collect Sherbet," he gloated.

"Is Koosta so determined then? He'll risk his gains?"

"Tanra gives the victories! We slaughtered yours."

"You mean the Tanra of the rock face, not He of the everlasting blue skies; certainly not the Father of Yesu."

"I mean the one to whom I offered blood in sacrifice. He gave me the girl, the money, the command that I longed for. He will give me the prince's house and I'll let his wife live and serve Sherbet, since they suit each other and I'll kill that cat that I owe for sacrifice," he snarled.

"My Tanra saves people from death and destruction. He forgives sinners who repent of the evil that they do and turn to do good. Yesu gave his innocent blood for this."

"Don't preach to me, your sister did enough of that."

"She's a 'Delight' as her name indicates: she delights to do Tanra's will. He desires that men everywhere repent and believe for salvation. Now is the acceptable time."

"I have time enough to finish the slaughter and send back to clean up the trash on the road," Han Lee retorted, as he rode away to catch his troops. Kaya watched him gallop off saying, "It's true, God does blind the eyes of the proud. He'll rouse up Khan Kinner's army."

HOT PURSUIT

"Your nation has embraced commerce for income and power. Your capital, Khan Kinner, sits on the main crossing of the Mother of Rivers. Your income has notably increased since the addition of the Don River bend. The Black Sea is accessible and the Byzantine ports open to you. Your power grows through the control of the routes of commerce." Ben Ishaak reminded his powerful friend.

The Khan sat before the council waiting for the preamble to end and he could present what he had already decided. He was happy, however, to read between the lines and know that the life of Judith, Ben Ishaak's ward, was much more important than the supposed death and burial of the name and their relationship. Both men would probably feel better about the marriage and the approaching birth of a possible heir in the shared grandchild. Now, they'd be able to talk about it.

The Khan spoke now: "The victory at the Don crossing has enthused our people. Now the news of defeat brings a need to decide our course of action. My son's personal guard, recently grown to five hundred men, can scarcely defend the Don crossings from an army of Huns. The moment has arrived for our intervention. Such strategic locations can't be left to be guarded by impetuous youths. I received notice by pigeon, from sources inside the Khazar Guards, of the ambush and brave stand by our fellow troopers. The time has come to move. I will personally lead the Royal and the West Guard armies to the Don River. Huns will not invade our lands."

> - - - - - - - >

"The scout rode day and night, killed his horse, to bring the news. We've over-reached, and we'll now suffer for it." Lady Judith declared to Sherbet as they rolled bandages with other wives and children of the estates gathered together at the prince's large house. "We can't hope to defend our homes individually. We're better to stand with the young and old together in one place."

"The weather has turned, Bayan, rain and fog replace the cold dry days," said a worn and strained Sherbet. "Like my hopes for the future."

Lady Judith lifted her little helper's chin, and shook her head gently, "How could you have known of Han Lee's plans? Marriage leads to many surprises. Men hide their deepest schemes, just as we hide our dearest hopes. There's no way you could have known." Tears surfaced on Sherbet's little face.

"Doesn't matter, what I knew, they're blaming me. Some won't talk to me now. I don't care, I hate them. Before he left, Han Lee was as indifferent and rough as the old cook used to be. It started when we found the pigeon cage had fallen and the door sprung. All the birds had escaped and there was a bunch of feathers and blood. It wasn't my fault, some cat must have done it. He was always angry after that." Judith patted her hand and sighed as she trimmed old cloth to shape into soft rolls.

"Tenderness is important in marriage. Men who've been brought up roughly have to learn. We have to teach them. You were abused early in life, so it's easier to respond in kind. Insult for insult, threat for threat. It builds to anger, confrontation and heartbreak. Our hopes and dreams are never realized without the help of *Adoni*."

Sherbet ducked her face to her hands. Her shoulders shook as she cried desperately. "He can't come back even if he wants to. No one will ever want me again."

Judith smiled sweetly, "Life is too full of surprises and unforeseen changes to try to predict the future. Only a fool would try."

> - - - - - - - >

"We've scarcely two hundred able men left, Prince Ilkin," Ozkurt observed, "to stand and fight on the steppes is folly with odds at four to one. They've been trailing us for three days. We're riding day and night and our animals are nearly finished." The prince was riding at a steady pace.

"True, but we are nearing our territory by this fast pace. You know that Atilla, the scout, came in this morning from the estate. Defenses are being readied on the Don. Rumors spread that my father is coming with the army. I wonder how many troops are actually behind us. Burning the winter camp was a stroke of good fortune for us." He turned in the saddle to address his men. "Now, dismount and share your food with your horse. Loosen the saddle and let it graze a moment." He turned to continue talking to Ozkurt, "After the feeding we will lead, dismounted, at a run for the men's exercise before riding again. I see some Hunnish scouts behind us, so the army can't be too far away. Atilla believes we can make the Breasts by afternoon."

"What if some of the men break and run for the border?"

"Announce that deserters will be shot. That'll make them think. I know a way to divide the enemy once we are at the Breasts. We'll try what you and Kaya did there. Half will wait near the shrine and the rest will go to the thicket and rest before returning or going on to the river." Ozkurt shook his head doubtfully at the thought then voiced his objection. "Han Lee and others know of that trick. They'll be sure to check it first."

The prince continued feeding a part of his bulgur, heaped in his felt winter hat to his horse. "If we're cut off, the hill is good defensively. I've checked it out. We'll counter attack while they're distracted."

> - - - - - - - >

"The Ukraine is large and the flat steppes seem almost endless. No one can search it out, but smoke, light or quick movement will attract eyes. You must live without them and even your food will be raw or slow cooked on coals. It's a question of life or death: your own and others." Kaya was exhorting his patients. "Hobble your horses down and sleep by day, let them graze by night between your rides. Small trips are better than long. Don't let the light find you out of the new hiding place. Carelessness equals attention and perhaps death."

One of the men spoke up, "Why do you have to leave, sir? You've been here with us for three days."

Kaya nodded in agreement. "You are all stronger now and over the worst. You can make it on your own now, if you're cautious. If Khan Kinner comes with an army, I'll have to leave as quickly as possible. He told us that to see his face was to die; and I believe him." The Khazar men's heads moved in unison; they believed it too. "It'll take three days more to gain the river, traveling by night." They wished him well and said they would miss the stories he told to pass the days. Kaya wondered what Ozkurt was doing and if he was aware that Kinner Khan would soon be on the Don River.

>- - - - - - - >

"Lady Judith, the Khan is here with his army. I dare not stay even a day in these parts. I must take Altom, the mare, and the colt born in our absence, and go down river."

"You can't take that cute little colt out in this wet, cold weather. Besides, what if Kaya comes, where will he find you?"

Ozkurt held up his hands to quiet her, "We knew we'd have to go by sea to Byzantium. There in *Rume* we'll find a way to go on. I'm leaving tonight."

"But where'll you meet? You can't be sure where he is now." Ozkurt jerked his head impatiently, negatively, "We'll meet in Kertch Port beyond the Don Mouth and the little sea of Azov. It's a Greek trade center. We'll take a freighter from there when the shipping season opens."

"That's a wild port, as I understand it. You may not be safe. It has all kinds of drifters from every nation.

"We'll have to winter there whatever the conditions."

"Crime and commerce go together, unfortunately. There are taverns and places to stay, but it takes money. I know a banker of my people there. I'll prepare a letter of credit for you."

Ozkurt looked puzzled and leaned forward saying, "What's that?"

Lady Judith leaned forward smiling, "I forgot, you wouldn't know. It's a permission to use my money for expenses. It's a commercial arrangement."

"Kaya worked on the Silk Road. I didn't."

"I'll make it out for both of you. He'll know what to do. The man has a room on the harbor where he fills orders and dispatches goods. I'll give you a letter authorizing you to represent the Prince in the Capital of Byzantium. Then, I also have a written offer to Khan Munzur to send with you. I'll ready them while you talk to Ilkin, he won't be happy without a goodbye from you." She motioned him toward an inner room.

He paused and added, "Kaya sent you a message, bayan, a psalm really, 140, he said. I don't see how a number can convey any meaning."

Judith paused before the open door. "It's part of our childhood memory work. We both memorized many Psalms, each has special meaning. Kaya is surrounded by violence; he needs our prayers."

"*Bir dakika lootfin*, Ozkurt bey," implored Sherbet hanum, "one minute please, I must give you something." She thrust some letters into his hands saying, "Kaya bey said he was responsible for my coming here. Said he would help me any time I asked. I don't know what to do with these letters. They're Han Lee's correspondence. They could endanger me. I want you to take them to him." Ozkurt agreed heartily and slid the papers into his shoulder bag.

Ozkurt entered the darkened room. Ilkin made a show of sitting up and smiling, though his face showed strain and dark circles showed plainly under his eyes. Ozkurt sat gingerly beside him.

"Your plan succeeded, Lord Ilkin, the army was scattered when they discovered our presence on the hill. You swept them in their confusion and your retreat brought them into ambush by the reserve troops. They won't stay at the camp."

Ilkin nodded in agreement. "Kaya had widened the path down the hill from the cross. We could charge in formation. Huns were dismounted, scattered, claiming tent sites. I caught Han Lee, the traitor, at the old command post. He was down, bleeding profusely from arrow wounds, when I rode up."

Ozkurt's eyes widened, "Tell me about it," he requested.

"His face held a smirk, and he taunted me. 'If you have sacrificed to the rock-face Tanra, be warned,' he said. 'He gives, but he takes back more than he gives. Fewsoon's Tanra takes, but gives back more than He takes.' " The prince shrugged and shook his head before continuing. "I couldn't understand his meaning and my heart was full of hate.

RIVER-BOAT LOADING

My arrow took him in the throat. An arrow took me in the shoulder seam back between the armor plates and I fell off on top of him. As I lay fainting I heard Gochen calling his troop. 'Retreat northward all.' I heard the Huns call their troops into formation and the onbasha led them after the retreating troops. I struggled up and mounted, the reins were tied to my wrist. The wounded in camp did not hinder me, so I gained the road and found your column."

Ozkurt nodded, taking up the story, "I remember, we were in control of the carts and were moving as fast as possible. I saw Atilla go over and support you. He said later that the arrow was Khazar."

Ilkin nodded slowly: "Friendly fire? Accident? Evil intent? Maybe a Hun borrowed a spent arrow? I guess I'll never know," he sighed deeply and lay back. "I was impressed that you could capture the carts and keep the drivers working."

Ozkurt laughed loudly then shushed himself, "I've learned from Kaya. I told the carters that they would be safe if they didn't try to run away. I promised them money and life if they would continue to the river. I told them they would be free to stay or return to the Huns. So we brought in the Hun's camping goods and food."

Ilkin agreed, "We can use them for our own advance. and recoup our losses."

"You men have celebrated victory enough for today," insisted Lady Judith, entering the room with an oil lamp. "But I insist that the mare's foal must remain. I promise to take special care of her. She doesn't have her mother's color; she'll be dappled. Let her stay here. I've included the payment in the letter of credit. By the way, what stallion did you use?"

Ozkurt smiled shrugging, "Kaya would like to know the answer to that. I think a little prince in Samarkand was impatient to get his promised colt and used the palace stud to hurry the gift. But then, we left..."

She laughed and responded, looking at her husband, "See, patience is the hardest of all virtues to acquire. It's practice is bought with tears." Ozkurt agreed and the formal words of parting were exchanged with a sad feeling of permanence.

"I've hired more men for my troop, Sherbet hanum. I'm to be an important man now. The prince needs me, especially with his wound. He depends on me for a stout defense if the Huns press over the Don. I'll never let them take us here." Gochen was full of assurances as he sat on a keg near the door of the kitchen watching Sherbet hanum in her work at an outdoor table set in the sun at a protected corner of the house. She was collecting and trimming dried meat from a rack and layering the cured pieces in a sack for hanging up in the food shed half buried behind the big house. When she had filled the bag he took it from her and carried it in one hand to the shed where he started to hang it near the door. She corrected him instantly.

"No, not near the door, it will attract flies in summer. Meats must be put deep in at the back."

"There's no flies now hanum, it's cold," he objected mildly. "You'll have eaten it all by spring."

"You can't be certain of that. Everything has its place; put it there." He was careful to do exactly as she said. After all, he had watched his mother go through widowhood and he knew that it was not a time for contradictions or quarrels. He wished he had words of comfort, but feared their rejection. So he came by regularly, helped as he could and spoke little. She worked feverishly: sometimes angry, sometimes sad. He always bore her moods with mild replies and cheerful cooperation. He brought new gossip as they all waited for Kinner Khan to arrive and take over the administration of the base.

SEA SPANKER PASSENGERS

PEOPLE, PLACES & PLOTS IN CHAPTER 12

Altom: a golden mare loses her foal, but gains new friends.
Ebenizer Effendi: Judith's banker has good advice for newcomers.
Fisherman: gets advice, a paying passenger and a big temptation.
Gochen: a war chief celebrates, happy to lose competitors.
Inn master: gets rich clients and new dangers.
Jinx: a drifter finds food for thought in many encounters.
Kaya: helps yet pays his way through trouble to safety.
Khan Kinner: faces new opportunities with enthusiasm.
Olga: a refugee finds opportunity to better her condition.
Ozkurt: must move fast into more discomfort.
Sherbet: a maid solves a problem and saves a cask.
Ship's boy: a responsible boy on sea and shore.
Ship's master: knows safety on his river and sea.
Stable boy: acquires a demanding customer.
Stable master: finds trouble without rewards.

GLOSSARY:

ah'kel-suz: stupid; dummy; brainless.
babam: my father; daddy.
ba-rak: leave it; leave off; don't do it.
bay effendi: My Lord; Dear Sir; (respectful honorific).
ben: I; me; myself; it's me.
binbasham: my general; head of a thousand; a commander.
dummkopf: stupid; dummy, Germanic expression.
effendi: Lord; master; an honorific used after the name.
ha'mom: Turkish bath with steam, hot and cold water.
im-kahn-sez: no way; impossible; it can't be.
kah-ret'sin: blast it; curse it; damn it.
kim' oh: who's there?; who are you?
kim gelior: Who's coming; Who is approaching us.
kommen katze trinken: come cat, drink; (Germanic).
soos: hush; quiet; shush; shut up.
ta-mom'-ma: okay?; all right?; agreed?
vah'she: wild beast; savage; wild child of the forest.

COME CATS AND KITTENS

"*Ah'kel-suz*, stupid easterner, one man can't load horses on a small boat. Doesn't matter how docile the mare. You need some pushing power to move them." Gochen walked up to watch, criticize and to help if need be.

Ozkurt angrily growled, "Go back to the *hamom*, you can find strangers to bully there."

Gochen threw back his head to roar with laughter, "That still burns you, right? Got you hot and bothered?"

"Just a big man with a big mouth, you try to throw your weight around, but I'm not afraid of you."

The big man reached over and picked up a barrel of wine stacked on the river bank and holding it over head walked to Ozkurt, "Here, catch!" He warned, "it's heavy." He held it over Ozkurt's head and let it lower until Ozkurt lifted his hands to ward off the descending weight. Ozkurt felt the weight of it and couldn't hold it. It crashed to the ground with a thump. The smell of wine filled the air.

"You crazy fool, you've broken it," Ozkurt exclaimed, "spilled the wine."

The giant hefted the barrel and laid it gently on the others. He laid a hand under the edge and cupped the drip, which he swallowed with glee. He motioned toward the drip.

"Come, drink! We celebrate your departure. Comrades of the battlefield should toast the fallen and fleeing. May your new destination be as profitable as your departure. You brought me the knowledge of where to find gold and buy new men. I've learned many other things. I'll not forget you, but I'm glad you're going."

Ozkurt did not know what to do. The boat man came over to sample the drip and motioned his helper to come. Several of the grooms from the stables came with cups and joined the samplers. They drank with gusto. The mare was left alone with the colt.

"So you party and get drunk while I delay and may have to face the anger and judgment of the Khan."

"Not so, little man," bellowed Gochen, "come men, all hands, move the mare." It was easier said than done. Altom resisted the manhandling with squeals and kicks.

"Men are so stupid. Bring the foal, I'll show you how." Sherbet hanum appeared and took charge. She carried the foal onto the boat, and with a whinny the mare followed. "Now, tie her in place and bring off the foal," she ordered and it was done, as the men grinned sheepishly at one another.

Gochen stood, liking the situation, chuckling to himself. "Neatly done, now let's toast the lady and the voyage."

"Not another drop, you've had your fill. Now bring the cask to the house. It belongs to the Prince and it's down half empty at least. You'll get no more." Gochen picked up the cask carefully and, meek as a lamb, carried it after the girl to the house.

Ozkurt, open-mouthed, stood watching the scene. The stable hands easily loaded the other two horses.

"Come, master Ozkurt, we mus' pass de guard posts by night 'er be taxed 'er stopped. Der' 're still 'Uns on de river below 'ere. Yur gold won' satisfy dem." Ozkurt boarded hastily. The boat's captain prepared to move them out and the helper loosed the halters and leaped aboard. Without a sound they left, but the distressed whinnies of the mare called long after that to her foal across the water.

> - - - - - - - >

"Dis is de last Khazar post. Dey don't need t'see our cargo. Jus' trust me an' we'll get by."

Ozkurt looked puzzled. "It's near dawn, how will they know?"

The captain touched his ear and touched his lips. Something rubbed the bottom of the boat and a distant bell rang vigorously. "Der's a rope jus' under de surface and when a boat touches it, it pulls a bell rope beside de post. Dey usually can know when boats passes. If I tries t' ignore'm they'll get me later."

A voice hailed from the shore, "*Kim oh*, who's there?"

The captain cupped his hands to his mouth to shout the name of the boat, "De Sea Spanker bound fer Kertch wit' refugees."

"*Kah-ret'sin,* Damn you! Can't you carry something of value once in a while?"

The captain laughed heartily. "I got orders t' fill fer de prince in Kertch, yu shares on mi return. I'll heave to and lets yu see mi cargo now."

- 136 -

"*Ba-rak'*, leave it, Bring a cask of red wine on your return. *Ta-mom'ma*, okay? Don't forget!"

The captain didn't reply. "Dey says dey'll pay fer it, but never does," he muttered.

"I'll buy one for you to take back," murmured Ozkurt, "even refugees have some pride." The captain smiled his agreement as the Sea Spanker moved on the Don current. "I never sailed on water before," Ozkurt said nervously, "I can swim a little in lakes and rivers, but it's different on a boat. I feel funny, this swaying gets you." He started to lie down on a pile of rope, then, he had to lean over the side, where he remained.

> - - - - - - - >

"We're 'ere sir, only a week from our start, a quick trip I calls it. You'll be feelin' better when you've been 'ere a few days. Mi boy 'er' e'll 'elp you t' de inn." The boy had his hands full with a sick man, and three horses to lead.

A girl dressed in a long, dark wool dress and kerchief ran forward. "I can handle the horses for you," she offered. Altom was being difficult and the boy was glad to be rid of them.

"I seen you afore doin' bits t' ern a penny, e'll pay right enough, win we get 'im t' de inn. De Golden Fleece is closer. De mare's a witch wid' out de colt. I don't milk 'er good, she kicks lots." Altom pulled loose at the moment of transfer and started to run down the street. The girl ran after her as the boy yelled. "Catch 'er an' bring 'er back, she be named Altom." He gathered the reins of the other two horses.

Ozkurt roused up sufficiently, to take in the escaping horse and girl in pursuit. He yelled as he stood swaying. "She's Kaya's mare, she's worth her name. I'll pay you." He lost balance and the boy steadied him toward the inn.

"Du na worry sir, Olga be a good girl, she bring Altom back soon." He left the horses at the stable and Ozkurt at the inn's table. Then, he went looking for them.

> - - - - - - - >

"I cetch't yur hoss, now gi' mi somtin' afore I givs up de rope." a tall boy stood holding the halter. He looked thin and hungry.

"I've nothing to give, but if you'll come to the inn, I think the owner will be generous." Olga reached out to take it.

"Why'd Jinx giv a perti an'mal like dis t' a skinny girl? I does better t' keeps 'er. She'd fetch a perddy coin a' de stalls." He snatched the halter back away from her hand. The abrupt action startled the restless Altom and she jerked away from both and ran back the way she had come.

The ship's boy stopped her this time. "She be one restless spirit, like a big blow i'na winter."

"She lost her baby. She's full of milk and needs relief. I'll milk her at the stables, but you must borrow a pail." He nodded agreement.

"Wad about mi?" Insisted the tall youth, "I stopped 'er. She'd be out da town, if I an't caud 'er. Yu promis some thin'. Yu can't leave Jinx wid out it all." Olga nodded as she patted Altom's trembling head.

"*Soos*, quiet, don't spook her, she's been on a boat and is tired, lonesome and in pain. You know what that's like." Both boys nodded in agreement. She led Altom forward. "We need to find the master and collect something for our efforts. I'll take care of her."

At the inn they sought Ozkurt who was gingerly testing his ability to keep barley beer down. He bought both boys a drink while Olga went to the stables and milked the mare. She put her head against the mare's flank and gently squeezed into the wooden bucket and softly sang a milking song.

1.   We are singing and dancing; we have fun, we do.
         Oh, but don't kiss the milkmaid until she gets through.
         We love music and laughter, good food for us too.
         You must wait for the drink 'til the milkmaid gets through.

2.   There is butter, cheese, yogurt, ayran, kumiss, too.
         Work while mother, wife, girlfriend can make it for you.
         Then we'll sing and be happy in all that we do.
         But you must thank the milkmaid who gets it for you.

THE MILKMAID

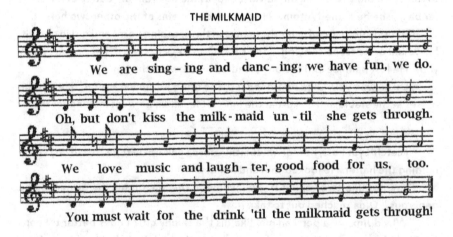

"*Soos*, quiet Altom. Not a lot here, you're congested." She first tasted, then took a swallow from the bucket. Then she picked up a wooden hay fork and refilled the manger. While she worked, she talked to the mare.

"You poor darling, they didn't even feed you properly. Altom, my gold, you've been neglected and got tarnished on the trip. You need a foal to reduce that congestion." Holding the fork before her she sought out the stable boy whom she found mucking out a distant stall. She stood her tallest and took a severe, badgering tone,

"Well, where is the foal? Not here in the stable?" He looked startled and stood open mouthed. "Well, don't just stand there like an idiot. Where is the foal?"

"Wid de dam out in de pasture." His eyes narrowed as he took in her dress, youth and size. "Why d' ye ask?"

"Never mind why, the master wants it brought here right now! Go get it. Leave the dam there." He left.

"Good breakfast, better lunch; God is good and that's no hunch." She looked around and drank from the pail. She tipped it up to drain all but the last drops and sighed: "Drink *heil. Kommen Katze trinken.*" She laid the bucket on its side and made a perfect imitation of a cat's meow. The stable cats poked their heads out of stalls and hay to make their way to the tipped pail. Its sides and bottom would soon be licked clean.

"Here be de colt. ware yu wan 't em?" The stable boy had returned carrying a small dun colored foal of perhaps two weeks. Olga looked it over critically,

"He's ugly! He'll need the extra milk if you hope to get a good horse to rent from this little guy. You ought to be paying for this extra food." She shook her head disapprovingly. "Luck for you, you get it almost free. Bring it here. Now, go in the golden's stall and bring some horse buns to rub on his hide. I'll get some hairs from her tail to wrap around his neck and face. He has to smell like her." The boy did as he was told, grudgingly. "So, now, put it under her so she can't see it too well, her head's tied she can't look round. Let him nuzzle and nurse. She needs that." There was a sound at the door.

"Who needs wat?" a gruff voice questioned. "Didn' yu finish muckin' out dose racks yet?"

The boy left complaining, "Just finishin' zir, she called mi t' 'elp." He had the shovel and was all energy at the stall.

The head groom swung to face the girl who stood by Altom's head. "Who be yu missy? Yu come in wit dat hoss?" he asked.

"Yes, and I'll be taking care of her. She's delicate and I'll be sleeping here to mind her."

He peered at her closely, "I seen yu afore, yu be Olga, from de docks." Dey say yor folks be dead. Who give yu dis mare t' watch?"

"I'm paid to take care of Altom until Kaya, the owner, comes. They expect him any time. The master arrived sick and is in the inn now."

The man turned away saying, "De boys un I sleeps in de loft. Yu finds sum'er else an no complaints t' de boss."

She looked at the man wisely, "I'll sleep with Altom and a hay fork, so spread the word. I'm going to report to my master now. Leave the horse as you find her 'till I get back." He didn't turn to look at her.

> - - - - - - - >

"Yu tooks long 'nough," the ship's boy declared when she came to the table. "Ere be Olga de Gott, she works de docks fer eats an' coin." He spoke to Ozkurt who still reflected the effects of the voyage. A food platter had been set before him, but he wasn't eating much -- the boys were.

"How's Altom now?" he asked.

She sat across from them and refused to be tempted by what lay before her. She took off her scarf and shook out her golden hair, running her fingers through it. "She's better. She has hay and an adopted foal I put to her after I milked her. She's congested and the milk was... well, I let the cats finish it." He nodded in understanding. "I'm going to sleep with them tonight and make sure she's taken care of. I'll apply warm wrapped bricks and a poultice if you've the means to buy it."

He took out a fat pouch and removed a silver coin. All three young people gasped and leaned forward. He also removed two copper coins and gave one to each of the boys. All motion in the inn had stopped, and every eye watched.

The inn master himself brought a bowl of flat bread and ask if he would be staying any time. Ozkurt agreed to pay by the week until his friend Kaya should appear. He offered a gold coin in payment. The inn keeper stood a moment in silent embarrassment. He held center stage for everyone. "Bey *ffendi*, my Lord, it's Saturday, the bank is not open today. I must see the money changer tomorrow for your money. Only the Jew and rich merchants and shippers can change such coins."

Ozkurt agreed and took bread, after a bite he laid it down and started to rise from the table. He checked, "I haven't eaten in so long I forgot to thank Tanra." He opened his hands and repeated in a low voice an ancient blessing by rote:

"God is great, God is good. So we thank Him for our food.

By His hand we all are fed. Thank You, Lord, for daily bread."

He stood up slowly, and sighed, "I'm so glad Yesu brought me through this last week. I hope I'll never go to sea again."

The teenagers exchanged glances and the tall boy, Jinx, said,

"Where be yu goin' when Kaya get 'ere?"

Ozkurt swayed and sat down again, his land legs failed him.

"He has a quest to complete. I'm going as a friend."

"Wat's a kwes'?" asked the ship's boy curiously.

"It's when someone makes a promise to do something that's hard, but right to do. You make it all your life and interest until it's finished, right? You always have to travel to do it. If you do that, it's counted by everyone as a win, but you sacrifice a lot to get it done."

The teen-agers were frowning and not sure. Then Jinx spoke up. "Wats de ting he got t' travel t' do?" The others nodded.

"He has to rescue his sister and marry his promised bride, who was captured and carried off by Huns near the Yellow River in China. We have come a long way, following them and still we haven't found her; much less got her back again."

"Two girls? A sister and a fiancé?" asked Olga.

Ozkurt's head jerked up in a sharp negative. He made a helpless gesture. How could he explain Kaya's past life? "The bride is a step-sister, raised together for part of his life, breast mates. He spent several years in the forest as a *vah'she*, a wild boy raised by bears. He was hunted and escaped several times. He went to school in a hermitage. When he returned to the tribe - the Chipchaks - they found he was the child of promise, the heir of the Khan his father, but the step-mother was angry. Her son, his friend, could have been the child of promise. He had to live with his ... almost a sister in the medicine hut." The young folks listened with open mouths as they tried to take in the life summary of Kaya.

"I need to sleep and I don't feel well." Ozkurt rose unsteadily, "I'll go up now, we'll talk tomorrow." He started away from the table.

"Can I take your unfinished bread for Altom to eat?" Olga held up the round bread with the missing bite. "You won't finish it."

"Take it all." The remaining bread was hastily split into pieces by several hands and tucked away.

"I'll sleep outside yur door t'nite," offered Jinx. "Yu'll be safer."

The inn keeper, with price in hand, was willing to provide covers for both hall and stable when the ship's boy started for the dock. "Dis Kaya mus be sometin t' zee, win 'e com'," he observed on leaving. "I comes back afore we loads de ship, an' fer supper too, yu 'ear?" But they were already happily leaving with warm bedding.

> - - - - - - - >

"You're in trouble. What can I do to help you?" Kaya stood on the bank of the river shouting to a man alone in the boat. The fisherman was struggling with a loaded net in the water, which was splashed white, as huge fish thrashed with resisting energy. The man was red-faced and panting as he tried unsuccessfully to bring the haul out of the water. He heard and turned toward the bank to nod and shout, but his words were not clear. His needs were evident and urgent.

A FULL NET

- 141 -

He couldn't let go the net's edge and lose the fish. One side hung from the boat and he held the other. The thrashing increased as he strained. The boat tilted, quivering at a dangerous angle.

"Hook the net's edge on the mast cleat," Kaya shouted.

The man heard and turned his head to see the cleat at the bottom of the mast. He was able to snag the net's lead rope over the cleat. He could let it take the weight while he tied up the leading and back edges so the fish could not escape. The boat was continuing to list; tilt toward the fish. Water was starting to splash over inside. The fisherman quickly seated himself on the high side board bringing a better balance to raise the net edge slightly higher.

"Bring the boat closer to the shore and I'll help you."

"Who be ye?" the man asked, "I never seed yu bout 'ere afore,"

"I'm serving with Prince Ilkin's forces. I'm called Kaya *Aya*, We had a battle and I was left taking care of the wounded. Now I'm trying to get across the river to safety."

The man humped skeptically, and still balancing on the boat's rim retorted, "A likely story, yu got beat and now ye be lookin' fer a way out. Yuz a refugee wid' out coin, robbin' good fo'ks t' eat. Like as not yu steals mi boat, cross de river wid mi fish t'boot."

"*Im-kahn-sez*, no way, I have money to pay for the trip. You need help with those fish; you can't do it alone."

The man looked angry, "Mi son be sick. Mi good wife keeps de home. De girl be married now, and gone. De wee ones is liddle. I'z good alone, 'cept for dees big sturgeon Dey's too big to eat, bedder I takes dem to port, selz 'im in de fish stalls. Bring many coin fer mi liddle ones."

"Could you take me with you?" Kaya asked, "I'd help all the way. You'd earn even more coins by taking me down to the port. Follow the Don to the sea on the current, no extra work."

"Dis be de Donetz River an' de 'Uns' garrison be at de mout' o' de river wear it meet de Don. Dats wear yu wants t' get bi."

"We can go after dark," Kaya countered, "slip by."

"Dey got big net wid floats at narrow spot, bells on buoys. Dey make big racket. De 'Uns shoots." The man looked down thoughtfully. "Yu swares on yu mudder's grave, yu tells truf? No tricks me?"

"I fear Tanra's anger against sinners and love Yesu for grace."

"I t'row yu rope, yu pulls boat over t' de bank. Yu helps bail water. Boat settle wi' de big fish, mo' water seep in. Yu pays coin first, I takes yu t' port. We go now, sturgeon stay alive in water, two, tree days. Dem 'Uns tired o' eatin' fish, no trouble t' us. I gets yu bi."

> - - - - - - - >

"You're better setup here than I imagined, son. Your men must be well trained to get through that ambush and turn them back before they could cross the river." Khan Kinner's tone was grudging as he stood over the bed.

"My husband is an accomplished warrior, My Lord," the lady Judith responded attentively. Father or not, Kinner was Khan, and their future depended on his good grace. Courtesy ruled.

Prince Ilkin submissively spoke from his bed. He lay propped up and looked spent. "What I have is all by your grace and permission, father. I hoped to do you good by clearing the river banks of Huns."

The khan sniffed his contempt of the words and his lips pinched tight. "That's why you got caught on the Donetz River? Clearing the Don?" There was a long pause while Judith had Sherbet fill the Kahn's drinking horn. "Why not admit your blind ambition; irresponsible risk taking? Why pretend that your troubles were the acts of a traitor? He simply gave you false information that you gladly took to be true. You wanted it to be true."

The prince nodded. "You're right as usual, *babam*, I wanted to impress you and make up for the flaunting of your will in marrying Judith." The khan's lips almost turned up. Instead, he buried his face in his cup.

"Why did you kill the traitor? He would have been able to give true information, had you kept him alive," he demanded,

Ilkin hung his head. "He was fatally wounded when I got to him. He fought bravely, but I was in a rage and didn't hear him out."

"And in your fury forgot to cover your back." His father said, "Many a prince has fallen in that way. Who was your back up?"

The prince shrugged doubtfully. "Kaya was wounded and remained behind. Atilla and Ozkurt were capturing the supply column. Only Gochen remained commanding his men. My troop was scattered, I was alone at the time."

"You lost control of the action for vengeance." The khan paused for effect, "What did he say? The last words of men are usually a revealer of character and purpose."

Ilkin sighed, "Something about the stone Tanra giving, but taking more than he gave. I supposed he meant the local worship place on the hill where they sacrifice." Everyone waited while Ilkin thought. "Then, something about a Tanra who took, but gave more than He took. He must have been delirious from his wounds."

The Khan made a snorting sound and walked to the door before turning to address Judith. "I'm interested in soldiers' fare today, horse meat shish kebob, flat bread, yogurt and bulgur. Have you got the makings of that?"

"We only have lawful meats in the house, My Khan: that which has a parted hoof and chews the cud; fish with fin and scales; and ducks. Will you join us with those or eat in the mess hall with the troops? My husband finds such an arrangement satisfactory."

"I should have guessed." He glared, then, proceeded to mock,

"Your uncle deems it improper to come at the time of the festival of lights. He will consider a later date."

She bowed smiling. "He'll come inside eight days with a Rabbi if the child is a boy."

"He'll shorten him, as they do all others then?" jibed Kinner.

"A prince is too important for my personal status to apply. The mother is a Jewess and the child must be connected to Adoni's promises and community," Judith explained.

"You've no objections? After the way they've treated you?" Prince Ilkin spoke up, concerned.

"I'm what I've always been. My offenses are my love for two men. Prince Ilkin my husband, and the Jew Yesu, my Messiah."

> - - - - - - - >

"Yu don't suppose 'e died 'n de nite? It be mid-day now. Naught be moven' in de room." Jinx was eating hard ship's biscuits with the ship's boy and Olga. They drank the mare's milk from cups.

"He and the mare were bad off. She's in a slump for her foal. I got an apple with the money for medicine, and she only took one bite."

"So as yu 'et it for 'er," sneered Jinx. She jerked her head up in a negative gesture. Then they heard a crashing sound from the room.

"I'll bets ye coin 'e's still loop-legged," proclaimed the boat's boy, with a knowing grin.

"Na', but I 'opes 'e's 'ungry likes I is now." Jinx replied grumpily.

"Good morning sir," ventured Olga knocking gently on the door. "We'll bring you breakfast if you wish, just tell us what you'd like."

The answer was a loud yawning and clearing of throat. The bolt drew and a disheveled Ozkurt appeared at the door half-dressed. "I need a bowl of ayran and gruel." They were stunned.

"Dat be soljer's fare, zir. Gent'mens eats bedder." Jinx stated.

"I'm a soldier and I'll eat what I'm used to, there's no better."

"I come to see be yu feelin' bedder zir, I'm goin' back t' de ship now, we needs more hans t' load de boat." declared the ship's boy.

"I'm needin' a job fer coin be yu takes me too," offered Jinx and the two left hastily.

Olga stood looking at him wisely. "You like the same food as the Huns order when they come here. Do you work for them? You're a mercenary?" Her tone was not friendly.

"Get the food first and then we'll talk."

She didn't move. "I'll not serve a bloody Hun or any of his supporters." She glared at him.

He scoffed, "I've been fighting them alongside the Khazars, girl, why do you think you know what they're like? They came through the Ukraine fifty years ago."

Her chin was up in stubborn defiance. "My folks took refuge among the Circasians, on the sea side of the mountains, when they attacked us. Opa Otto and

Mutter Helga were fighters there when they lost his little brother, Grossunkel Fritz. They told me all the stories. How they escaped to the mountains."

"I'll hear them later. Now, I'm paying you for the mare's care and mine. I've no doubt you've fed her. Now, I need food: plain food, soldier's food, something – anything! I've starved for a week."

> - - - - - - - >

"The inn master was in for change this morning. Word has gone around town of a rich soldier. I've been expecting you." The skinny Jewish banker observed courteously.

"How did you know I'd come to your bank? There are at least two other men in town." Ozkurt was feeling better after his brunch.

"A pagan and a heretic. The Christians and Jews here would rather deal with me. The ship's master brought me a letter from Lady Judith. I gave him the money and credit to buy the needed supplies for the Estate and army too."

Ozkurt looked the man over carefully. Ebenezer *effendi* looked hunched and old, although black hair yet mixed in his gray beard. He was dressed simply in black wool. "The lady's very able in her dealings." The long beard and side curls moved as the banker silently laughed. He motioned grandly for Ozkurt to sit beside a table full of papers. "The Don River projects move on her money and ability to manage his financing. Now she is financing the purchase of an expensive foal and travel costs for two of you. Where's the other man?" Ozkurt looked curiously at the short skinny Jew. How much did he know? He had the sound of one who knew a lot. He must find out.

"Kaya was wounded at the battle, but promised to come here or to Constantinople if I had cause to move on."

The banker paused to consider these facts before speaking, "You'll be here a while then. It would be safer to leave part of your gold here. This is a dangerous town, robbery is a daily occurrence. Word of your wealth has already spread."

"I thought of getting civilian clothes, since I'm not on duty. I can do my purchases first."

The man nodded, doubtful but agreeable. "I know a Jewish tailor who can do finished work in two days. It's Sunday and many other shops will be closed."

Ozkurt nodded, "Why not? I'll go there now, it'll fill the day."

> - - - - - - - >

"*Kim geliyor*, who comes here? Hold and identify yourself," the sentinel shouted.

"*Ben*, 'tis me, de fisherman. I needs t' pass de gap."

"It's nearly dark. Come back in the morning. We're closed." Another voice had joined the exchange.

"I caughts dree sturgeon 'n mi net. I needs t' get dem t' de port stalls afore dey dies. I'll 'ave coins den. I'll give yu de liddle un fer de favor."

The Huns laughed, one stuck out his tongue. "Waagh, fish and ducks! That's our fare every day, week after week. Go sell the little one and bring us meat, I'll even eat goat."

"Don't listen to him. We want horse meat, like the old days."

"You got anything else in the boat?"

The fisherman poled his way through a gap in the net and bell barrier, near the shore. He laughed and waved as he put the pole down and upped the sail. "Sure, I gots a sleepin' bear in de boddom o' de boat. I wakes 'im up fer youse."

The Huns doubled in laughter, and waved him on. Others added bits to the joke. "You do that, we need some excitement around here,"

"It's winter, better let him hibernate or you'll be sorry."

"Don't forget our groceries when you come back; horse meat: dried or fresh." The dark settled around the coasting boat.

"I wondered if you would sell me out to them, since I had already paid you. This bear is grateful." Kaya quipped softly.

The fisherman's laugh came through the dark as he set sail.

"I admits t' de idear steerin' trough mi 'ead, but foolin' 'Uns iz more fun... It make a good tale fer wintertime."

> - - - - - - - >

"So, you boys have worked hard today and the boat is loaded for a return trip up past the Don Bend?" The ample supper met the children's hopes and expectations were high for additional perks.

"De skipper buy all de stuff 'n de mornin' an' de brings zit t' de wharf after we leaves 'ere today. Cold win' blow, but we sweatin' plenty," proclaimed the ship's boy.

"Yea, we can't see nothin' inside de ship's 'ole when nite com," complained Jinx.

"We leaves first lite in de mornin'," the ship's boy announced.

"We 'elps a big Khazar river boat tie up, but de soljers don' give nodin'." Jinx complained. "Jus more work, but no gain." Ship's boy disagreed hastily,

"Skipper, 'e buy us drink an' meat skewers atween deliveries."

"Jes once, no more. We works all afternoon t' nite." Jinx voice showed dislike of work and disappointment.

Olga spoke up, "Altom is better now. The swelling and congestion are less. The foal is getting the best part of two sources and the cats are always there when I milk."

The ship boy laughed, but Jinx, bored, reached for bread. A group of three older men entered the hall and sought out a table. They were dressed in Khazar officers' uniforms. The ship's boy noticed immediately. "Dey wears de uniform, but I don' knows dem from d' Estate." Who be dem?"

Ozkurt rose slowly from his seat. He recognized the rank. His heart was pounding and he gasped for air.

"Who are you soldier and why are you here in Kertch?" asked the man of highest rank, a general of the Royal Guards. The other two men gathered around the table curiously. The young people froze.

"*Binbasham*, My General," stuttered Ozkurt, "I'm sent by my Lord Ilkin with the Estate boat, to buy supplies and pick-up any wounded from the battle on the Donetz; comrades who may have survived. Particularly an officer named Kaya with whom I travel to Rume, to Constantinople." Ozkurt was sweating at attention when General Alsin nodded approvingly. His staff exchanged glances and smiled.

"You're a fortunate man to survive that debacle. I'd like to hear about it first hand, if you can spare the time. Has the officer Kaya arrived yet?" Ozkurt's head moved up in a negative. "Well, we'll all be traveling together, if he arrives in the next three days, when the Sea Witch sails for Byzantium. Come to our table when you finish with your helpers." The group nodded pleasantly and proceeded to a private room guided by the ingratiating inn keeper. The youths watched the procession in silent awe.

Ozkurt slumped trembling and breathed a sigh of relief. He smoothed his plaited queue. "I went to the church after the tailors and prayed thanks for the escape, my arrival, and many other things. I'll have to go again tomorrow."

Olga alone nodded agreeably, "I'll go with you master."

> - - - - - - - >

"So the prince had to accept all three: cat, bear and Sherbet as a condition of his wife's confinement." Ozkurt finished, as the Khazars roared with laughter. The officers had finished their supper and were in their drinks when Ozkurt joined them with stories of battles and intimate details of Ilkin's life.

Alsin said, "We will be in close contact in Constantinople, we must form one delegation to deal with the Empire. We, Khazars and the Greeks, are natural allies against the Huns. Our wealth and commerce will grow mightily. You will benefit as much as we."

TOASTING VICTORY

PEOPLE, PLACES & PLOTS IN CHAPTER 13

Altom: the golden mare continues her journey by boat.
Binbasha Alsin: a Khazar general sent as ambassador to Byzantium.
Captain: takes the Sea Witch on a late delivery of wheat.
Chavush: an experienced relative of the general sent to serve.
Ebenezer: Judith's banker and agent in Kertch Port.
Fisherman: carries sturgeon, a bear and a jinx some place.
Ishaac: is expediting the importing of refugees from 'Rume'.
Jinx: a boy of loose ways, seeking his fortune.
Kaya: new to the sea finds much to interest him.
Magda: aunt in charge of the governor's daughter.
Merien Papasion: attracts the young men's attention.
Olga: the young Goth continues to work as Altom's caretaker.
Ozkurt: goes from bad to worse as they continue to sail.
Yuzbasha: a young Khazar nephew sent to serve in Constantinople.

GLOSSARY:

baluk: fish of most kinds.
Binbasha: general; military title: head of a thousand.
Chavush: sergeant; military title: ranking above an onbasha.
duenna: a female companion for marriageable girls.
dummkoph: stupid; dumbbell; brainless (Germanic origin).
effendi: Lord; Sir; title of respect for an important person.
hamom: public baths with steam, hot and cold water.
Hesus: Jesus, in Greek usage.
kafkas: Caucuses Mountains between the Black and Caspian Seas.
kalk: stand up; get up; arise.
kebab: skewered food cooked over open flames.
Kurios: Lord; a Greek word for diety.
luff: to turn sharply into the wind; to spin and accelerate the ship.
oraya bach: look over there; just see that; what a sight.
tamom?: okay? alright? do you agree?
uyan: wake up; awaken.
yuzbasha: lieutenant; head of a hundred men.

ALOUPKA ENTERTAINS

"I tell you the truth gentlemen," Ozkurt stated, "my guard was sleeping outside my door. I saw him this morning and the change purse was still on the table when I came here. After breakfast it was gone. The room was locked so it must be one of the servants." A yuzbasha came running into the dining area. His face was anxious and worried,

"Sir," he addressed his General, "I was out to check the stables, I heard a commotion, when I got back to the room my dress knife was gone." He stopped for a moment to listen to the indignation and protests. "I had closed the door, but didn't lock it; I was coming right back. I didn't expect a delay." The sergeant left to see the room, while the general called for the inn keeper.

"What was the commotion that delayed you?" Ozkurt asked the Yuzbasha anxiously.

"The golden mare was raising hell with the stable boys. The girl you hired to nurse the horse was hiding beneath her with the colt and the mare protected them. She had kept the boys away by kicking at them. The girl was shouting insults in some foreign language and they had wooden forks that they tried to use on her. They were screaming that they would get her and she was yelling *dummkopf* at them. The stable master intervened and sent the boys packing to the loft, then he ordered the girl out with the horse. They followed me and the master took the colt back to its mother. The girl tied the mare and followed me to the rooms. The door was open and I saw my knife was gone from the table."

"Look to your own people, mine were working in the kitchen," protested the inn keeper. At that moment the general's other attendant, the sergeant, returned to solemnly report: "Sir, there are two knives missing, your gold handled one from Khan Kinner, for distinguished service."

The *binbasha* paled and tried to recall the details of the room. "It was hanging on the bedpost.

"You're sure?"

He nodded. "Was the official roll and commission there?" the sergeant nodded again. "Good, we are dealing with thieves not spies. Bring the boy and the girl."

The girl was outside with Altom, but the boy could not be found. The girl's small bundle was examined and then she was sent to the ship to house the mare for the voyage.

> - - - - - - - >

"Yur price be too much, I've fambly t' feed," The fish master protested to the fisherman offering three large sturgeons at the dock. The fisherman shook his head wisely,

"Day 'z live an' flippin' day sells all 'n dis day, 'n yu takes de left overs 'ome t' de fambly." Silver reluctantly changed hands. The dock help was called to hoist the fish to be carted to the stalls. His passenger, in uniform, left the crowd to walk down the dock toward the Sea Witch, now busy loading.

A skinny youth joined the crowd. He had wandered up to the fisherman's boat to watch the action. He asked, "T' where be yu goin'?"

"Where'z yu wan' t' go?" responded the fisherman.

Jinx shrugged and moved down to the boat, "Up river fo' sure. Where ye goin' to?"

The fisherman smiled slyly and put his money away, "Up de Donetz and wear ever more far de silber takes ye. Yu wan' t' go far? Yu fambly not goin' t' miss ye?" He inquired carefully while folding up the net.

"I comes from de *Kafkas* Mountains, De fambly be far away now. Never wan' t' go 'ome. I wan' t' zee de worl' an' travel. Yu takes mi up river t' de village dare?"

"Yu pays mi de silber now *tamom*, okay? I takes yu t' de bes' place for wat you wan'."

The boy scanned the wharf, and smiled knowingly, shaking his head. He jingled a purse in his hand. "I gots it all 'ere yu sees, but I pays win we gets dare. No' be for." The boy tucked it into a belt which held an army knife.

The fisherman nodded, "Yu gets wa' yu gives. Trus' fer trus' an' skin for skin. Yu sits en' waits wile I goes t' de stalls an buys meat fer de return 'ome. Yu bales

- 150 -

water on de trip up an' I gets yu wi' men who teach yu t' ride an' shoot. Den yu sees de worl'." The fisherman left chuckling.

> - - - - - - - >

"Why are you taking that horse aboard that ship, girl?" Altom neighed and shook her head vigorously as Kaya walked up to pet her nose. The girl looked up startled and then broke into a beautiful smile.

"You're the Kaya we're waiting for! I'm Olga and I have a quest too, so I'm going with you."

Kaya smiled in return. "Altom must trust you, so I will too. I need to go to the *hamom* now. When do we sail?"

The girl nodded and instructed him: "Not today. Go to the inn, the Golden Fleece, there on the harbor front first. Master Ozkurt's there now. He'll take you to tailors, banker and church after baths."

Kaya nodded his approval and set out. Everything happened just as she said and a clean and fed Kaya found himself measured for travel wear and off to the banker.

Ebenezer *effendi*, after careful inspection, admitted them.

"You're spoken of very highly by Lady Judith, she certainly has trusted you with a great layout of funds," explained Ebenezer indicating a rolled letter. " I know the skipper and will send the passage money directly. You won't have to do that chore."

"I understand you have three horses as well," he continued. "I'll pay the total bill. You must realize that you're starting very late and most shipping is closed for the winter. The ice is growing on the rivers. Your skipper is a risk taker and is hoping for a late sale of wheat. There is a shortage in Byzantium this year. He won't get insurance from me this voyage, so take care. I will pay your bill for clothing directly. I understand you bought much fine cloth." He indicated Ozkurt, who had indulged his love of color and quality. Both men nodded their assent.

"I understand you've already been robbed. I warn you again not to carry money about."

"It was the change purse, I sleep with the gold," Ozkurt said boastfully.

"Men get their throats slit for such," gestured Ebenezer. Then he changed the subject. "Ben Ishaac has sent authorization for more refugees of our people from the port to be sent on to Gechet City. The Khazar boat will take the latest arrivals here to the Don Bend. The lady Judith will receive and help them winter there. It will be the last boat until spring when the ice goes out."

Kaya said, "How do you interpret her continuing help to your troubled community."

The banker shrugged, "Her expulsion was an act of a Rabbi, who, although important, is only one. The guardian is angered that she didn't support his choices, but other Jewish maidens have done as much. Her choice of Messiah is more serious. It is hers to make as long as it does not offend the first, most important, commandment: You shall have no Gods before me. You Christians take a human for God, but there can be only one; not three. Adoni is not dividable."

Kaya answered slowly, "Tell me, what will the Jewish reaction be to the Messiah when he comes. Will you obey him as you obey the Law of Moses?"

"Without a doubt! He will rule as king among us and make us great. The world will become as paradise because peace rules."

"A worthy dream, He will be as a son to his heavenly father; knowing his father's will and mind. Will he love your people?"

"As a husband loves his bride. This is His promise to us."

"We share the same dream and promise. A Messiah, bonded to the Holy One, bearing His will, mind and strength is worthy of obedience and honor. Could Yesu not be that one?"

"He was rejected by our high priest and leaders. He may be worthy of obedience by the other nations, but not by us."

"Why are you different from others?" inquired Ozkurt. "Your leaders never make mistakes as others do?"

Ebenezer drew up to his full height and showed himself at his proudest and best. "Adoni has promised to guide us. We cannot be wrong. Personally wrong, perhaps, but as His people never. For this reason we await His time and revelation to Israel. He will come as it is promised."

Kaya nodded at the little man's certainty. "How will you be able to be sure of the right one? Do you have a High Priest?"

"Not in our present exile, but we will know. Something inside here; His spirit will tell us."

Ozkurt said thoughtfully, "A spirit that speaks of the Holiness of God? We believe that too. The Holy Spirit is part of God's being, a part of three that make one Supreme Being."

Ebenezer sat down abruptly, moving rolls. He explained as if to a child. "Adoni is not plural, He is one. He does not share His glory. Other Messiahs come and go, but the one we wait for will rule forever from Jerusalem."

Kaya responded, "Yesu has promised to return to receive his faithful ones. He will judge the world."

Disdain filled Ebenezer's face, "Your people always seek to take our promised heritage."

"Like Jacob took his brother's birthright when Esau despised it and sold it for food?" countered Kaya.

The banker replied carefully and coldly, "We cherish our heritage. We have not sold it, but you want it. You people envy our prosperity. Neither I, nor Israel need salvation, now in our dispersion or returned to the land. You do need a savior from your sins. I and my people do not want what you need. Our refugees are expelled from Byzantine provinces by Christians. If you have no further business, I bid you good day. I have accounts and important letters to do." They departed quietly.

Outside, Kaya said, "They intend to help only their own. We must obey Tanra and help everybody, All need Yesu's salvation. After all, no one else has ever offered to save others."

> - - - - - - - >

"Why sleep here on the boat tonight? The longer I can stay off it, the better I like it." Ozkurt's complaints were coming thick and fast. "We don't leave until first light. After a week on the river I was hoping to never travel on water again. Look how small our quarters are. There's no place to exercise the horses. You heard the stories about pirates and ship wrecks, how can you be so calm? Don't you care if I die?"

Kaya lay yawning, ready to sleep. "Did you pray for a safe voyage in the church? Yes? Then why worry? Do you think Yesu is deaf? If he could forget, wouldn't his mother remind him? Trust him and rest. I'm going to sleep now."

Ozkurt was not assured and went on deck to talk to the Khazar officers and a few passengers willing to risk a winter's trip to Byzantium. He inspected the horses. They were well foddered and blanketed against the cold. Altom looked groomed and splendid. The little Goth had done an excellent job curing her. He had paid her well at the Golden Fleece and said his goodbye and thanks. He had a favorite cousin at home only a few years younger. He sat on the deck and thought of her and about home for a while. Then he went down to the cabin. A ship docked and secured in its berth doesn't move much. He fell asleep on top of his bunk.

> - - - - - - - >

"*Uyan*, wake up! I wondered how long it would take you to come alive. It's windy on deck, but we're through the Straits of Kertch and the Sea of Azov is behind us." Kaya was up, warmly dressed and in a teasing mood as he shook his friend.

"I was hoping it would freeze up before now, so we couldn't leave," groaned Ozkurt from the bed. "Why was it late this year?" he moaned. Kaya's laughter filled the small cabin.

"Fresh, moist winds are blown from my Yownja, in the west. I know where she is now. I must close the distance." He prodded him. "*Kalk*, stand up! Soon the wind will change to the east and the real winter starts. In Kertch you would freeze as stiff as the rivers." He pulled him to his feet. "Up my brave warrior." He pulled at the resisting Ozkurt.

"You're crazy, I'll be sick if I stand up. Let me die here."

He collapsed on the bunk again, hitting his head.

"You can't die till the quest is over. Tanra forbids it."

"Am I to be pummeled to death by you and the ship too?"

"Come, Altom awaits our attention, she needs milking and petting. She will feel neglected if we delay."

Ozkurt sat, rubbing his head gingerly and grimaced wryly, "Why make these planks so hard? You could break your head."

Kaya smacked him with a pillow saying, "You want to get beaten with a soft club? Or would you like the board to break and the cold sea water wake you?" He laughed and hit again.

"I'll show you, no bear can beat me, even if he sleeps with tigers." He stood and the ship shuddered, lurched and rolled as the steering brought them to a new heading. Ozkurt fell again.

"We've changed course. We're quartering now. The captain told me this morning. We sail south-west, almost into the wind. It's slow; they come back three times faster with the West wind behind them."

Ozkurt began dressing on the bunk. "I think you planned to do that. Knock me down with only a pillow in your hand. Ruin my reputation. Wait till I'm up again."

"You'll have to catch me," shouted Kaya running from the cabin. When Ozkurt got to the deck, Kaya was up the main mast waving. "Come up and see the view. It's beautiful! It's clearing. You can see the Mountains of Crimea."

"Bears always climb trees to escape danger. Come down and face me."

His answer was a peal of laughter and an invitation, "You come up and bring breakfast with you please."

"I'll bring you milk and sea biscuits," shouted a thin girl's voice. Olga was below in her wool hood and cloak. Ozkurt gasped at the sight of her and forgot his pretended vendetta.

"I paid you off at the Golden Fleece. How do you come here?"

"You paid my passage, master, for my quest. I told the captain that I would be traveling with you to care for Altom. He sent the bill and you paid it. I came on last night when I heard about it."

Kaya descended from his high perch while she explained. He made a laughing comment. "Altom will be happy you're here."

She agreed cheerfully, "The milk is still warm, sir. Drink. I'll be no more expense. I can buy my food. I sold my family's boat, so I have something to use on my quest."

Ozkurt's voice was stern, "For what are you questing, girl?"

Her voice was timid, but confident. "I must find my great Uncle Fritz. He is with the Ostrogoths that fled west."

Kaya looked concerned, "How will you know where to find him? Have you ever seen him? Know what he looks like?"

She nodded and explained, "It was a long time ago, but the scars will still show. I'll know how to find him."

Kaya and Ozkurt locked eyes and nodded. "It's true that you have no family left here?" Ozkurt asked, still tying his belt.

"When Opa Otto died the neighbors took our land and I stole the boat and escaped to Kertch. I fished some and worked at the port some. Now I can care for Altom while we travel west."

"The milk is getting cold," said Kaya. "We had better finish it."

While they ate a figure warmly dressed in wool hood and cloak approached them. The beautiful voice held an accent of southlands and city culture. "Olga, are these your friends? They take you west to our great city? Yes? They are noisy in their games; like little boys? No? They like to make fun? Yes!" Both men were suddenly tongue tied and awkward.

"Yes, Merien, to all your questions," Olga replied with vigor. "Masters, this is Merien Papasion, daughter of the governor of Kertch Port. I took her out fishing in my boat once."

Merien smiled and gestured prettily. "Yes, my father was furious when he found out, but we had -- what is the word -- *baluk*? Yes, fun and fish *kebob* that morning. We have been friends since then. Yes. She helps me this morning, when Magda, my companion is ill. So you must treat her well for my sake." Her whole being seemed to sparkle excitement.

Ozkurt's soul was in his eyes as he gazed at the dark-eyed beauty. "Of course, she is invaluable to us." He looked down to see that he had come on deck without his shoes. One foot tried to cover the other one, embarrassed, as the ship heeled over. Ozkurt went flying. Kaya caught him as he neared the rail. "Excuse me, lady Merien, I must finish dressing." he implored while the ship's compliment laughed heartily.

> - - - - - - - >

"Sail ahoy, to the south, a galley be passing east around the cape, like a hound going for a hare," the lookout shouted. "She has a war look, got a beak for ramming."

The passengers flocked to the side to see the sight. A week of viewing only water and distant mountains had whetted their appetites for watching anything different. Ozkurt was keeping the company of Merien Papasion as usual. She was flanked by the young Khazar officer, who had also fallen under the spell of the governor's daughter. Kaya and Olga were not far from the three. Aunt Magda had kept to her bunk.

The captain cupped his hands to shout: "Any pennants or flags for identity?" His voice was tense. The passengers listened attentively.

The lookout shouted: "Aye, a black triangle from the stern, skull and crossbones on the main sail. She's changing her course. She's seen us and is bearing round."

A second sailor shouted, "Abkhasian pirates. I've heard about that raider. They were pillaging the Byzantine Pontic Coast where the Laz carry cargo."

The shrieks of dismay were deafening, but the captain's roar was noted by the crew. They looked at each other in shocked dismay. They had rarely heard this drastic command under these conditions. "Rudder, hard over, luff her, spin and steer north. Attention on the main sail. We're going to slow by bringing her around, into the wind. Lively now, brace for acceleration after."

The forward motion of the ship slowed as she came into the wind. The sails were in chaos as the prow swung past west to the north, toward the Peninsula of Crimea. The sails filled again, and the mast groaned as the crew strove to realign the ropes and angle of the sails. The sail filled suddenly as the ship spun past north to north-east. The west wind drove the nose down to lift water. The ship heaved and shuddered. The timbers groaned with the passengers, who were falling or clinging to rails and bulk heads. The captain was disregarding all consequences for an escape. Spray filled the air. The acceleration was felt by everyone. They clung to their place of safety, even the captain, as they waited to see the results of this drastic action.

"A variation on Asop's story of the tortoise and the hare," shouted the captain. "We have been the slow one, but now the sleeper has awakened at the smell of the wolf." True enough, the loaded ship which had plodded slowly west, quartering by zigzags into the wind along the Crimean Riviera had become a bird skimming the water under the power of the west wind.

"Ahoy lookout, what of the galley now?" the captain shouted.

"Flummoxed, Sir, they come out of the cape's current to our east, the wind be in their faces." Satisfaction showed,

"Have we a clear shot at Yalta harbor then?" he retorted.

"They're breaking out the oars, Sir, they'll cut us off."

"Then it's north to Aloupka. Let's hope the harbor defenses are not manned by volunteers."

"Won't matter, Sir, we'll be seen easily within the hour."

"And how long do we have?"

The lookout paused to watch. Everyone waited anxiously. "About the same time for contact. They're professional and strong, pulling well, but the ship is loaded, going home with the season's loot, no doubt. It'll depend on the wind at the bay's end and harbor mouth. I'll wager on a touch near the island."

There was a moment of silence as the captain considered the situation. Then he turned to address the anxious passengers, who were now adjusting to the changes. "Break out your weapons to repel boarders, gentlemen. We may have to fight our way into the safety of the harbor."

> - - - - - - - >

"This will be an occasion to match our skills," said the yuzbasha. "We Khazar think ourselves the best archers in the world." All the men of the ship were on deck fully armed.

"We've defeated Huns, so, you'll have to match your words. Pick your target: deck or shrouds?" said Ozkurt pleasantly.

"No, boys, we'll take all the men on the sails." said the sergeant, "Your uncle and I are not to be cheated of our part. You two take the drum and tiller, there lies the test of skill."

"Tiller," said the Yuzbasha, "it's a long difficult shot. I'll pin him with the first two arrows."

Chavush smiled, "The drummer is closer, but partly hidden in the pit. You'll both be champions if you make it clean."

The women and children had clumped together near the mast, unwilling to go below and miss the action, yet nervously excited by the anticipated clash. Kaya was at the stern with Olga looking at a small metal anchor resting there.

"What is it for?" he asked.

Olga smiled wisely and answered, "It's an anchor to dig into rocks or sand and hold the ship in place or to slow its speed in deep water. She sat on a large stone wrapped in a rope net.

"What's that thing you're sitting on?" he asked.

She pointed to the attached coil of rope at the stern. "It's an anchor weight for a soft bottom, it drags and slows."

"Will this anchor slow the galley?"

She shrugged and with a little laugh said, "Not unless it's attached to the galley. Here's the mate in charge, ask him."

A red bearded giant appeared behind him and immediately took charge. "Ye best go forward to the mast," he said. "I got to ready this deck for defense." Another sailor came up to help.

"Could I have a minute of your time when you're through?" Kaya inquired.

"If there be time, of course."

> - - - - - - - >

As the shore neared, the wind became less forceful, the mountains were blocking it. They passed a scrubby, pine-covered island on the right and entered the bay. The galley, which had trailed behind, now appeared around the island. It was within shouting distance, preparing to ram the cargo vessel. A cry of shock and dismay came from the passengers.

"Surrender or we ram and board," a voice roared. The answer was a flight of arrows from the men of the Sea Witch. Both drummer and steersman fell dead; the galley lagged and veered off course. As arrows were exchanged men fell down from the rigging and the ships sailed parallel for a moment. Grappling hooks flew over the side to the larger ship and pirates heaved on the lines to bring themselves close.

Kaya jumped to cut one rope; Binbasha Alsin cut another and the pulling men fell in a heap. Kaya, with the freed hook in his hand, ran to the ship's stern.

A horn was blown from the peninsula nearest the island. Port security had spotted the fight. They were warning the Aloupka authorities. The port's fort appeared in the distance as the bay narrowed. An answering horn echoed from the docks.

Kaya had the help of the red bearded giant to secure the line. The grappling hook and shortened line thrown by the expert hand of the seaman, caught in the stern of the galley and pulled it toward the heavier cargo vessel's own stern. The oar strokes pulled the line tight between the two ships, sinking its hooks into the wood. The galley was hooked!

A ballista rock, the size of a small keg, splashed into the water just before the bow of the galley, sending a plume of water as high as the mast. Artillery from the fort had just commenced. The galley oarsmen backed water to get out of range, but their tail was tied. The weight and counter motions pulled the galley, reversing quickly, tail first behind the Sea Witch.

Then Kaya and the giant heaved over the anchor rock into the water. The galley's stern dipped when the rock's weight on the line stopped their motion. The galley swamped and slowed. Pirates cut through the anchor rope, but the chance for a quick escape was lost. Screams and curses followed the Sea Witch into harbor. A ballista at the fort sent a rock crashing into the oars, still thrashing in the water beside the struggling galley. Another followed near the stern, the catapults had the range and no more time was spent on useless shouts. Now a small flaming ball of pitch came crashing into the sail of the galley. On contact, the ball collapsed as it slammed into the sail, and a jet of fire exploded from it. A black stain of fire followed the jet down the sail and droplets of flaming tar spread havoc on deck. Another ball of fire followed, but the mass fell among the oars and it exploded and dropped to the water where the oils stuck to any surface or floated away burning. The pirates spent all energy on suppressing the fire and getting out of the bay into the sea and away. They rounded the peninsula with the remaining oars. Friendless, they would scarcely find safety outside their homeland. What they took to be an unexpected stroke of fortune had proved to be their disaster.

The cargo ship, a tortoise transformed into a hare, sailed into the harbor in triumph while everyone cheered. The town turned out to welcome the victims, who owed their lives to them.

> - - - - - - - >

"Can we visit your forts?" was Kaya's first request of the armored guards that lined the dock where the Sea Witch had berthed. The Dock Master conferred with the Captain.

Olga, jumping with excitement, added, "I've seen the ballistas at Kertch. The Lady Merien got us in. She knows all about them." She continued breathlessly, "They have the fire balls too, all the Greek cities do."

"No passengers are allowed to leave without permission of the Dock Master -- not even the captain." the guard responded. "You barbarians must learn to wait for instructions from our authorities. We can't have ignorant people around, poking into everything without supervision."

Ozkurt heard, "Who are you calling ignorant, soldier? Better guard your tongue," he responded heatedly.

Kaya laughed warmly, "He's right friend. We are innocents on the water. I'm just curious." He addressed the soldier, "We are actually very grateful for your protection. The raiders would have overrun us in sight of the port, except for the catapults."

The soldier nodded and sniffed contemptuously. "Your captain is a fool to leave port in winter. We have to suffer the cold for his folly." He rubbed his hands together in the chill, his weight shifting from foot to foot.

Yuzbasha, the Khazar, joined them near the gangway. "The Greeks are tender, like their olive trees, to the cold. They lack the heartiness of the apple." The group laughed.

"But, no, my friends, you are wrong. I, who live in the capital know. Yes, I tell you true. Sometimes snow, she falls on our Golden Horn. So pretty, the snow on the palm trees, no?" Graceful little hands described the action graphically.

Yuzbasha couldn't pass up an opportunity, "When the Volga freezes over, we'll export a bit to you at your harbor Horn. You send some of the Golden to us. *Ta mom?*" Everyone was in a silly mood, so they laughed.

"Come, Olga, I tell the truth, they make the joke, yes? Maybe they never see palm trees? No? We visit captain, yes? Make sure we call on port authority and fort together. More fun than silly friends." Olga was quick to match steps, while Kaya tagged after. Merien called over her shoulder, "Come, Magda, you will feel better on shore."

"Yes, my little dove, but slowly please, remember your poor aunt's week of indisposition." A large, plump matron moved languidly, huge in size under a heavy wool dress, cloak and muff. She sagged and rolled as she walked unsteadily to the gangway down to the dock.

Yuzbasha, chagrined by his put down, leaned over the rail, "Kaya bey would have sunk the pirate's galley if he had used her as the anchor weight." Every one pretended not to hear, but the chaperone looked back for a long minute.

> - - - - - - - >

"The fort commander was so nice to us. No, Magda? He showed us his ballistas. Oh, so impressive! Yes, he let me shoot to the practice range on peninsula. Bomba! The rock she go very high, bang, crash. The missile, she land just so, in target clearing. Olga and Kaya have big eyes, oh, so surprise. Magda, she get dizzy." Merien was seated on her couch while those reclining around her watched with fascination as her hands described each part of the story. All were smiling and laughing pleasantly. Greek music came from one corner of the large room. Plates of cooked grains and meats wrapped in grape or cabbage leaves were brought by servants. Small spits of roasted meats and vegetables were offered to each of the invited guests of the Aloupka city's mayor.

Olga, listening on an adjacent couch, spoke up, "He showed us the fire balls, really leather skins dabbed with pitch and with a little bit of petrol or something inside that becomes steam and breaks out to burn when it hits. The mixture is a secret." Her eyes shone with excitement and her dress, a loan from Merien, was of flowing silk and fine angora wool. Even Magda's bulk was becomingly sheathed in the style of Byzantine ladies. Olga pierced an olive with the small fork shaped like Neptune's trident. She held it up to describe the trajectory of a missile and popped it into her mouth. She ran over to Merien's couch and hugged her. "I think he would have given the secret to us, if Merien had asked for it." All laughed in agreement as the girls sat together hugging; a contrast of hair, eyes and complexions.

"Come with me to Kaya's couch," Merien whispered to Olga, "I want to hear his story and you can play the *duenna*. Magda is too tired." Olga's eyes brightened and her head nodded agreement. She knew enough to want to know more of his quest. They left together for the ladies' room; it would not be seemly to go directly to a young man's couch and the master of ceremonies might make comments. Returning, Olga went directly to speak to Kaya, and Merien, after stopping to speak with Magda, joined her. They stayed so long the Master of Ceremonies noticed and they left reluctantly after his jokes.

"A forfeit or penalty from the ladies for over-long visits. The rest of us are jealous. One lucky young man will spoil with so much attention. Fine or forfeit, one must sing and one may dance. Come now, you're taking too long to decide. Make up your minds! We might each get a kiss if the penalties apply. Let's have the song and dance." The two girls happily consented. Merien sang of the sea: Her song was Sea Fever.

1.   Up anchor and off we go! She blows!
       Feel salt sea spray in our face.
       Soon before the wind we'll race.
       Port behind us, we seek space.
       Set the sails, we'll cut the sea. She blows!

2.   Farewell friends and home folks too. She blows!
       When we return to our place,
       T'will be from far lands by grace,
       Stories rare our journeys trace.
       Wind picks up, we're out of sight. She blows!

3.   In a calm the oars we take. We row.

Beat the drum in cadence pull.
Shed the tunic and the wool.
Burning sun will dry us cruel.
Pray that God will send wind soon. We row.

4.   Breath of evening cools the cheek! She blows!
Thankful then our fast we'll break.
Singing, happy jests we'll make.
Longing, rest by night we'll take.
Good wind bears us down for home. She blows!
She blows, whoosh.

SEA FEVER

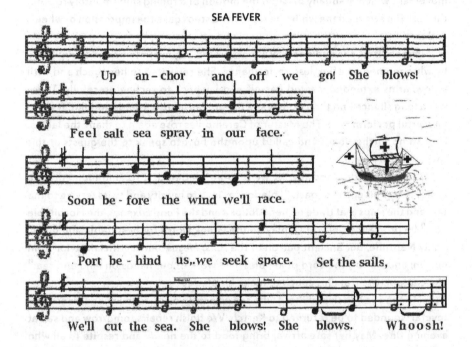

Up an-chor and off we go! She blows!

Feel salt sea spray in our face.

Soon be-fore the wind we'll race.

Port be-hind us, we seek space. Set the sails,

We'll cut the sea. She blows! She blows. Whoosh!

She made the sound of wind by whistling or softly blowing off her hand and illustrated the rowing and other actions. Every one watched her fascinated by her gestures and song. They cheered with enthusiasm as she finished.

The Master of Ceremonies thanked her for the sea voyage, but did not like the rowing part. Exercise, on a full stomach, was bad for the heart, he reported. He also complained of motion sickness which he claimed was bad for digestion.

Olga had gone to Magda's corner couch and that formidable lady had ably taken to readjusting all the necessary tucks that had been made to reduce the dress to Olga's size. The skirt was lengthened to touch the floor and the bell bottom stiffened and the hips enlarged. Now after the applause and admiration expended on Merien subsided, she stepped forward to indicate an eastern melody to the Greek musicians. They started a Georgian song used by many of the varied people of the vast Caucasian region for a stately dance.

Taking tiny mincing steps, unseen under the stiffened skirt, Olga seemed to glide gracefully around the center of the room and around the couches to the Master of Ceremonies and her arms waved slowly. Every action was smooth; without jerks, angles or hurry. It was as if she were mounted on wheels. She advanced toward him and with a brief pause reversed away from him like the rising tide.

She continued the action drawing closer. Then, almost ready to reach out and touch, she melted away and the tide receded. Withdrawing to start a bird-like arm movement which gradually became the motion of a rolling ship smoothly rocking through the swells all the while the rapid little steps gave the impression of wheels and mobility.

Immobilized, the audience lay almost breathless, hypnotized and tranquilized by what seemed an effortless performance. She retreated to her couch and with a bow, arms extended, seated herself and lay back to recline gracefully. There was a long silence and then sighs while the applause rose. Heads nodded; it was a masterful performance. The Master of Ceremonies rose again to thank the ladies. He had no further jokes and called upon the host to speak to the guests at this special victory meal.

The feast ended and thanks were to be rendered; a solemn moment. The mayor raised his cup in a toast. "I pledge my love to my city and to its service to the sea, and the ships that trade on her. Aloupka and the Pont-*Euxenos*, the Hospitable Sea," he proclaimed making a play on the Greek words for hospitable and black. "May Neptune, our ancient patron of the seas; *Hesus*, our sacrificial Savior from our sin; and *Kurios*, the Lord of all, bless the work of our hands on land and sea." The captain rose from his couch to make his pledge.

"To the Sea Witch and those who sail on her. Two are dead in her defense and several wounded to be returned to Kertch. We finish repairs tomorrow and sail at evening tide. May her safe arrival bring food to the needy and respite to all who traffic for life and profits on our smooth yielding waters and its dangers." After the meal the ladies retired, while some of the men went on drinking.

> - - - - - - - >

"*Or'aya bach*, look over there, the island and harbor." Kaya spoke to the cavalcade of horsemen.

Merien called, "I see the ship, how tiny, like a child's toy."

Olga added, "But the people are not dolls, they're fleas, too small." Everyone laughed.

Ozkurt yelled and motioned up. "Last up to the top will lead the horses down."

Yuzbasha raced past him with a ululating cry of victory. All spurred on eager to reach the top of the mountain. The horses had been restless after a week of shipboard and were responding eagerly to the excursion. All were dressed warmly against the mountain chill. Magda had elected to stay in port, which made the young people even happier.

"I can see the other side, I win." yelled Yuzbasha.

"Not so, there's a trail to the very top," answered Ozkurt.

The rivals raced on for the highest point and look-off.

"Let's stop at the next open glade and eat there; I'm tired, cold and hungry," complained Olga.

Merien spread her hands wide to include all. "Here is the land of my people. The Hellenes, Greeks have been here even before the time of the great Alexander; a warm garden by the sea, watered and protected by these mountains."

Kaya looked around carefully from the pine covered peaks to the plain below, "Then you must protect the mountains. The interior is short grass, steppe country for grazers. Put your forts there, below these passes to hold the coasts." He then spoke to Olga, "Go on up, I'll lead the horses back down after." Unnoticed a black dot appeared on the distant horizon.

CRIMEAN MOUNTAIN VIEW

PEOPLE, PLACES & PLOTS IN CHAPTER 14

Altom: the golden horse is admired and coveted.
Binbasha Alsin: commander of a diplomatic mission.
Captain: owner of the Sea Witch faces new challenges.
Chavush: a Khazar on duty to travel to Constantinople.
Kaya: continues west on his quest for his bride.
Koosta: the Hun commander of the Ukraine and Crimea.
Magda: aunt of the Kertch Port governor's daughter.
Merien Papasion: travels to the Golden Horn, her home.
Mark Thorstroom: is left to spy, but persuaded to guide.
Odin Thorstroom: elder brother of Mark loves gain.
Olga: is set on a quest to find her great uncle in the West.
Ozkurt: finds excitement and rivalry on his trip west.
Yuzbasha: a nephew of the commander on mission.

GLOSSARY:

cheush: whoa; stop; halt; for animals.
evit: yes; I agree.
goozelim: my beauty; my pretty thing.
Hesus: the name of Jesus as in Greek.
janum: my lovely, my soul.
jezza olson: there is a fine; punishment is due.
krym: Crimean Peninsula, enters the Black Sea from the north.
yavol: yes, truly; of course; certainly. (German)

THE PIRATES' GALLEY

"You're sure you saw approaching horsemen, Kaya bey? It wasn't a drove of animals for market?" questioned the mayor of Aloupka suspiciously. "We get our meat from both steppe and sea here."

Kaya moved his head up in the negative gesture, "We all saw them after the picnic on the look off. They are about two hours away now. The others went to the ship to tell the captain. The presence of the Khazar officials will bring an attack from the Huns. You will be blamed -- we must leave before they get to the pass and see our departure."

The mayor agreed, "The sea is only the end of land for the Huns. We have avoided occupation because we seem so unimportant.

I'll order the captain to leave, but I must call out the guard, too, as if you have escaped. The vessel can be seen for an hour out to sea."

The ship's bell was clearly heard ringing an alarm and the wharf was a bee hive of activity. Ordered out or not the ship would leave, but the wind was still. No land or sea breeze fanned the sails now being set in the hope of help. Row boats were let down from the ship to act as tugs and without further fanfare the ship moved sluggishly out of harbor. No one waved farewell as the volunteer guards took their posts on wharf and fort.

Near the island a fitful breath of air shook out the sails. The captain ordered the tugs to move out between the island and peninsula and head the Sea Witch south, away from the sheltering coastal mountains. At that moment a fire ball was lobbed from the fort to burst just in the wake of the ship. Another followed, but the fire was blown out in trajectory before hitting the sail. A black tar stain remained as the tarred skin fell to float in the water. After that a stone hit the target area on the peninsula, raising a cloud of dust. The fort was putting on a good show. The watching passengers and crew cheered as the tugs returned to the ship. The sails filled as a chill, yet gentle, west wind moved the cargo ship south into the Black Sea, so much less hospitable than it seemed before. A wisp of high cirrus clouds appeared above them. A change was due in the weather.

A greater change was due in Aloupka as the Hun authorities arrived to assume control of the port. The mayor stood in chains. "I'm informed by the Yalta garrison that this little town has been very active in receiving and dispatching ships this fall. Such activity is unwarranted for an area of farming and fishing. You allowed that boat, rescued by your hand, to escape. *Jezza olson* there is a fine; failure bears punishment. You will in the future bear the expense of a garrison and increased taxation. As punishment a tenth of your villages, fields and boats will be destroyed, and your youth mobilized for the army. We are also to investigate the possibility of direct attack on Khazar and Rume shipping from here by order of Commander Koosta, protector of the Dnieper frontier.

> - - - - - - - >

"I can't understand why we escaped from that fire shot, he hit our sail." Ozkurt exclaimed to Yuzbasha and Kaya.

"A hasty shot usually steadies by the second round," stated Yuzbasha laughing. "So they got our sail, but then, on the third they lost us for the practice field."

Kaya disagreed strongly, "They didn't intend to hurt us. I was at the fort I saw the ballistas working. They shot us a cold round. They didn't want us to burn, they wanted proof that they tried to stop us."

"Exactly, it is so. Yes, we know the commander," Merien insisted heatedly. "The Hun will kill in cold blood if we don't act, no? Proof appears on sail. Poof, black spot shows! Even on mountain top they see." She finished with a flutter.

Olga started, "*Yavol*, yes, truly, the fire balls are delicate. The steam inside is not always manageable. Too hot, they blow up before contact. Too cold, if the fire goes out in the air."

Ozkurt snorted derisively, "It sounds too dangerous to use at all. Give me a composite, recurved bow and bone shaft arrows for accuracy and power." All the men nodded in agreement. Tradition was safer than new unreliable toys: foolish innovations. Only Kaya seemed less decisive.

Yuzbasha noticed this and quipped before them all, sarcastically. "How many kills did you score before you started making a splash by throwing stones, Kaya bey?"

Kaya smiled modestly, "I wounded two in the legs, I think. They sat down hard. I cut the grapple and used my time on the anchor stone to make a big splash. How did you score?" Everyone knew that answer. He bragged about it constantly for two days as he and Ozkurt competed. Their rivalry had become intense, but Merien now favored Kaya with attention and conversation. He was jealous.

"You seem reluctant to kill for our protection," Yuzbasha accused.

Kaya nodded in agreement, smiling. "*Evet*, yes, because the wounded help us more, by impeding the effectiveness of the attackers. They cause distraction and lower morale of those still fighting. Dead men only anger those still fighting and cause revenge to animate them."

"Dead men can't fight any more; the wounded can."

"The wounded need attention and distract those fighting."

"That's a coward's argument."

Ozkurt was spurred into opposition. "Kaya has even challenged a tiger with a wooden club when it attacked his herd. We fought Huns together. He is as brave as I. My score is as large as yours." The two were faced off, glaring.

"The Huns massacred yours at the Donetz." Yuzbasha replied hoarsely.

Then, stepping between them, Merien spoke up, "You men are such brave protectors, no? You will guard us from the enemy, but here we are all friends, yes? Friends must not quarrel. Come Olga, Kaya, let us go up to see the captain together. The weather she change again, no?" They left with the two rivals chagrined, but trailing behind. The captain confirmed their fears. Within an hour all were forced to walk with care, the wind had changed and the sea was rough.

"I thought I had gotten over my dizziness the first day, but I don't feel like staying on deck," Ozkurt stated. Olga came over to help him go below. Kaya took his friend's side and they got him installed in the bunk with a potty near his head.

He moaned, "How do you and Olga manage to avoid this?"

BALLISTA'S FINAL SHOT.

Olga laughed, "Opa used to say I was cradled in our boat from the first week of my life. We fished and farmed between the sea and the high mountains. There was no other way to live."

Kaya chuckled as he offered his view-point. "Bears fish a lot, but, also, they walk with a seaman's roll. It must be the reason why it doesn't bother me."

Ozkurt sighed as he struggled to sit up in the bunk. "Promise you'll not bury me at sea. When I die, let me be buried on land." They agreed, trying to keep a solemn look, between snickers.

The Sea Witch sped south without knowing the results of their Crimean stop-over. They were too far away now to see the smoke of some villages burning. Clouds swept in from the east on cold winds that caused sea mists to form in wraiths of obscurity. The waves were mounting higher and the sail was taken in and the ship was faced east and anchors were dropped to ride the wild, blustery torment. The storm drove them on.

The anxious captain groaned, "We have escaped the frying pan, to fall into the fire. In port we would be safe. Now, we must pray and out-last it." The sailors worked doggedly, with one ear cocked, listening for breakers on the western shore. The wind and current bore them northwest.

>------->

"Land ho, on the horizon -- low flat country," came the cry from the mast lookout. All who braved the biting winds looked carefully at the frost-filled white and brown line just in sight. They shuddered. It was better than ship wreck, but there was no joy in their salvation from the relentless wind and current. Here, unlike their last port, there would be no temperate, hospitable place of refuge.

"I judge it to be the mouths of the Danube River," said the captain. "We will turn and make way in, when we spot a wide or deep mouth. We must avoid sand bars."

"Ship Ahoy, to the north, oars out, heading for a deep channel." Eyes from the deck strained to see. "It looks like the galley, no rigging or mast visible. Now, she's into the channel going out of sight." The others caught only a glimpse of what the lookout saw.

The captain shouted. "Come down now, I need fresh eyes to find us a safe landing." He motioned to the red bearded giant. "Up you go, my lad, you'll land us safe I'll wager."

Yuzbasha said, "This will be their repair base and summer home. They can swoop down on the traffic of almost every port from here."

Ozkurt, looking pale and weak, objected, "Their homeland is on the opposite coast. Why come here?" Clinging to the mast, he shivered in the cold.

"The west wind is the rule on this sea," replied Kaya. "They take advantage of the fact. I understand that their land is like Crimea only wetter; they must be home-sick now."

"Aye, that they must be, but I wish them nothing but misery for the damage they do us each year. The swamp land here is not controlled by the Huns or any authority," the captain stated vigorously. "It's filled with refugees and law-breakers. We will double the guard while here and get out as soon as we can." The passengers nodded gladly.

"View ahoy, a deep mouth due west, the wind'll bear us in, Sir."

The captain frowned for a moment then shouted. "Bosun, get all hands on deck, up anchors, break out the jib. We'll not back in like an old cow into a stall." The icy deck was suddenly filled with men pulling on the anchor ropes.

"Heave ho, mi lads, give it a grunt now," shouted the boson. "Together now, fore and aft look alive, heave now, heave, pull me hearties, up anchors. We'll soon be out of this bloomin, icy blow for extra rations and a warm berth, when we snug her down."

The captain's voice ordered men about like a puppeteer moving his puppets. "You men up front get that jib set. Tiller hard over, we're coming round. Hang on for a flying entrance, gentlemen." Each crewman had a function, a role to play, like a part of machinery or organism that pulsated with artificial life. The freed ship moved into a Danube mouth with men forward throwing a measure weight to warn of depths and sand bars.

> - - - - - - >

"Your last dispatch to the Khan must be in his hands now, Uncle." Yuzbasha questioned at the family gathering on the bow. Binbasha Alsin assured him that all was as planned. "You can be sure all is in motion to build the boats. The landing in Aloupka was an unexpected bonus. We saw, first hand, that they are lightly guarded and that the climate is rather mild. Conquest should be easy, but Koosta may buy peace with Byzantium by giving them the Krym ports. They are one people and their history and culture relate. We must prevent that until the spring invasion starts. Kertch port is ready to surrender the moment sufficient troops are present to repulse any attempt of occupation by the Huns. The governor has sent his daughter and sister away with us just in case Koosta does something from the Donetz River base. That, of course, is our first objective to be taken by a boat landing on the Azov side below, and an army moving south from The Bend. A threat to the Dnieper line will keep Koosta spread defensively and assure light occupation elsewhere. He is stimulating commerce on the river, and the building of the new base is causing vast imports of lumber. Their grain and lumber trade with the empire will promote Hun attempts at peace."

Chavush agreed. "They will paint us as the barbaric threat to their own territories. We must demonstrate our ability to repopulate, stimulate trade and rebuild with those willing to receive our troops. We must do nothing that will upset Rume's opinion of us as allies."

Alsin resumed the lecture, "Which means, Yuzbasha, that you must keep your head about this girl. You must not fight with the easterners or provoke dislike by the Rumans. You will want to marry into one of the noble families of Khazars to assure your success as a commander. Careers and marriage are usually closely related. It's an important thing to remember when you're young and impetuous."

Yuzbasha replied, "I'm perfectly able to handle the two Chipchaks, and my plans for the girl don't include marriage. But tell me why I should tolerate those two criminals. They were jailed and exiled by our Khan."

General Alsin laughed, "Because they are protected by our Khan for the son, Prince Ilkin's sake. The wife finances them and she will bear an heir to the Khan's delight. Our interests are with another younger son, who rewards us for our help, but we must be careful. There must be no blood on our hands, there are other ways. Our patron will not want the prince to be represented in Constantinople. But hush, someone's coming." Kaya approached the men at the ship's bow.

"We have the captain's permission to take the horses ashore for exercise and salt grass. Would you join us?"

"I'll gladly go," exclaimed Yuzbasha, now tired of the talks. "You'll go too, Chavush?"

Only Alsin objected. "I've an important dispatch to write. We must record the pirates' base on the channel north of here. The Byzantines will also want to know. It will be a good basis to start our sharing of commercial interests."

> - - - - - - - >

"Let's go ashore, Magda, you do so much better on land, no? I'll fix a basket for an excursion with our friends."

"As you wish my little dove, but frankly I've no liking for the Khazars. For all their vaunted tolerance, these horsemen are barbarians resembling the Huns far too much for my taste."

Merien gave a little laugh and shook her head. "They will help father's resistance to Hunnish demands and protect commerce. That is certainly different from the Hun's disruptions, no?"

Magda shrugged her shoulders, "The Huns too, show more concern for trade and gain in ways other than destruction and expropriation. They learn on long contact with civilization. Even the barbarians learn, Merien."

Her answer was a trilling laugh. "We must be their teachers, yes, Magda? I would like to instruct a certain young stranger in the ways of love."

"Your father will be offended. He has political hopes in view by an alliance. Your husband-to-be will not like an early affair to shadow your value as mother and wife."

"You are so serious, Magda. We speak of possibilities, not certainties, yes? The magic of might be; not the surety of will be. It's an opportunity to test the human spirit, no?"

"You adventure at risk, I warn you as an aunt should."

"Noted my dearest, for confession, should it be needed, but for the moment an excursion on the island fits the bill."

> - - - - - - - >

Tall grass and brush covered the soggy soil of the nearby islands. The maze of water and land continued miles up the river where salt and fresh mingled in the slight ebb and flow of the sea's tides. The Sea Witch had anchored where the channel narrowed and the bottom was scarcely detected. The ship nestled on a mat of green reeds which cushioned the margins of the island. A long gangway bridged from ship to shore. A descent down the hollow sounding boards took the animals to the safety of the shore. Wood was sought for repairs. Ozkurt brought their baggage ashore to air. Olga explored the large island on foot while the men staked out the horses. Merien and Magda watched the activity as they selected a high, sandy, drier area for the picnic blanket and plates. After which, Magda found shade from the sun and shelter from the cold wind. Merien, however, walked to the circle that Altom made on the marsh, as she was allowed to run at tether length around Kaya.

He shouted encouragement. "*Git, goozelim*, go, my beauty, run hard, the air is cold and the sun warm. What a day for a run!

A MAIDEN'S APPEAL

- 171 -

Gel, janum, come, my lovely, show your best."

Merien waited until the horse passed her and ran to Kaya. She ducked under the taunt leash as it passed by over her head. She laughed with glee as the horse's run continued. Kaya, then, alternately faced her and turned away following with face and eyes watching the movement of the horse.

"It's a game like skip rope, no? Only, it hurts more if you get caught by the rope, yes? I like games with risks. Altom is the lucky one, no? She is loved and pampered." Kaya's answer was a laugh of exhilaration. She continued, "Will you also take such care of a girl you love? Yes? Suppose the one you seek is married and with children. Will you take her from the man? No? It's like being caught with the rope and hurt, yes. Very sad, when the heart hurts. I bring you a gift to remember: wood from the Mount of Olives, so you don't forget." She slipped the cross with a thong over his head and dodged the rope as he continued to turn. "You come back to the Golden Horn. There is medicine I have, yes? It will wait for you there. No? I'll show you our house in the city. We have a country house too. You see them next week, when we get there. Yes, I'll show you, so you can come back, if you're hurt." She was crouched below him, eyes upon his face, ducking and standing as he turned with the motion of the horse. If he heard, he gave no indication. Then he slacked speed.

"*Cheush,* whoa," he shouted, and the leash went slack. "You've had enough, you beauty. Better things wait for you. Rest a bit, you're too worked up now. Travel lies ahead of you. *Soos,* quiet, enjoy the moment. Tanra gives recovery and rest to the weary. Trust him. Things will be different later, you'll see. You must rest quietly now." He walked forward to the horse, leaving the girl listening to his patter as if it were meant for her alone. Above, Magda came into the sunshine shivering and calling them. "Let's eat and get back on the ship, it's too cold for this kind of excursion." Every one gathered, but the mood was quiet as they ate the lunch together.

> - - - - - - - >

In a thick willow stand Olga heard a boat approach the place where she stood. Someone spoke in a foreign tongue, neither Greek nor Hunnish, yet she understood his meaning! It was her family's language. A punt approached and two men talked.

"I'll be back just before dark. See how much damage they have and when they are ready for sailing. Stay out of sight and don't get caught. The Ahbakanies pay good for a job well done." The listener was a boy of ten or twelve who seemed reluctant to embark on the venture. The man stood with pole in hand holding the boat to the bank and the boy jumped over and held to the willow stems as the man backed the punt away and set a course west, up river.

"If you'll stay and talk I'll keep quiet, but if you run, I'll scream and they'll hunt you down." Olga spoke quietly in Gothic and the boy froze in position looking for her.

"Where are you?" he asked softly. "Show yourself."

"I'm hidden like you are; but I can get men with weapons here very fast if you don't stay and talk," she whispered.

"You speak our language. You're not of the outsiders. Why help them?" he asked.

She thought hard on his question. "Why do you help the Ahbakanie? They're not our people."

"They got money and let us work on the repairs. I don't like them, but the money helps." She smiled at this answer.

"I like the people I travel with; they're honest and good." She moved forward, "I'll keep your presence a secret and you can get your money, but you must talk to me. I have a knife here, so you mustn't act like the pirates."

His voice rose in hot indignation. She saw he was younger and smaller. "You don't need a knife with me. I'm not wild." He did look wild, but she couldn't tell him that.

She asked, "Do you know any old men, Ostrogoths, from the old Ukraine, with a scared face? His name is Fritz." She slowly continued to move toward him through the bare willow stems. He had found a log, perhaps washed ashore in a storm, to sit on. She came over and sat facing him.

"Not here, not from the old country, but there be folks up in the mountains. They're like that, battle scars and all."

"I want to go where they are. I have friends who will go with me. Would your people let us pass? Even show us the way? We could pay. I have a silver coin from my boat."

"You have your own boat?" He was impressed.

"Yes, it was our family's boat, but I sold it to get here. My name is Olga. My friends are Kaya and Ozkurt."

"My name is Mark Thorstroom my brother is Odin. I can ask my brother, he knows all the people around here and he'll do anything for silver."

She changed topics, "Why do the pirates want to know about the ship? What do they plan to do?"

He looked uncomfortable, "They want to catch you, when you leave the river, and take you back with them to their country." He blurted hastily. "They blame the Sea Witch for damage to oars and mast and the storm for driving them back here to the old base camp. In two days they'll be ready to take you, but they don't want to get near the Bosphorus water, there be war ships on patrol near there." There was a sound nearby.

"Have you found a friend, Olga?" Kaya's voice was soft.

"Yes, he is a fellow countryman who may know how to get us off the island and on the west road." She answered in Hunnish. Then in Gothic she said "This is a man you can trust completely, he will help you and pay well."

"You're sure of him? He's not a Hun?" the boy asked.

"He is the opposite of them." She replied, still in Gothic.

"Give me the silver for my brother and I'll persuade him. I'll tell the pirates you'll leave tomorrow evening. Is that alright?"

She gave Mark her silver coin. He tucked it away and said, "You are in the southern mouth of the river, the galley is in the middle stream. You can outrun them if you lay on all canvas and take the night wind. It's strongest toward the dawn."

She nodded agreement and added, "I was brought up with boats and water, but how do we get the horses off the island? The river is too wide to swim them across."

Kaya walked to the water's edge and looked up stream to the west. Mark shifted to watch him carefully, while he answered her query. "There's another island just above this one the next channels are low and easy to cross. There are two islands and channels to cross before you can get to higher, drier ground, but if you go toward Constanza you'll meet Huns. They always attack delta people, just like they do in the mountains."

"We want to get to the mountains first," she said, "then after that we'll worry about Huns."

Kaya turned to look. "What did he say?"

She told him in Hunnish and he agreed, "We will have to leave before dark. We mustn't cross in the dark. We must tell the captain so the ship moves as soon as it's dark." He placed his finger on his lips in a sign for silence, and went off to seek Ozkurt. Then they both followed the passengers to the ship and Ozkurt sought the captain to warn him of the danger.

"You must take the ship out tonight. You can leave here after the spy meets his brother. He must see the ship and have news for the pirates to get his job done tonight, and put them at ease. Otherwise they will be suspicious."

> - - - - - - - >

"You must accompany us across the two islands, Mark. Then you come back to meet your brother. We'll meet you tomorrow up river, so you can take us to the mountains. Bring a horse. We'll pay your price there." Kaya spoke slowly, but Olga said it off quickly in her family's language and the boy led the way. It was slow, hard work moving through brush and cold water, but they got there. They made camp close to the water while Mark returned to meet his brother. Odin was late, and didn't bother to get closer to the ship.

Yuzbasha and Chavush were bringing in their three horses and Merien stood on deck watching the return of the last arrivals. She ran to Yuzbasha and complained loudly, grabbing his arm. His gaze held contempt.

"Where is Olga? I haven't seen her since lunch." The words tumbled out. He sneered, staring down at her.

"Is it her you're worried about or another?"

She huffed, "Where are the other horses?" ignoring his query, her face reflecting concern.

"Why should you care for the stupid easterner? You had better offers." He persisted, grabbing her arms. She twisted away to free herself. Noise came from the ship's side as the sailors pulled in the gangway. All was noise and distraction as the ship cast off and the girl squealed.

Yuzbasha attempted to silence her with a kiss. Merien's call was a muffled shout and a great arm reached around the throat of Yuzbasha and a hard voice grated into his ear. The giant form of the red bearded mate lifted the man. "Release her or feel the water over your head." Attention focused on the struggle. Magda appeared to embrace Merien, almost pushing the two men overboard.

Benbasha Alsin intervened quickly, "Go below, nephew, and don't leave the cabin until we arrive at the city." He turned to address Magda, "My apology to your brother, Madam, the boy will be punished, assure him of that." The mate released the youth and then moved to confront the weeping girl.

"Your pardon, lady, the other passengers won't be going with us. Kaya bey sent his regrets, he said that he has a quest and remembers your kindness. They leave their uniforms to the general. The girl, Olga, leaves her many presents from yourself for another whom you will befriend. Ozkurt bey sends this silver fish for a chain to remember them." The tiny, shining, fish-like form was composed of jointed segments that could move.

She thought. 'But the one I wanted got away.'

The ship was gathering speed now, under the steady power of the west wind and the land breeze from the mountains.

> - - - - - - - >

"There be a ferry here to cross de Danube," Mark reported in Hunnish, with difficulty. "A drachma should pay our way and get change you need later. Huns don't come here, this deep in swamps is dangerous for them." Then he and Olga went into a lot of chatter that only they understood.

Olga stated to the others, "The best way to the mountains is to go north of the Buz River where another shorter stream goes directly up. Then in the high country you go through the upper Buz to the Ult River, where the Rumans live. You follow up stream to the highest peaks and beyond. The Goths live in the high country scattered in the woods." She stopped and they talked more before she concluded.

"The sheep are off the high alpine meadows because of the snow. The woods are sometimes open, but sometimes snowed up. There are not enough women for the Goths, so some marry Ruman women. Retired soldiers - many are Goths - come from the empire to take land and marry their neighbors' girls. But the Huns changed that and rule the people harshly. They take boys for military service and tax people heavily."

Ozkurt and Kaya exchanged looks and asked, "Does he know where the patrols ride? How can we avoid them?" She and Mark took longer on this one.

"Patrols are constant on the north to south roads between the delta swamps and the mountains. We'll pass over them by night. No trouble, he says, we always do it. His brother Odin is to meet us there." They looked doubtful, but there was no other recourse but to go on.

"Is your family Christian, Mark?" Kaya asked.

Olga spoke to him at length and reported the story. "He says that his mother is Christian, but his brother is from his father's first wife and he keeps the old ways. Mark works with his brother for money, but they don't live at home any more. The swamps are dangerous, but more money is made there. Mark will take us up to his father's house, but Odin won't go there."

Ozkurt asked the question, "Are you and your brother able to visit villages? Move around freely?" The answer was a cautious yes.

"You're not considered enemies of the Huns?" The answer was a shrug. Kaya took up the line of questions.

"Do the Huns give rewards for information?" The boy looked angry now, and walked ahead of the group.

> - - - - - - - >

"Come my dove, you've prayed long enough. *Hesus* forgives, when we ask it from the heart, and the Virgin is tired of your complaints." Magda observed, "Marriage and heavy family responsibilities come soon enough. Don't try to do things too fast. Life will go quickly enough anyway."

Merien, still kneeling, looked up at her icon and sighed loudly. "I didn't know kind words could hurt so much. He spoke to us both, the mare and the forward girl. Yes. A barbarian showed mercy to a headstrong fool of a girl. No?"

"You said we must teach, Merien, but one who teaches learns more, dear. Your encounter with the young fool, Yuzbasha, is more important, for your father will hear of it. The Khazars are the growing power on our sea. We must not offend them or trust them overmuch. They wish to win the north side of our sea and our ancient posts in Crimea are in danger. Your father balances on the knife's edge."

"I'll pray for him while I'm about it," she paused, "I'll be civil to that brash boy, but he'll get no smiles from me."

"I doubt that you'll see him again, dear. The Uncle is anxious for the favor of the Emperor. Diplomacy always hides dirty laundry."

Magda busied herself with folding clothes. "Will you keep the silver fish from Ozkurt bey? He was certainly impressed by your beauty."

Merien laughed now, "He was nice and so loyal to his friend. Yes? I'll keep it to remember them by." The ship lurched as the tack was changed. Now the Sea Witch sailed south to the city.

> - - - - - - - >

"Is this the village where we're to meet Odin?" Olga asked Mark, "It looks deserted." They stared into the gloom wishing for the moon or some light to brighten their way as they walked forward leading their horses. They stopped in the mist.

"It's too quiet, something's wrong." Kaya whispered. "I smell horses but don't hear them. They're being muffled."

"I have my knife in your back, Mark, so don't try to run," Olga hissed, "Your brother intended to sell us out, didn't he?" Mark Thorstrom said nothing, but their horse's ears were cocked forward, listening. Ahead a horse whinnied beyond the village.

ENCOUNTER AT THE CAPE

PEOPLE, PLACES & PLOTS IN CHAPTER 15

Alsin: the General loses documents in the Danube Delta.
Chavush: attempts to trace suspects.
Evran: is a suspicious general whose name means dragon.
Gochen: seeks advancement at the Don River bend.
Hans Marker: a young warrior, eager for fame and revenge.
Kaya: perseveres in his quest taking the name Aya.
Magda: comforts her niece and readies for their arrival home.
Merien Papasian: feels regrets over the voyage and loss of friends.
Mark Thorstroom: guides, yet leads his friends astray.
Olga: continues to seek her lost Uncle among the Goths.
Ozkurt: slogs on, shortening his name to Kurt: Wolf.
Ship's boy: back from the trip gives news of Kertch Port.
Wolfgang: a messenger boy sent to warn the mountain Goths.
Yuzbasha the Khazar: hopes for new opportunities in the city.

GLOSSARY:

bailer: gentlemen; my dear sirs.
boo tarafa' gel: come this way; come over here.
dekot: careful; watch out; attention; precaution.
duy-doon mu? did you hear that?; feel it?; sense it?
effen'di: Lord; sir; used as, pardon? when something is not heard.
er'dash: fellow soldier; comrade: trooper.
gel: come; come on; come here.
ha'at: a net; network; system of roads and routes.
hazur ole: ready; prepared; be ready; are you ready?
ismim: my name is ___; I'm called_____
kah'ret-sin: curse it; damn it; hell, man.
kyoo' ni fe, man'ta, and pot'la jan : luxury foods.
olabilir: possibly; it could be; perhaps.
oraya bach: look over there; see there.
pa paz': a Christian priest.
Tanra-ya teshekur: thanks be to God; thank God.
yol achen: open the road; get out of the way.

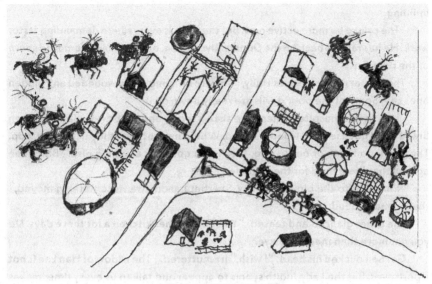

A TRAP IN PEACE VILLAGE

"*Dekot*, pay attention! Make way boy! Don't crowd a lieutenant in the bath house. I have to visit the Estate and see the Lady Judith." The giant Gochen proclaimed at the door.

The ship's boy hastily drew aside to avoid the big man. The boy was now considered too old to go during the women and children's hours, but he was still careful around the many garrison men who came early. He resented the juvenile treatment meted out by some of the crude men.

"Wait now, aren't you the ship's boy?" the loud voice of Gochen came again. "You be back from the port with news?" The boy, speechless, nodded agreement. "What happened to the easterner, Ozkurt? He went there with the mare."

The boy gulped and found his voice. "He be some sick on de river and he stay at de Golden Fleece till he recover good. Khazar officers make friends for trip to de city on Sea Witch. Dey wait for dat Kaya."

"I never seen such lucky people. I learnt lots from them. They acts weak and timid, lettin' other folks get their way, even helpin' the hurtin'. They must do somethin' right. I try to do like they did. I even go to church, but I don't really understand much yet. But I got friends here to help, now."

Gochen stood blocking the door to the public bath. A man stopped behind him and spoke. "*Yol achen*, get out of the way, Yuzbasha. I ain't got all day, while you jaw with that kid."

Gochen smiled and stepped aside. The ship's boy used the action to escape inside the door, while Gochen followed the soldier to swap news about the boat building.

"The prince be more active now. But the Khan is everywhere demanding faster work. He has raiders back on the Donetz River again. but they haven't moved south of the river yet."

The soldier nodded respectfully, "They're bringing in the wounded and hidden ones still. Some of the poor devils are really down on it."

"I go by the hospital, where the sisters work, and visit every day," Gochen bragged. "I got a few old troopers hired. When they get well, they'll join my troop. The rest'll go home or out to beg, they're no good for anything else." Both men agreed that life is hard for the wounded.

"I'm to go to the big house now. Sherbet hanum, wants something moved," the big man added.

The other glanced and teased, "You get into her kitchen a lot these days. Do you get more than meets the eye?"

Gochen ducked his head, "I wish," he muttered. "The widow of Han Lee is not a push over. But the Lady Judith seems to appear and talk to us every time; makes me feel like I'm really welcome, even when Sherbet is cranky."

The soldier waved him off. "You go over to the high and mighty, while I drill and build, work and exercise. Some men get all the luck."

"Some men make their luck," Gochen said as he left.

> - - - - - - - >

"*Boo tarafa gel*, come this way," Kaya whispered, "Remember the proverb: 'Whoever puts their trust in the Lord shall be safe.'" They led their horses left, away from the village, down the crossroad west, holding their mounts noses so they wouldn't snort or whinny. A light flared beyond the village and a horseman with a torch upheld started moving down a line of men where more torches flared. Each shared his light with another. A similar light was suddenly displayed behind them on the trail where they had entered the crossroad. Ahead of them two horses were running down the road toward them in the dark. A reckless and frightening thing to do! They quickly parted and pulled their animals to the side where bushes brushed them. In a flash, two forms went racing past to pull up at the crossroad and stop. Two torches were lit to help form the circle that now surrounded the village. Another racing horse came toward them, and they froze in the increasing light as a man, now more clearly seen, raced his horse to join his companions. The late arrival shouted an order.

Quickly Kaya moved to get away from the brightening light. They now moved single file up the road. Even as they ran, the light grew as fire was put to the little houses that formed the village core. The barking of dogs and the scream of women and children echoed as a few villagers fought to escape the doomed barns and houses. The Huns killed everyone, including the animals. But the dazzling light dulled the eyes of those watchers, so they did not see the forms moving away in the dark on the west road.

The boy, Mark, remained quiet until they had distanced themselves from the burning village. Then, he sobbed in broken Hunnish, "It wasn't me, Odin thought you would be worth more than silver to the Huns. He didn't tell me where they would wait, but I knew it had to be around here. We had friends in the village. He's gotten them all killed." No one answered him. "I'll take you home now, he won't dare go there."

Olga sniffed contemptuously as they mounted to move quietly westward. "Why should we trust you now? He'll have a party of Huns waiting there too."

The boy's voice carried anger. "He'd be a marked man, if he hurt our father. The Goths would kill him."

Ozkurt turned to Kaya and asked, "Why did you lead us west?"

Kaya chuckled. "Any animal will run to safety on known trails, not in new directions. They'll hunker down and hide if they can't run. The Huns would expect us to do the same and run for the swamps. They'll reinforce that side."

"So they expected us to panic and run back?"

"Certainly, they burned the village to make sure we didn't hide. They control the roads and presume we won't go there. For us it's the only way to the heart of the empire and Munzur Khan's presence."

Olga looked at them hard, "So you are going to befriend the Huns?"

Kaya agreed, "We must seem like others to pass their territory. You must be the slaves and we'll get you home free," he quipped. "Odin has never seen us and will only have what Mark told him."

Olga transferred her glare to Mark. "And how much did you tell about us, Mark," she started in Gothic. A long angry discussion followed.

>- - - - - - - >

"You're sure it was our village, Hans?" the boy, Wolfgang, asked.

"What would you say?" the man replied in Gothic.

"I didn't want it to be ours." The voice held a sob.

"They intend to exterminate us. Their submission gave them no security at all. I told them it wouldn't help them."

"They paid the tax and gave up their boys for soldiers. Why would the Huns burn them out?"

Hans' harsh laugh was angry and he drew himself up to spit down the slope. "We fight for freedom in the mountains and in the swamps of the delta. The Huns can never accept anything but a slave's abject groveling. We offend their pride, because they desire to control and play God. They hate our ability to survive their brutal rule. They want to enslave us like the Rumans here."

"But what can we do? We're scattered across the peaks and forests and are separated from the delta people by the roads and troops." The man cupped the boy's face and smiled.

"We can die for freedom Wolfgang, run risk for contact, and brave dangers for solidarity with our people. We can inspire others by our brave liberty. We will not be slaves. You saw the burning of slaves last night. It meant nothing to the Huns. Our attack next week will mean much to them. We will cut them off at the direct road to their devil Khan. We will slaughter all who seek to pass through our mountains. Mountains of Goths will oppose them. God in heaven will remember our efforts and there will always be our people here in these mountains He has given us for protection."

"But the Rumans help them," Wolfgang protested.

WATCHING BARISH BURN

"They obey only when they are sure of the situation. Rumans pause to wait and see when the outcome in not clear. Some share our blood and our desires. They will pause, even if hurt is threatened by the Huns." Hans stood, and gathering his weapons turned his back on the mountain overlook. "We must gather the army to attack Ruggenfurt. Come, you know the route you must take to spread the news. The planned moment has arrived with the offence to be avenged."

> - - - - - - - >

"*Oraya bach*, look over there," Olga shouted, pointing. A column of riders appeared, leisurely moving south along the road they were approaching.

Mark's voice rose, "Huns, run! They're soldiers!" He spurred his black horse into a gallop. Kaya raced his Altom after the boy and soon caught him. He returned to Ozkurt and Olga leading Mark by the reins of his horse. Moving ahead of them, he hailed the leader of the column who had calmly watched the action on the hill. Mark's face showed tears and terror.

"We are messengers from the Ukraine. The boy has misled us and tried to get away." The man looked coldly at them and motioned them to his side in a haughty manner.

"These scum are not worth the price of a slave, even. They should be exterminated. Why do you keep them?"

"We needed a guide and the girl is a good cook."

"Be careful lest she poison you. They do it with mushrooms and roots. What are your names *beylerim*?"

"*Ismim*, my name is Aya and my friend is Kurt."

"Mine is Benbasha Evran. *Ha'at Effendi*, Lord of the net of roads. So, by your names, I conclude that I have a bear and a wolf of the Ukraine passing through the land of the dragon."

Kaya smiled broadly at the jest and Ozkurt rode closer to salute with a bow. "You have, no doubt, heard of the battle at the Donitz River? We were present there during the hard fought battle."

The general smiled his satisfaction for the first time and warmed slightly as they continued southward. "Building on the new base progresses well, I trust."

"We saw little of it, my Lord. We saw the old base burn, but we have been traveling since that fight," Kaya replied.

The general nodded understandingly. "There are more battles shaping up. The Khazars rape and rob endlessly. Barbarians must be resisted. You are on Koosta's staff then?" Ozkurt exchanged glances with Kaya to say, "We were more associated with Han Lee, his adjutant."

"They are all men of the left hand armies, even as you are. Correct?"

Ozkurt answered this query carefully, "We have come from the far east with Koosta leading our way. We have followed him until our service there, in the Ukraine. Now, we seek the capital with much important information."

The general inspected them closely. "This is why you have no insignias, your present task is to return with dispatches and letters? I notice your friend, the bear, wears a tribal badge and the symbol of the Christians. Is this true? I have met so few among our people, although, there are enough of them among the local people."

Ozkurt bore on, "There are Christians among the tribe where my friend lived. I have been under his influence and find it uplifting in times of trouble. We have needed stamina. My Lord will not believe what we have suffered to fulfill our task. We have lost many things in all we have endured with the promise of more to come."

The general laughed, "It is the cost of duty and greatness. Which road do you follow across the mountains?"

Ozkurt was now bold, "We thought the boy would know, so, he led us in the swamp. Now, we seek our way to the west."

"You must be careful. There are rebels and robbers in the mountains. You should seek a larger party to pass there. In fact, you would do better to go south. Follow the Danube to the Iron Gate and pass there into the edge of the plains. It's longer but safer."

Ozkurt's head jerked up, "Impossible, time is pressing and we must seek speed over safety."

General Evran smiled now, agreeing. "I'll dispatch a squad and my onbasha with provisions to speed you on your way. He will get you to the pass. You will have to do the descent alone or with another squad."

"*Tanraya teshekur*, thanks to God," interjected Kaya," now we are sure of a safe arrival. We will praise your name to Khan Munzur. May he repay you a thousand times over."

"I regret that they can't continue all the way, but I need my men back here without delay. There are reports of an enemy ship from the Crimea here."

Kaya countered, "Pardon, my Lord, but troops of Huns occupy that land. How could there be any but trade ships from there?"

"The reports are inconclusive and from unreliable sources, so we can't be sure. We must always be vigilant to protect ourselves from attack or subversion."

"Probably they're survivors of our recent storms, My Lord, wrecked or driven ashore," Kaya insisted.

"*Olabilir*, possibly, we are checking all the information now. Men are rewarded for accuracy and punished for lies. I'm awaiting reports from a village east of here. We'll stop for the night, soon, at a little town ahead. You will feast with me tonight and in the morning you will travel west and we south. But I want to hear more of your stories of the fighting."

Ozkurt laughed loudly. "You'll get your fill tonight, I promise you."

"Look my dove, there is a war galley at the Bosphorus mouth. We are safely home in a few hours. The City waits."

"Safe, but alone, Magda. Father and friends are far away, no?"

The aunt studied her niece carefully and resolved to speak to her brother, the father, about the need to move forward on his marriage project. She decided on a policy of distraction. She pulled her arm away from the rail, "Come, we must choose the clothes to wear as we disembark and go home. Your brother will be beside himself with joy. He will tease you forever if you are out of style or distraught in any way."

On deck the new Khazar ambassador scanned the landscape, but could not keep his mind from his loss.

"*Kah' ret sin*, damn it Chavush. I was reading the instructions from Kinner and from our patron. I left at the captain's call. Ozkurt was there with news. Kaya was leading the horses away. I stayed above talking, but the papers were gone when we cleared the river. Who has done this to us?" He stared at the blue waters of the Bosphorus.

"You have the letter to the Emperor, it's all you need."

"The letter from our patron could be used against us; but who could have it?" the general insisted. Chavush shrugged.

Below deck Yuzbasha, observed the villas and roads along the waterway. It had an opulence and strangeness that promised compensation for his chagrined arrival. As the new power in the north, the Khazars would rate deference and, for him, opportunities for distraction.

> - - - - - - - >

"You will forgive my frankness when I say I don't trust your commander Koosta. He is a new recruit from the Far East and is a novice to the changes we make in our execution of war and terror as policy in the west. Since you are from that far region I don't expect you to agree." General Evran stated in an aside to Kaya or Aya as he was being called. Aya, seated on the binbasha's left, agreed amiably and explained their situation.

"I've had a number of conflicts with Koosta, short thumb, from school days to the present. Han Lee reported that he left my breast mate and foster sister in the capital to gain favor with the royal house. This is another reason why I'm impatient to get there with the messages and documents we carry."

Evran smiled agreeably. "I heard reports of a fiery-haired beauty in the forbidden area, the harem. Our Khan has the best selection in the world. My wife would poison any I brought home, or even me, if she felt threatened or frustrated. She vows to rule alone, so I let her." He laughed and did not seem to feel defrauded.

The general and his guests sat on a raised platform on a bench with a low table before them. It was covered with foods for the expected governor's garrison, who sat on benches one level below them. Their food was soldiers' fare and little extras accumulated on raids or by confiscations. Men who had a nose for the discovery of hidden delicacies were valued members of each troop. Some of these men were shaman with resources that reached into the spirit world. At this moment many of the men were more interested in drink and entertainment. Every troop had a paid singer. One of the men of this garrison was famous for his songs. He was starting a chant, which he sang in the three voices practiced by tribes north of the Gobi Desert. The head or child's voice, high and clear falsetto; the adult voice: baritone in this case, and the spirit or inner voice, where the bass sound seems to swell from deep within the chest of the singer. The man moved easily from verse to verse and voice to voice to the admiration and spontaneous acclaim shouted by the garrison.

HUNS' WAR SONG

1.   Sprinkle the earth with blood of heroes.
        Cut through the lands that we may thrive.

- 186 -

Comrades of men who thrill to battle.
These are the brave with whom to die.

Chorus:

Ride on to battle.
Champions lead your conquests.
Fight onward. Win riches.
Sharpen your arrows,
Bend your bow to victory.

2.   Warriors arise to seize the bounty.
Spatter their blood to feed the ground.
Let all their tears flow down like rivers.
Horsemen will rule the world around.

Chorus:

3.   Take all their flocks and keep their chattel.
Treat human kind like herding cattle:
Some for your work, and some for your treat,
Some for your leather, horn and meat.

Chorus:

One time through was not enough, for the men demanded more. So, he sang the same again and again in the different voices he commanded. All joined the chorus. Noise increased as more drinks were passed around. Evran ignored them.

"Tell me more of the double role played by Han Lee. I know that every wise general has his agents placed to send reports and cloud judgment of the enemy forces. But what were the orders through him?"

Aya smiled confidently and leaned forward, "He was to play on the ambitions of the Prince Ilkin and to lure us ... them, into premature action before Khan Kinner had time to draw up his army. An overwhelming defeat would delay the yielding of the Ukraine front."

Evran chuckled softly. "The Ukraine's been picked over and will cost two generations to restore to productive abundance. Our cousins the Khazars are welcome to it as long as we don't look bad. So you and Kurt had a hand in training the Khazar troops and exaggerating the ease of conquest. I take it you were successful." Kaya looked at Ozkurt, seated on the general's right side.

He agreed. "They thought it would all be theirs in a week. Koosta made enough natural mistakes on the river raid that the impression was exaggerated even more. Sums of gold were left to be found and desire heightened." The general's laugh was echoed by the two bodyguards standing behind them with drawn swords. They were the only men with drawn swords in the room with the general. Ozkurt grimaced, but went on. "So the impression grew and the ruse was easily fanned to high flame. Giving up wealth was to make a great victory by a slaughter of Khazars, but it turned out otherwise. When the troops viewed the helpless camp on the Donitz and Han Lee rode off as if to the spoils, only one troop broke rank and followed. The rest kept formation." Evran was in his third cup and expected his companions to keep pace with him. Only the guards were abstinent.

"*Dough rue*, right," the binbasha echoed, "Yes, one of the commanders yelled: 'Hold it's a trap' and the horn was blown. A sweeping victory lost for Koosta by a wise man and a quick command by Ilkin." The friends exchanged glances across the general's chest.

"You have previous knowledge of the battle, My Lord Evran?" Kaya inquired tentatively.

The general pointed to their platters. "Blood sausage, roasted head, tripe, bulgur and lions' milk, eat up, *erdash,* comrades, enjoy our modest meal. Tomorrow night I'll be happily home, *potlajan ezmesi, manta* and *kyoonyfay* will be served. My wife is anxious about my activities away and her closest companion is a Rumen woman. She was an ugly left-over from a mountain raid and no warrior wanted her. My wife is jealous of any beauty but her own: so I took her home. They became close companions and she runs my household now to my wife's complete satisfaction. They even have daily prayer and readings by a *papaz*." He laughed, "They want to build a chapel for our increasing staff." Everyone laughed.

Kaya suggested, "Perhaps you too, find redeeming qualities in their faith in Yesu?"

"Some is good, some foolish to my mind. All I seek in life is found by taking, keeping and demanding more. My wife desires that I not be injured or killed while she enjoys what I've got. Our manager wants personal safety, tolerance and the freedom to serve her God. So, all are happy as she prays for us."

Ozkurt objected, "But every man resists losing his goods. The odds are that he will scheme and fight to hold onto his possessions. The evidence is overwhelming. The risk of injury to those who attempt to collect it is great."

"For which you share a part of your goods for the hired hands to do your dirty work. Why be strong except to gain? What kind of warrior does a Christian make? How many did you kill in Ukraine, Aya bey?"

Kaya shrugged and half-smiled. "Perhaps more than I would have liked. I counted double hands of wounded during the battle."

Evran frowned saying, "A score, twenty is not bad, but why did none die?"

"I shot for arms and legs. Heavy losses in wounded always discourages the enthusiasm of an attack. The wounded demand attention and distract those still intent on fighting. It discourages the weak and green men."

Evran sneered sarcastically, "You think mercy wins battles?"

Kaya answered slowly, "I think that wherever mercy and generosity are shown to the opponent the others respect and respond with the same qualities."

"You make war and kill nicely, in a merciful way. While actually less people are killed when the action is sharp and fierce. Terror enforces obedience and conforms the defeated to the will of the conqueror. Slipshod local administration is changed to outside foreign control, where local politics has little bearing, and efficiency is achieved."

Ozkurt responded now, "Resentment and frustration grow to test the strength of the dominant authority. Which conflict leads to freedom or increased retaliation and deaths."

Evran smiled broadly in his triumph and said, "To the victors go the spoils. Every warrior knows this. Even God must rule through conquest and theocratic dictation or suffer neglect and disobedience as we see now among Christians. God must show Himself strong to reign on earth."

Kaya disagreed, "God's chief weakness is to love his creation and the humans he left in charge of it all. For this reason he sent a sin- bearer. He is willing to forgive those who earnestly seek his pardon for offences. His weakness is stronger than the hatred and greed of the world. True love reconciles, it doesn't force obedience. True love teaches. Careless Christians have a life-time of suffering, further learning and experience. A dead renegade to God or to the authority you describe, whatever it's beliefs, has no time for repentance. I conclude that the present precarious condition of the world is to bring us all to repentance and growth in humanity and knowledge of God."

The general responded cynically, "It's a sloppy way to run a world. Almost like wealth and skill didn't matter. Better that a man go for all he wants now, any way he can get it, and let the chips fall where they may."

Kaya quoted: "What does it profit a man to gain the whole world and lose his only soul? What would you give for your life? Have you ever thought about such an exchange?"

ARMED RECURVED BOW AND QUIVER

Evran lost his pleasant look. "Is Tanra against wealth and prosperity?" He hissed angrily.

"Only when gained by exploitation, deceit and murder. He has made many saints wealthy through righteousness."

Evran turned away to face Ozkurt. He changed the subject, "Do you use boats in your home country, Kurt bey?"

"To cross rivers or gather wood, or fish, but we are largely horsemen. Why do you ask, Binbashim?"

Evran's smile showed teeth, "I was wondering how much and where you've traveled. Here, drink up."

> - - - - - - - >

"Oh, my head hurts! Why are they making all that noise?" Ozkurt complained piteously.

Kaya leaned over, "You drank too much. I hope you didn't talk too much." He pulled his friends arm. "They're preparing to leave. It can't be soon enough for me. I've prayed and am ready, so let's get you set up to travel."

Olga came to speak to Kaya. "Did you pack your weapons last night?"

"They were hung on the center pole when we left for the banquet. Did you ask Mark?"

She fidgeted, nervously, "He was sent to the kitchen. I was taking care of our horses. It was dark when we returned." Kaya shrugged, "We'll inquire when we're ready to go. It's their doing."

"I have my knife," she patted her waist under her dress.

"I think we all have them," Kaya pulled Ozkurt's from under the pillow. "But he couldn't have used it anyway." They laughed together as Ozkurt, fully dressed, even as he had slept, sat up painfully holding his head.

An outside voice shouted into the tent. "*Hazur ole*, be ready, it's almost light now. Assemble in the town center."

Ozkurt cringed, but Kaya ran out to ask: "Have you secured our weapons?"

"They're packed away for travel," was the brusque reply. "You have a squad, why would you need them?"

"We're ready, bring the horses," Kaya replied.

"I'll get them," responded Olga. "They're not used to strangers. I've already milked Altom. We can clear out now."

"I wish I were dead," groaned Ozkurt painfully.

"You may get that wish answered before nightfall," Kaya replied. "Look alive now and we might make it through."

SOLDIERS' BANQUET

PEOPLE, PLACES & PLOTS in Chapter 16

Evran: torments his wife and plans his clever strategies.
Hans: a Goth, an angry young warrior, intent on revenge.
Kaya: honored guest or prisoner going to Munzur Khan.
Loki: a Goth, dealer in stolen horses and portable goods.
Mark: finds his father in the midst of misery and danger.
Martim: an attendant and administrator of a Royal Yurt.
Olga: reduced to the rank of a slave, does her duties.
Ozkurt: given the name Kurt, finds new, dangerous adventures.
Saraijik: resents her father's treatment of herself and her mother.
Steiner Thorstroom: a warrior and freeman finds his son.
Wodan: the best horse breaker and trainer in Transylvania.

GLOSSARY:

duy-doon' mu: hear that? Did you feel it? Do you sense something?
gel: come; come here.
hisar' im: my fortress; my castle.
hyer: no; not at all; to the contrary; a denial.
kan'der: It's blood; It has to be blood.
soos: hush; quiet; silence; listen.
yorgan: a quilt stuffed with wool.
ya-ha-yu'-wee: a berserker war cry.

THE GOVERNOR'S LADY

"You are not permitted to ride up here at the head of the column, Aya bey. You must go back to the center with your companion."

Kaya looked reluctantly back. "My friend is hard to endure after a night of drinking. He's in misery now and he makes it contagious."

The cool corporal warmed a little and laughed. "Few can keep up with our General Evran cup for cup. No sensible man would try. It's always our custom to keep important persons in the center of our columns, so you must return there anyway. General Evran wants you to take good care of his golden horse."

"I suppose we should be thankful we're not in chains." He said to Olga on his return. Mark rode glumly beside them on the pack animal, his face matched that of Ozkurt.

"How much do you think they know?" she asked.

"Enough to suspect our story and to desire further inquiry into our presence."

She scratched her head sadly. "Then why not chain us?"

Kaya laughed loudly, "What would happen when they discover we have such letters and information for the Khan? Open private letters? Chain the official messengers of an authority? Too risky."

"Please, no more levity. It's inappropriate to the present moment," sighed Ozkurt. "How much longer will this ride be?" The two conspirators exchanged glances of keen amusement. Kaya started humming to himself.

Olga said, "They said we'll be near the foot of the mountain by tonight. We'll stop at a Hun base camp there." A groan was the only answer. The information was not appreciated.

> - - - - - - - >

"You took your sweet time on this excursion. Did you accumulate superb rewards for your retinue or find the Insurrection's leader?" The Lady Saraijik questioned him coldly.

"All in due time my little partridge. I'm weary of travel and ready for treats and a suitable welcome to our yurt." Evran, Lord of the lower Danube, looked with satisfaction at his princess of cold, aloof beauty, his chosen lady.

He thought, 'she's as deadly as a well aimed dart; as quick and unexpected as a serpent's strike, so is my lady.' Her finely embroidered wool coat covered red shalvar pants and tunic as she bowed in mock humility. Pride seeped from every movement and word: a princess aware of her power and vulnerability before the strength of a ruthless dragon, warrior and master. He smiled sternly. Parry, stroke and touch for the blood of anguish, this was the object of every encounter. Here, indeed, was a game better than the torture of enemies. It was a game that hurried his steps from the boredom of enduring servile peasants, long weary journeys, and soldier's fare to the duels, excitement and luxury of the home harem with its one object of his passion. Like an unbroken horse or an unyielding town, she held his attention and admiration.

Her answer delayed to the fringe of rank insolence, as she straightened and proudly answered. "My Lord knows that the steam room, bath and kitchen are always at your command as are all the attendants of my yurt. Your rest, however, is delayed. We have not finished the drying of the *yorgan* and blankets. But all else is ready." Behind her the ugly lady steward and an attendant eunuch bowed with the household servants.

The mounted troops drawn up in the column exchanged glances and from the back ranks a faint chuckle echoed. The troops knew of the Lord Evran's high-born wife and her peppery ways. The general's cold gaze swept the blank faced ranks of troopers seeking the culprit. All was silence and respect. At a nod, the Yuzbasha at Evran's side took command of the troops.

Evran dismounted to penetrate the thorn fence of the forbidden area. The lady led the way to the entrance. She turned and asked seriously, "We saw the lights and smoke of a burning village in the north two days ago. What happened?"

Evran's face became less serious, even smiled, "We burned out the Ostrogoths near the divisions of the Danube into the delta."

Her face registered shock. "But they were the first of the Goths to make peace. Why burn them out?" They stopped near the harem gate.

"An informant said that spies from a ship were to pass there from a Khazar boat. We thought they were unknown collaborators of rebels armed with Khazar gold and promises. We decided to make an example of them."

"It might work for a weak, submissive people, but the Goths are fighters. You light a fire behind Koosta's back. You hate the fact that Father makes much of him and his East Huns."

"Why waste men and gold on a devastated land? The Goths in Italy and the empire of the Rumens wait in the south with their cities that hold the wealth of the world. The Ukraine is finished: we must leave it."

She smiled; half contempt and half admiration showed briefly. "You devil, you're forcing his hand. You're fanning the flame behind Koosta."

He studied her pert face and answered slowly. "My goal is protecting the future of the Hunnish people. Only great wealth accumulated by greedy empires can preserve a people like ours. Cities, not villages, hold the wealth we need."

Her glance was provocative; contemptuous. "Villages provide, taxes, labor, and food we need to rule."

He lowered his face to hers. "Warriors require expensive up-keep and rewards for risks. We can't hold our fighting forces without hope of great gains. *Soos*, hush now, no more questions. I need to do something. Wait for me here."

He returned quickly to the magnificent command tent. He left the princess waiting as he performed some real or imaginary task with the clerks and scribes within. He emerged smiling as the frowning princess waited impatiently.

He answered her angry look of inquiry, "A letter is needed to advise our Khan, your father, of two important messengers dispatched this morning. They bear watching."

She laughed, "My ungrateful father needs no one to tell him about suspicious watching and conjectures. He is as fidgety as a fox in a barnyard. Look what he did to my poor mother because of vicious gossip. She was virgin and he is my father despite all they say." He frowned, but agreed in a soothing voice as they walked through the entrance.

"Saraijik, I could never have had you from his harem, only from your mother's clan could such a match as ours be had. So evil was turned to good."

She cast him a disdainful glance. "Perhaps, for you, but for her there is only sad exile and barren childless existence far from her husband, my father. I was left, orphaned." Her voice quivered with passion.

But you have never known him, you were isolated, except through reports and gossip from court visitors. She shook her shoulders indignantly.

I know him like I know myself, intimately. His blood tells me all that I need to know about him. I read his mind from afar. He ignores and despises me. He refuses to acknowledge my rights. I hate him."

He answered coolly. "He permitted our marriage, which is recognition of a kind."

She sneered her contempt, "The delivery of a dangerous prisoner to a faithful guard who delights to do his master's bidding."

He laughed and moved to embrace her. She ducked, "The delights of faithful service are many," he affirmed. He moved toward her, but she evaded him.

She retorted with contempt, holding her nose, "Go and bathe, I smell the stink of you from here."

> - - - - - - - >

"Its been a hard week and it isn't getting better in this snow," complained Mark. He was riding on the same horse with Olga, now that the pack animal had burden enough on the mountain climbs. He sat the saddle before Olga and they were wrapped together with a blanket about them.

"Do you have snow in the delta, Mark?" inquired Kaya carefully. Mark's Hunnish was limited.

"A little around Christmas, but nothing like this." He put a hand out reluctantly to indicate the forest of beech and pine. Olga nodded agreement, as she shivered. "We could see it in the mountain tops when we fished. Uncle Otto said it happened often in Ukraine, even on low ground."

Kaya decided not to tell them about winter at home. He looked at the still silent Ozkurt who had not kicked his earlier depression. Kaya leaned over to request, "Would a copper coin buy your thoughts?"

Ozkurt grimaced, "I was thinking about snow on palm trees being rare and pretty. I think of my little cousin in the hill country and a warm yurt to pass winter days." He paused, then, slowly continued: "I'm thinking that a great warrior's reputation does not balance a life of comfort and safety. I think that a wanderer in his cups should not match wits with a cunning general of the dragons." He shook his head. "I wonder if we don't get better than we deserve from God Almighty, ruler above. I wonder if I should confess my weaknesses here at advent time. I wonder why my friends and Yesu put up with me." There was a silence as the troop continued up the snowy valley following the upper Ult River westward.

"It would take a fortune to buy the answers to all those thoughts," Kaya replied. "Only Yesu has paid the price and has the knowledge to save us from this pressing world and hopeless despair."

Mark's excited voice broke a long silence. "It's the fort. There on the rise, see? I saw it once in summer when the delta was swimming in heat and humidity. We came home for the last time." He stopped abruptly, while others strained to see the grim lines of log and mud daubed walls surrounding a stone core of towers. Squat, ugly, but strong, the guardian of the pass stood inviolate, a guarantee of safety and suppression.

"We call it Ruggenfurt," Mark continued. "Only the high alpine meadows and upper forests escape its rule."

Kaya agreed, "At least, we'll be warmer and rest until we know the next part of our adventure."

Ozkurt grunted and added, "You mean, learn our fate."

> - - - - - - - >

"The men are in place, the attack is ready, it's almost dark enough to start," an impatient youth reported. The grimfaced, old warrior grunted and rubbed his hands together,

"*Ya*, we have a long night for this, son. There's a group entering the gate now, late arrivals for our planned party. It's a squad, plus two men and two children, prisoners of some importance. They're not much help or hindrance without their weapons."

Hans, the angry-faced young man retorted, "A squad more won't affect the outcome."

"The men look like Huns, the kids look like ours, a strange prison mix. We can investigate, if we live 'til morning." He turned to look behind them. "Let's get back to camp and see if the outlander troops have arrived. Our sentries will watch for us and prevent any more coming or going from Ruggenfurt."

The young man smiled a snarl. "Now, all our mountains will see the bravery and daring of Hans Marker. Valhalla prepares a banquet for heroes, while we prepare one for the ravens. We have a good night for great deeds to be done." The old man put his arm around the boaster as they walked down the hill.

> - - - - - - - >

"*Duy-doon mu*? do you sense it?" Kaya whispered.

"What? Feel what? It's cold and dark. Go on with your prayers: why wake me?" Ozkurt grumbled, turning.

"Something is happening outside. Listen, hear that?" Several crisp, clacking sounds occurred in sequence. Tick, clack, tick, clack came from different directions outside their room. The windows were vertical slits with shutters locked closed. Ozkurt protested as Kaya got up and opened one to stare out in the night. He stood sniffing the cold night air.

"*Kan'der*, it's blood I smell. See, men coming up over the walls? They're killing sentries! Now they're sliding down their ropes to the courtyard. Some are using the stairs to the gate towers. The gate is unbarred; it's open. A mob of bearded men push in, a group with battering rams." The screams and shouts proved Kaya right in his observations. Ozkurt jumped to his feet and joined Kaya at the tower window to stare below.

A gang had formed at the door of the barracks. The door was forced open, smashed by the ram, to reveal men dressing and seeking weapons for defense. The sounds of hand to hand fighting were heard.

Everyone was awake now and their companions joined them to watch from another window. A tower sentry was aiming arrows at the running shadows below. An arrow from a dark corner below caught him and he fell over the parapet. Something flashed up and the tick, clack sound was heard again. A wooden grapple and rope caught and a dark figure climbed the rope to the tower top, then another followed him up and another sentry's body was flung over. Now, a flash of light as a man bearing a torch appeared from what must have been the kitchen. Men ran out with sacks and bundles toward the gate. More torches were fired and darted through the night. Fires were being lit. Oil was spilled against the wall and lighted. Wood was piled near the gate. The victors had no intention of keeping the fort. Everyone could smell the beginning of the burning.

"Father, come! I'm Mark Thorstroom," shouted Mark, repeatedly, through the open shutters.

"They'll be on us in another minute," Kaya said. "Dress quickly, but don't offer resistance. This is not our fight."

"They're talking Gothic," Olga said, "I'll go to the door and try to explain our situation."

Mark stood beside her, "I'll go with you, father may be among them."

"*Ya ha you' wee*," a berserker war cry sounded above them. The sound of chopping came. They were breaking down the door below. Screams and cries followed the progress of the attackers. No one was being spared. Warriors, wives, cooks, slaves, or stable-hands; all were struck down except the few who could speak the victor's tongue. Prisoners were released on the same basis.

The horses were run out of the stables and driven through the gate. Other livestock followed. A cart of hay was pushed against a wall and set fire. Smoke and heat were now felt everywhere.

Pounding was heard on the locked door of their room. Olga began to plead in Gothic and Mark called his father's name repeatedly. The sound of the ax followed. The crash of the door brought three figures into the room. One snatched up Mark and laughed triumphantly. The other two stood swords in hand to watch the two men while Olga stood between them talking excitedly and indicating Kaya and Ozkurt with sweeps of the hand. She ran over and held up the olivewood cross on Kaya's neck. The two blood-spattered, bearded warriors stood mutely regarding the scene. Below, a horn sounded the retreat amid the crackle of the mounting flames as the logs of Ruggenfurt brightened the night with light that would reach the plains of Wallachia and the coast. The cycle already set in motion would continue: blood for blood and blow for blow.

"Bayan Saraijik, come see to the northwest, high in the mountains. Fire light shines on snow and peaks." It was the time before first light when the work began in the Royal tent. Martim Cristescu stood, fully dressed, her mouth open at the astonishing sight. Saraijik arrived trembling with a woolen blanket around her shoulders. Her face was alive with emotion. Binbasha Evran stood beside her, bare sword in hand.

"Does the forest burn?" she whispered.

Evran growled, "*Hyer*, no! *Hisarim*, it's my castle in the pass. Our short cut to the capital is cut. We must sound the alarm and ride. It'll take most of a week and winter pursuit is near futile, except for the few that leave a trail and can be burned out. We'll simply have to clean the mountains of people."

Saraijik drew closer to Evran and whispered, "Do you think the two messengers you told us about are there? The bear and wolf are at the pass?"

Evran nodded agreement, "Alive or dead they should be at the castle by now." Beyond them the garrison had come alive with the alarm of horns and cymbals and the shouts of the officers. Men were dressing, arming and readying their mounts to form their squads.

Martim Cristescu made the sign of the cross, head and right shoulder first: as did all under the influence of the East Rumens. "May the Father, God of Yesu, give the messengers grace and mercy in time of danger," her staff of servants echoed the amen.

"Now will be our opportunity to observe if these Christian's prayers are answered," said Binbasha Evran to his shivering princess.

> - - - - - - - >

"We will return to our own stockades to celebrate. We can't let the Huns catch us in the open ground. Their bows and horses make a dreaded combination there." Warrior Steiner Thorstroom declared. "The outlanders are a Goth force from Siebenburgen, the little mountains in Transylvania. They take their part in horses because it's easier to take them home. We keep the food supplies and other goods with only a few horses as needed." Mark walked with his arm around his father's waist.

Olga spoke up, quickly, "We need our horses. We have four. What of them?"

"You must bargain with Loki Rothander their Thane. See, over by the herd, the man with golden hair."

"*Gel*, come Kaya, we must hurry over to claim our horses or lose them," she called as she ran.

"I see you like my spoils," the plump man declared. "It's easier to carry coins than herd horses. I'll sell you some."

"You speak Hunnish?" Kaya asked, surprised.

"I heard the girl call you in that language. My stockade is surrounded by Hunnish neighbors. I need to talk with them that they might leave me alone, even as I respect them. I must gain my profits from afar; not from nearby."

"They permit such an arrangement in their empire?"

"As long as I don't provoke greed, and pay regularly. An attack would be extremely costly to them."

Kaya laughed, "But you attack them here."

Loki smiled pleasantly, "Others will take the blame and the retaliation. I'll claim to have bought the stock at discount. Who will know?" Olga was busy spotting and sorting out all of the ones she knew and put the salvaged bits and blankets on them.

"The black, red and golden, plus one for packing, these are ours," she quickly pointed out. Kaya soothed Altom, who nuzzled him.

Loki watched them closely. "I can't sell the golden, she's too valuable. We need breeding stock and she's ideal. I'll sell the other three and you choose another for four."

Kaya looked thoughtful, "You won't be able to ride her or even lead her where she doesn't want to go. She'll break out of any fences."

"I have riders that can't be thrown." Loki bragged. "Come, Wodan, show this mare who is master." A tough, thin man of medium height and weight walked over to look at the mare. He nodded for Kaya to move away. He jumped, and so did the mare. He landed, but not balanced. She reared and he clung on. When she bucked her head came around and teeth came back to catch an out stretched leg. He yelled as she jerked. Altom sat down and quickly rolled backwards and Wodan yipped and jumped free. Her head and extended neck fell across his legs as he tried to get to his feet in the snow. Now she rolled to her feet and ran after him neck out-stretched, teeth open to bite. He flung himself behind the laughing Loki, who was bowled over while Kaya stepped in to quiet his angry mare.

Loki and his rider got up painfully wiping off the snow. He looked the golden over sadly and shook his head. He walked to Kaya, smiling slightly and shook Kaya's hand. "I see that you're an honest man. You can have her, but I must have gold for gold."

Olga stepped up and pulled a knife from beneath her kirtle. She presented it handle first. "Will this be enough to pay her worth?"

Loki looked at the gold handle and hefted it knowingly. In admiration he examined the inscription and tried the keenness of the blade on a horse hair. He chuckled his satisfaction. "This pays all the animals and there remains only one debt. On my part, I owe you hospitality at any day or night of your adventuring in our land. But come I must have it's history and origin.

Steiner interrupted the conversation. "Shall we sit here then and wait for our enemy's cavalry to find us? On your invitation they may visit and entertain you, but this is neither the time nor place."

Loki looked up, "Yes, you're right. We must clear the pass and not meet anyone to report our participation. Come, promise to visit me, it will bring joy." Kaya nodded his acceptance and the man rallied his men and horses to leave.

Ozkurt frowned, "So it was you who took Binbasha Alsin's knife? How did you manage that?"

Olga hung her head and muttered, "I knew Jinks had taken the money and soldier's knife to defend himself. Both doors were open, so I took the gold knife and hid it in your room. I thought I would have to pay my passage to find uncle. Now we're here, but I haven't found him yet. God must be angry with me."

Kaya listened with care. It was the first he had known of it. They brought up the rear of the column that moved west toward the high mountain peaks. Kaya, riding beside her agreed, "We often disappoint God, but that's why we confess sin and find forgiveness and pardon to reform our lives."

The snow continued to slow the carts and horses. "Any fool can see our tracks to the stockades," murmured Ozkurt as they rode in the gray of mid-morning.

"It feels like snow by afternoon," Kaya countered.

> - - - - - - - >

"Thank God for warm halls and hot cooked food." Mark exclaimed, "I'm home again with mother's cooking."

Olga said, "Why would you leave this for the delta, Mark?"

"Dad lives up to his name, Steiner, always in his cups, and he quarreled with Odin constantly. Odin wanted to make peace with the Huns to live well. To survive as hunted animals was not his choice."

Kaya spoke up, "I wonder what the Huns have done to him. His information was flawed."

Mark shook his head, "I don't know, but I see he was wrong. Freedom is worth more than money."

A group of warriors came into the hall. Mark's mother sent out the drinks while they talked. "Fritz Marker is coming to the banquet tonight, snow or no." The group agreed happily and some displayed new loot from the burned fort: jewelry, weapons, and clothing.

"With more victories like yesterday, we can control the valleys," one of them enthused.

Another disagreed, "We have called attention to ourselves by burning a fort."

A brother took up the same line of argument. "They'll decide that punitive action is the only cure. They'll burn us out with an army."

An older man objected, "Not so, they're committed to war in the Balkans."

"With the empire? Don't be ridiculous. Only we Goths have ever conquered old Rome. The new Rome will defeat Huns."

"They'll do well to hold Adrianapolis," stated the old one dogmatically, "or even the city against them."

A younger man who had held back ventured tentatively, "I understood that they were going up the Danube to the Rhine River."

A general groan followed the declaration. "What fool would go north through the Black Forest for gain?" There was a general consensus, nodding heads.

"Italy and the cities of the south are a stronger magnet."

"But westward gains give the control of everything to them. With Gaul they'll own the western world!"

"Bosh, the old Rome held it, but couldn't cross the Rhine even if they did cross the channel against the Celts."

Agreement was general at this point and more drink was ordered as more warriors joined the celebration. Toasts were pledged to leaders, causes, and victories; ancient or modern. More joined the gathering in the hall. A few had reached the sentimental stage and started asking for song.

"Sing: Mine Liebling von der See," one voice requested.

But someone had started The Freemen's Song and all joined the singing, keeping time with the mugs in their hands, beating the tables rhythmically to the music:

FREEMEN'S SONG

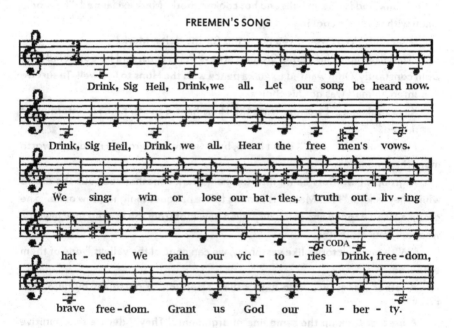

1.   Drink, Sig Heil, drink we all.
        Let our song be heard now.
        Drink, Sig Heil, drink we all.
        Hear the free men's vows.
        We sing: win or lose our battles,
        Truth out-living hatred.
        We gain our victories.

2.   Come brothers, brave brothers.
        Give our telling glory.
        Come brothers, brave brothers.
        We will not be slaves.
        We sing, with our heads up high,
        We'll see it through or die.
        Free men, we toast victories.

Coda:
        Drink freedom, brave freedom.
        Grant us God our liberty.

The cups were emptied and refilled as the celebration gained volume and enthusiasm. No thoughts were wasted on possible counterattacks or defenses.

RUGENFURT'S FALL

PEOPLE, PLACES & PLOTS in Chapter 17

Biorn: top man at Loki Rothander's base in Transylvania.
Evran: the general rebuilds his fort at great cost.
Fritz Marker: a thane of the Ostrogoth people in the mountains.
Hans Marker: son and heir, resents any claims of kinship.
Kaya: freed by Goths, he is a prisoner of circumstances.
Kline Marker: Hans' brother and younger, tallest son,
Loki Rothander: leader of the Goths of Transylvania.
Merien Papasian: home in her city, remembers friends.
Olga: finally finds more than she was looking for.
Oren: Evran's adjutant and yuzbasha shares a secret order.
Ozkurt: meets new challenges and finds danger present.
Saraijik: proves a princess can command and, also, obey.

GLOSSARY:

a-tesh': fire; conflagration.
bach: look; see it!
bash ooze to nay: As you order; it will be so; I obey, sir.
kalk: stand; stand up; get up.
Mine Liebling von der See: my darling from across the sea.
ora-ya git: go there; get over there.
ompa: grandfather. (Germanic)
ordu ev'e: army headquarters; military command center.
ooyan: wake; wake up; look alive.
raiya: the enslaved people of eastern conquerors.
shim'di: now; immediately; this minute.

SCARFACE DEMANDS A SONG

The horns were being drained now and the spirit of the men rose with the temperature, and action. Food was served by the host's serving men and women. The guests were becoming boisterous as jokes, boasts and arguments were heard, the liquor loosened their tongues.

Again the demanding voice came, cutting through the excitement and chatter, requesting his favorite: 'Mine Liebling von der See'. Kaya recognized the old leader he had seen in the courtyard directing the fighting. Gradually the toasting warriors recognized the voice of their leader. Laughter and respect mingled at first then quiet prevailed. Men exchanged glances and grins, they knew what to expect. The young messenger boy, Wolfgang, Hans and Kline Marker sang the song together. They, too, knew their Thane's favorite song:

1.   I have lost my darling,
        Far across the sea.
        I wait for my darling.
        She'll come back to me.
        We'll rejoice to see her here,
        Living happily.
        I am waiting, soon she will come.

2.   She'll return to seek me,
        From across the sea.
        With great joy she'll greet me
        Then her face I'll see.
        She'll be glad to join us here,
        Singing happily.

I am waiting still, she will come.

3.   I dream of my darling,
      She must dream of me.
      God knows how I miss her,
      She means so much to me.
      She will come to seek me here,
      Crossing land and sea.
      Wait with patience 'till she can come.

MY DARLING OVERSEAS

I have lost my dar-ling, far a-cross the sea.
I wait for my dar-ling. She'll come back to me.
We'll re-joice to see her here, li-ving hap-pi-ly.
I am wait-ing, soon she will come.

The sad face of Fritz Marker showed clearly in the torch light. Two great white scars showed on his cheek: one from ear to chin, the other from nose to jaw; an X of past pain and humiliation. His grim visage softened and his eyes glistened in the dancing light.

Respectful silence filled the hall, until, from beside Ozkurt and Kaya, Olga stood and in a trembling voice questioned, "Grand Uncle Fritz? You're my grand uncle Fritz? *Ompa* Otto's little brother from the old country, in the Donetz valley before the invasion? I've come from Otto over the sea. He told me to look for the scars."

The old man stared at the girl, his eyes wide and startled as he stood gasping. "Helga! Helga, my love, is it you? You've come back to me." He swayed and stumbled forward. His son, Hans, caught him.

"No, impossible," he grated out. "She's young, father."

"I'm Olga, Helga's my grandmother. She told me all about you. How she cared for you after the battle. How much you loved her. But *Ompa* Otto took her away from the battle front to save her life. She loved you both."

> - - - - - - - >

"It's well we rode ahead of the troops. We won't bring them closer than a half hour's ride of this ruin, Oren," Evran ordered.

The Yuzbasha at his side, shook his fist at the blackened ruin and spoke through gritted teeth. "We'll deliver the earth from such blood thirsty rebels. Our vengeance will sweep the mountains clean."

Evran agreed, "Naturally, but first we will entice them here to correct what they have permitted, or participated in destroying. Send out an offer of great rewards for information and workers to help us."

"I don't understand sir! Offer them great rewards?"

"Reconstruction is our first priority. We will need laborers and material so we will offer high wages and buy material here on the mountain. The guilty will hide, but those who stood by neither warning us nor participating in the actual attack will come to offer condolences and help. We will use them until the construction is finished and then exact our revenge."

"And the information they provide will be our guide in finishing the cleansing of the peaks!" the adjutant finished, his face bright with excitement.

Evran chuckled, "Such men will implicate others to excuse themselves. Our scribes will be busy. This plan must be known to us only. The troops will complain, but if they know, it will leak out and a general flight will result. I hold you responsible, Oren. No one must know."

"*Bash ooze to nay*, I obey my Lord. I will send messengers to the villages and strongholds to offer rewards for news and laborers. Work must come before pleasure."

"Good, meanwhile get in two squads to identify what remains of the bodies of our defenders for burial. Let them have a good look for friends and acquaintances. We will have to control them when local workers arrive, but it will be more convincing," Evran smiled grimly. "I want news of the two messengers that passed here. The big one called the bear and the tough skinny wolf. You understand?"

Oren nodded, "I'm curious too. The garrison was only about two hundred men I've been told."

Evran grimaced sourly, "Thanks to the Khan's policy of reinforcing Ukraine. Bad counsel drains our resources. Perhaps this will modify or reverse that foolishness of wasting fodder on a dying horse."

> - - - - - - - >

"I've told you all I know about Olga," declared Ozkurt. "The governor's daughter knew her before that, but who could have known her before she came to the port? Only the Circassians or other Goths from there could know."

"That is not proof of kinship," countered Hans Marker the son of the Thane. "An unknown girl comes in claiming kinship to my family with only a cooked up story of her supposed grandmother and grandfather who claimed kinship to a Thane of the Eastern Alps."

Kaya spoke up strongly, "He was only a warrior, a little brother, as far as she knew. She told us about a recognizable scar on his face. She didn't know where he would be found. Her story is true and your father recognizes it as true."

Ozkurt added, "Your father gained his present status, after their exile and separation, by hard work and leadership of his beaten people. He took refuge in these peaks."

Hans screamed, "No, it's not true. I'll not share my inheritance with a girl, a relative I've never even heard about."

Ozkurt replied, "Your father's favorite song should have clued you in about a lost love overseas. You've probably never shown interest in your father's life in Ukraine."

Hans retorted, "You say this because he's invited you to spend the winter here. He accepts every suggestion she makes. You're in this as much as she is."

Ozkurt insisted, "The whole stockade heard her declaration and your father's recognition of her accounts. They sat there and swapped stories for hours."

Hans Marker would not listen to more. He rose, grabbed a cloak and stormed to the door. "You've even persuaded Kline, but I'm not fooled. I'll not stay here. New snow or not, I'm leaving for my hunting lodge. I'll never come back until she's gone."

> - - - - - - - >

"You were gone when I woke! Where've you been?"

The young boy of nine pressed his head against Merien as he hugged her. He looked up admiringly, "Magda didn't know?"

She pressed her fingers to her lips and giggled, "I went to St. Irene for prayer. Yes? Our secret."

"You go a lot now. Magda says it's dangerous."

"No, night celebrations are over, only busy, early morning workers are up and about. Most people sleep."

"What's this?" He pulled out the silver fish on a chain that graced her slender neck.

She blushed and explained. "It's a gift from my travel friends: to remember, no? I pray for their safety among the Huns. Yes, it's a big danger."

"I wish I'd been there to travel with the golden horse, a bear, a wolf, and a Goth. Magda says they're barbarians."

"She told me to teach them our good things, yes."

"Are you the fish or the fisherman?" he asked, still working the joints to make it wiggle.

She laughed and smoothed his curly, black hair tenderly, shaking her head. "You're too smart. Who can say, maybe both, no?"

"Your hands are like ice!" He jerked his head away. She pulled away to shake out her cape and hang it on a peg. "But why go today? It's so cold out. The snow hasn't melted." He pouted, following her as she walked to the brazier that was burning in the middle of the room, to warm her hands over the heat.

He volunteered, "Magda promised to make snow candy if the snow stayed over night." They both stood leaning over the bank of coals absorbing the warmth.

"I had to see the palm trees with the snow glistening on the fronds. Yes, they lean over, oh so heavy, so tired. Then suddenly the snow shakes loose, the branch jerks up, so high and proud again. I enjoy its beauty always. One man did not believe me, no, but it is all

I said, yes. You must see to believe. The Emperor's garden is silver and green. It's so pretty at every season, our great city. I want my friends from the ship, Sea Witch, to be safe and, if God wills it, to come and know its beauty, yes."

> - - - - - - - >

"Here is the letter from My Lord Evran's hand, Bayan," the messenger began. "The cleaning and burials are over and the repairs on the buildings proceed rapidly. Another month and the basic repairs will be over and the summer will see a new fort in the place of the old one. Only one tower is being rebuilt. It suffered damage from fire weakening the mortar. The stones were largely salvaged. All the other towers and the palace are still complete."

She listened to the recounting of events with patience and then started her questions. "You have been there a month. How're the living conditions, and the food?"

The messenger replied, "The camp is cold and rest is possible, but not comfortable. The food is better than foraging, but monotonous and not agreeable."

"Are there women in the camp?" She scrutinized him coldly as he paused and sought a suitable answer.

"Some of the trooper's wives have arrived and local women also sell near the fountain in the meadow. None are allowed near the construction or the work and storage grounds."

She grew colder, "There will be houses of pleasure for the troops. Are they comfortable and the women suitable?"

The messenger wished himself elsewhere. He tried to think of some manner to go on. "I've been too occupied with my duties, My Lady."

She cut in angrily, "You have heard; men talk about such places and people. I will hear about it from you, now."

He squirmed uncomfortably. "It's a small yurt of little comfort. They joke that the madam stutters and her girls are cross-eyed and one's a harelip." The man paused, "I beg you lady, let me say no more. It is not seemly that I should repeat the jokes of the men."

She smiled coldly with a nod. "Tell me of your master, does he joke and laugh? Is his hair combed? Is daily sword drill maintained? Does he sing the soldier's songs after the evening meal?"

The messenger rose and bowed, "I have other letters to deliver and a short time to complete my work and return. I'm sure My Lady will find much more than I have said in the letter."

She let him go without thanks and called Martim. "I have a letter to read and it will tell me nothing of what I wish to hear, except his devotion. Leave the tent to a few trusted servants and prepare a departure for five persons. We will take the cooks and Joseph and leave at dawn. Those who remain will pray for us each day, just as you have prayed for the two Christian messengers."

"Is there news, My Lady?" Martim inquired.

Saraijik sniffed, "Nothing fully trustworthy, palliatives, and smoke screen for the calming of this camp. I understand that more wives wish to join their men. Invite them to join us. So that they will not be hindered or turned back by guards on the road."

She opened the scrolled letter and remarked almost to herself. "How fortunate my uncle taught me to read. He said I would prosper only through intrigue and manipulation. How right he was. Today I'll write to that wretched father of mine and warn him of the dangers of a weakened Danube force. I'll say the two messengers can tell him of the dangers. That will assure them of a good reception when they arrive. With Martim's prayers they certainly will have escaped. Father won't deign to answer me directly, but he'll read it. He knows how to appreciate information and sure sources."

> - - - - - - - >

"They're rebuilding the Ruggenfurt. When they finish you will feel their wrath. We must strike while they have limited safety and are exhausted with toil," Hans Marker urged his friends.

"How can we, when they are here in strength? A direct attack would be fool-hardy," one of them objected.

Hans insisted, "The work is too much for horsemen, they depend on the conscript labor."

One of the young listeners agreed, "We could disrupt their labor base and ambush their foraging squads and work details. We'll get them in the forest."

"If we burned a few villages, the Rumens will have to move or stay away to protect their farms. Above all we must act now before the early spring work. Winter storms will still cover our movements and impede the horses," Hans declared. All were agreed, enthusiasm grew with more drinks.

"My father is warm and comfy reliving old times with the sea witch. She has him bewitched, but I'm not fooled. I'll lead the fight and put things right. He's too old to lead anymore. I can force his hand and make him active in supporting our attacks. I'll be your war chief." They drank to that and sang rousing songs.

> - - - - - - - >

"Oo'yan, kalk, awake, get up, My Lord Evran," exclaimed Oren the yuzbasha. "There's fire reported in the villages of our workers. The men in the labor camp

- 210 -

are rioting and leaving to rescue their wives and children. They have overpowered the sentries and escaped. They raided the camp armory, too."

Evran was instantly awake his dagger was in his hand ready for defense. His orders were concise. "Send three squads after them and kill all who resist. Send a squad to check out the villages, but if there be no traceable trails, return immediately. Now, turn out the army to reinforce the guards."

As he spoke, a new cry was raised in the noisy confusion of horns and cymbals outside the headquarters tent. Yuzbasha Oren shouted from the door. "*Bach*, look, the supply depot! *Atesh*! Fire! They're firing the supplies and lumber."

His binbasha was now fully armed. "*Ore' ya git*! You go there," screamed the commander. "I'll go to the fort. We must save it." Squads of armed men were forming up on the open ground before the *ordu evi* where the commander slept. The officers were preparing their men to ride. In moments like this, promptness and action could merit future rewards and promotions. His personal orderly was bringing his horse to the tent door. Oren rushed off to get his mount and depart. The commander called three squad leaders and was soon racing to the fort, half an hour away. As they rode the light began to grow in their eyes. The fire was well lighted and bright, but not beyond control when they arrived. A squad was sent to fetch water. They were ambushed before they reached the fountain. A pile of brush roasted the new mortar on the rebuilt tower. Any wood or fabric was now afire in the apartments and halls. A few Hunnish arrows found living targets, but the attackers faded back into the forests leaving dead sentries and damaged goods everywhere.

Morning found the commander in the courtyard amid the smoke and ruin of his fort. A few men with buckets ran from the well above the courtyard to splash any smoking remains. Some of the damage was superficial, but widespread inside the buildings. In a few places only ruin remained.

GOTHS RAID CASTLE

- 211 -

The yuzbasha Oren came back with squad leaders, *chavush* and *onbasha*, to report. All were travel worn and dirty, cold and soiled with black and wet. One had a face wound and blood showed.

Evran scanned them sourly. He could read the signs and they were not good. "*Shimdy*, now men, you have conspired to come as one trooper to report. Can it be that bad?" Then Oren moved his horse forward a few paces. None dismounted, they were more comfortable mounted even in conference.

My Lord," he began, "the villages are near a total loss. With the men away working, the old men and boys were not able to put up any defense. No alarm was given. Many were burned in their beds. Had the attackers remained they could have slaughtered everyone. There was no trace of them, all lost in the forests." We left the *raiya* to save what they could. None had seen the attackers. The tracks were few, perhaps a half squad of men."

Another spoke. "We pursued the laborers who deserted. We caught one group who were returning to their village. We had to kill two before they were willing to comply and come back with us. There were fifteen of them. My comrades traced other groups, but they were lost in the woods. Some must have decided not to return directly to the villages to avoid us."

Evran held up his hand to silence the babble that followed the report. "You should have brought the villagers here to force the *raiya*, human cattle, to return here to work. Go back and get the villagers and bring them here." One of the men rode away at a gallop to call for his squad and send them into action. "If none of you saw the enemy, why do I see blood?"

The man who showed the stain replied. "*Aga-m*, My Lord, we were following the tracks from the burning of the supplies and fort. They were fired after the villages, you remember. In an open alpine meadow we spotted two groups of men afoot, running toward the high pine forest beyond the peak. They wore strange flat boards tied on their feet. Our horses were tired plodding through the snow. It was over shin deep there. They made amazing speed on their boards, they left flat pressed trails. We followed as fast as we could drive the horses. In range we started shooting and one of the men fell. The men with him gathered around him and put up their shields in a wall facing us, while others tried to help the downed man. These men were armed with spears, axes and swords only, so we could close the range. But the men were as tall as a mounted man, so we didn't consider hand combat. We surrounded them and they formed a circle like a hedgehog around him. All their shields, spears, axes and boards were raised to protect themselves. We managed to wound a few more, until finally they decided to surrender."

"*Ney oh*! What's that! Surrender? They might have run you out of arrows had they waited." Heads nodded; the enemy was weak.

"Yes, but another squad was coming up to reinforce us and their friends had disappeared down the slope. These would not abandon their chief and I think they hoped to save his life. They waved a rag and put their swords down. We motioned for them to march toward camp and when they were in line we killed them and left them there." Heads nodded approval. Cowards deserved no mercy. Men who gave up easily, did not have the courage to die. They were fit only to be *raiya*: cattle, without rights or security. Such animals depend on the good judgment of their herders.

"You brought me not one mouth to answer my questions. Who are these rebels? Where is their camp? Am I to consult the shaman to know something of them? Are my officers without wits?"

"There is one, My Lord. A tall, skinny child of smooth face was at the end of the line with the fallen chief. He had kept his shield at his feet. When we started the volleys he grabbed it in time to deflect the arrows and he ran toward the slope where the others disappeared. An arrow caught his leg and he fell, but he kept his shield and drew a long knife to wound me when I came close to finish him. My blow hit his helmet and he blacked out." The cut on the jaw of the officer spoke of the boy's courage in the face of the attempted death blow.

Evran nodded his complete understanding. "Where is the boy now? You didn't let the men finish him off?"

"We dragged him by his heels in the snow until he woke up. Then, I gave him a horse. I lost three men and one horse to spear throws in the conflict, so I had a horse for him. I put him with the Rumen laborers they brought back."

Evran looked about him. "We'll see how much of a man this boy can be. I want him here now." Another officer set off at a gallop. Evran continued, "What happened to the other group that did not pause to fight?"

Now the officer paused, he paled and stuttered, "Sir, they were out of sight and hearing. The mountain sloped away, but none were in sight, only the trail of the boards down places that were very steep. Our own reinforcements could not follow the trail. The horses fell, some balked. I called them off." All the men were staring at their horse's necks. They did not wish to shame the man more.

Evran let the silence grow long. Then his face softened and he spoke softly. "It has been a hard day for all of us. We will remember the lessons learned. We will all be better for this day of humiliations."

At that moment a parade of horses and riders in colorful coats and shalvars came through the open gate of the castle. The sun came out from behind the clouds to shine briefly on the sight. A cavalcade of women arrived with only two squads of warriors guarding the head and foot of the assembly. Mules and pack horses outnumbered the riders, for the ladies had come to stay and comfort is gained only with goods sufficient for a family's needs. In addition, all were talking, pointing and gasping at the damage they were now witnessing.

Saraijik rode through the guards to greet her lord. She deliberately smiled into his grimness. "Surprised my dearest protector and husband? I thought to put myself near, so you may faithfully fulfill your promised duties. I see the quarters are cleared, but still a trifle grungy. We've come to put that right." Evran sat glaring at his nemesis, his face red with silent anger. She ignored this and started ordering her servants, sending them to the royal quarter. Her manner was imperious for she had no intention of arguing the point of staying.

She observed from her mount the wound on the onbasha's face. She checked and demanded, "You have a cut on your face, come up immediately to the royal state room. I'll have Martim treat it for you." The man looked at his sullen commander and hesitated. She reached forward with her little quirt and slapped the horse's haunch. The tired beast moved forward and she neatly placed her horse in the vacated space. She smiled her sweetest at her husband. "I know how much you value your men."

Then, through the crowded courtyard rode a group of armed guards with a tall, gangling, smooth faced boy in chains. He was on foot, but stood as high as the little riders who surrounded him. His face was dirty and his wrapped pant leg was wet with blood. He favored the leg slightly as he walked and his face reflected defiance and exhaustion.

The guards stopped before their binbasha who spoke. "I have questions for you, rebel. Answer, if you wish to live. There is boiling water in the kitchen we can begin by washing your hands in it to learn what you know." The commander let all the suppressed emotions boom out through his voice. The swaying boy stared back silently. One of the guards shoved the boy and he staggered forward, dropping to his knees where he stayed.

The princess spoke regally, urging her horse forward. "You see, My Lord, the child submits. He clearly recognizes your authority. Now, he needs food and medical attention. The boiling water will be for tea. Come to the state-room in an hour for an afternoon meal. The boy will be ready to talk, and answer your questions." She didn't wait for a reply, but motioned with her head and the guard yanked him to his feet, and moved toward the door followed by the pert princess. The officers waited, watching their binbasha lose the contest. They exchanged glances behind expressionless faces. The exchange said: that's what comes of marrying a Khan's daughter. However, there was a measure of humor in watching the mighty man suffer a dose of arbitrary medicine. Now, some were slowly detaching themselves from the commander's presence to look for their own wife or family. Others moved to where a wife meekly waited. Then, Evran looked up and became aware that he was alone.

> - - - - - - - >

"Yes Biorn, I've seen the smoke this morning. A surprise attack; they didn't bother to invite me." Loki Rothander snarled at his top man. "How then can we turn this to our advantage?"

The tall, bearded man said, "Dis attack could jus' move de army. It comes jus' six weeks after we got back wid de horses. We've just sold 'em, marked-down, t' de gen'ral."

Loki smiled broadly, the presence of the army had opened a new source of wealth, which he was starting to exploit. "Yes, he was generous and asked few questions. He'll report a higher price to his Khan and keep the difference."

Biorn stroked his beard thoughtfully. "He haf t' spend it t' buy favors later. I doubts de army 'ull want t' move. Dey still settin' in winter camp. Dere more fires on de mountains an' only one's from de place o' Ruggenfurt."

Loki grinned, "The general will want to move. He would like to be in charge of more than Transylvania."

"It's 'ard t' know wat dese fires means in damages, Zir.

I sends some o' de men t' find out."

"No, too dangerous, Huns will be swarming. The binbasha will get his chance if Evran doesn't move fast. We got pigeons from the old Thane on the last visit didn't we? I'll send another message. The army is newly in residence here now, but ready to move. Stop all attacks and make up a hasty peace. Otherwise, they'll clear the mountains."

SHIELD WALL

PEOPLE, PLACES & PLOTS in Chapter 18

Ansgar: teaches an old skill to gain fame abroad.
Evran: under attack faces the danger of demotion.
Fritz Marker: finds his lost love only just in time.
Hans Marker: finds success often hides unforeseen failures.
Kaya: serves as an emissary to offer peace at a price.
Kline Marker: the younger son is offered freedom at a price.
Loki Rothander: has surprise visitors and finds riches.
Martim Christescu: Evran's efficient Christian stewardess.
Olga: the grandniece from overseas finds home at last.
Ozkurt: moves from freed prisoner to truce maker.
Rolf: turns failure into success by keen observation.
Saraijik: finds war an excuse for intervention and letters.
Sven: finds his search abroad for fame ends in frustration.
Yuzbasha Oren: a Hunnish lieutenant learning hard lessons.

GLOSSARY:

aga'm: my lord; sir; (the g is silent here).
ay'ney shay: The same; the same thing; identical.
bash- ooze to nay: I obey; I will do it; as you say.
tom-mom': okay; all right; I agree.

FUNERAL PYRE

"A clean sweep! We cut off their tail," exalted the youth carrying his boards on his shoulder.

The ski troop arrived at the door of the hunting lodge in the pine woods in an exuberant mood. One chortled, "Did you see how fast we left them behind when we reached the down slope? Their horses were bogged down in the snow. It was so easy."

A tall rugged blond, who had to bend over to enter through the door, exclaimed with a strong accent, "I tell you this from beginning, but you laugh at me. 'Stupid little Norseman' you call me. Our snow only stays four months, you say, not like North Country, but you learn good when you see advantages."

"Heinder, didn't. He fell on his butt three times."

"Rolf hit a tree, I saw him. Good thing it was at the bottom."

"How's your arm, Hans? Where the sentry cut you."

"Just nicked me on the elbow. I don't even feel it. I was busy keeping him from yelling an alarm. I didn't even see his blade."

"Let's have some food, I'm starved."

Another went to a keg. "Let's have a drink, I need to celebrate."

"Old scar face was having some trouble there when we left."

"Yah, one or two down, but they were over the climb to the meadow. They probably made it." Another came in late with blood and scratches on his face. One of his board skis was broken. He limped and seemed stunned. They all took it in and laughed. "Rolf, brother, were you wounded in battle? Tell us how you got your scars." They laughed loudly.

Rolf shook his head to clear it. "I stayed; I saw old scar face Fritz go down from a lucky long shot. His squad tried to get him up, but these boards are tricky or he was hit too bad. They formed the shield wall when I followed you. I was too far to go back and help them." Silence descended on the crowd.

Hans' face turned angry red. He burst out furiously. "I told the old fool not to try the skis. He said that if the young could learn it, he could too. That witch has put this idea in his head. He's young again. They were a pathetic lot falling all over the slope."

Rolf looked at his leader critically, "He did well enough to get to the target and back to the mountain. We just skimmed through. A squad of Huns came over the slope after us, but the horses fell or balked. That's the last I saw, likely they were recalled."

Ansgar, the Norse, looked around with mournful eyes and suggested, "Shouldn't we go back and look. If some escaped we could help them in."

Several shook their heads in mutual disagreement. "Once they form the shield wall they can't leave."

"The Huns will use the bodies as bait to get more of us back there."

Hans spoke quickly, "Ansgar, grab some food and come with me. We'll go up the mountain and have a look from above. Then we'll know what to do. You are the skier and I know the country. A small team will be best," Hans ordered.

Rolf objected, "I want to go too."

Ansgar denied his request, "You're hurt and would slow us down. I'll take my cousin Sven. We traveled the rivers together to adventure and win a name. He's good on mountains. He'll be our rear guard."

"Make sure the two groups are reinforced: first, the hunt for Rumen laborers. You must continue a sweep of the upper Ult River valley and the tributaries. Second, the trap on the alpine meadow must include troops at the bottom of the slope where the first Goth troop disappeared. Keep out of sight until they try to recover the body of the leader and his guards. A leader like Scarface Fritz Marker might command a rescue by a thousand or more men, so be prepared."

"Sir, it's dark and you've been up since the burning alarm, before dawn. Your lady will have made food and waits your return to the castle. You should return and rest."

Evran reacted with anger. "Do I need an adjutant for nursing care? I will go to the supply depot again for inventory and then to interrogate the prisoners."

He could not admit to himself or others that he dreaded to confront his nemesis and passion and try vainly to send her home. He recognized the futility, but could not leave the need to assert his dominance. Yet up to this moment the passionate arguments that led to intimacy were his delight. His obvious humiliation by only four dozen enemies had weakened his position in every level of his authority. His Khan, Munzur, would make inquiries. His position as son-in-law was not one that held assurance in every circumstance. He was vulnerable, which took away the edge of his enjoyment of his wife. He delayed his encounter with her.

> - - - - - - - >

"We can't leave Uncle Fritz and his guards dead, left out in the snow. They must be gathered and burned as heroes who die for their people's freedom." Olga cried out between sobs, "We must declare a truce. We have to get his body back!."

Kaya spoke earnestly, "You can't get a truce on demand unless you're winning by pressing the attack. However, a peace conference might get you a chance at recovering them. You haven't the men and supplies to win this conflict, but they might make a treaty of some kind to cover the loss of face and damage you caused."

Ozkurt, nodded his agreement, "It's been nearly six weeks since the first attack on the fort. It's near the Lenten season now. The forest trails will be open to them soon. We can make some kind of treaty before the big attacks are launched against us."

"Hans and his young men are pressing the attacks. They wanted war so they would become heroes and have things to brag about. They deserted Uncle on the high meadow when they were attacked. They wanted him to die and don't want peace," she affirmed.

"Your uncle's councilor said that the members are ready for peace at almost any price. Loki sent his letter advising an end to hostilities. An army is moving east from the capital. The burning of Ruggenfurt is an affront. Khan Munzur is offended by the disruption of messages and contacts east. I think Evran bey would be glad to have some kind of victory before another general arrives to take over. Submission might get you good terms if you act now."

"We have no way to get an offer of submission or talks to the General. Rolf brought us news of the massacre, but he would be treated as an enemy as would I," Olga countered. There was a moment of silence.

Then Kaya spoke, "I can go with a truce and an offer on your part to meet, but I can't do the negotiations. You or someone else will have to do it. After Hans left, your grand uncle took you into every decision he made and his happiness was clearly shared by everyone. You're an heir. He joined the burning of the workers' villages and the fort, so Hans would not be careless and irresponsible in the attacks. He knew that the destruction of your people would be certain after the reconstruction and strengthening of Ruggenfurt. So he was willing to attempt the disruption. Now Loki sends this new message about troop movement from the capital, but it's too late, received today, after the burnings. It sounds like the Huns plan to raze the mountains. We need to submit before they are close. Yesu teaches that if a stronger army comes against you, it's wise to send an embassy of peace before it gets to you. Let's follow that advice."

> - - - - - - - >

"I suppose you have healed and dispatched the wounded, set up the kitchen and fed them all. You will have the prisoner rested, fed and encouraged. You'll know his mother's name and any possible love interest in his young life." Evran's tone was bantering, but his voice was hard, cynical and resentful.

She appraised him coolly, "Jailors are rewarded for garnering information of value. Is this then the reward of the Lord of the lower Danube? That his source should be rewarded with mocking? Or that his agent become his enemy for efficiency?"

He stood in a confusion of emotions. "Why did you come into danger? You move without my consent. You interfere in my business..."

She interrupted. "All Huns live in constant danger. Your herd cattle rebel when they are oppressed and damaged. You need me here and here I'll stay." Their eyes locked.

"I'm in command here. You are duty bound."

"I'm bound by a union that we both wanted. The gifts and money you gave were not for a purchase, but for an investment to have the benefits of a yurt, a wife and a home of your own."

"Where I would be master and benefactor."

"Have you lost control in your command? Look elsewhere for the fault. I am here to benefit you, not to take command."

"But you didn't ask. You just came with all those families."

She smiled now. "Love called us to come. I would rather die with my family around me. Others feel the same." They stood glaring till she reached out a hand and brushed his face fondly. "We have roasted hare, Joseph set a snare last night. The rest is soldier's fare. It will take time to get better food here. Come, enjoy what we have."

A guard rattled the door shouting: "*Aga-m*, My Lord, a troop has arrived with two East Huns. They request an audience immediately."

Evran grimaced and pushed her hand away, He turned his back murmuring, "If these are the ones I think, *Aya and Kurt*, the bear and wolf, I'll have come full circle from one little misstep to a larger one. Is it too late to change destiny?" Then he yelled at the still closed door. "Send them in." The pair came in with guards.

The onbasha reported carefully, "They rode in on the west road. They were without weapons except for short knives. They claim to have been taken by the rebels."

"We seem destined to meet after sacrificial burnings. The bear and wolf in the wild are survivors. Thus, those are suitable clan and personal designations. You survived the attack and the detention. Do you still have your letters?"

The princess smiled and squeezed in a comment, "You are the messengers I never got to meet. Welcome to my yurt."

Kaya, obviously surprised by the warm welcome stuttered, "Thanks, My Lady. Yes Sir, we have all our papers unopened and a message from your rebellious subjects as well. They're willing to meet you and discuss their grievances. If you will meet them and extend a guarantee of safety."

A surprised look marked Evran's face. "Discuss grievances with an enemy! Why did they attack us if they wish to discuss grievances? Talk should come before action."

"*Ay'ney shay*, the same, they say this too! Why did you burn a village formed under a peace agreement and why resent a counter-attack? They say you started this war."

Evran snarled, "And I'll win it, too."

Ozkurt interjected a withering word, "No, you'll be replaced. Another army is on its way to take over the task. They've given you a last chance. They don't understand how it started and will kill everyone. The country will be people-less, burned and desolate."

"Is this true, Evran? Is all this from the village you burned? My father will be overjoyed to replace you and humiliate me again." The princess' face was set and intense. Her eyes burned brightly.

"The village housed spies from the boat." Evran protested.

"No, My Lord," interrupted Kaya, "we were on the boat and escaped the Khazar embassy to Constantinople, to get our messages through without the knowledge of either Khazars or Rumens in our party."

Cold anger filled Evran's face. "Why wasn't I told this on our meeting?"

Ozkurt quickly answered, "You had already burned the village. We would have been killed without a chance to explain and prove our case. You would think us spies. We had time to present our credentials that way."

"You may be spies as far as I know," he replied.

Kaya smiled, "You could open the letters and scrolls to the Khan Munzur."

"There is a death penalty to reading his letters, as you well know."

The princess held up her hands to prevent further talk. "We have roast hare to improve the bulgur tonight. We will eat now and talk later. Surely there can be an accord before my father's army arrives.

> - - - - - - - >

"It was so easy to carry out the attack and retreat. Why is this reconnaissance so tiring?" Hans complained wearily.

Ansgar laughed as they crawled forward, "Going to battle is usually easy. Returning victorious is full of satisfaction. We are dodging patrols and climbing the mountains; arduous business in the snow."

Hans looked worn and dirty. He wore a sling around his neck to support his left arm. "I thought it would be a matter of a few hours trek. I didn't expect we would be pinned down and have to spend two nights here. Now, we are so high, I doubt we will see more than dots on the snow."

Sven called back, "I can see the meadow below. There are many people gathered there." Hans moved over to look.

"At least we can see today, yesterday's clouds and mist are past," Ansgar said, as he crouched down beside a boulder.

"Sven, what are they doing down there? Is it a house they build?" asked Hans, "My head is throbbing, it must be the height."

"They are laying logs in crisscross pattern. It's a funeral pyre they're building. It has three layers. Fritz Marker is probably the figure on top. The guards will be on the first level, others, freemen above that. They're getting ready to light it" Ansgar gasped, "There are mourners present, a party of Goths there. There's a party of Huns, too. I see the figures of women and children: families are there. Look, your brother is there."

Hans, forgetful of hiding, stood and exclaimed. "No, it can't be! No peace with the Huns. They burned the peace village. Kline, remember, we must continue the war."

Ansgar pulled him down. "Hush, we're hiding. We don't know the conditions of the truce. You risk our necks."

Hans lay back holding his arm, moaning, "It burns." he said.

Ansgar agreed, watching the action below. "A small woman walks forward with Kline, both with a torch and yes, it's lit now and burning."

Sven, however, bends over Hans and touches his face. "He burns as well. The cut on his elbow is poisoned through his neglect. My mother always washes wounds."

Ansgar shrugged, "Too late for your mother now. Let's take advantage of the formalities below to go down the mountain's backside, straight to the lodge. He'll need a lot more than washing or peace." They roused Hans and got him to his feet to help him stumble down the slope.

Behind and below them the pyre blazed while a hymn was sung. The immediate hopes and ambitions of men and women were paused to focus on a reality few prepare to meet.

1.   I come to You with empty hands,
Left jewels, gold and precious lands.
To stand alone with all I've done:
Decided, chosen, doted on.
As I have come, so will I go,
With nothing but my life to show.

2.   All-Father in the vault above,
You know my weakness, sin and love.
Clothed in my pride to stand accused,

By all defrauded and abused.
As I have dealt, don't deal with me,
For so should I forever be.

3. In halls of heroes and the brave;
To live with such is what we crave.
Let love take flight and gain great height
So let me live for what is right.
The Thunderer calls us to be,
True men in Christ, forever free.

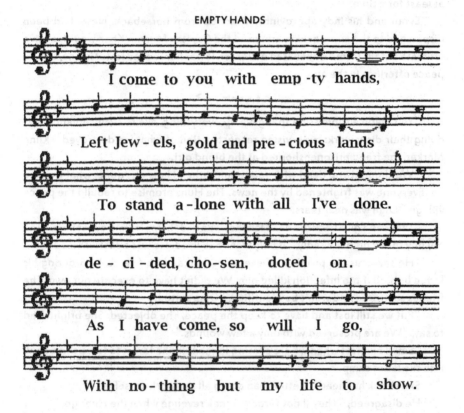

EMPTY HANDS

I come to you with emp-ty hands,

Left Jew-els, gold and pre-cious lands

To stand a-lone with all I've done.

de-ci-ded, cho-sen, doted on.

As I have come, so will I go,

With no-thing but my life to show.

The men were armed and the women shrouded, each racial group stood apart distrustful, for the idea of co-existence was new for the Goths. Both understood treaties as expressions of weakness or as postponement of the final drive for dominance. However, the high mountains were simply an impediment to easy communication; there was nothing of great value to covet for the Huns.

Necessity, as ever, is the mother of new attempts in human relationships. The boy prisoner, a grandson of Fritz Marker, was released unharmed. The Goths had to make restitution by hunting the scattered Rumen laborers or supply the labor themselves. They had to supply timber and other materials for the construction. They would supervise others in their work for the Hun.

The peace village was to be rebuilt and inhabited. Odin, the informer, was released to the Goths to be punished. This was almost an apology, by the rulers.

Herders use dogs in the control of the herd. The animals are useful and for this reason respected, but hardly equal. So the Huns would regard the Goths and the treaty of submission.

The Goths on the other hand would see it as recognition of their self-rule as a tribe. The ring leaders of the revolt would be sacrificed, but the people preserved; at least for a time.

Evran and his lady approvingly watched from horseback. News had been dispatched to the approaching army and the Capital. Munzur Khan would receive intimate details from an alienated daughter. It was her second letter in one month; peace offerings in the air.

> - - - - - - - >

"You made a submission that gave up everything. We're their servants now, doing their dirty work: supervising reconstruction of what we destroyed." Kline Marker, the freed prisoner shouted at the blond girl.

"We thought you dead with your grandfather. Hans was gone, what was I to do. Everyone was frightened by the news. The Huns promise to rebuild the peace village." Olga was near tears.

"They can't give back the dead families. We had them cleaned out of here." The tall boy shook his head sadly, "If only Hans had lived. He was a real war leader."

"He saved us the problem of executing him and his friends by ordering his lodge burned if the infection killed him. We didn't have to execute our own. The friends scattered and won't be identified," Olga stated.

"But we still lost and have to keep the peace," he objected. She brightened to say, "We are preserved with only a few wounds."

"Small comfort when we are chasing Rumens in the forest to force them back into the labor camp."

She shook her head, "Better than doing all the work ourselves."

He disagreed, "They'll not forget to seek revenge when the Huns go."

"Who knows when that will be? Meanwhile we're safe."

"No one who holds the tiger's tail is safe."

She started to cry. "Uncle Fritz is dead. I found him only to lose him. My friends, the messengers, have left on their quest and I'm alone again. Just like the time Ompa Otto died. The neighbors took everything, but I took the boat. What will I do now?"

Kline reached over impulsively and hugged her. He whispered to her, holding her very close, "It's alright, you have a place here. He loved you. He was so happy and he stopped singing about a lost love overseas. We'll get through this. Your place is here."

"Well, My Lord, the Khan, my father, has relaxed. He even thanked me for my letters. There is resistance along the Rhine River kingdoms to making an alliance with him. He will send the eastern army to reinforce the western. He thinks the threat will be sufficient to convince them of the need. He instructs me to make sure the back door is guarded."

Evran lay on the divan before the fire. He chuckled and stretched out an arm in invitation as he replied, "He even said that the Goths' submission was good and its promotion would insure a time of peace. Said it was unusually mild for me to let off the rebels or admit that burning a village was a mistake."

She came to stand beside him, "Martim would say the Christ has softened your heart toward mercy."

He chuckled amused, "The Goths would say we have learned that the wolf has sharp teeth."

She nodded her approval, "Father's getting milder in his old age and I suppose you are too."

"Who said anything about me being old. Come here, I'll show you how old I've become."

She escaped hastily, laughing. She teased, "You said you had a busy day, so you'll be too tired to chase me."

He leaned back and grinned roguishly, "I don't have to chase. Here, I command. Those are my wife's words, when she came to bring the yurt to our construction site. She is a choice woman who tells me the truth. So, I'm master, I command."

"I'm sure such a woman would keep her word," she whispered, smiling her prettiest.

"Blow out the candle and come," he commanded. "It's time we had a son to start our family."

"*Bash ooze too nay*, as you command," she murmured.

THE SUMMONS

>- - - - - - - >

"I am fascinated by the happenings in your mountains. I'm so pleased you accepted my invitation to stop by for a visit." Loki beamed happily at the visiting messengers. "Naturally, I've heard of the rebuilding and burnings. We have an army here in Transylvania, but they have camped now. News of the submission and the burning of the rebel headquarters has put Munzur's heart at ease."

"The lodge was burned around its master, the instigator of the war. He wanted revenge for the burning of Peace village," Kaya replied. "Retaliation is an endless game."

"Meanwhile, the army has brought a large market and an unruly menace to our region. Fortunately, we are clear of them here in these little mountains, but the surrounding plains are full of troops who exact tribute and food from the people."

Ozkurt asked, "Why would they be considered a market for you if they are extorting food for their use? They aren't paying money for it."

Loki grinned smugly, "There are goods in demand that they will pay well for. Goods that make hard, dangerous service seem worthwhile, if it buys such pleasure. They don't always have gold or coin, but other goods can be traded for pleasure."

The messengers exchanged curious glances. "It sounds as if you were providing some of these goods."

"Only as a supplier, others handle the deliveries and supervision. I don't have to collect from the men. That's why I couldn't afford for the army to move on up to Ultania. It must stay here for my profits."

Ozkurt nodded his agreement, "No one wanted it there. But will it stay here long?"

Loki shrugged and smiled observantly. "Men get restless for action as time and pleasures decrease and wealth and ambitions remain unsatisfied. Munzur must make war on rich lands to satisfy his soldiers and great men. He rides a tiger."

"So, he will move west or south as he is able?" Kaya asked.

"As sure as the sun rises in the east and sets in the west."

"We will have to go on to the capital with our letters."

"From what you have told me, I'm sure others will have passed you, while you were detained. Your news will be outdated and useless for prompt action. You can make much of your adventures on the Ult. The Easter season of your faith is past, stay a while with me until summer while your horses recover. We smuggled you in, we will smuggle you out as the army starts to withdraw."

The two friends exchanged glances again. Ozkurt put his head back and stretched, "It's nice to be out of the continuous cold and snow. It feels like spring is already here. We will enjoy a short rest."

Loki smiled, "*Tom-mom*, okay, we'll make you comfy. It's too bad your little blond friend, Olga, didn't come too. I would have had good use for her here. Such are in demand."

Kaya tried to explain, "Her duties in the royal house keep her busy. She is very apt and is taking an important role in the working out of the agreement. She both bosses and cajoles the young heir, Kline, the grandson. They fight and make up. The tribe will survive."

Loki replied with a smirk, "She is well traveled and worldly wise, she'll make a good queen someday. Better than the dolt of a grandson. He was supposed to become a priest. He wouldn't have had the sense to seek out and marry one like her. I'll be sure to go up when the wedding is announced." He laughed suggestively.

"They are very young yet, it could work out differently," objected Kaya, annoyed by the man's cynical statement.

"A burning candle brings moths by night; and dead meat, flies by day. I'll wait for the announcement this summer.

"Here we run a tight establishment and have little leisure. You, however, are our guest and may enjoy your stay. We have no chapel or people of your beliefs hereabout, but you are free to practice your faith privately. However, most of our people guard the old ways; so don't offend them with your notions. I'll not be responsible for what will happen if you should preach your ideas to them. So be warned," thus Loki terminated with final instructions to his two attentive 'guests'.

"You're free to go now and explore the chateau and grounds.

I have letters to write. Go enjoy the garden or a ride. I have two servants assigned to your protection. They will always accompany you everywhere."

LAST FAREWELL

PEOPLE, PLACES & PLOTS in Chapter 19

Anders: finds his job more interesting with Turks.
Biorn: The bearded giant enjoys prison supervision.
Evran: keeps to a building schedule and listens to gossip.
Kaya: makes new discoveries while enjoying his stay.
Loki Rothander: is vigilant to keep his plans profitable.
Myra; a slave and small part of Loki's plans for wealth.
Ozkurt: fears treachery and finds good reasons.
Saraijik: finds life in the castle enjoyable and tells father.
Wodan: learns a few new tricks on horse handling.

GLOSSARY:

cha'buk: hurry; be quick; speed it up.
dough rue: correct; right; true; It's okay.
fur-lot: cast it off; throw it up; set a sail; launch; hurl.
shim'dy: now; this minute; at the present.
soos: hush; be quiet; don't talk; calm down.
tom-mom: okay; I agree; give permission.

WINDOW VIEW

"What's happening Kaya? Why are you up?" Ozkurt's voice boomed in the dark of the room. Kaya was standing at the window with the shutters open and the cold spring air caused his breath to show in the moonlight.

"Quiet, they may hear you. Men are loading bales of something from a cave in the side of the hill. I recognize the smell. They used it at the public baths during a festival in Epec Kent."

"What is it and why keep quiet?" He sat up and peered about in the dull light of the dying hearth fire.

"It's opium balls. He must grow the poppies. It's contraband for the troops. He'll not want us to know. Our two guards must not see any changes in us. Our host is engaged in criminal activity and is holding us for some purpose."

Ozkurt's voice queried, "What value would we serve for him?"

Kaya stood silent then he asked, "You left the packs in the stables?"

Ozkurt stood thinking, "*Hi'yer*, no, we carried them in, remember, little Mark brought in the skins and letters. He put them there in the corner, before he left for home." He pointed with his chin and they moved over to the loosened pack.

Kaya spoke, "I don't remember opening the letter pouch. Do You?"

"Not since we showed them to Evran bey," Ozkurt whispered as they felt through their packs.

"The pouch feels empty!" Kaya's voice came thickly. They stood speechless pondering this development.

Ozkurt sighed, "I wish we could light a candle."

A high shriek came from outside the window. A woman was protesting and struggling. "I won't go, you promised us something better; a house to work from, not a tent in an army camp."

Another woman's voice cut in, "Come on Myra, it's only for a short time before the army moves. After that, you'll be settled into a place with more comfort."

Another voice chimed in to encourage the protesting woman. "Sure, you may get an offer and travel with the army. It's better than being stuck in the village with a farmer the rest of your life."

There was a murmur of agreement among the several women in the cart. The woman's protesting voice came again, "Well, tell this animal to get his dirty hands off me. He can't do this to me without paying."

There was laughter as a commanding voice shouted into the moving shadows. "Leave her be. She'll wake the dead with her complaints. Now, get in the wagon freely or stay for a beating you won't forget. Your choice!"

There was a moment of silence and then the woman said "I'm not a cart horse to be prodded and driven. I'll get in on my own, thank you." And she proceeded to do that. A chuckle came from those in the cart and from the men who drove and protected the goods.

"*Tom-mom*, okay get out of here. You men are responsible for their protection. Don't spoil the goods. Remember your pay is held.

I don't forget a good turn or a bad one. You don't want me for an enemy." The cart moved out with the urging of the driver.

"Let's leave too," murmured Kaya, "Where are our weapons?"

"In the corner by the fireplace," Ozkurt replied.

Kaya groped near the fire. "There's nothing here but the shields," He held up the small round shields. "No swords, bows or arrows have been left."

"I'll check the door," Ozkurt whispered.

"They're still around, so be careful."

Ozkurt crept to the door. He lifted the bar and eased the door open. All was silence outside. He leaned out to look in every direction and his foot touched something yielding, but firm. A rumbling voice arose below him.

"What's yu nosin' about? Stay: an uder step an' yur dead!" A huge darkness rose up and the scrape of metal sounded.

"What are you doing here at our door?" Ozkurt snapped.

"Guardin' yu! Yu can't go about by night. 'T'aint safe. Orders be t' keep yu safe. Yu go's back in an' closes de door. I don't likes bein' woke up." The silhouette of a large man showed against the starlight.

"Who are you? What's your name?"

"I be Biorn, yur guard."

Ozkurt paused and tried again. "Some noise woke us up. Someone screamed," he said.

"Anders an' 'is wife 'ave a fight; 'e 'its 'er w'en 'e's drunk. Like I say, go back t' sleep or I'll 'ave t' report it t' de master. He an' yu wouldn't like dat."

Ozkurt withdrew and barred the door. "We're prisoners." he reported quietly. "House arrest by night, and escorted by day until they decide otherwise."

> - - - - - - - >

"I have an unsolicited letter from father. I would say he is trying to convert me to be his eastern eyes," Saraijik said.

"Every wise commander has eyes and ears among his men and also among the enemy. As long as you and I see the same, I find no problem with your occasional correspondence."

She laughed, "You don't fool me. You'll want to read and even dictate parts of the letters. I'd better warn father that he should have secured a less zealous jailor and guard for me. Perhaps he can find me one closer to the capital," she teased.

Hands on hips, Evran tried to stare her down. "There is no better guardian and it may be time to teach you a lesson in duty and submission."

She stared back coolly with a smile. "Martim is coming with food now. Who knows who she reports to?"

Evran sniffed contemptuously and brought his face close. "You don't fool me either. She reports to me, you, and Yesu, regularly. She, at least, is transparent. It's people with secrets to hide that are the source of trouble."

She shrugged a shoulder provocatively as she walked to the window. She pretended interest before turning. "He's gotten a ransom note and a teaser document to prove they hold the two messengers. Someone wants money for more documents and the messengers."

Evran folded his arms over his chest. "Not the bear and wolf again! Aya and Kurt, how much bad luck can someone have? The documents will be ancient history when they get there."

She imitated his movements, "Yes, Aya and Kurt again!

I liked them. Someone doesn't want them to rescue the promised bride. Daddy doesn't know that part, it's our secret and I won't tell."

Evran scolded, "Don't mock me, young lady, or I'll forget about food." He reached for her.

"Stop! I just remembered something Olga hanum told me." She reached out to push his hand away.

"You're talking a lot with that Goth," he said critically.

"I like her, she has traveled and is in love. She hates Hun warriors, but considers me a victim of war and capture. She talks about Kline, her groom to be, also she has heard that a Goth, a big dealer in the Transylvanian hills, is offering a golden mare in the Summer horse fair. Aya has a golden mare. Could it be the same?" She moved closer to his side and took his arm, concerned.

"They're rare." He paused and affirmed, "Yes, if they're to be ransomed, their goods will be pilfered. Get the name of the horse dealer next time."

She nodded and walked to open the door for Martim. "Yes, working for daddy may have its bright moments."

> - - - - - - - >

"Merien, where have you been?" A young boy shouted. "You have a letter off the first spring ship from Ukraine. Magda has a letter from Father. Kertch port has accepted an alliance with the Khazars. They have launched a spring offensive and are rolling up the Donetz River." He paused out of breath. She bent slightly to kiss his cheek. He shrugged off the accepted token to insist, "Where have you been?"

She hung up her fine, red wool Easter cloak before speaking. "I have a letter also, but not from the ship, no, from an old friend who is soon to marry in Rumanian country. Yes, I got it this morning from the Hun's embassy here."

"That's up near the stadium. Were they racing this morning? There is an official game on Saturday." He was excited by the new distraction now.

She giggled and cocked her head, "Yes, Stefan, the young men are there and they watch the horses and others as they pass. Is old custom, no?"

"I won't tell Magda," he grinned, "but you must tell me about it." He followed her to where she sat down in the patio.

"I tell you nothing. You will learn too soon from them. No, I tell you about friend Olga from Kertch port. She finds her great uncle Fritz, yes. So happy for a month, then he dies and she is all alone. Grandson of great uncle is new leader of tribe. They are Goths you remember, no? He wants to marry Olga." She held up her hand and counted the fingers. "Olga, then Father and mother, grandmother Helga and uncle Otto who is brother of grand uncle Fritz, is grandfather of Kline." She touched the last two fingers lightly and closed her hand to a fist. "Is good marriage no? Family blood strong, but not too close. Yes, I wish her much happiness. She is very young yet. I'm much older." She sighed deeply.

"How did she get the letter here? You didn't say she wrote. I thought all barbarians were illiterate," Stefan stated.

"She has important friend, a Hun princess who wrote for her, yes. You remember the wolf and bear, no?"

"The men with the golden horse? Sure, are they there now?" He fidgeted with excitement. "I wish I were there!"

She didn't answer immediately, but stared into the fountain for a long time. "He goes to their capital city, yes. He will finish his quest or die, no? It is beautiful and sad too. Only heaven can save him now."

> - - - - - - - >

"I don't know how much more I can take of this confinement. In Samarkand we at least had the run of the city. You entertain yourself gentling and making friends of horses, but I can't do that. They won't let me practice with the bow." Ozkurt was complaining again.

"Let's ask for permission to hunt," Kaya suggested. "The birds are flocking north and new meat will be welcome."

Ozkurt smiled in relief, "I hoped you'd say that. I know you've given promise that you won't attempt an escape, but we ought to know the lay of the land and the roads at least for a few hours ride."

Kaya chuckled and smiled at his friend. "Remember, Yesu will set us free at the proper time. We can't start anything premature." He thought a moment, "They will give us extra guards, birding arrows and weak bows and no maps or road coaching at all."

Ozkurt grinned and winked, "Some things we learn by the seat of our pants."

"So, Tanra has to let horses, dogs and opponents apply pressure in that seat to keep us in line and careful." They both laughed.

Outside the door Biorn waited and hearing them laugh reported to the new guard, shaking his head, "I never seen such men as deez two. Got no sense o' danger, no worries. W'ere others would be glum or angry, dey seem t' like workin'. It's like havin' two new hands t' share de jobs wit. Beats me!"

Kaya was talking gently to the nervous filly, moving slowly toward her as she skittered at the end of the rope halter. Ozkurt and others stood watching. Would he mount and take a terrific ride or would he simply talk and stroke as he did on some occasions. He slowly reached into his sash pocket and brought out a bit of dried honeycomb and slowly placed it under her nose in an open palm.

Wodan whispered, while Ozkurt held his breath, "I got m' hand bit by a stallion de last time I tried sometin' like dat." They watched and sighed in unison as the filly sniffed and then took the proffered gift. Nibbling it from his palm she relaxed even as the watchers did. Still talking gently, Kaya turned his back and hand in sash walked two steps forward, stopped and held out his hand with the tasty nuggets. She took two steps to eat the sweet offering. Heads nodded and chuckles arose from the audience as the horse now followed the walker for treats. They walked the fence line to the approval of all. She even trotted once to keep up with the generous Kaya. They finished and he slipped a bridle over her head and they walked together with no pressure on the reins.

Kaya took the bridle off and turned to the men. "Put her in pasture to think over our little exchange and tomorrow we'll get on with it." One of the hands lowered the bar and she moved out walking, not running to get away. She nickered and looked back once.

"Yu gets a civil goodbye, all I ever gets from 'er is a snort an' head toss." Wodan complained.

Kaya laughed, "Some creatures won't be won by force and threats. Only respect and cooperation for mutual gain will win them over."

"De wranglers I learnt from, all use strength o' will t' dominate an' break 'em."

Kaya nodded his agreement and understanding, "There are wild, rebellious mavericks that will learn no other way, but you lose a third or fourth of your horses by breaking them. A befriended horse will give more power, stamina and obedience to their master and companion than an animal of broken spirit. Learning is promoted through friendship."

"Well, I done learnt lots from yu," Wodan stated honestly.

"We're friends who don't cause you trouble," said Kaya. "But we have the problem of my friend Kurt. The wolf needs to hunt and keep his teeth sharp, otherwise he becomes morose and angry. Kurt needs outings, would you permit us to go birding? Migration is on, the air is full of flocks; the meat is good. Let us hunt for the household and families."

Wodan was thoughtful, "Yu got t' speak t' de boss," he murmured. "I tink he say yes."

Kaya nodded and said quietly, "I'll talk to him after dinner tonight, I'll let you know then."

> - - - - - - - >

"You've paid for your keep so far and given me no trouble," said Loki, "You will be given your hunting gear." He smiled, I'll send some men along for something bigger if you run across them. Please don't try to leave. I'll tell you when it's safe to go."

Kaya smiled broadly. "Yes, we understand and wait for a timely word. You have other things to concern you."

As they left, Ozkurt said, "We wait for a timely word? You're going to let him tell us we can go?"

Kaya nodded, and slapped him on the back. "God will tell us when. He's brought me safe this far. I'll trust Tanra's timing for the rest of the journey."

Ozkurt sighed, "I don't know who keeps me frustrated and on edge more, you or your God, Yesu. I want to run and both you and Tanra say 'not yet.' Tanra seemed better when he was a distant creator and impersonal. Living close to Him and His will seems so much harder. But till now I thought it gave more good results."

"A keen observation, my friend. It's more fruitful, yet it does take more trust and willingness to have His will, not our own. I'm praying that when the moment comes you will feel it as definitely as I do."

Ozkurt nodded in agreement, "But I'll probably be too distracted to notice, until He kicks me in the pants."

Kaya turned and brought a knee up, "You mean like this? You want to be kicked?" He ran away from the house.

"Just a minute I'll show you exactly how hard I want it." Both were in full flight through the garden and into the pasture. Ozkurt made a flying tackle and brought Kaya down. Laughing they tussled on the spring grass. Kaya's weight should have given him an advantage, but Ozkurt was all wire and sinew and the struggle left them both breathing hard, lying on the grass. Ozkurt brought over a foot and bumped Kaya on the rear. Both laughed breathlessly.

Ozkurt gasped, "There, paid back with interest. Why don't you treat your horses this way?"

Kaya shook his head, heaving. "They get their release from running. People need struggle to gain good sense."

Biorn came walking up to where they lay. He grinned broadly at the sprawled figures. "De master, he say yu can hunt birds, an' has named de equipment. We makes up a party an' starts t' morrow afore dawn."

Kaya poked Ozkurt in the ribs saying, "I know you are anxious to get practiced up again, but how would it be if I take the Loki's Peregrine. It's being neglected. I'll get as many birds as you, as long as you hit the prey and not my predator."

"It's a bet, I could beat you with one eye closed."

"Better use them both, the Falcon is sharp eyed. The reward is half a day free from chores and the loser skins the birds."

Biorn grunted in satisfaction, The boss was right to test these foreigners with little liberties. They were very different from the people he knew.

> - - - - - - - >

"They rode into a dawn; clear, blue and fresh with the cool mist still clinging to the ground, but already the sound of waking bird calls and movement could be heard. Five men rode with them. The Peregrine was chained to Kaya's glove and Ozkurt held a slight birding bow with arrows that had an inverted V at the point with tiny barbs to hold the bird snug in its embrace.

Kaya nodded amiably to Biorn. "You're dressed for war not hunting. Why the armor?"

"Der be reports o' Huns about. We needs t' be on guard. We knows we's bein' watched."

"I thought Loki said he had an understanding with his neighbors?"

Biorn indicated with a motion of his head that they were to ride on. Ozkurt was arming his bow and fitting an arrow. They chose a path leading to a nearby lake. "Neighbors be one ting, de army be an uder. Anders an a friend be ridin' wid us," Biorn growled. The attendants rode in pairs, far out on the flanks.

"I thought they intended to kill us," Ozkurt whispered. "I intended to go out with a fight even if the pronged v wouldn't kill, it could take out an eye." They were home now and the afternoon was far spent.

Kaya smiled indulgently. "Is that why my bird collected more than your arrows? They thought we might make a run for it and were prepared. If they intended to kill us they could do it just as well in our room or anywhere on the property. Why pretend? Anyway," he chuckled, "you cleaned the birds."

Ozkurt protested, "I was distracted, and anyway that bird can fly beyond arrow range of these little birding bows."

Kaya looked over their stored luggage and rising, stood sniffing suspiciously. "Something is different here. Someone's been here."

Ozkurt poked among the baggage. He held up a small satchel. "The messages are back in the case. Someone returned them here."

Kaya took the case and sniffed it. "I wonder if they changed anything. I'm sure they read them. It's beginning to look like they intend us to live and deliver them."

Ozkurt grabbed the case and counted the documents. He took one up. He liked to show off. His new skill at reading pleased him. "We ought to read them to see," he offered eagerly."

"I'm almost sorry I taught you to read during our frequent stop-overs. Now you ask even more foolish questions."

Kaya's complaint fell on deaf ears. He continued lecturing his unheeding friend. "The army is still here and hasn't moved into the mountains. Evran must still rule the roads and lower Danube. If the Goths were fighting we would know that too. Everyone must be busy with calving, sowing, fishing and hunting. An army has no such responsibility and will be restless. The men with us were ready for a chance encounter. The troops must be moved soon or there will be trouble of one kind or another. Perhaps Tanra will let us move too."

Ozkurt scratched an itch, "Do we dare carry old or doubtful messages, even if they are our credentials for passing army checkpoints and get an interview with Munzur khan?"

Kaya shrugged, "We don't dare get rid of them, we keep getting more like the ones Olga gave us from the boat, but we can't leave them lying around any more. Where could we hide them?"

Ozkurt scanned the room. "Not outside we're always watched there."

Kaya moved over to the fireplace and examined the rock facing carefully. "Look here," he called "This one is loose." He started moving a large rock and scratching at the dry mud and mortar around it. As he worked the stone free, a space was revealed between the walls and the fireplace foundation.

Ozkurt chuckled in triumph. "It'll fit the letter packet and even more."

Kaya added, "The Janovar skin will fit if we wrap the letters. They'll be safe until we know what to do with them." They replaced the rock and moistened the dirt and mortar powder and tried to fill the edges of the seams.

"It's there if we need it. It may be better for the Wolf and Bear to become a Pure Free Fighter and a Big Rock when we leave here," Kaya mused thoughtfully as they finished.

"I'm glad, although being Wolf was not too bad; except for the other meaning." Ozkurt looked chagrined when Kaya pronounced his name separating the two syllables. Then they laughed together. And Kaya threw his arms around him. "Pure and free fighter, wolf or worm; I love you. I hope I'll be in a position to reward you when this quest is over."

> - - - - - - - >

"*Fur'lot*, launch, launch de falcon," Biorn cried, "Dey's escapin'." With a flurry of sound and action the geese were paddling themselves into the air. Wings waving, feet splashing, they gathered speed. Kaya already had the hood off the bird and was swinging his arm up and out and the bird was in direct flight toward the prey. Kaya fletched an arrow,

Ozkurt was in a frenzy waiting for the birds to fly over land so his arrows could be retrieved. He had already lost several over the lake and could afford no more loss for they would be permanent.

Anders and Biorn composed a team with them now. Summer hunting had formed a bond between them. An easy camaraderie existed between guards and guarded; Goth and Turk. They honed their skills as providers of meat for the work crews at the chateau.

"*Shimdy*, now, shoot!" Anders shouted in excitement, "Dey's turning over land; de falcon done spooked 'em." Ozkurt quickly launched two arrows and took the lead bird and a follower. As the flock split, the falcon overtook one and fell with his talons buried in its head. Biorn had also shot a bird, but Anders in his excitement missed his shot.

Teasing began as Ozkurt shouted, "I got two. Someone else can skin them."

Biorn added, "I got me one, I'm off free."

Kaya laughed and said, "My arrow missed, so I guess Anders and I will do it."

They retrieved the arrows and birds. They left the falcon with the heads. As they worked Biorn stood scanning the view.

"Der's smoke on de skyline," he observed. "It has t' be de chateau. Dey's under attack." Everything stopped, as all stretched to look at the distant smudge.

Ozkurt said, "Huns; they've traced us. They'll take out everything."

"Gretchen an' de kids?" said Anders anxiously. Biorn shrugged and turned away. He stooped to take up the knife and finished the work. Tears wet Anders' face.

"We gots t' go back an' check on everbody," Biorn stated. "Den we decides wat t' do."

> - - - - - - - >

"They hain't left nothin' liven' or useful" Biorn noted sourly. The shell of the buildings still smoldered.

"I wonder if anyone escaped," Kaya mused. Anders rode off to examine his home area. Kaya rode to the corral now empty of men and horses. Ozkurt went to the chimney of their prison building. Biorn went to the main building and each looked for tracks or counted bodies.

"They took the horses and the livery equipment," reported Kaya as the group came together again later.

"Loki's not dare among de dead, 'e's runnin' free, gone fer cover," Biorn stated.

Ozkurt disagreed strongly, "No, he's wounded and taken alive. They'll force him to reveal where his money's hidden."

Anders came crying, "Gretchen be dead, but de kids hain't dare. Dey gone t' cover." The others did not look hopeful.

Biorn said, "We hain't searched de woods yet. Might find lots o' bodies dare."

Kaya rode over and gripped Biorn's arm. "You must run, escape to the mountains. Olga hanum will give you refuge. Take this bird and tell her it's from me; say you have heard the good news."

He passed the falcon to Biorn who took the bird, but objected. "Loki, he say t' kill yu if anyt'ing go wrong, so's I can't leaves yu go free. Better we all go's t'geder t' de hi mountains. He be plenty mad at me if yu not wid us."

"When the Huns finish with him, he'll wish he was dead." Ozkurt observed, "After you tell them what they want to know, they kill you and you're glad to go."

"*Chabuk*, quick, a squad of Huns from the spring side trail." Kaya yelled in alarm. He urged Altom into a run. Biorn glanced over his shoulder and set his horse in motion. They rode back the way they had come, but that road too, produced another squad of men bearing down on them. The Goths veered left and the Turks right. The Huns after a pause chose the Turks.

"Meet a' de lake," Biorn cried out, as they thundered away; the Huns from the spring following.

Ozkurt griped, "Here we are with birding bows and arrows; no way to stop them. Defenseless in a fight!"

Kaya snapped coldly, "Then we can concentrate on escaping. If these men have been trailing us their horses will be as tired as ours. Lets go to the thicket."

Ozkurt agreed heartily, "*Dough rue*, right, that's a maze of trails and swamps."

"If you recovered the letters we'll make contact farther in, closer to Munzur Khan's headquarters, with people less eager to kill us, somewhere far from these blood-thirsty troops,"

Ozkurt swore, as a spent arrow fell behind them. The horses were heaving now as they raced down the hill. Ahead the green jungle of bog and dark trees waited in silence. Summer heat radiated from the valley.

"No more talk from here on," Kaya warned. "We have to lay up for a few days and get clear of these squads. They'll expect us to head for the Alps, but we'll go the other direction."

"I did get the letters and skin, we'll have to be messengers when we report or when they catch us."

"It's important not to get caught around here or anywhere else for that matter," Kaya replied.

"Mosquitoes by night, gnats by day, green water and cold rations for days," groaned Ozkurt as they entered the brush.

"*Soos*, hush," hissed Kaya, "Dismount and run."

"I'm making progress in the use of prayers," Ozkurt whispered. "We need them so frequently." A branch slapped his face as they dodged the thick stands of scrub. In a few moments they were lost from view as the Hun troops pulled up to dismount and set trackers out to trail their prey. Wary of ambush, they traced the escapees in squads spread through the bog and scrub, while the onbasha angrily saw the hoped for rewards for a golden horse diminish with the passing hours.

BIRDING WITH HAWK AND BOW

PEOPLE, PLACES & PLOTS IN CHAPTER 20

Attila: nine-year old son of the Emperor, already superb with a bow.
Brahin: giant lover of the Princess, being married off to one of her maidens.
Chee'chek: the princess' attendant and singer.
Evran: finds new areas of conflict with his princess.
Fewsoon: attendant to the Princess Yetkin by gift of the Koosta mercenaries.
Kaya: arrives at last to the West Hun capital with Altom.
Munzur Khan: Emperor of the right hand Hun Armies.
Ozkurt: finds relief from travel boredom for excitement in the capital.
Princess Yet'kin: a spoiled girl and elder sister of Attila.
Saraijik: finds new concerns and old conflicts renewed.

GLOSSARY:

ah-tesh': fire; release; shoot.
es-ear' lair: war prisoners; captives; P O W s.
evit: yes; of course; sure.
getch kalda: It's too late, too much time has passed.
gel: come; come see; look at this.
git' mem lazum: I need to go; I must go now; I'm going.
ha-zer' ole: get ready; be prepared; take aim.
hoe'sh gel-den-niz: happily you've arrived; happy to see you.
hoe'sh boll-duke: happily we got here; glad we made it.
jan'o-var: monster; great beast; dragon.
ya-bond' jee-ler: foreigners; strangers; outsiders.
yorgan: a puffy quilt or comforter.

A MAD MOB

"The inspection went well, I see," Saraijik said with a wry smile, "your work was approved and you fooled them about the unfinished parts."

Evran scanned her scornfully, "Let's say, rather, that they understood the scope of what has been done and ignored the little incomplete bits. Your father's ministers are competent; regardless of what you think of him."

She sniffed contemptuously, "Ever the loyal minion and guard of royal property."

He bowed slightly and came close to where she stood. "The privileges of faithful service are my need and yours, I might add. You profit no less than I from my duty."

"They brought news of the court; come tell me of the latest scandals," she coaxed. He knew she would not leave the room until her curiosity was satisfied and smiled accordingly. Now, she would wait until he was satisfied.

"Let me start with good news first. The house of Loki Rothander was destroyed and the drug traffic to the army camp disrupted. The golden horse was spotted, but lost. It may have been ridden by the ringleader himself. The facts were given by a Goth named Woden before he died. They did hold the two messengers at the camp, but they were not found."

She looked pleased and nodded thoughtfully, "Then they must still live. Martim will be pleased; our prayers prevailed."

His eyes bore into hers. "You said 'our prayers'! Do you pray to her Yesu?"

"When good things are sought, our hearts should agree."

"That was not my question. You've entered into this soft, sentimental belief of forgiveness and mildness?"

"The surface seems meek and mild, but at the core is a fierce loyalty and faith that does not falter; it takes courage to live it out."

His jaw dropped in shock. He wondered how this would affect his accustomed role of antagonist lover. "I forbid it! Your father would be shocked," he thundered.

"Evit, yes, I knew he would. It must have been part of the attraction. I am learning to forgive his suspicion and folly."

"You can't do this! I forbid it! We'll get rid of Martim. You agreed that I command here. So, you will give up this rash foolishness now." He continued to pour out arguments and threats, which she silently disregarded.

She walked to the window to gaze on the summer verdure, she then looked into the silver plate reflector to compose her face. Then she turned, interrupted, to smilingly say, "*Gitmem lazum*, I need to go; Olga has a new peregrine falcon to show me at the Gothsruck's meadow. She'll be happy to hear about the messengers. She is full of sweet wedding plans. I'll get the other news later."

Evran, Lord of the routes and the lower Danube, stood perplexed while his victim and his moment of domination and satisfaction left him, closing the door firmly behind her. His heart tightened, raged and trembled before the new unexpected discovery. His antagonist had taken on a new role and a new and challenging aspect. He was at a loss to know how to deal with it. Now, he must learn more of this faith to combat it.

> - - - - - - - >

"See, we have arrived safely in spite of everything that happened," Kaya commented as he rode Altom toward the shining Danube River ahead.

"Well, it took us long enough," complained Ozkurt, riding beside him. "Being a prisoner again is not my idea of a safe arrival anywhere."

It was a late summer afternoon when the escort squad arrived at the large city beyond the great Hungarian Alfold where they had passed hundreds of herds and their keepers. At last, they had come upon a vast new city with streets that ran from the first yurts at its limits to the Danube River. Many yurts were fenced off with felt, cloth or rope. The yards were designed, not for beauty, but to hold animals in as well as keep intruders out.

Like most nomad towns made up of herders' homes, there were yurts and tents scattered about the area where water could be easily obtained. From Manchuria to Poland they were found, usually on a temporary basis, wherever sufficient reason of power, wealth and necessity called them into existence. They could disappear almost instantly through defeat, disease or change of trade patterns.

If a feared authority had a good street master, he assigned the families their place; then straight lines and order ruled. If the authorities were weak and the underlings corrupt, disorder and self-serving prevailed. The roads would be twisting paths, the properties guarded by jealous partisans.

Agricultural people marveled at these centers of authority and trade for their ephemeral nature was easily apparent. Personality, power and strategic position were more clearly seen as factors of key importance in herding societies. In contrast, the same factors were present, but not always easily recognized in agricultural societies. There towns rested on land potential and their owners. The stability of crop-based towns blinded the occupants to factors that nomadic people instinctively grasp. This gave a ready superiority to mobile grazing societies evident since the times of Abraham. It also issued in an instinctive antipathy between the societies thus formed.

Kaya's escort, being careless of their prisoners' value, allowed a mob of dirty urchins and curious adults to follow the small party of horsemen down the broad passages between yurts. More of the idle were attracted, as they moved toward the Khan's tents near the river.

"Ya bond jee lair, es ear lair, gel! foreigners, war prisoners, come see!" The cry went out, calling even more to the mob. In an army town, strangers and war prisoners were taken as the same thing and of interest to those who wished to easily acquire others' goods.

Rough, dirty-faced, little boys started urging and daring each other. One ran forward and shouted a dirty word, and all laughed appreciatively. With this another blew his nose on a small stick and threw it at them. Catcalls, whistles and hoots followed with some small rocks. The crowd laughed and shouted encouraging words. Dust and trash filled the air and showered the two riders and their beautiful mounts.

One of the laughing guards unlimbered his whip and threatened the mob, but they drew closer together and growled menacingly. The mob moved forward angrily, purposefully.

The guards stopped their laughter and worried. They began to trot the horses toward the Khan's large tents at the riverside. A shout went up from the mob. Jeering and whistles followed their movement. The children ran shouting and throwing things from behind. The horses began to gallop. They rushed toward the gate and its few guards.

As they arrived at full gallop, the captain of the guard had called for reserves from the barracks with the blast of a brass trumpet. They came flooding out of the tents facing the palace. Still arranging the details of their dress and arms, they drew up into a double line facing the palace. They were strong men in their prime, armed with saber and bow. At the sight of them, the mob slowed.

"*Hah zure ole*, get ready," shouted the sergeant as the two lines swung to block the passage behind the panting horses. The shouting line of pursuing boys drew near. At the sergeant's command the men armed bows and notched ball-tipped arrows in place. As they drew the bow, the attackers suddenly skidded to a halt and by evasive running and darting made a vain attempt to thwart the soldier's aim.

"*Ahtesh*, fire" came the cold command. The flight of knobbed arrows produced a volley of thumps and howls. Some boys ran crying from the scene, the braver carrying an arrow in hand as a trophy. A few lay unconscious on the ground. Others limped or stumbled feebly from the scene. Two soldiers moved forward to collect the spent stun arrows where they fell. The children were left to recover or be removed by crying relatives or friends. The double line of soldiers, another arrow notched at ready, watched without concern as the mob drew back and started to dissolve into its individual elements.

"Good work, sergeant," shouted the lieutenant, as he left his vantage point near the gate. The escorts brought Kaya and his companion to the door of the huge royal tent, where the yuzbasha intercepted them.

"We have intruders, Yuzbasha," they stated. "We took them between the mountains and the great Alfold Plain. They are Chipchaks from the east. They seek our Khan Munzur. They claim to bring messages and tribute from a far land."

"*Hoe'sh gel din niz*, Welcome!" greeted the Lieutenant, "Come into the secretariat tent. We must register the messages and the tribute. Have you eaten? No? We will bring ayran to refresh you. Here, sit." He indicated a rug.

"*Hoe'sh boll duke*, you honor us, thanks, bless the hands that made your rug. We've come a six-day ride from the mountains and are tired and thirsty." So the exchanges continued as the vital information was recorded on parchment. The secretaries sat on the rug behind small wooden tables and made ample notations on the day's roster. A token of wood was given to the escort guards to exchange for their food and accommodation for the night.

Han Lee's letters, Prince Ilkan's offer, and the Kazar secret instructions were taken to a Secretary of Documents. The prisoners were taken by guards to a detention tent to await the Khan's pleasure.

> - - - - - - - >

Munzur looked at his newest tribute, the large skin of the Janovar critically. The reptilian quality of the skin left little doubt of its origin. The Khan shook his head in admiration.

"I have heard stories of these monsters from the time I was a child, but I have never seen the proof; only old bones of giants and creatures long dead. Here is the closest to living proof for my eyes." The Khan paused and looked at his son. "Accuracy is the secret of victory; here," he pointed with his finger, "you see only the slightest of damage to the skin at the eye. Remember that when you are called to practice your aim."

The child, Attila, a short and stocky nine-year-old, handled the skin, his dark eyes shining in excitement. He stroked the skin with his hands and looked admiringly at Kaya.

"Tell us the story again," Attila demanded.

"Later," the Khan countered, "I'm appointing them to the personal guard, and you can command their time then." He turned to Kaya and Ozkurt again. "You are both valuable men, and I willingly accept you into my service. However, you must understand that I cannot allow strangers to disrupt the camp with charges against other mercenaries who arrived before you. Personal matters are laid aside here. Crimes committed in other places are left to the past and the revenge of Tanra in the future. I will remove any head that differs with my laws."

"Sir," Kaya began deferentially with a bow, "our quest is the pursuit of the captors of my sister. Justice must be done, and she be released unharmed."

"My Lord, the Princess Yetkin arrives," shouted the door guard. Indeed, the princess was already inside the tent, and bowing to her father and little brother.

She said, "I heard we have visitors or messengers newly come." She and her laughing, bright retinue were dressed in simply cut steppe dresses over baggy silk pants. Pausing as if mesmerized, she looked the two men up and down, and her face showed complete approval of all she saw. She stepped up to Kaya and said cheerfully, "You're the new guard now and you'll come to my party tonight. I am marrying off one of my slave girls." Smugly, she pointed with her chin to one of the girls just entering the tent. "The sad-faced one will be made happy."

"Yownja, *janum*, my love, you're here!" Kaya replied in stunned surprise and opened his arms.

Yetkin stepped into them, saying, "Yes, I'm here." She put a hand on each side of his face and kissed him lightly.

Fewsoon looked up startled, gave a cry of despair and ran off crying, "*Getch kalda!* Too late!"

Khan Munzur glowered in anger and shocked disapproval.

Well before dark, Kaya and Ozkurt arrived at the gate of the forbidden area behind the administrative tents of the palace. They were dressed in their new uniforms of royal guards and were met by a guard with their names on the roster of invited guests. They were searched and surrendered their weapons on entering the guarded sector. They were warned not to stray outside the Princess' tent. This excluded them from the Khan's private quarters, his wives' and children's homes and school. The heirs' quarters for marriageable sons and daughters were in the sector near the only gate which pierced the thin wood palisade with its cut piles of thorn bush around outside and deep ditch inside. There they were guided by the young Attila to the Princess' tent.

"She likes lots of music and drink for all her special celebrations." Attila explained. "I like the food best."

Kaya laughed and said, "And the sweets and candies too, I'll bet."

Attila laughed and admitted to the charge. "She never lets me stay after the food. I wish you would ask if I could stay longer."

Kaya looked surprised. "Ask your father when he comes."

Attila, stared at the two strangers and then shrugged, "That's no good."

"Your father won't let you stay?" Kaya asked, puzzled.

The boy laughed, "He doesn't even come. He always sends an excuse, too busy or tired or any thing else to keep him to his tents. He only eats with generals and ambassadors."

They entered a large tent the size of two rooms; entrances to smaller tents opened on three sides away from the main entrance. Trunks and boxes around the sides were padded with cushions and throw rugs. Two magnificent rugs covered the floor of the tent house. An ensemble of strings and flute played soft music around the center pole. A small tambourine-like hand drum punctuated its rhythm. The small, round-bottomed violin stood like a cello to be played.

Guests were seated on the rugs in small groups. Young boys and girls the age of Attila were busy serving the groups with bowls of *chay*, tea and other drinks and with dainty pastries for snacks. One of the boys rushed over with bowls on a tray as soon as they sat near one of the tent side entrances. The smell of food wafted from the door.

"How did you score in archery today?" Attila inquired of his serving friend.

"Two birds and a perfect in hoops," he answered, "But I lost an arrow."

"I got a perfect three, today," Attila boasted. His friend looked with admiration and envy at the heir.

"You always do," he replied with resignation.

"Bring on the food," ordered Attila, "I and my friends are hungry. Then come, sit and hear their story of hunting the monsters."

> - - - - - - - >

"I'm told you have a letter from your father, the Khan, today." Evran inquired, grinning knowingly. He loved to boast of his control over her life.

She glowered and spit fire, "News from your sources won't give you the contents."

"Your use as eyes and ears interests him, but what can you tell him now?"

She averted her face and caught a sly glimpse of his expression. Her smile was triumphant. "I know you're planning to start to exterminate the Rumen, who stood by silent during the attack: all the men who rebuilt your fort. The Goths suspect some treachery as well. Married life doesn't occupy Olga to the point of disinterest."

He stood silent a moment; startled that his secret was out.

"I wouldn't believe everything a young bride imagines. Being a Christian doesn't give power to read minds."

"It may give one power to discern evil, and prayers to disarm it. If Yesu can reconcile some, He may also prevent the evil of others."

Evran chuckled and smirked arrogantly, "Come, tell me of the letter, Saraijik, your indoctrination attempts are futile."

She inclined her head coquettishly, "I am to contemplate a move. I'm invited to the Autumn Festival." She shrugged, "It might lead to consultations, recognition and reconciliation. I've heard that the present princess, Yetkin, doesn't please him."

Evran cocked his head smugly to prod her pride, "You're useless for his political agenda; you're married. You're more valuable to him here."

She showed her teeth, "Widows are sometimes considered more valuable than young virgins who lack political sense or discretion." His jaw dropped and he stared at her silently. She continued smiling sweetly and moving toward him, "I've almost decided not to go. I have hopes that the fall will provide tranquility and bring a soothing of all irritations. Peace at home and abroad would seem a worthier goal than revenge."

> - - - - - - - >

The Princess Yetkin sat on a special rug near the entrance to her private quarters. A large communal dish of bulgur, steaming whole wheat kernels, sat on a beautiful cloth in the middle of her group of ladies. Smaller side dishes of meats with sauces were arranged around the centerpiece. Guests would wander over and speak to the princess and her women there. When dismissed, they would go back to their place, marked by a similar large communal dish. A buzz of genial conviviality punctuated by laughter filled the tent. After the meal the sweets were passed: fruit and nut-filled tarts and pastries arrived. As the children and mothers thanked the hostess and retired, drinks stronger than *ayran* appeared.

Fewsoon sat in her best, most colorful outfit with flowing trousers and a garland crown of flowers woven close together on her head. She blushed as her well-wishers came over and had their say and made their jokes. Her companions laughed and made repartee.

Another dish on the opposite side of the room was base for another stream of well-wishers. There sat a tall, blond giant of a man in high-ranking guard uniform. The men at his side were likewise in guard uniform. They were drunk, laughing outrageously as the party went on. Brahin, the hero, wore a flower crown that had slipped to one side of the great blond head and sat rakishly tilted over one ear.

Those who went with congratulations inevitably returned with less firm steps, as they were plied with drink from great goblets of bone or metal.

The Princess Yetkin invited Kaya and Ozkurt to her circle and seated Kaya beside her. He found himself telling the Janovar story again. He stressed the story of his search for his sister and the result of the trip through the Kyzel Kum.

Fewsoon sat before him, pale and serious, occasionally she made the little head jerk upward that means 'No' in Chipchak. Her lips were drawn into the pouting thin edge of a dime, tightly sealed. Frown lines stood between her eyes.

The princess shifted to face Kaya. She would interrupt the story with a grape or small pastry, which she fed him. She rested her elbow or wrist on his knee or shoulder. Her face was always close to his, peering into his eyes and watching his mouth with a rapt expression. The story finished, she leaned over and planted a kiss full on Kaya's lips and sighed. She arched back languidly and spoke softly.

"Cheechek, Flower, dear, sing us your little song." The plump girl next to Fewsoon stood and going into the small tent produced her long necked saz and picked out the tune singing in a slow sleepy voice:

1. Dally a while with me, Love,
   Stay and play with me.
   Talk all the night,
   Kiss, hug or bite,
   Love's a delight.
   Let's do it right,
   All through to light.
   Dally awhile with me.

2. Dally a while with me, Love.
   Give or take a kiss.
   Stay wide awake,
   Dance, priss and shake.
   Let go for now,
   Sing, take a bow,
   No matter how.
   Dally a while with me.

3. Dally a while with me, Love.
   Drink or smoke a line,
   Let's dream away,
   Till comes the day.
   Love makes no haste,
   Come take a taste,
   We've time to waste.
   Dally a while with me.

4.   Dally a while with me, Love.
              Come and stay with me.
              Tickle away,
              Touch where you may.
              Life's a dull fit,
              Push it a bit,
              Use your sharp wit.
              Dally a while with me.

DALLY A WHILE WITH ME

Dal - ly a - while with me, Love. Stay and play with me. Talk all the night, kiss, hug or bite, Love's a de - light. Let's do it right, All through to light. Dal - ly a - while with me.

While Cheechek sang, Yetkin occupied herself with Kaya who sat as stiff and rigid as a statue. She primped his hair and straightened the wrinkles and tucks of his uniform. He let himself be examined and arranged to her satisfaction.

The women in the circle exchanged knowing glances and made quiet comments between giggles as they started to prepare the long stem pipes for smoking. On a small low table, brazier and pipes had been placed with a twist of hashish and an opium ball at the groom's and bride's places.

Kaya kept trying to meet Fewsoon's eyes, but she had her head bowed and sat behind the princess. So he had to lean his head to one side. Then, Yetkin would move his head to another position.

After the song, the volume increased at the bachelor's area and laughter augmented. The tall Brahin and several companions came to the women's circle. They bowed low as they thanked the princess for the party. Brahin especially tried to hold Yetkin's attention, which she kept returning to Kaya. This vexed the big man.

"Does my outfit please you, my lady, Yetkin? It's one you selected for me." He smiled, and she spared him a glance.

"Yes, have Fewsoon arrange the shoulder belt. The buckle needs rotating a bit left." She adjusted Kaya's buckle.

Brahin frowned and tried again. "Should I have the shirt collar embroidered?"

She glanced again, shrugged, "Yes, have Fewsoon look to it." She ran her hand around Kaya's round collar. "You need a thumb width of height here," she said to him, ignoring the frustrated man, wearing a crown of flowers, standing before her.

"Would you hear a poem I have composed in your honor, Lady?" he asked her.

She stopped and stared into space a moment before answering. "I have all your heart's best outpourings, according to your word, what need have I of more?" She smiled, "You have given me the gems of your love. I am rewarding you as best I can." She sighed, "I am only a prize mare in my father's stables, reserved for royal decree and political breeding." She shook her head distractedly. "Give it to Fewsoon. We will read it together later." Fewsoon reached up and took the proffered scrap from Brahin's numb hand. He looked around like a man just awakened from a bad dream into a prison bed and liking neither. The circle again returned to its activities.

Unwilling to retreat, Brahin pounced, "This must be the Janovar with the large skin." He looked smirking at Kaya. "I have heard that tall stories are coming out of the east. Fantastic stories no one could possibly believe."

At these words the circle hushed suddenly, and all listened. Fewsoon stood and said, "Here, allow me to fix this buckle." He pushed her hands aside and continued to stare hard at Kaya. "Some gain advancement through the credulity of their audiences; story telling is an art for the tavern."

Kaya stood, "Truth from afar is always suspect. I was fortunate to have the skin as proof," he smiled. The princess, too, stood and stepped slightly before Kaya.

"Serpent skins cleverly cut can pass as pelt when well sewn or pasted," Brahin affirmed.

"Only to the blind and dumb," countered Kaya.

"Why came you to these parts?" shouted Brahin.

"To seek a beloved sister and wife, stolen by bandit mercenaries," replied Kaya.

"Now, you have become one and joined them in stealing what another loves," declared Brahin violently. "By Thor's hammer I'll make you sorry."

A moaning sigh brought everyone's attention to Yetkin as she slowly slid against Kaya and slipped to her knees. Kaya grasped her arms, and Fewsoon stepped between Kaya and Brahin who shoved her aside vigorously. Others were now around the limp figure of the princess and Cheechek was directing her group into the small tent entrance.

A great fat eunuch with smooth face and egg-bald head stood before the tent entrance and spoke in a loud contralto voice demanding all the guests retire from the guest tent. Many were unwilling to go and congregated near the main entrance talking in low voices. Others left to spread the news of the near fight and scandalous behavior. Some paid no attention and continued their drinking or smoking. A few lay bemused or asleep.

Inside the small tent, they lay the princess on some pillows and thick *yorgan* quilts on the rug. Kaya was pushed aside by the crowd of attendants and stood to single out Fewsoon, trailing the group. Brahin had stayed with Yetkin, imploring her to speak to him. He kissed her limp hand.

The joy Kaya had expected was diminished by the situation and the solemn expression on Fewsoon's face. Her misery was plain. He led her to a quiet corner and put his back to the crowd and shielded her from view. He took her hand. "Tell me all that has happened to you since these two years." She leaned her head against his chest and quietly started.

"Koosta was greedy for gain, so I threatened murder and suicide if they touched my virtue. He protected me for the ransom. Later he learned to respect me and admired my nursing and cooking skills. That and my threat held the group in check, as the hope of ransom faded. I became a big sister who quarreled and scolded to keep them clean and working as a disciplined band, traveling from one court to another.

"When they were able to sell their services to the Khan, they gave me for a slave to the princess to advance their cause, thinking me safe in that household. They were wrong. The princess is neurotic and addicted. Undisciplined wealth has produced a corrupt family. The princess takes lovers, and when she tires of them she marries them off to one of her attendants. I am to be married to the latest of these." The insistent wail broke through their concentrated talking.

"Fewsoon, where are you?" The penetrating call came again. Hurrying toward them, the trembling princess grasped her hand and said in a tense, hysterical voice. "The Spirit of the Ancestors has spoken to me now. We are to advance your marriage date!"

THE PRINCESS' PARTY

PEOPLE, PLACES & PLOTS IN CHAPTER 21

Atilla: gets in on his sister's parties, if he won't tell their father what happens there.

Blume: a nun and royal nurse in charge of harem children.

Brahin: gets a gift from his chief interest, the princess.

Chee'chek: sings a new song to Princess Yetkin. It may prove dangerous to her, as a friend of Fewsoon.

Fewsoon: is paralyzed by fear and depression. She must get a message to Kaya.

Kaya: is the object of attentions he does not want.

Memmur bey: a captain of the guard of the harem.

Princess Yet'kin: insistent on having her own version of everything.

GLOSSARY:

is-ah-niz'lee: with your permission; permit me; farewell; let me leave.

do'er: stop; stay where you are; don't go.

effendiler: gentlemen; lords.

Kum-mool-da-mah: don't move; don't try anything; stay still.

TRICKY TANTRUM

The young boy stated the invitation in a memorized rote way. He did it twice without variation, which to Kaya verified the message. It was a scarcely masked command by Princess Yetkin to come to the royal tent for a private dinner that night. He looked at Ozkurt who was staring bemused as the well dressed child retired. Kaya blushed as their eyes met and held. Ozkurt laid his hand on his friend's shoulder and smiled, "Mother used to warn me about playing with knives or fire." He chuckled and squeezed Kaya's arm. They were on the practice field and had duty in the afternoon roster as guards till sunset.

"I must see Fewsoon. We need to talk." Kaya shook his head, "This seems to be the only way. We must pray for the opportunity to be together." Ozkurt looked at him kindly, pity filled his eyes.

"We've become accustomed to deception and half-truths since we left the Sea Witch at the Danube Delta," Ozkurt began. "It has not improved the speed nor conditions of our journey. Just the opposite. It's beginning to bother me. I'd like to change our ways now. We need to get right with God. You may do yourself harm pretending a visit to one in order to see the other. Remember, 'Devious decisions develop drastic damage.'"

Kaya threw his head back in a long laugh, "Maya said it constantly in our play times."

"Just remember that it's still true," Ozkurt warned, "even for boys who sleep with tigers."

> - - - - - - - >

Fewsoon was not in sight when Cheechek met him at the tent door and he was taken straight into the center opening to the small tent behind. It led to the private quarters of Yetkin. He sat on one of the covered box seats against the side of the tent. Cheechek went through the inner door opposite and immediately Fewsoon entered the main door. She put a hand of caution to his mouth as he started up from his seat. Hurriedly, she whispered. "Do not mention me to the princess. It will hurt us. I will talk to you inside the main gate as you leave." She was gone even as he stretched out his hand to touch her.

There was a sound of giggles at the inner door and the smell of perfumes as several figures passed into the room bearing a large spread of delicacies, which were placed on a cloth on the rug. The sculptured heap of boiled wheat, *bulgur*, sprinkled with pine nuts, resembled a rose. The cooks circled the large metal tray with several smaller dishes of fragrant meats and sauces. Wooden spoons were placed in two bowls of soup. The cooks set out the dishes, bowed and left by the main door.

The princess entered from the inner door. She stood waiting as he stood and bowed deeply. She smiled and made a motion toward the food. He came and seated himself cross-legged at the rim of the tray, pulling the edge of the cloth over his lap. She came likewise and seated herself on his right side, leaning on her left arm with her feet tucked up beside her. She turned her face up to his and said softly, "What would you like first?"

> - - - - - - - >

Kaya was full and weary as he looked up from the meal, the remains of which were whisked away by the kitchen help. The constant need to balance between deference and intimacy, both of which the princess demanded, was difficult to maintain. She had occasionally kissed or stroked him and invited the same between courses. When he did not respond, she would frown and pout. She would try to hand-feed him, and when he ignored the morsel, she would throw it down angrily. She would alternately smile sweetly and throw a tantrum: a juvenile performance which shortened both their tempers.

The couple stood up as the servants cleared the dishes and lifted the cloth, folded the crumbs inside and carried it back. A small low table with a little brazier burning and a pipe and dish of ingredients was brought in. Yetkin smiled and stretched her hands as if to warm them in the glow. "Here we have a treat for us, as intimate friends. You will not have experienced this special indulgence." She started the preparation of the pipe with opium mixed with aromatic herbs.

"We know this custom in my country," cut in Kaya, "and I abhor it." He reached down and broke the pipe stem, "It ruins good people and makes them useless."

"But it brings such beautiful dreams," cried Yetkin as she watched in shock as Kaya stood and threw the mixture on the brazier releasing a cloud of pungent smoke, which dissipated slowly. He, bowing, exited to the larger tent. She ran sobbing and clung to him, her body trembled. "Come, I need your love; comfort me." Her urgent voice commanded him. Placing her right foot behind his left knee joint, she pulled herself up close. Then she seemed to swoon and let her upper body fall back. Her two arms were fastened around his neck. Her weight and pressure of her foot caused his knee to buckle, and he found himself kneeling over her sprawled body. Her mouth slightly open, she continued to pull his neck toward her. He had put both arms out to break their fall to the rug. She pulled herself near to stroke his hair and bite at his ear. "Love me," she cried.

"Princess Yetkin, stop, think what you are doing!" Kaya's right hand found the neck of the frantic woman and pulled her away from his body. He struggled to his feet while holding her away. Suddenly, she went relaxed in a faint. It was like holding a limp little kitten by its neck, and he laid her down on the rug inside her tent. She was panting, weak and out of breath. Kaya looked round and saw a small gong near the pillows. He hit it with his fist.

"Mistress? You called?" A voice said, and Cheechek appeared hesitantly at the inner door. Her startled face took in the scene in a rapid glance. Quickly, she took a small lacquered porcelain bottle from her waist band and pulled out a small wooden stopper. She tilted out about five drops in the slightly open mouth. She laid her ear over the woman's breast. Hastily, she hit the gong then started to rub the arms of the limp figure. Two more women entered the room. After one look, one disappeared while the other joined Cheechek to rub the legs. Fewsoon now appeared at Kaya's side and motioned with her head for him to go to the outer door of the room in the larger tent. She took him to the yurt entrance nearest the gate.

"Here in my quarters we can talk." She began, "All will be flurry and worry in her tent." They paused as the heavy tread of one of the eunuchs ran by. "She has tantrums and fainting spells when defied. Her staff is terrified by them for the Khan would kill them all if something harmful befell her." Kaya looked puzzled and worried.

"You talk like you know what happened in there," Kaya objected. "She just fainted."

Fewsoon put her hand on Kaya's cheek and smiled. "Yes, when you refused her bold advances." She chuckled and pinched his cheek between two fingers as if he were a child. "You are not so hard to read bold warrior and shy lover." He blushed and hung his head at her words, and she giggled like a little girl.

"Oh Kaya, how I love you," she kissed his forehead. "Now you must go home and stay out of her sight. Refuse any more invitations. She will be a witch for several days until her fancy lights elsewhere." Fewsoon shook her head knowingly, "I am essential to her tranquility and will be busy with her. Don't try to see me. I'll let you know when and where we will meet again to plan our escape."

"What about this marriage of yours?" Kaya ventured. "Isn't that something to worry about?" Fewsoon shook her head and took his hand between hers.

"It's not a love match. She was simply dumping a lover and offering me my freedom." She smiled confidently, "I know my way around her. She would change her mind several times before it happened."

Kaya frowned and stood. "I have little respect for wavering and frightened minds. Why does she allow herself to be mastered by smoke and passion?"

Fewsoon stood and put a hand on his arm. "She is weak through riches and indulgence. The father loves her little, and she is a pawn in the kingdom's politics -- as she well knows. Her contact with normal outside life is limited and cushioned. Pity her." Kaya sniffed indignantly. She stroked his cheek, smiling. "Come, I will walk to the gate with you." Fewsoon walked to the tent entrance. "With the princess ill, the household will not notice us; the guards know me."

Kaya went reluctantly. "What of our plans?" She put a finger to his lips and shook her head.

> - - - - - - - >

The princess, robed in splendor, was enjoying the attentions given by her frightened staff. Entertainments alternated with medications in an impressive attempt to pacify her whims. She wanted new songs, new distractions. Only Cheechek and Fewsoon dared try shock therapy. Cheechek entered with her saz and bowing low explained. "Fewsoon and I have written a new song for you to make you laugh and cry. I will sing it if you promise to take your medicine before the song."

Yetkin pouted, "I hate this foul-tasting brew. I will have the song, but no medicine."

Cheechek made a shocked face, touching her head with both hands. "Alas, in this moment I have forgotten it completely."

Yetkin stuck her tongue out at her. "I know your childish tricks, you will forget until I obey the medicine man. Why do I have such useless companions?" She grimaced, "Bring the medicine, better to die of poison than boredom."

Cheechek giggled and tuned her saz while Yetkin drank the potion with gagging and choking sounds. Cheechek strummed the chords and started:

1.   Why do I think of him? Why do I sigh?
        He will not kiss me; Kiss me and care.
        He will not miss me if I'm not there.
        I'm the best dressed at the parties.
        It's tailored to fit my fine form.
        I say bright things and am charming.
        Why do I think of him all the time?

2.   Why do I think of him? Why do I sigh?
He has not hugged me. sought me and cried.
He will not talk or stay by my side.
I'm the bright light of the boys here.
The one that is courted and sought.
I have both riches and talent.
Why do I think of him all the night?

3.   Why do I think of him? Why do I sigh?
He's gone and left me, left me to cry.
Life is so lonely, I feel I will die.
I miss the sound of his laughter.
I miss the warmth of his smile.
I miss the meaning of joy now.
That's why I think and cry all the time!

WHY DO I SIGH?

Why do I think of him? Why do I sigh:

He will not kiss me; kiss me and care.

He will not miss me if I'm not there

I've the best clothes at the par-ties

They're taylored to fit my fine form.

I say bright things and am charming.

Why do I think of him all the time?

4.   Why do I think of him? Why do I sigh?
         He's not so tender, so feeling or bright.
         He's not attractive now in my sight.
         I have new choices and options.
         I have new faces to see.
         Life will go on to new joys now.
         Why should I think of him to the end?

The song finished with a flourish, and the hush caused by its daring also ended. Yetkin had cried during some parts of the song, but she did not go into hysterics. She sat, looking in a polished metal mirror thoughtfully, repairing her face. She said, "Yes, I must put this thing to an end and pay everyone. Send for Brahin to call tomorrow. Old loves will have their uses, too."

> - - - - - - - >

To the esteemed Princess Judith,
Greetings. I was both surprised and honored by Your Grace's letter. As daughter of the Governor of Kertch Port, I was aware of Your Grace's royal position in the Don River Estates. I know Ebenezer Bey, your Grace's banker. Trade with the Estate prospered our port. And, therefore, all the history of your presence there is known to me. To serve Your Grace in any way is, for me, a great honor, yes.

I traveled with your Khan's embassy to our capital last winter and quite understand your reluctance to use their services for your inquiry about the Hebrew refugees. My aunt Magda knows the governor of Pontus and assures me that he will co-operate with the investigation. She, however, will not be able to travel until the fall season arrives and the heat has passed. Meanwhile I will do what I can to provide information from here. This will be satisfactory to you, I hope.

You ask about two men from your staff, dispatched to the capital. Kaya and Ozkurt, effendiler, are dear friends of mine. They left the ship on the Danube River. I get news of them through another friend now settled in the old Rumanian lands north of the Danube. The Princess Olga manages to get a letter to the Hunnish embassy here by the hand of a powerful friend, the Princess Saraijik. My last letter stated that the two men are now serving in the Royal Guard at the Hun Capital. This seems too good to be true, so we pray them every success as they continue their quest, no?

Be sure of my attention to Your Grace's request. I will be prompt to inform Your Grace at the first opportunity.

Please convey my greetings and prayers for a complete recovery for Your Grace's royal husband, Prince Ilkin, Yes.

Thanks again for Your Grace's attention to her most humble servant,
Marian Papasian

> - - - - - - - >

The scream pierced the moonlit night like ice water on a sleeping face, snapping every head awake. The scream came again, more urgently, and the whole camp was awake. Kaya was up and running to the entrance of the forbidden zone. He had recognized the source. Fewsoon was in trouble!

The three guards stood at the gate facing inward toward the source of distress. They were uncertain as to their duty, which normally was to keep the gate against outsiders. Should they abandon the prime duty to bring help? They stood like statues; ears fixed on the sounds, as Kaya pushed past the gate and ran toward the yurt beside the large royal structure. As he passed, they were suddenly set free. Two yelled and set off after him. One remained at his post.

The yells of the guards now mixed with the short urgent burst of sound from the yurt where the sounds of blows and angry curses came. A fight was in progress. Kaya found the door flap open and entered in a rush with the captain of the guards on his heels. In the inside gloom they could make out the form of the giant royal bodyguard hunched over the body of Fewsoon. One hand was on her chest holding her away from his face. The other hand was on her knee trying to force her legs apart. The large framed man was on his knees and tried to use one knee for balance and the other for a pry against one thigh.

The girl was screaming in short breaths of anger and distress, clawing like a wild cat at any part of the arm or face her hands could reach. She was kicking with her legs, vigorously, but the huge weight of the man could not be deflected. He was pressing his body between her legs and had moved his forearm against her arm and throat where he allowed his weight to stop her breath. He gave a chuckle of satisfaction, as his body flattened on her.

At that moment the accelerated weight of Kaya hit him on the shoulder and head, overturning and pinning him into the back edge of the yurt. Kaya tripped over the body of Fewsoon and fell on top of Brahin. The men lay stunned where they had fallen. Kaya was conscious of the odors of alcohol, perfume, blood and sweat: a sickening stench.

Fewsoon was the first to recover and pulled herself back from the two, instinctively pulling her torn clothes about her body. The captain of the guard had managed to stop before colliding with the men and stood over them drawing his dagger.

"*Do er, kummul da my yan,* stop, don't move," he ordered, shouting as the other guard came panting up. He looked at the bleeding face of the girl.

"Go quickly and tell your mistress. Have her come tomorrow and lay charges. I, Memmur, am a witness." He spoke kindly in Chipchak. They bound the hands of the dazed Kaya and unconscious Brahin.

"I am glad you came for the lady's sake," the captain continued, addressing Kaya, "but you are in trespass, and there is a penalty. Much will depend on the witnesses and interpretation of the events." A groan announced the awakening of the giant blond guard, Brahin.

At that moment, the princess arrived. Every hair in place and fully made up, she looked like she had not slept, but was prepared for audience with a king.

Fewsoon accompanied the lady with a royal robe thrown over her torn disarray. Her face still blooded and hair wild about her head: a golden halo.

ARREST AND ACCUSATIONS

"What is the meaning of this uproar, Captain? Have you disturbed the Khan's peace for brawlers?" Her voice was theatrical and smooth.

"I came in answer to summons screamed by this poor maiden. Your guard has gone berserk. This man and I answered her cries for help." The Captain indicated the two men as Kaya stood and the second guard continued to tie hands.

"And how do you explain this disruption of the camp's rest by your partying?" The princess turned to stare at her servant with cool appraisal.

"Brahin forced entry here, assaulted me. Forced me, Lady." Fewsoon's voice was high and edgy, "but my brother rescued me." Her look of infinite warmth and thanks touched Kaya.

The lady saw the look, and a flush of jealousy crossed her face for an instant as she spoke. "Brahin has been in love with you for months, and though he pressed his offers, you have paid no mind and given him no hope. He has become depressed and taken to drink. It is natural to act as he has." Her tone was now very self-righteous, prim and hectoring. "It's not safe to play lightly with a man's affections."

"You know, My Lady, that I have fled his presence and avoided his crude attentions," she shuddered, "You aided me until the coming of my brother. It was then your heart left me for him."

"Shut your mouth, you slut. I know your sly ways. You always pretend great virtues to your companions, and yet, are, even as they, a fox bitch in heat." She turned to the captain with a smile, "Disregard her." She touched the captain's arm with a finger.   "Drunken men brawling over a pretty bed partner. You can leave them to me, Captain. I'll punish my guard and the intruder. The girl lacks discretion." A venomous look at Fewsoon accompanied her words.

"I hold both men guilty of breaching the Khan's peace. They will be charged tomorrow, My Lady." The voice of Captain Memmur was hard and sharp. "I trust the maiden will be safe with you. Tomorrow without fail she must bear witness of this night's events."

"Surely, Captain, the Khan is too busy with affairs of state to be bothered by a midnight love tryst and fight between rivals." The princess was at her seductive best and her whole attitude was of soft imploring. "Leave them here, Memmur. We will celebrate your capture of two such strong, brave men with a drink or two. Come please. Tell me how all this happened." She motioned toward the royal tent. The enchanted captain was at the door of the yurt when he recalled his duty and turned to his guard.

"Take the men to the gate. I will be there after arranging for the girl's protection and appearance tomorrow. Call the reserve to help with the prisoners. Let no one interfere." He glanced at the princess.

"I insist, Captain, they are my prisoners, taken in my quarters. You are in charge of the outer gate. Here we are inside." The princess smiled triumphantly. "Understand?"

"When on guard, my orders supersede all others save the Khan's. I judge the woman unsafe while the attacker remains here," He gazed steadily into her eyes, "Understand?"

The Princess Yetkin was all smiles, coyness and sweet pretense. She called a hovering, curious servant of the royal tent, "Cheechek, go call my guard to accompany Captain Memmur's guard to the gate." She turned to Fewsoon. "Go to the yurt of Bayan Blume. She will help you cure your hurts." She smirked on the last word and waved her hand in a contemptuous dismissal. "Come Memmur, we need to talk of this disgrace. I need your council." Her glance was warm and intimate, pleading. "Leave Brahin in my care, after all he can sleep it off in my jail as well as yours. My men will question him. I'm sure his many romances are well known to the men."

The captain's negative shake of the head, jerked up indignantly, stopped her, and she tried again. "After we drink a cup, you can question them and him. I have sent for them. You can establish his habits. His conquests make a long list." She smiled with cool superiority. "A love-struck girl can be let off with a lecture." She smiled and added insinuatingly, "Strong men like you, Memmur, have your way with any you chose." Her eyelids fluttered.

Outside, the sound of the princess' guards echoed. A handsome guard entered to nod his obedience and presence.

"She is only an insignificant serving girl, Memmur, not worth making a fuss over. Men like you must look higher for family and wealth that do not fade with the years as a pretty face." Yetkin and her guard blocked the door.

"You misrepresent the situation, My Lady Yetkin. I was a witness to rape not romance." He spoke firmly, "Add that to trespass; The Khan's orders are positive on both counts. Punishment must follow."

At that moment the reserve, called by the remaining gate guard came and surrounded the yurt. They outnumbered the princess' own guard. When their captain entered, the Princess and her guard exchanged glances, yielded and stepped from the door. The reserve bore the two prisoners away despite Brahin's protest of innocence.

"I meant no harm. She invited me in." He swayed as he passed the entrance. "I drank too much. I don't remember what happened." He straightened up and looked around at the guard forming about them. "Help, comrades; I'm the princess' guard. You can't do this to me." He struggled, pushed and shoved, but none of his companions helped him. Kaya said not a word and followed meekly. Memmur bowed low.

"*Is a niz lee*, with your permission, Lady Yetkin. I will accept your kind invitation another day," Memmur stated, as he moved away after his men. He ignored the intense expression of frustration on her beautiful face.

"Leave, Captain, but do not expect future favors for today's slights. You have earned an enemy, where fortune could have been found. Tomorrow you will understand."

HAREM GATE

PEOPLE, PLACES & PLOTS IN CHAPTER 22

Brahin: suffers a hangover and offends everybody.
Cheechek: gives a medical report on a friend.
Chief magistrate: a political appointee from a rich family.
Fewsoon: turns on her tormenters with anger and contempt.
Igor: a slave, a trainer of athletes, a fight manager.
Kaya: gives a resume of his life.
Memmur bey: gives an accounting of what happened.
Munzur Khan: seeks political satisfaction and a good show.
Ozkurt: is not allowed to help his dearest friend.
Princess Yet'kin: must sit by and watch all her plans change.

GLOSSARY:

Bin-bash'a: head of a thousand; a general.
dee'cot: attention; be careful; watch out.
hock'soz: not just; without justice; unjust.
seraglio: the harem; a forbidden zone for procreation.
Janovar: monster; savage beast.
yasa: the traditional laws ruling the tribe.

COURT QUERIES

Kaya awoke at dawn and rose to face the growing light. He began his morning prayer as the noise of the waking camp grew around him. He made the sign of the cross and rose from his knees as a sleepy guard came with a bowl of food. He hummed as he sat and ate with chained hands and tranquil face. He smiled as he overheard Ozkurt's raised voice arguing with the guards at the gate, demanding to see Kaya. "He doesn't remember I sleep with the tiger," he mused.

> - - - - - - - >

The trial was set for the afternoon, and all business of the kingdom was stopped by the magnitude of the offence and the importance of the participants. The newest hero, messenger and killer of the *Janovar* was involved with the princess or at least the princess' attendant, also loved by the giant guard from the north, who had a secret assignation with one of them. Things became violent because of drugs, drinking, passion or some other trigger and the *seraglio* was invaded. Someone rescued a lover, whichever one it was, and someone was held on charges. A dozen versions of the events were circulated all morning long. Everyone was wild for the details of the true story, but each had an adopted version they hoped would emerge as that truth.

The procession was almost as large as a dress parade. The weather permitted the raising of the sides of the tent, and the field before the Khan's tent was filled. The guards marched in first; they were commanded by *binbasha*, generals no less.

Then the resident diplomatic authorities came, because all those involved, except the princess herself, were foreigners. Then came the experts: lawyers and judges, because it was a perplexing legal tangle. The law must be upheld. The royals found themselves filling in the odd spaces left as the chief magistrate called for order. The princess' retinue, arriving late, squeezed itself into the area occupied by her father, Khan Munzur, to his discomfort. The court clerk demanded the attention of the assembly by thumping the butt of the large metal staff on the dais floor. After the resounding beginning, the charges were read, and the prisoner spoke.

Kaya spoke quietly, but his voice filled the tent of judgment. The assembled authorities and friends of the Khan, crowded to the very limits of space available, listened quietly without comment. Word of the event had filled the morning with wonder and gossip. No one wanted to miss a word.

"My Lords, I am called Kaya Aya, the Bear because my earliest memories are of being just that: a bear, and not even a very good one. I was weak and cold, incapable of a full winter's hibernation.

My jaws could not break bones or tear flesh, and while I was more agile at certain things, I lacked strength to compete. I was a failure as a bear, and I was often grieved over my situation, but I found no remedy."

"The life of a bear is really rather pleasant. We eat and sleep in a relaxed, regular fashion. We eat as we encounter food and sleep when tired. Our life consisted of sound and smell; motion and color; family and friends; hunting and fishing; gathering and exploring; mating and bearing cubs. Our only effective enemies are humans." He looked round his now fascinated audience.

"Driven in fear by enemies to the point of death, I discovered refuge and mercy at a hermitage where I was able to become a human. Again, I found that I was not a very good one. I was stronger than others my age, but a human must think and know. There were delightful new things to learn: talk and music; math and measure; letters and poetry; cooking and preserving; geography and language. To be human and learn is a delightful thing, but not easy. There are internal and external impediments," Kaya paused to shake his head.

"Indeed, there was in me laziness and gluttony that kept me from learning all that humans should know. The other children knew this and took advantage of me, even as the bears had done. However, a few accepted me, even though I was disadvantaged, and they guarded my good. To be human is better than being a bear.

"During the years of learning to be human, I discovered something else. One could become spiritual. It was most clear in the hermit himself. He was more than human. At first I thought it was a part of being human, but that I and most of the children had not arrived at the proper fullness of humanity. I thought that it would come of itself, if given time, but it did not." The listeners were quiet and attemtive.

"Humans can sing the hymns of beauty and say words of wisdom, but still remain only human, and as limited in being, as bears are limited in their being. I longed for the attributes of spirit: joy and peace; acceptance and love; purity and virtue; justice and grace; brotherhood and cooperation; discipline and control; meditation and prayer; the knowledge and forgiveness of God. This desire for a spiritual nature led me to Yesu, who is God's word and message to mankind."

"When I was a bear, there were activities that were normal for bears, but not possible for humans. I had to change my ways and do what was not natural for bears in order to remain fully human. In the spiritual life I had to curb and change things that are natural for humans, but contrary to spirit. I did this because I wish to remain spiritual; it is a better life. There is yet another higher thing than spirit. Holiness, however imperfectly lived, will lead to the enhancement of spirit-filled life. Paul, the apostle of Yesu, spoke of this perfect spiritual obedience and oneness in community with the believers and with God: being one body, though we are many. I seek that..."

The magistrate's voice rose to angry scorn as he shouted laughingly, "You seek more than God when you come to the royal encampment and enter the forbidden zone." Raucous laughter followed this pronouncement, and a buzz of loud conversation filled the tent.

The captain of the guard pounded his spear butt on the floor of the dais to bring order. The magistrate smiled maliciously as quiet was restored. He pointed at Kaya with his chin, his voice rose and he spoke coldly.

"You are a petitioner who comes with complaints against mercenaries of our lord, the khan. You tell stories of gold taken in the land of the Han people and of a rich merchant and a robbed sister. Your use of the word *hock'soz*, unjust, is reported. Now on top of this fantastic story, you disturb the khan's peace and enter the forbidden zone, penetrate the yurt of the slaves of the royal house. You attack a guard of the princess whom you accuse of assaulting the princess' attendant." He shook his head in disbelief.

"Now, you claim to be not quite or is it more than human, and talk of a Roman God who has no authority here. You cloud the issue with words of our enemies' God. You will, no doubt, like them, offer us baptism for our submission." He snorted his contempt and nodded to the officer beside him.

"Bring in the accused guard," his harsh voice commanded. He waited while the tall prisoner stooped to enter the door and standing touched the roof of the pavilion with his wild blond hair. His massive face bore the marks of nails, and he glared angrily at the authorities before him. He was muttering and shaking his head. A hangover was evident.

"So I diddled a girl; she wanted it. They all want it, if the truth were known." He looked about defiantly. "She was only a foreign, serving wench. Besides I had permission of the owner. Said I could have her." He nodded affirmatively, frowning to remember. "Why all this stir? I'll pay her if that's the trouble." He ran his hand over his face and winched. "Just look what she's done to me. What about that?" He groaned as he clutched his head suddenly. "Oh, it hurts."

"This is the princess' guard, My Lord," Memmur, the gate captain stated, "he was taken in the act of violating the princess' attendant. I am a witness."

"The princess likes them by length." The lord magistrate observed to the audience: "The longer the better." His sally was answered by raucous laughter from the audience. "All right, Captain, give us all the details. Leave nothing out." He leaned forward his face avid with lustful curiosity.

> - - - - - - - >

Fewsoon stood like a victim in the arena, surrounded by lions. They growled in unison as she entered, and now licked their chops in anticipation of what they would hear. Lecherous eyes probed her robes and penetrated the mask she wore of cold control. The autumn had been chill and all were dressed accordingly, but she was naked in their eyes.

"We have heard the other witnesses," stated the judge as he ran his tongue over his lips, "now it is your turn."

"I am the daughter of the Chipchak Khan's commander-in-chief. I was raised in the yurt of Merien the medicine woman and was breast mate of the Khan's son. According to tribal law, I was engaged to that son by promise and oath." She looked at Kaya and blushed. "I was captured on a caravan trip with Jomer, the merchant, and after much trouble, I was delivered here to the princess, whose companion I became. The guard, Brahin, showed me unwanted attentions from the time I came to the princess' tent. His affections were actually directed toward the princess and several women attendants were party to his games."

"Are you virgin?" inquired Munzur, interrupting the witness and the judge, anxious to pass over to the point.

"Does this, in any way, affect the nature of the crime?" inquired the bold Fewsoon, after a pause.

"It affects the nature and extent of the damage done," the khan leaning forward, smiled wolfishly.

"But it does not affect the facts of trespass or violence toward me, an illegal assault." She was pink now, "Unless there is bias in the judgment."

"We will know the extent of the damage," he showed his teeth again, smirking, "Unless we are to take the evasions as being related to a negative answer."

"Since I cannot see clearly that part of my anatomy, why do you ask me to assess the damage done?" She was as red as her hair now, angry and fists balled up to attack. A laugh had passed through the attentive crowd and the guards moved forward, unconsciously, while Munzur sat up gesturing for silence. He looked at one of the princess' attendants, Cheechek, for an answer.

"There was blood," the girl affirmed, "and pain."

"That was not the question," the Khan glared at the serving girl. "Was she virgin and did he penetrate her?"

"She was examined by the eunuchs on admission to the royal quarter and was up to standard. She is a virgin." The girl continued, then nodded and remembered how vigorously Fewsoon had resisted the first examination and shaving of her pubic hair. "We are not sure about the second part. There was only a little blood, but a lot of hysteria and anger last night." She smiled wanly at Fewsoon, "She was promised by her Khan to his son, whom she loves. She has lived in fear since her capture." Cheechek, too, knew that fear.

Fewsoon scarcely heard. She was in reverie. Her mind had found a moment of emotion in the past to anchor her thoughts. She felt the cold sweep over her and heard the wind of winter. The whole scene came before her: the woods, the cave, and the icy night. She wondered to what degree she was still virgin after that storm. She knew she was no longer innocent, but they were promised before the khan that very summer. Her mind moved toward that event, but a voice caught her attention. The judge was speaking:

"We have heard all the evidence and will withdraw to consider the matter in consultation with Munzur Khan. Sentencing will be at this time tomorrow." The Judge looked grimly satisfied. There was much to think about, and they were all stimulated by the events described.

> - - - - - - - >

Kaya in his prison tent sat dolefully thinking. He was not too sure of the outcome of the judgment for his little Yownja. He had no idea of what the princess would do next to revenge his slight. Their love was an offence to her. It was something she had never experienced. So she envied them. Her jealousy was unbridled. She would extract her pleasure from the situation. For himself, he was sure of death. The illegal entrance into the forbidden zone was always death, whatever the reason for doing it. Only the Khan could relieve him of that penalty, and he could see no reason why he would.

At that moment two guards entered the tent with a chesty, strong but short man with a small trimmed beard. He was older, near forty. The man was protesting vigorously in accented Hunnish. He shouted and tried to use his hands, which were manacled, to emphasize his explanations.

"I have to work with what I'm given. A stupid man makes a stupid match. Let me find my own men, and I'll face any champion in the country. My man will win. What does the Khan expect when I have to take bums to make champions?"

"Don't fuss so much. It's only a week for drunkenness, insult, assault and failure. You got off light at that. We'll take good care of you, so don't make any trouble." The guards grinned appreciatively as they sat him on the wooden bench. They started to take off the manacles.

"Anything you want, if there is a bonus in it for us." They laughed broadly and bent their heads over the cuffs. Suddenly, he flipped the manacles' chain over their heads and had pulled it tight round their necks, bumping their heads. He hissed at them his face red with anger.

"You scum will get nothing but trouble if you try to squeeze me. I'm going to train a champion, and he'll demolish you." He flipped the chain off their necks and held out his hands. Breathing hard, they finished removing the cuffs and, angry now, departed without a word to him, but cursing him under their breath. He stretched, laughed and looked around him.

"Hey, big boy, what are you in for?" He inquired slapping Kaya on his arm jovially.

Kaya smiled weakly. "Trespass in the forbidden zone."

"You stalk big game, son. Did you collect anything worth talking about? I've heard the Princess Yetkin throws some pretty wild parties." He winked jovially and slapped Kaya's knee vigorously.

"The princess is out for my hide. I was promised in my country to her attendant, Fewsoon. I came to collect her, but the princess had other plans."

"I heard a story about a guy from the east called Rock or Bear or something like that. Got Yetkin all riled up and flustered." He looked at Kaya speculatively.

"I'm Kaya. It means 'rock', and I'm called 'bear' too, because I lived with them when I was little." He bowed, smiling at the whimsical man.

A TOUGH MANAGER

"I'm Igor, a Slav, captured as a boy, enslaved, sold several times and finally owned by a man who was a merchant and trainer of fighters. I trained and fought successfully and got both freedom and enough to start my own string of men. The Khan likes my champions, but he tries to run my work and make my selections. Then he blames me for bad results." He took Kaya's arm in the Roman fashion grasping the forearm above the wrist. Kaya had seen it before.

"You look like a bear, too. I could make a man of your build a real performer among the heavies. You must be a fighter, you wear an ivory badge. Do you wrestle?" He smiled on Kaya's assenting nod. His hands were on Kaya's shoulders, feeling the muscles there.

"Train with me, and you will so please the Khan that he will forgive you any transgression short of the wives in the royal harem. I hope you haven't been trying anything there? No? You can still blush! You're my boy. Let's start right now."

"Guards," Igor bellowed, a guard stuck his head in the door flap. "Move your lazy tail. We need my training stuff here and take off this man's irons. This is our next champion."

The guard looked unimpressed. "The captain is away. We'll ask when he returns." He looked Kaya over critically, "He's too young, lacks staying power and experience." He shook his head, "I'll give you two for one he'll lose to any of the old hands." He withdrew as Igor shouted abuse and made demands for his release.

"Don't worry. We'll have the chains off in an hour," Igor confided. "Now, here are our first exercises." Kaya listened obediently. There was no other hope in sight.

> - - - - - - - >

The convened court was as crowded as ever, and the Khan was in a happy mood. His spies from within the princess court and his captain of the guard had reported in full. He had a plan for teaching Yetkin her place. She was flaunting custom and important families were complaining of scandal.

Igor stood by Kaya's side and the princess' handsome captain stood by Brahin. The royal court consisting of the princess and young Attila sat behind their father, the Khan. Counselors stood on every side; important families, ambassadors and military heads were beside them.

The charges were read off. The *Yasa*, traditional laws, were applied by the court. They could be modified by the Khan, but they could not be ignored. The pressure of public opinion was behind every jot and title. Today there were mitigating circumstances in both cases, and the case was being argued in every yurt and at every campfire. How would Munzur resolve the contradictions? Everyone waited with bated breath. The Khan delivered the verdicts.

"Kaya of the Chipchaks, you are guilty of trespass in the forbidden area. Though you had frequently been guest of the princess with pass to the social tents, at the time of trespass there had been no permission extended. This calls for the death penalty. However, you rescued your promised bride who, however, is now a slave of the princess. This good action mitigates the severity of the law. Your sentence can be commuted to punishment and exile." There was a flurry of comment and a pouting pucker took possession of the princess. The young Attila smiled his approval.

"Brahin of the islands of Thule, You are guilty of assault and rape in the harem. You were of the princess guards and had a pass, but you abused your position. This calls for the death penalty. However, witnesses say you received verbal assent of the princess that you could have her slave as wife. This permission mitigates the severity of the law. Your sentence can be commuted to punishment and exile."

Now every one started commenting vigorously, dissatisfaction seemed evident; Brahin was not well-liked. His crime scandalized many. Why should he escape and have his victim to wife as well?

"*Deecot*, attention," ordered the court convener, using his staff loudly.

"There is a matter overlooked in this case," continued the Khan with a superior smile. "The slave woman is Chipchak. We Huns can make slaves of our enemies, but not of our kin people. The princess obtained the right of service, but the woman belongs to the free people and cannot be disposed of like a horse or household goods. The princess having surrendered her rights to service permits me to take the girl's future in my hands." He stared round at the family to see if any dared object. None did.

"We must decide on a husband for her. We must celebrate the marriage at the fall festival," He smirked. "Then a summer-born child will have a father and a yurt."

The buzz of conversation erupted again. They anticipated his hints and approved. Only the Princess Yetkin looked disapproving. The convener used his staff.

"Both these men desire her as is evidenced by their actions. Each has a certain legal right to her. Let their strength of will and body be tested at that festival on the first day and the marriage consummation on the last day. The punishment for both is combat and a reward for one, the winner, is marriage. Both will go into exile within thirty days of the festival's ending." The Khan smiled hugely. He had pulled off a coup that would paralyze all criticism of his easy-going lack of discipline of the family.

"You have participated as wrestler in your country. I'm told you are quite good." Munzur leaned eagerly forward as Kaya nodded in agreement. Munzur shifted his gaze to the tall form of Brahin.

"You have bragged often enough of your strength and power. Are you willing to prove it?" The Khan was gloating now, and the glow of anticipation showed on his face.

"I can tear any mere man into pieces." Brahin looked at Kaya with a snarl. "Let me at him. I'll take him apart finger by finger."

RIVALS' MATCH

PEOPLE, PLACES & PLOTS IN CHAPTER 23

Atilla: is loyal to his friend, Kaya, and wants him to win.
Brahin: is boastful and contemptuous of his enemy.
Blume: is a teaching sister of harem children.
Cheechek: fears the princess' wrath, goes with her friend.
Fewsoon: takes refuge with Blume, the Christian teacher.
Igor: as a freed man has something to prove.
Kaya: his life depends on this one test of strength and skill.
Match Master: will referee the fight; will he catch tricks?
Munzur Khan: loves contests of skill and bravery.
Ozkurt: is powerless to do more than pray for Kaya.
Father Yohan: an old priest claims to have visited China.

GLOSSARY:

Altai-don ay'ya gal- lip-gel'den: bear from the Golden Mountains you conquered.
ay'ya dar, yawl nuz: he's only a bear; just a bear.
baw'sh lie'yen: start; you may begin; have at it.
core'room-ma: protect; defend; watch over; cover.
em'dot: attention; notice; help.
gay bear ta jam: I'll slaughter you.
gel: come; attend.
go'beck ott'ee yor-sun: to toss your navel; means: to belly-dance.
no-bet'chee: guard; night watchman; to be on duty; to be on call; to be one's turn to serve.
peech: bastard.
sair-sairy a-dam: tramp; worthless man.
tamom: okay; agreed; permission granted; it's alright.
vise bar kum: come, white bear; an incantation.

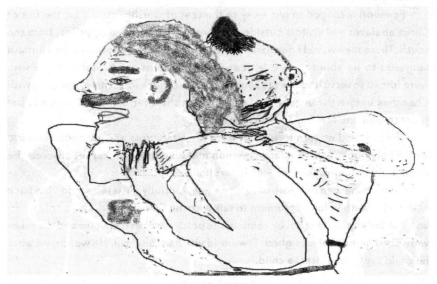

THE HEADLOCK

Practice started in earnest at the tent of Igor. Food was plentiful and good. Kaya put on weight and muscle with the constant practice. Igor also started to lay down rules for procedure in the fight.

"Always be alert for treachery: some fine sand in the waist-band for your eyes or a hidden knife or salve that burns the skin. This man will do anything to win. The more points you win the greater will be his desperation. He will buy curses and fetishes to weaken your spirit and purpose. You must be alert, but not afraid."

He smiled in enjoyment and continued enthusiastically. "Munzur will love it if you wear Brahin down with a few spectacular throws and clips. He is big so any movement of his body is dramatic. Make him move or throw him. Keep him hot. He will not be able to keep up the pace and will tire gradually. He is slow and deliberate; use speed and skill to keep him moving. You must not let him rest or use his strength against you: use his weight to trip and unbalance him. He has the reach on you. Don't let him get you stationary. Keep on the move, surround him." Igor laughed loudly, "That's it, surround him constantly." They both laughed together.

>-------->

Guards moved Fewsoon and Cheechek out of the Princess' tents and into those pertaining to the small children. Life was simpler, but they were very busy as teacher or nurse. A sweet motherly nun, Sister Blume, was permitted to work there. She, too, had red hair and spoke fluent Hunnish. The girls had little time for brooding on the trial.

Fewsoon managed to get away to the tent of worship placed for the use of Christian slaves and visitors outside the harem. It was tended by priests from the south. These men would know Greek or Latin, but learned enough of the Hunnish language to be able to use it with enslaved northern and eastern people who were forced to serve and use the tongue of their conquerors. There, kneeling with Cheechek before the unadorned Latin cross on the altar, she could pour out her heart to God and feel her anxieties dissolve.

The tent had no furniture apart from the altar, cross and a wooden lectern, with a holy book upon it, a large maroon and blue flowered carpet covered the straw padded floor where the worshipers knelt or sat.

Father Yohan, an old Goth of extreme age, tactfully puttered around the back of the tent, waiting for his moment to talk with the Chipchak girl. The whole camp knew of the impending trial by combat; the betting was extravagant and the jokes were outrageous. Yohan sighed. The world was hard and evil. He wondered what he could say to comfort the child.

> - - - - - - - >

The day arrived with fanfare and pageantry. The contestants clad only in belt and scant loincloth, which did not conceal much, paraded on opposite sides of the village of tents and yurts. Each was accompanied by a band of drums, bronze horns, cymbals and a primitive glockenspiel on an overhead pole with bells distributed on the cross arms. All were playing loud music.

The route was planned, controlled so each group with its enthusiastic crowd of followers did not meet until they neared the tent of Khan Munzur in a square surrounded by soldiers. There, they were allowed to draw near. Large carpets covered the combat area.

The October sun was pleasant and the fall had proven to be fruitful. The ambassadors with their retinues of servants, secretaries and guards were clumped in little self-satisfied knots enjoying, but contemptuous of, the barbarians' splendor around them. They always contrasted the 'them' and 'theirs' to the 'us' and 'ours' that pride demands.

The contestants faced each other, attendants beside them, and they began to grease their bodies with fat and perfumed oil, prepared for such occasions. It prolonged the contest and gave time to appreciate skill as well as power.

Munzur had young Attila on his right with Yetkin and other royal children. They used chairs in the European fashion. The mother of the heir sat on a large carpet, on the left with other ladies. Cheechek and Fewsoon sat among them. Many, conscious of the stares of the crowds and aliens, modestly covered their faces with their scarves.

The two contestants moved toward the Khan and each other. A master of the fight with a long blunt-ended staff, the height of his head, moved between them. They bowed before the Khan who examined them critically.

"You know the traditions. I want a fierce fight, but when the master of the fight touches you, act quickly or suffer a beating until you do." He peered into the face of each. "You are winner only if I declare it so. Better please me, right?" He smiled wolfishly and nodded to the master.

"*Tamom, bawsh lie yen*, okay start," Khan Munzur ordered. The master retreated three steps. And before the two bowing men had turned away from the Khan toward each other, Brahin had thrown his arm wide and back to hit Kaya across the face, throwing his weight after the arm.

Kaya did not escape the blow of the arm, but gave way before it. So he was a bit distant when Brahin's body touched his. Kaya got the full weight of the tackle below his knees taking them out from under him. He fell on rather than away from the blond giant. Kaya got a head lock on the man, jerking the head toward his chest vigorously twice. The giant roared in anger and kicked vigorously and forced himself along the rug to reach under Kaya's left arm to get a pry on his neck and push him away, breaking the hold.

They now pulled back and assumed the wrestlers' position facing each other, hands slipping and sliding as they tried to grasp the other's head or shoulder. Brahin then tried to block, but reach past Kaya to get a leg, crashing his body into him with all his force, but as he slid past, Kaya raised his foot and brought it under him to drop on Brahin's back and try to grab an ankle and reach back to put his right arm round Brahin's neck. The ankle slipped away and Brahin had twisted round to pinch Kaya's neck under his elbow and was trying to squeeze him and get his weight above Kaya. However, Kaya was on his knees, pulling away now, keeping his body away from Brahin's weight. He stood and pushed at the opponent's elbow and wrists. His hands slipped and slid.

Brahin brought his free arm up between Kaya's legs with all his force. Brahin felt the descending rod of the match master on his back, but he repeated the blow. He was beaten again, and he felt the rod slide under his elbow and force open his arm. Kaya fell back and rolled in agony. Screams came from the women's carpet, and the crowd roared in anger and frustration.

The match master rested his body's weight arms extended on the rod and pushed Brahin's unwilling, thrashing body back away from the groaning form of Kaya. Brahin was screaming insults in a blind fury.

"*Peech! Gay bear ta jam*. You bastard! I'll slaughter you. Let me finish him off now." He rubbed his wrenched, tender neck.

The form of Igor was dancing up and down, shouting at the outer edge of the carpet, trying to get Kaya's attention. Finally, he darted forward and rolled the boy into a sitting position. He pressed his hands behind the stunned man's ears shouting encouragement.

"Get up. Don't let him catch you again. He means to kill you. Keep your distance, wear him down. You'll be numb down there now, so don't worry about it. He outreaches you. Remember what I told you. Keep your elbows near your body. He has broken training most of the time. He can't last. Hurry, your time is over. Kill him!" With a pull up and a slap on the back the stout, squat man was gone. Kaya stood swaying uncertainly.

"But I can't kill him. He's human," Kaya shouted drunkenly toward Igor. "We can't revenge ourselves; vengeance belongs to God. 'You shall not kill.' Moses commands us. He is human. I'm only a bear who became a man." His face reflected his misery.

The match master moved aside and allowed the shoving man to pass him. The giant rushed forward and threw himself at Kaya who promptly stepped aside hitting the man's lower back in a backhand swing as he passed, carried by his own momentum. Brahin tripped and fell off the carpet into the crowd who scattered yelling.

Shouting insults, some kicked and hit at the blond stranger, who had gotten such promotions from the princess. Others pushed him away laughing. He stopped and hit several in the crowd who had landed kicks and blows. Curses and shouting followed and it might have developed into another serious fight, if the match master had not intervened.

Now they strained head to head trying for a hold on their opponent's oily body, Kaya on defensive evading, dodging successfully the aggressive dives and checks of the larger man. As they grappled, the giant Brahin hands seemed to be trying to get a hold on Kaya's head, but the movements were wrenching an ear and bashing a thumb into his face near the eyes, when the match master could not see. Kaya began to bleed from around the ears and near the eyes. The blood was making a red haze on all Kaya could see. He shook his head repeatedly to clear his vision.

Once Kaya evaded a rush and then grabbing the belt behind the wrestler and slung him off balance into the crowd again. This time the punching and blows were more intense and angry. Again, the match master waded in to the rescue.

Both men were panting and tired, sweat and oil dripped from their bodies. They strained against each other. Brahin's arrogant disregard for training rules was telling on him. He was breathing hard and looked exhausted. Kaya's face was a sticky mask of red.

Brahin suddenly stepped back and made a wait sign with his hand while he fiddled with the adjustment of his belt and reached inside to the bottom of his loincloth as if to adjust some binding. When his hand appeared it held a small transparent bladder filled with fine ground quartzite sand, which he emptied with a backhand motion of his left hand into Kaya's face. Kaya rocked up and back before the motion dodging, but still got some of the powder on his face. Kaya grappling, was driven back to the limits of the rug. Spectators were trying to evade the rush. His opponent held his headlong charge and Kaya fell. Brahin's knee hit his head, flatening him.

Squeals of horror came from the women's rug and some covered their faces in fear. The princess leaned forward in eager anticipation, triumph showing on her face. Fewsoon's hands clutched a rosary, "Yesu gel! Yesu gel! God help us!" She wept.

Brahin, now on his knees, reached over his enemy's body. He had Kaya around the waist from above and behind and was lifting him, head down feet up. Kaya blinded and helpless tried to lock his legs around Brahin's head and drummed his heels on his back. Brahin still on his knees tried to bang Kaya's head on the rug mat. He tried to struggle to his feet and get more power in the blow, but overbalanced and fell on Kaya. Quickly, Brahin reversed and took Kaya in his arms between the neck and shoulder locking them together. Brahin growled and shouted in Kaya's ear.

"*Optal*, stupid fool, do you think you fight a mere man? I was washed in the blood of the great white bear of the north, when I was but an infant. I kill you now with his powers." The great pressure of Brahin's encircling arms caused Kaya's head to press into his own shoulder painfully. Brahin started an incantation.

"*Vise Bar, Vise Bar kum*, Oh, white bear come." He pressed harder on Kaya. Kaya had ceased to listen now. He too was starting to talk painfully.

"*Ay'ya dar, Yawl nuz*. He's a bear! Only a bear! He's a white bear in the form of a man. *Yesu Gel*, God help me, He isn't human! Humans control animals. We dominate them for our needs." Though exhausted, Kaya seemed to gather new strength before everyone's eyes.

Kaya's scrabbling hand found one of Brahin's locked fingers and was able to bend it back painfully. The hold was loosened, again the oil and sweat allowed the positions to switch. Kaya's actions seemed vigorous and sure, as if he had rested and eaten.

Kaya pressed Brahin's head with his right hand while he scooted his body away from Brahin's at a right angle to bring his head out behind Brahin's back. Then he pushed forward and managed to get his left arm under Brahin's arm and locked his fingers behind his opponent's neck. He applied pressure vigorously and something popped. The sound was as clear as a bell and was heard by everyone. The match master stepped in and separated the two. Brahin lay with a dazed expression in his eyes. All his strength seemed to have departed. A trainer entered and knelt beside him feeling the bones with delicate fingers. Then he consulted with the match master. He shook his head and motioned for men to come forward to carefully carry the disabled man off on a litter to a healer's tent. He motioned toward

Kaya who stood unseeing, equally dazed by the sudden turn of events. Igor came forward to lead the blinded Kaya tenderly toward his helpers. They ignored the court and left to attend his wounds.

> - - - - - - - >

Munzur smiled with grim satisfaction. He was not displeased with the results, though his daughter sat angry and pouting behind him. She was destined to be a tool of politics and make a dynastic marriage to an ally or enemy, to seal an agreement or peace. It was better to have the source of temptation away from her presence in the camp. He hoped that he was not too late. There had been some disquieting rumors in the spring. If she had been careless or promiscuous, it would mean future beatings by a jealous husband and a possible source of strife between kingdoms. Fortunately, there was another, Saraijik, a yet to be fully reconciled daughter that could be used in a pinch, even if it meant losing a general. But there was a tender spot there; he would have to admit to a wrong. His mistake in harsh treatment and judgment of a wife. It would be necessary to publicly make known his error, even apologize. It was a necessity he had never faced before. He would have to think on it more. Nevertheless, family discipline for the young must be preserved; the dynasty's reputation and power must be upheld at all cost.

Then, he thought of the message from the Master of Documents, the messengers' letters were very valuable. One could be used to black-mail the Khazar ambassador in the great city. The other, an offer from Prince Ilkin; a way to save face and make peace. All that was necessary after the Kazar spring and summer conquest of Donetz basin and some of the Crimean ports. He could give a few ports back to the Greeks and break up their alliance with the Khazars. Trade competition would level the playing field. Only Han Lee's letters seemed dull history. This occasion and the merits of the winner deserved a notable reward, he thought, something memorable, expensive and even extravagant.

He had the victor called forth at the celebration banquet before all the powerful and important warriors to hear his decree and reward.

"*Altai don aya, gal lip gel den*, Bear from the golden mountains, you have won. In seven days you will be married to the girl promised to you before your father and confirmed by me now." He glanced at his daughter and raised his voice. "It is good to let one's life follow where the wise father has shown the path."

Kaya bowed deeply. "I long to return to my father's yurt. There I can tell of Khan Munzur's greatness and generosity."

The Khan smiled and nodded. He motioned to his ministers. "Give him twenty men from the east. Let him choose them. You will equip them with three mounts each from my herds, and supplies for the journey, as much as will fit on the horses. You will have an honor guard."

Munzur smiled again; he was creating a legend for his people to think on and remember. "Write: 'Let there be a safe conduct out of the camp and our large territories. Food will be provided at all army garrisons. An honor guard will travel with your twenty from camp to camp.' In this way your treasures, wedding presents and friends will be safe."

He smiled again. "The man with the ivory Swan will lead the flock. To the victors, go the spoils." He glanced at the Byzantine and West Goth ambassadors to see if they caught the double entente in the quote. The legend of prodigious generosity was for them. "I sponsor your wedding and will receive the gifts for you and provide the banquet." Deep bows were exchanged by all except the Khan, who bowed to no one.

All present realized that the gifts had to be worthy, yet would indicate to the Khan the state of each man's wealth, which was constantly assessed. Loss of favor or position would be with confiscation. All were enslaved by their fear of loss. They groaned within, but few opted out. Status and importance depended on being close to the Khan. His favor determined life or death.

> - - - - - - - >

The week passed quickly, while Fewsoon and Cheechek joyfully wrestled over details of the wedding. Should the bride wear a red shalvar and blouse under a white coat or more effectively white under red? Should Koo'chuk's gift be made into a blouse or form part of the veil to display distant love? What color and part should a vest play under or over the ensemble? Then, the delightful debate came over material: silk, wool, linen or cotton and in what weave? Combinations of materials were important to give the best effects. What about her hair? How could you control it and put it up? Or perhaps, down? Cut here or there?

Kaya, meanwhile, chose and equipped men who were both outstanding and desirous of returning east. All were Chipchak or other Turkish related peoples willing to serve under the ivory swan, Kaya's badge of office. Many more wished to go than could be taken. Their pleas were heard and evaluated.

Kaya limped from interviews to feasts while Ozkurt or Igor did much of the leg work of preparation for the long journey. The three had their heads together and sharpened their plans and timing. The necessary passes and safe conduct documents were gotten and guarded. The chosen men started to train for the nuptial parade, which included racing and archery under Memmur's practiced eyes.

> - - - - - - - >

The evening before the wedding, the women of the forbidden zone had a farewell party for Fewsoon who would soon leave the women's quarter to live in the main town with a husband. Cheechek put on Fewsoon's daily work clothes at the party for a skit of her arrival at the compound: a free woman learning the restrictions of harem life. She was unconcerned with the social classes in the harem and even talked with the guards.

The women roared with laughter as Cheechek mimicked her interest in horses, war and trade. With her hair pinned up, Cheechek looked like a plump Fewsoon. She strode boldly to two girls dressed as guards, too small for the baggy male clothes that hung on their shapely frames.

"I saw a large caravan enter from the east gate. Are they from Crimea or the Caucasus?" She peered boldly into the face of the first pretended guard, who stroked a frayed rope mustache with serious mime.

The petite guard replied, tittering occasionally. "It was from the Crimea, Lady, and brought wine for the Khan and wheat for his table." The hand transferred its attention to the eyebrow.

"But I saw silk and cotton-baled cloth goods," Fewsoon's twin said in an impatient manner.

"True, Lady, there was a cloth merchant who gave the Khan first pick of all his merchandise" The pseudo guard shrugged and transferred his stroking to his hand.

"Will we have no chance at the goods until the court has picked over the lot?" she exclaimed indignantly.

"The chief eunuch will bring over the nicest of the goods." The guard had surreptitiously started patting the lady's hand. "Don't worry your pretty head about it."

"They will all have the best of it before we even see the poor remains." She stamped a foot and shook her head. The guard was patting her arm now.

"I'll speak to him about it, little love. There will be something special for you from him and from me too if you like. I'm off duty tonight. I know a quiet dark place to meet." The guard reached beneath the arm to pat, with a leer that twisted his face. The lady hit the guard on the temple with such pretended force as to knock him flat. The audience of women shrieked with laughter and nodded in agreement. That was their beloved Fewsoon.

"*Sair sairy a dam*; tramp, stupid man," she screamed above the noise. The second guard helped his companion to his feet, while the lady stepped outside the tent door and pretended to call more guards to denounce the errant guard.

"*Kore room ma, no bet chee, gel*; Protect me, guards, come. *Em dot*, help," her voice was sharp with urgency. With this more laughter arose inside the tent.

She stood in the last light of the day, terror on her face. Something flashed. Cheechek's scream was piercing as she fell backward into the tent. A long feathered wooden arrow stuck from the front of Fewsoon's best work coat.

There was a moment of shocked silence. Then the screams began in earnest as the women scattered like partridges each to a separate hiding place.

Fewsoon ran first to the door, where she scanned the outside perimeter. Then she returned to her dying friend as the guards came running. The court buzzed with gossip; a black eunuch was found in a nearby tent. He claimed innocence and died while being questioned. The gate guards were also put to the question, but could not explain the large bamboo bow found abandoned near the tent. Fewsoon's friend, Cheechek, was taken to Sister Blume's quarters, but she was clearly dead, so they left her there to await a quiet moment for burial. They were unnoticed while the celebrations continued. Fewsoon put aside her bridal plans for one day and attended the quiet ceremony in the small Christian cemetery outside the city. Father Yuhan presided and comforted the bride. "If you name a girl for her, she will be with you to love again."

> - - - - - - - >

Because of the murder and fear of another attempt at murder, the women did not parade the bride through the streets. The Khan insisted on the groom's participation in the parade, but he wore his warrior garb and armor. Small cuts and scabs were evident on his head, where Brahin's work was clear a week after the fight. A sticky white clay had removed most of the glass-like particles imbedded in the skin, but had left the skin a blanched contrast to the red pocks and cuts.

The chapel tent was open, the altar and cross outside, where all could see the ceremony. Since the couple did not understand Latin or Greek, the ceremony was to be in Hunnish, much to the disgust of those Westerners who preferred the 'Civilized' languages of old empires. The old man who claimed to have visited China was to wed them. His daughter, Blume, was a bride's maid. At the chapel all was bright with autumn fruits and many colored leaves. The two choirs, one of women and the other of men and boys sang during the nuptial of the two lovers.

First came the introduction as the groom and his attendants, dressed in the guards' uniforms, came forward to stand beside the minister. The church choirs stood inside the tent facing the assembled people and notables who sat in attendance. These were the words of their joyous celebration.

> Shout for joy, their wedding day.
> Sing of love's great power to stay.
> Pray them happiness always.

1. The day has come all are waiting.
Joy fills this great marriage festal.
Their wedding day, happily play.
We celebrate blissf 'ly.
Let us sing a song of sweetness,
Love and joy are waiting,
Calling those who're true to them.

Shout for joy, their wed - ding day.

Sing of loves great power to stay.

Pray them hap - pi - ness al - ways.

The day has come all are wait- ing.

Joy fills this great marriage fes-tal.

Their wed - ding day, hap - pi - ly play,

we ce - le - brate. Bliss - ful! Let us sing

a song of sweet - ness Love and joy are

wait - ing. Cal - ling those who're true to them.

They began the wedding march and the standing crowd parted to allow the party to pass to the chapel tent. The bride wore a white silk shalvar and blouse under a forest green, knee-length coat. A red cummerbund was worn for good luck. Koochook's gift of tiny meadow flowers embroidered on white appeared as the crown from which the white veil hung. This was worn to show modesty, but not to completely hide her face. The crowd gasped at the glimpse of pale beauty, showing joy touched by grief. Patience, confidence and love seemed to shine from her visage. She serenely moved forward to join her beloved before the altar. The church choir sang the processional. The men's voices took the first phrase: 'Comes the bride', and the women responded 'Oh, how beautiful.' This pattern continued with each line. They waited at the altar until all the singing finished. Then the priest commenced the readings and vows.

2.   Comes the bride. Oh, how beautiful.
Waits the groom, Oh, how fortunate.
Friends have come, let their joy abound.
Maids attend, see their beauty round.
Say the words, in this holy place.
Make the vows, God will give them grace.
Sing of love, let their hearts be one,
And their wills bring sweet success.

COMES THE BRIDE

Comes the bride, Oh, how beau - ti - ful.

Waits the groom, Oh, how for - tu - nate.

Friends have come, Let their joy a - bound.

Maids a - tend, See their beau - ty round.

Say the words, In this ho - ly place.

Make the vows, God will give them grace.

Sing of love, Let their hearts be one.

And their wills, Bring sweet suc - cess.

3.   Come give thanks. Joyful let us sing
In chorus of the love that bore us;
When our fathers took these vows we hear.
Through future days, love and obey,
This is God's way for us.

4.   Come to the chapel to see them.
Feel their joy touch every heart.

Repeat 2x: Hear the bells a-ringing.
Joy bells and their singing,
Glad days they are bringing

1ST   love to all of you. 2nd   happiness.

Repeat 2x: Joyful singing, music ringing,
Presents bringing, toasts proclaiming

1st   marriage bliss. 2nd   happiness.

AT THE ALTAR

Father Yohan's flawed but understandable tongue pronounced the sacred words that bound them together. The crowd listened as the enthusiastic singing continued. The celebrants left the chapel as the choirs sang *Ardent Love*, a parting farewell to the champion and his bride.

A banquet and the delight of seeing expensive gifts awaited them at the Khan's palace. The people wanted to congratulate them, and press flowers and gifts on them as they passed.

5.   Look at the face of the bride and the groom.
           They're so happy and joyful today.
Repeat 2x   Young dreams seeking, longing,
           Finding one another, warm love,
           Deep devotion,
1st) joy will shine.   2nd joy divine.

ARDENT LOVE

6.   Let rejoicing now begin,
      Drink to love which has no end.
      See its beauty shine within.
      Ardently love now forever.
      Have a happy wedding day.

Even the critics from the West said it was a most impressive wedding. The joy was apparent among the population in general.

All felt that justice had been served.

The couple was taken and presented to the court where Munzur was already starting an early drinking session. The banquet was long and boisterous and they were glad to leave early with permission and several bad jokes.

The Hunnish Empire celebrated for a week: the time of nuptials, harvest, fullness and bounty. After, they plainly advised the newlyweds that they had three weeks to clear out of the territory and begin their exile. The *yasa*, law, was not lenient with laggards.

Igor took full charge of departure, to Ozkurt's disgust. The men always looked to Kaya for confirmation: a nod of the head or slight movement of hand. The Slav was alternately bossy and humble in serving the Chipchaks. They were moving up the Danube River toward his country, and he knew the way to it. He would tell funny stories, buy fruit or equipment for Fewsoon or others, when the need arose. He ordered people about, sent off hunting or fishing parties. He gave specific instructions about where and how to proceed and about what to do next. The humble, earnest, squat man was a brave leader, dutiful nursemaid, and annoying pest.

QUEST COMPLETED

>- - - - - - - >

Esteemed Princess Judith,

Thank you for your kind letter. I will try to give you an answer before the winter closes off the Don River. Aunt Magda is ready to travel now and we leave this week for Pontus. She knows the Governor there, and believes an appointment is assured. He will be open to your kind offers.

Yes, I'm sure the matter of the Hebrew refugees can be solved. I will write to you from there and perhaps send it with some responsible person from among them.

Thank you for your offer of friendship and your request not to use the titles. I am overwhelmed by your generosity. I find it hard to put into words, no? I think few persons have had the privilege of being so regarded by a person of your rank. Yes, we do have precious friends in common. I have just heard from my new friend Saraijik that Kaya has won the hand of his intended, Fewsoon, and she promised to send details in the next letter. I will pass them on to you immediately. They have been in great danger, but surely, with God's help, they will emerge safe.

Princess Olga is expecting a baby next spring and is full of happiness. How wonderful are the ways of married life. To love and be loved, to the exclusion of others, by a person of honor and tenderness is thrilling; truly a gift from God.

If you would include more details of Prince Ilkin's symptoms, my Aunt Magda will get some helpful information from our family doctor and send you his advice. In matters of health, second opinions are important, no?

I would like you to tell me more of your baby's doings, it's so interesting.

Your grateful servant,
Merien Papasian

SPRING STEPPE FLOWERS

Kaya and Fewsoon found themselves with baskets assigned to gather berries. They left the horses hobbled, grazing in a small clearing. In the woods they found a silence they had not experienced in months. They smiled at each other and were suddenly timid, awkward and embarrassed.

"Our friend has planned this," Yownja whispered.

"Let's enjoy it. We are almost alone," he said.

"Almost? Someone else is about?" she worried.

"There's a solitary bear over near the stream. I think he's fishing." He smiled reassurance.

She fidgeted, "He won't come to investigate?" She sat with her back against a tree, running her hand through the fallen leaves.

He sat beside her. "If he's full, he'll go away. If hungry, he'll likely eat berries and pay us no mind."

She sighed and pulled him around to face her. Each looked into the other's eyes. "How do bears make love? Do they pair for life?"

He put his hand on her cheek. She took his head in both hands. He laughed as she pulled him closer. "During courtship there is usually resistance and protests, but after pairing they indicate to each other when they wish to be served. Why be coy when you have need? Love gives all."

Her eyes grew full of surprise. "You mean they have ways of showing desire? Signaling?"

He laughed fondly and patted her cheek. "It's just like people signal their wants."

She inched her shalvar a few fingers lower so her belly-button showed, and waited for his response.

He leaned back to see and laugh, "*Go beck ott'ee yor-sun*? Tossing your navel? You'll do a belly dance?" He chuckled and made a circle with his finger on her quivering tummy.

She grabbed and held his hand, laughing. "Well, I won't dance above you like some of the shameless ones do. You won't have to pay." She guided his hand, "I'm ticklish, so please don't try."

He nodded obediently, saying, "Love gives all and longs for more to give. You've already cost me more than you'll ever know. I'll probably be paying the rest of my life..." She cut off his words and the woods sighed with the breeze.

BERRY PICKING